UNMASKED
&
UNDRESSED

Edited By
ERIC SUMMERS

Herndon, VA

Published in the United States by STARbooks Press

PO Box 711612, Herndon, VA 20171

Many thanks to graphic artist John Nail for the cover design. Mr. Nail may be reached at: tojonail@bellsouth.net.

Cover Photo Model: www.justinwoltering.com

Cover Photo Courtesy of www.photosbyjae.com

Printed in the United States

Herndon, VA

Contents

ANIMAL MAGNETISM By Rob Rosen

When last we saw The Otter, our intrepid hero, righter of gay injustices, hirsute do-gooder in purple nylon, he'd just bedded his soon to be boyfriend and faithful sidekick, The Twink. Sadly, the relationship turned sour shortly thereafter. Suffice it say, egos clashed. As did costumes. Because, come on, purple and lavender simply do not go with yellow and tangerine. And though opposites do indeed attract, the divinely hairy and the stunningly hairless being as opposite as two people can possibly get, in this case, it didn't work in their favor. Think of an all-over rug burn, and you wouldn't be far off the mark.

"Please, shave it just a touch," pled The Twink. "My skin is raw."

The Otter merely shook his head, his seemingly alive chest-matting rising in apparent indignation. "My strength resides in my hairs, every last follicle imbued with the ancient power of my amulet. Cutting them is like cutting an electric wire, thereby short-circuiting the entire main-frame." He stared down at his partner, frowning now. "Look what happened to Sampson, my love."

The Twink sighed. "Delilah only had a head of hair to worry about; I've got your back, which would make a shag carpet jealous, and your chest, which hasn't seen the light of day in well over a decade. And let's not even discuss that unkempt bush of yours."

And so, the two parted, each with one half of the amulet, sadly fighting crime alone now. The Otter had his lethal body hair, The Twink his very skin, so smooth as to be blinding. Together they were unstoppable, but apart their once-solid chains, so to speak, now had kinks in them. And not the good kind of kinks either.

See, the Otter, with his advanced degrees in archaeology, was sometimes too cerebral for the tasks at hand, too busy analyzing when he should've been acting. The Twink, younger, more footloose and fancy free, rushed in, headlong, not always thinking before acting. Meaning, crime got fought, but crime frequently fought back, and, on occasion, won out.

Such was the case with Sir Magnetism. Evil as he was handsome, this menace to society had powers that easily overcame the authorities, superheroes included. His magnetic field made him impenetrable to mind control, to bullets, to rushing gusts of wind or freezing blasts of cold. Laser beams bounced off him, as did fists of steel. Women swooned in his presence, men feared for their precious egos. In other words, he rampaged through the city, stealing to his wicked heart's content.

The Twink encountered him after so many had failed. In truth, his powers might have been enough to bring Magnetism to his very knees. The glow of him was no match for sunglasses and could be witnessed even through a magnetic field, felt even, burning through you until you collapsed in agony. Very few, in fact, could stop The Twink once his shirt was opened and his fleshy brilliance revealed.

But Magnetism wasn't like those very few. Or anyone, for that matter.

"Stop!" shouted the Twink, rushing into the jewelry store just after the magnetic menace had burst in, breaking the locks with his magnetized eye beams, the security system immediately fizzling out with the enormous surge of current that came off his stupendous frame.

Magnetism turned, ultra-black costume fluttering, locking eyes with The Twink and smiling brightly, his teeth a dazzling white. "Stop?" he practically purred, voice so syrupy sweet as to rot your very teeth. "You mean here, so far away from you?"

The Twink flinched, jaw dropping and, truth be told, crotch bulging. And, no, nylon does very little to keep you in place. "Stop or I'll ... I'll ..."

"You'll what?" cooed Magnetism, inching in, closer, ever closer, eyes sparkling even brighter than the diamond rings encased on all sides of them. "Part your outfit for me, reveal that stunning torso of yours, blind me with your beauty, shine through me until I beg for mercy?" The villain made it all the way up the hero, The Twink powerless against his foe's intoxicating charms. "Or poke me with this fetching wand of yours?" His hand reached out and cupped the nylon-encased cock.

The Twink's eyelids fluttered, just for the briefest of seconds, but that was all Sir Magnetism needed. It only took a concentrated dose of his field to bring the amulet up and off The Twink's neck before it found its way into the rogue's grip. Only then did the hero know what had happened, what had been lost. Because, without the amulet, he no longer had his stupendous powers. Though, of course, he still had that raging boner to contend with.

"You evil, sinister fuck," The Twink spat out, once he realized the dilemma he was in.

Magnetism chuckled. "Flattery will get you everywhere, my lithe, little friend." And then he pulsed, shooting out an invisible magnetic beam that instantly brought dozens of metal necklaces and anklets and bracelets to his side before they instantly wrapped around The Twink's ankles and hands, binding him in tightly.

"Let me go," growled the trussed champion of the downtrodden.

The rogue leaned in, lips a hair's breadth away. "Your mouth says no, but your cock says otherwise," he rasped, reaching inside the costume for a grab and a squeeze and a stroke. "Mmm, mind if I have a look at it?"

"Let me go," repeated The Twink, though his eyes were now aflame with something other than mere anger.

"But of course," cooed Magnetism, menacingly adding, "Just not yet."

He lifted his hands in the air and, all at once, three metal chairs came flying in. Two flew in below The Twink's calves, the third beneath his head, until the hero was floating atop them in mid-air, thrashing about in an attempt to break free from his expensive manacles.

"You'll never get away with this," cried The Twink, soon exhausted, floating just beneath the evil one's hands, which were gently prying the costume off the young body below, until the hero was naked, shivering, cock ramrod straight, poking up like a ship's mast.

"My, oh, my," groaned Magnetism. "They should call you The Club, my adorable friend. Think of all the damage you could inflict with this weapon of yours." Said weapon was down the ruffian's throat in the blink of an eye as his hands traversed the soft, supple peaks and valleys of the floating Twink's nimble body. He popped the prick out of his mouth. "Your razor bills must be astronomically high, I would think."

"I'm naturally like this, you foul fiend," replied The Twink.

"Lucky you," said Magnetism, zipping down his fly, nine thick inches of meat soon revealed. "Or should I say, lucky me." He stared down at his prisoner, smirking as he stroked both their turgid tools. "Now then, would you like to see a neat, little trick of mine, oh stunningly smooth one? Something that doesn't involve breaking so much as entering?"

The Twink glanced down at the marauder's hefty appendage, with equal parts fear and lust on his chiseled face. "No way is that fitting inside me."

Sir Magnetism also stared down at his prized slab of meat, then shrugged. "Pity," he said. "Then how about a substitute, yes?" Again he lifted his hands, the chairs pulling slightly apart, taking The Twink's legs with them, the pink, crinkled hole quickly revealed. Then, in the blink of an eye, a sterling silver cigar case came floating in, very tubular, cock-like, in fact. Lastly, the vile villain found a tube of grease beneath a counter. "See, I'm not so bad," he said, lubing up The Twink's ultra-tight tush.

Again he stood to the hero's side, slowly stroking the stiff prick below with one hand, his own mega-sized rod with the other. His body pulsing again, the cigar holder eased its way inside the spread apart cheeks, until both super villain and superhero were moaning in unison, the bottom getting slowly fucked by the silver tube, the top watching in rapt delight.

"Fucker," growled The Twink.

The silver tube picked up speed. "Why, yes, I am."

And then both pricks were getting jacked, lightning fast. Minutes later, they came together, the cock below spewing up and out, the cock above, down and in heavy streams, both hefty wads quickly pooling on The Twinks expanding and contracting belly before dripping down to the floor below in thick, white gobs.

Magnetism bent down for an unreturned peck on the lips, then stuffed his shrinking willy back inside his black as night costume before promptly robbing the place blind, all while The Twink watched on, miserable at his inability to prevent it all. "You'll get yours in the end," he shouted, just before the villain left the shop, massive bag of merch in hand.

With a sinister laugh, Magnetism rubbed his tightly encased ass. "Only if I'm lucky, adorable, one. Only if I'm lucky."

And with that, he was gone, The Twink falling to the floor, the silver tube popping out of his ass. Thankfully, the constraints loosened, as well. Though, sadly, Sir Magnetism left with The Twink's magical amulet. Powerless, he frowned and whispered, "I'll get you Magnetism, if it's the last thing I do."

But the villain was long gone by then.

Though, of course, not forgotten.

Because that jewelry store wasn't the last place robbed.

No sir, no how.

Dozens followed. Banks, too. Convenience stores. Restaurants and movie theaters and ATMs. Nothing and no one were immune to his powers. Or his charms.

No one, that is, until The Otter finally caught up with him.

It was at a nightclub this time. Place was packed to the rafters, too. Meaning, the registers were crammed full. Naturally, the safe in back was no match for Sir Magnetism. Nor were the guards, who sat bound and gagged and out cold on the floor outside the once-locked room, the cash quickly stuffed inside its waiting bag.

"Not so fast," said The Otter, arms akimbo, blocking the doorway.

Sir Magnetism jumped up and pulsed, all of the loose metal in the small room instantly flying toward The Otter. In the blink of an eye, the hero's chest hairs flew out and formed an impenetrable plate, the hairs beneath his armpits snaking out, as well, whipping the debris to the ground, until all of it lay strewn out around them.

"Sexy," said magnetism, eyes lighting up, mouth in a delectable pout.

The Otter laughed and pointed to his ears. "Nope, you horrible hoodlum, my ear hairs have plugged up my drums, too. Your words have no effect on me any more than your magnetic powers do." He moved further inside the room. "Hands behind your back, ruffian. I'm taking you in."

Magnetism winked. "Dirty talker," he mouthed, so that even The Otter knew what was being said. And that was enough to at least clog the hero's brain, sufficiently beguile him so that the wicked one could pulse and shoot his field at the amulet. Though where The Twink had no protection against such powers, The Otter had all that luxurious hair, which quickly coiled up, wrapping around the amulet and keeping it locked in place, tight as a steel vice.

"Your powers are no match for mine, Magnetism," said The Otter, until he was within a couple of feet of his nemesis.

For once, the super villain looked nervous. Though he was, of course, as ingenious as he was immoral. Meaning, as quickly as it had disappeared, his captivating grin again broke free. "No, bushy one, I can see that, but perhaps your powers can be turned against you." The smile grew as Magnetism's hands rose in the air, every last ounce of his magnetic field concentrated into one beam that quickly radiated outward, landing full-on atop the amulet, instantly changing its polarity.

The Otter yelped as his allies turned on him, chest hairs clamping down, leg hairs breaking free from their nylon constraints and forming shackles, razor-sharp goatee suddenly jabbing at his jugular, and underarm hairs lashing him to the wall. In an instant, the hero was subdued. "Let me go," he grunted, shocked at the sudden turn of events.

But Sir Magnetism merely chuckled. "Your smooth, little friend pled the same way." The wicked one pulled the other half of the amulet from his back pocket. "It didn't bode well for him either." The villain closed the gap between them. "I mean, up until the point when he shot that hefty load of his."

Since The Otter's hairs were no longer protecting him, this he heard, loud and clear, and it stung him even more furiously than his goatee, which still held his head against the wall, one wrong move sure to end his very life. Still, The Otter was not without his cunning. There were, he knew, other ways to skin a cat. Or a skunk, as was the case. He'd just have to try and distract his infuriating foe and hope to be able to break free somehow.

"And was my ex-partner a willing mate?" The Otter asked, seductively.

Sir Magnetism inched in, mouth to mouth now. "Not exactly."

The Otter moaned, his tongue splicing the air between them. "Then perhaps I can be more amenable."

Their mouths, in an instant, joined, a near visible spark sizzling down both their backs, cocks steely stiff. Again The Otter's hairs reacted, as they always did when sexually aroused. They flicked and swatted and sprang free from their confines (while still holding the Otter captive), the hero's costume shredding upon impact, cock released, bobbing up and down as it shot out like a fifth limb.

Magnetism glanced down and moaned appreciatively. "Now I see what that twink saw in you."

In fact, that twink in question was standing there watching, waiting for his moment to react. "And still sees in him," he informed, the battling pair swinging their heads up to see who had interrupted them.

Magnetism roared with laughter. "Be gone, little one. Without your powers, you are but a pesky fly buzzing in my ear."

The Twink shrugged and grinned. "Oh, I still have powers all right. And don't call me little one. It's Delilah to you!" And with that, he let the razor-sharp knife fly. He'd taken it from the bar outside when he noticed The Otter up to his heroic ways and then overheard the scuffle inside the room. But instead of cutting lemons, it would now be used on hair. Not strong enough to cut an entire lock, it at least had the capabilities of sheering off a lone strand. And, as The Otter has promised, cutting one would short-circuit the entire main-frame. In other words, like Sampson, The Otter was quickly without his strength, the manacles of hair releasing him, the goatee no longer pointed at his jugular.

The naked Otter fell from the wall and onto Magnetism, both of them instantly wrestling around on the ground, punches flying, POW! WHACK! BAM! Thankfully, the villain was taken off guard. Deflecting the blows, he no longer had the mind to call on his magnetic powers. This gave The Twink ample time to rush in and retrieve his half of the amulet, which had since fallen to the floor.

In a matter of seconds, it was around his neck, the buttons of his shirt opened, smooth chest a blinding white. Magnetism covered his eyes and howled in pain, sending metal debris flying out in all directions. Not sharp enough to cut flesh, they still did their damage, the heroes wincing in pain as they tried to avoid the objects hurtling their way.

"The amulets!" shouted The Otter. "Join them!"

The Twink, at once, knew what his partner was ordering. He jumped up, dodging the flying metal as he pressed his half of the talisman to The Otter's. The two halves had not been joined in many centuries, its power many times stronger now, so that both crime fighters were instantly one mighty fighting force. And, finally, an unstoppable one at that.

Newly invigorated, The Otter's hairs flung Magnetism to the wall, while The Twink pulsed so brightly as to knock the scoundrel out cold. "You saved me," cried The Otter, fighting to catch his breath.

The Twink nodded and laughed. "Well, couldn't let the authorities find you like that."

The hairy hero stared down, dick dangling, nary a shred of his costume still clinging to his fetching form. "I see your point," came the reply, a slight blush creeping up his neck.

"And I see yours," said the young superhero, pointing midsection. "And I ... I missed it." Both of them were now blushing. "And, uh, and you."

The Otter walked in and grabbed his partner in a tight squeeze, his fine hairs once again slicing through the air. "Even these?" he asked, brushing his hands through them all, caressing them like long lost friends.

The Twink ran his own hands though his lover's bushy backside. "Especially these. They make you unique, make you who you are. Make you hot." The hands reached in further, parting the granite-solid cheeks, fingers caressing the crinkled, silky interior.

"What about him?" the hairy avenger asked, his voice husky now, lustful.

"He'll be out for at last an hour. And the guards outside even longer, from what I know about Magnetism's powers." A wink joined the smirk on the young one's adorable face. "And you are naked already, I mean."

The Otter glanced down, his dick already arcing up. "And hard."

"Be a shame to waste it, right?"

"A damn shame," came the reply, hands already working off the younger man's costume, the amulets temporarily off, protecting each of them from their respective powers.

And then both of them were naked, hard, dripping with precum, hands roaming etched bodies, one soft as a cloud, the other fuzzy as a, well, an otter, of course. "God, I missed you," moaned The Twink, dropping to his knees, downing the massive cock in one fell swoop as he yanked on his partner's lemon-sized nuts.

"Ditto," came the reply, the cock shoved in to the throat's hilt, salty jizz gliding down.

Then both of them were on the floor, one on the bottom, the other on top, face to cock, cock to face, yin to yang, so to speak. Mouths hungrily sucked and licked and slurped on thick, hard, pulsing flesh, while fingers grabbed and spanked and probed, bodies drenched in sweat, bucking and grinding happily away.

"Close," The Otter soon groaned.

"Closer," moaned The Twink.

They both jacked faster now, each with a finger deeply entrenched up the other's ass, balls bouncing in sync, eyes watching, waiting, eager for the spectacle.

The Twink, on the bottom, shot first, entire body twitching as his cock spewed, streams of aromatic cum flying up, one load after the next, all hitting the top's cheek and lips and chest before dripping back down. A split second later, The Otter shot, cock so thick it was almost impossible to grip, bands of man-sap flying down, coating the bottom's face and neck and floor. Both of them moaned, loudly, sweat flinging to and fro, bodies practically on fire from the heat and friction.

And then, they collapsed, side by side, chests rapidly rising and falling, the younger of the two giggling. "He missed quite a show," said The Twink, pointing to the still-unconscious Magnetism.

The Otter laughed, as well. "That's okay, I caught it, and that's all that matters." He pointed to his still stiff prick. "Standing ovation, in fact."

The Twink flipped around, so that they were now face to glorious face. "Heck, I'm already ready for the encore."

The kiss that followed was soft and wonderful, perfect as any kiss ever was. And then was repeated, over and over and over again. "I think we should bring him in first because that's one show I wouldn't want repeated. Too close for comfort, if you ask me," said The Otter, already hopping up. Only, he quickly realized he didn't have any clothes now, his costume in tatters on the floor.

10

The Twink pointed to Magnetism. "Take his; he won't be needing those fancy duds where he's going. It's orange jumpsuits from here on out for the likes of him."

And so, The Otter and The Twink got dressed and cleaned up. Then the hairy hero started laughing again, snapping his fingers as he retrieved the one piece of his costume still intact: the lavender O. This he stuck onto his new, sleek, ebony costume. "Guess what?" he asked his lover.

"What?" asked the young buck, admiring his boyfriend's new threads.

The Otter pointed to each of their costumes. "We don't clash anymore, my love. In fact, we look better than ever."

The Twink pulled The Otter in tight, a final kiss offered before calling the authorities. "Oh, we're better than ever, all right," he said. "Better than ever, forever and always."

"Forever and always," agreed The Otter. "And, man, do I like the sound of that."

PANIS ENVY By R. W. Clinger

SWIM TALE 1 – POOLSIDE PLEASURE

I put Michael Panis to the test, although I shouldn't. What kind of naughty superhero am I to question his survival skills? I honestly want to know what makes him tick. How much superhuman power does he really have?

Panis, as I like to call him, can do some uncanny things in the water: like hold his breath for over an hour; like have extra superhuman strength in liquid; like talk to undersea life; like …

It's a typical August day at the local pool in Cinn City. I swim for an hour in the deep end, dive to the bottom, surface, and stare at the sexy-hot lifeguard, who just happens to be my nemesis. My view scans Panis again from head to toe: twenty-years-old, six-one, 200 pounds, flash of yellow-gold hair, crazy-blue eyes, Greek-sloped nose, fish lips like a Hollywood star, broad shoulders, pumped pecs of steel, rigid torso lined with swollen abs, no hair on his chest, Baywatch-like trunks against his tight middle, and long legs with very little hair. I have the eyesight of an owl, one of my superhuman features, and digest the mound of meat between his legs, under his bright red trunk: seven inches soft, rolled to the right, uncut, clean-shaven balls, and very little hair above his knob.

The jock makes eye contact with me: scowling, unhappy to see me, rather disappointed in my poolside presence. His stare says to me: *You don't humor me, Seale. You never humor me. Go play in someone else's pool.*

I give him a wave, smile at the stud, and sink to the bottom of the pool, willing to drown myself … just to see if he will use his superhuman powers to save my ass.

The problem is rather simple, though: I can't drown, even if I try. Troy Seale (me!) is just like Panis. Same superhuman powers. From the same planet — Jount. Same knowledge degree in Superhuman Underwater Arts. Our difference is rather noticeable: Panis is Mr. Good Boy, and I'm naughty. For all the good he does, I do bad in Cinn City. He saves ten people from drowning in the Pacific Ocean, and I decide to tip a liner over, sinking it to the bottom of the ocean. I don't save whales. I don't worry about polluting the globe's water. I'm about as nasty as they come. This is my game; this is what I do; this is how I swim. Look out.

So I can't drown. But, I can pull three sexy eighteen-year-old boys under the water without their Marco Polo playing cohorts even noticing. The only witness around the pool that can see my action is simple: Panis. Just as I want him to, of course.

The scene that unfolds is rather disturbing. Swimmers, readers, and sunbathers alike, beware. I wrap a spiral of wicked water around the trio of young men and secure them to the bottom of the pool. They gasp for air. They try to escape my hold. They panic, which only thrills me. Their cute little man-faces turn white under the pool's surface as they begin to drown. Oxygen is lost. Limbs become tired and weak. If I have my way, each will drown today ... and three funerals will follow. Kudos to me. This is my game; this is what I do; this is how I swim.

Panis comes to their rescue; just as I suspect he will. He wrestles me under the water, preventing my ability to carry out an octopus-like tentacle to keep the boys at the bottom of the pool. In doing so, the boys swim to the shallow end of the pool and climb out among all the spectators. In the meantime, Panis's pert nipples graze one of my shoulders. His right thigh brushes one of my palms. His cock meets my mouth, and I attempt to bite at its trunk-covered mass. Panis is strong within the Olympic-sized pool, almost masterful, such as my skills. We wrestle wildly under the water as the trio of young men surface. Punches are thrown. Underwater tidal waves are shared. And, Panis attempts to cast a spell on me called Waterlogged, which works; something we both have learned at The School of Jount some five years before.

I am careened to the bottom of the pool and end up next to the filtering device. Here, I become dizzy, unable to breathe under the water, light-headed and numb. Waterlogged is a special spell that only the strong on our planet can perform. Its side effects are rather potent: lung-paralyzing, brain-freezing, and … dick-shriveling. To no avail, I become motionless on the bottom of the public pool, face-down, helpless, and …

Panis would never let a Jounter die, not even me. Never. It's not part of his code. He drags me to the pool's surface and lifts me out of the water. Here, I lie on my back in the summer sun on cement blocks that surround the pool, under his care. Humans stare at us as he performs CPR on me. The half-man/half-fish connects his mouth with my mouth, fills my system with air, and …

I come to, surfacing from my semi-consciousness. I whisper up to the chiseled hero, "You know you wanted to kiss me all day. You couldn't keep your hands off me, Nemo."

He backs away from me, realizing that I'm perfectly fine. The nemesis studies my body for the umpteenth time: five-eleven frame, 190 pounds, also twenty years old, black hair, matching eyebrows and eyes, ripped chest that is decorated with coal-black hair, dented navel, rounded hips, and deflated knob in my sunflower-yellow Rufskin trunks.

"You're evil," he whispers to me, obviously obsessed with my body, and everything I stand for.

I smile up at him and take in his charming looks. "You want to be just like me."

Anger blooms on his handsome face. His cheeks turn an enflamed red. His chest firms up with a frigidness that is unbreakable. "One of these days you're going to be sent back to Jount for your wrongdoings."

"Never," I whisper, egging his anger on.

"I loathe you, Seale."

"You adore me, and know it. Stop lying to yourself. You want me all to yourself … naked."

"Everything about you is foul."

"Except what you really want from me." I wink at him, discreetly roll a hand over my Rufskin-covered middle, and tease him yet again.

Our scene ends rather abruptly. Panis rises from my side and walks away from me. I observe his tight ass in his red trunks, lick my lips, and desire nothing less than to have my eight-inch triton jammed into his bottom or mouth, wherever I feel like sliding it.

SWIM TALE 2 – UNDER MY SPELL

Horrible events transpire in the city, no thanks to me. The Briscoe Tunnels become flooded. All the tanks at the Nachette Aquarium explode. The sewage system in the city is completely demolished. Swimming pools, both public and private, are all emptied. I bust my hump in destroying my surroundings, overjoyed with my naughty tactics.

Panis doesn't bother me; he's too busy cleaning up my messes. I have a big surprise for him, though. Tricks up my sleeve. Superhuman me has a great plan to carry out for Mr. Goody Two Shoes. Get ready for the surprise, Mr. Panis. Here I come …

I sneak into the man's mansion on Highdale Hill. Booker, the stringy and older handsome butler, is knocked out with a simple fist-punch to his face. Panis is sleeping alone in his massive bedroom, which is comprised of a mahogany bed, matching chairs, a crystal bar, a fireplace, and numerous Oriental rugs. The fish-man has some good taste, especially in his men — me!

Once Booker is unconscious, I stand over Panis in his bed. No surprise that the watery superhero is naked. Here, I visually consume my nemesis and practically drool: seven inches of soft shaft lies against his rigid skin; the tip of his uncut cock touches his hairless navel; clean-shaven balls are motionless between his legs. The half-man's chest rises and falls … rises and falls. I lick my lips, adjust the goods between my legs, feel a bubble of ooze leak out of my shaft's cap, which generously coats my navy-colored unitard that I do villainous battle in. Now, I move forward, lean over Panis's middle, outstretch my tongue, take a lick of his superhuman cock's stem, and brush the tip of my nose against his hairless scrotum. I take in a whiff of his sweaty and potent goods, smile, and eventually stand.

More cream leaks out of my hose, into my unitard. I rub my nylon-covered cock, which is a steeping eight inches, sigh with delight, continue to smile, and reach out one last time to strum the man's balls, which causes me to glow with deep-seeded satisfaction.

Within seconds, I place my lips against his lips, brush the four together, suck in the man's breath like a vacuum, continue to do this for the next minute, watch his eyes open in a struggle and wriggle on his California king-sized bed.

We meet eyes, locking them together. One set exemplifies pain while the other states pleasure.

I wildly sneer, thrilled because of the moment.

He continues to writhe on the bed, incapable of speaking. The half-man/half-fish goes white in the face by my heedless gig of suffocation.

Excited by his asphyxiation, noticing that he is unable to lie still, I giggle above him, and whisper, "You're right where I want you, bud. Make sure you enjoy what's coming next."

I pull out a pink test tube at my nylon-covered hip. The tube is filled with Cellulite, a pink gas from our planet that can cause us both to become sick with radiation-like side effects. I approach Panis's mouth with the plastic container, hold it next to his lips, pop it open with a few free fingers, and watch him consume the toxin.

Panis searches for oxygen, swimming in confusion. He inhales all of the pink gas, immediately poisoned by the Cellulite. The man suffers from a dizzy spell, caught under my unsuspecting control. He lets out a murmur of discontent, attempts to shake his head, but can't. Tears begin to fall out of his eyes, which roll down and over his cheeks. A groan exits his lips, and he collapses in a state of unconsciousness — just as I have planned.

Less than a half hour later, I have my nemesis exactly where I want him. Underground, below the subway and city's graves, is my lair. Here, I place Panis inside an empty, trapezoid-shaped fish tank constructed of durable plastic. Cellulite gas slowly leaks into the aquarium from a vent on one of the walls, keeping him handicapped and under my supremacy. By the look of his swaying, the fish/guy is quite dizzy. Dehydration will set in rather quickly. Memory loss will transpire in less than an hour. Scales along his legs will begin to dry up and fall off. All of his super powers and underwater abilities will vanish by dawn. All of Cinn City will belong to me in just a matter of hours.

Three semi-naked jocks with muscles out the wazoo surround me; my beautiful boy-help. Adam. Aaron. Alex. Each is blond, blue-eyed, and a starlet in the movie industry. All three are eighteen years old. And each adores me with their masculine kisses, cock-rubs, and sexual hungers. My pets. My caretakers. My trio of fun. They study me as I study Panis inside his upright aquarium. I tap on the thick plastic as if the superhero is more fish than man. I drag nails over its plastic shell, which creates the most annoying sound and drives my find and keep insane.

My nemesis comes to from his dizzy spell; I've instructed one of my blonds to lessen the Cellulite that seeps into the aquarium … just for this moment.

Panis groggily asks, "What do you want with me?"

I hear him through the tank's dense carbon-based walls and reply, "What I've always wanted … Your demise."

"I'll give you anything … as long as you let me out of here," he helplessly says, obviously drained and without spirit. The fish/man resembles something spoiled while in the process of dying.

"What do you have in mind?" I inquire, sounding sinister and badass all the way, just as I want him to perceive me during this hostile takeover of his virtuousness.

"You can't keep your hands off me, can you, Seale?"

He's right: since our school days; a few years before; and now. I've always been interested in him. Cautiously, I nod my head and agree with him.

"My body … You've always wanted to get close to it," he barely has the strength to say this inside the tank, almost choking on his words.

"Yes. It's the truth. I won't lie, although I'm known for lying."

"This can be our agreement. If you let me out of this tank … then, I'll let you fuck me."

I think about this for the longest of minutes, studying his naked body: nicely built chest that is bare; firm nipples; almost invisible patches of smooth scales along his hips; barely a noticeable triangular patch of pubic hair between his legs; the seven-inch limp knob hanging between his muscular thighs. "My lust for you has always been untamable. You know this. Have you ever not known this?"

"No, never. And now you can have what you want from me, as long as you let me out of here." His right hand falls to the shaft between his legs, which he begins to stroke up and down, causing it to grow hard. His balls swing dramatically to and fro, enticing me. "Let me out, Seale. Have your way with me. You've wanted my skin next to yours for the longest time. Now you can finally have me. It's your only chance before I die in here."

SWIM TALE 3 – NEMESIS RISING

I instruct one of the three blonds to turn the vacuum on inside the superhero's aquarium. When this is accomplished, the tank empties of the toxic gas and is replaced with breathable air. I now excuse my blond helpers, sending them away and leaving me alone with my nemesis. "Run along, boys. Find something else to do." Listening, the trio of boys scamper away to fuck around with each other in one of the mansion's underground rooms.

Within seconds, I stand at the aquarium and see a peach hue seep into Panis's face. Oxygen is discovered yet again, and his chest rises and falls with simple movement. The man still holds his dick within his hands, but stops stroking it. He says through the thick plastic, contained in his cell like a packaged fish, "Are you ready to fuck me yet?"

"I'm merely waiting for you to adjust."

He shakes his head. "You don't have to wait for me, Seale. A man with your desire is unstoppable."

"Are you afraid I'll wreak havoc on your ass like I do with this city?" I sneer at him, proud of my devastation, thrilled that I have Panis under my care, and overzealous that I finally get to grind his tight rump with my extended chub.

"Something tells me you're all talk."

I wave a finger at him and bristle with a smile, "You're in no position to be rude."

"If you're going to hurt me, get it over with."

"Patience, my toy. This is going to be a fine moment for me. I'm just building up to it."

"Fuck you!"

I roll my eyes, sigh heavily, and respond, "You can be such a boy sometimes, Panis. Shame on you. Spoiled, little you. The biggest pain in the ass in this city. Someone who isn't special at all."

His cock is limp now, hanging over his balls. The man places his palms on the plastic wall in front of him, sneers wildly, and glares at me with fury. "Fuck me, Seale. Fuck me hard and fast ... before I change my mind."

He's a game for me, I realize. Nothing more than a little puppy in a cage for my playful pleasure, care, lust, or whatever else I want to carry out with him. Again, I study his beautiful body from head to toe, lick my lips, and desire our abnormal flesh and transparent scales to mix. I laugh at him: heartily, with my head back, villainously. Now, I say to my kept puppet with his special water powers, "You're giving into my needs rather foolishly. I do expect a little fight out of you."

"Our powers are equal. We can't fight each other."

"It still makes you foolish not to try."

"Just do what you want with me. Have me if you want to. I realize the position I'm currently in. You have all the power over me."

Again, I laugh, knowing that what he shares with me is true. I do have all the power over him; something tells me he wants it this way, completely. "Panis, you're simple. All your good-doing. All your fans supporting you. All the praise from the mayor and how this city backs you. It makes me sick. For once, I would like to see you suffer. This is why you're in the position you are this evening."

"You're horrible. You already know that, though."

It's time to climb inside the tank. In doing so, I confess, "Horrible and horny." Once inside the tank, I stand behind the fish/man and supply his naked and tight bottom with a light smack, which is accompanied with an antagonistic laugh. "I do hope you're ready for some naughtiness, my friend."

"I'm not your friend." His left cheek is pressed against an aquarium wall. The superhero's back lifts and falls as he slowly breathes the human air. Between his shoulder blades are a number of almost unseen ventricles, which allow him to breathe outside of water. Minute and indiscernible fish scales cover his sides and the nape of his neck. A small section of greenish-white-blue scales are also discovered at the base of his back, which are identical to my own.

"How can my nemesis make me so hard? This is what I want to know."

Surprisingly, Panis quickly raises his left arm, swings it backward, and attempts to bash his fist into my beautiful face. This devised action doesn't surface into fruition, though. Instead, I block the hit with a palm, squeeze his hand and fingers into a tight ball, and begin to chuckle. "Petty you. You're always looking for the easy way out."

"Fuck you," he whispers.

"No," I laugh in a wicked manner, "I plan to fuck you."

SWIM TALE 4 – AGAINST THE WALL

Panis is exactly where I want him to be: upright, inside the empty tank, on his knees, and facing one of the walls. Here, I position myself behind him, spank him again, take in his fishy but desirable smell, and say down and over his back, "I hope my cock hurts you and you like it."

Does the half-man/half-fish show fear? I do believe so. All citizens of Jount have fear, among other humanlike emotions.

Now positioned on my knees, I pull his bulbous bottom apart and share, "No more comic book franchise for you, motherfucker. It's over. You're over. You'll just have to get used to it."

He's quiet and obviously ready for my work, which now involves my outstretched tongue lathering the perimeter of his narrow hole. My action is quick and prosaic, salty and sweet at the same time. The tip of my tongue quickly darts into his center, pulls away, and darts inside again.

Panis is simple in front of me. Murmurs of delight escape his mouth, and he begins to pant with excess excitement. My nemesis finds pleasure from my tongue-act, and practically begs for more robust action between us.

Again and again, my tongue delves into his system. Quick juts are applied to his alien rear. One tongue-ram turns into dozens as I hungrily go to town on his bottom, ravishing his insides to my fullest potential. Lick after dip after lick after dip ensues. I become ravenous for the half-human, into my face-fuck with his rump, so very satisfied with our connection.

"Now I want you to suck my pole, man," Panis instructs, playing me this whole time, into our gig, and into my body. Perhaps he has a crush for me like I have always had for him.

I rise from my knees, complying to his wish.

He faces me: eyes to eyes, noses almost touching, lips practically brushing together, without kissing. In a matter of seconds, he stretches his arms out from his sides, backs into one of the tank's walls, and slides upwards, against the thick plastic. Here, he hangs on the wall like a type of leech, aquatic lizard, or scum-sucking fish. And here, his ten-inch cock is hard and stiff, positioned at the center of my face, he begs, "Suck it, Seale. You want to. Don't tell me you have no interest in it. Suck me off. Pleasure the both of us."

I do have interest in his spike: fully, without conditions, perhaps eagerly. I lick my lips, take a sniff of his offered prize, and study its length, girth, and the accessorizing thin patch of yellow-gold hair above its hearty swollenness.

"Play with it. Tease it. Don't just stand there and look at it."

I'm completely caught off guard by these comments, which inevitably prove that the superhero isn't afraid of me and accepts this naughty connection between us with deep satisfaction and allure. Hearing him beg for such action is music to my ears. Perhaps someday soon, I can lead him into carrying out my dark ways, becoming more like me, and causing damage and inhalation to the world. In the meantime, I will surely take what I can get from him, finger the erection at his middle, snap it against his rippled torso, lick the tip of its length, and treat him as the toy I want him to be for my needs.

Nipples are pinched. Abs are fingered. The apex of his knob is sucked numerous times. His thighs are bitten with such zeal. And, his droopy balls are teased by my fingers in a whimsical manner.

My touch sends the half-man/half-fish into a spin of ecstasy. He gurgles something I cannot understand. His eyes glaze over, and his mouth hangs wide open. Panis is still on the tank's wall, though, motionless and in a state of full pleasure. Here, he attempts to buck my throat with his hips, wanting to plunge his shaft into my system, but his rump-cheeks stick to the wall.

I continue to blow him: wildly, ravenously, and relentlessly. My head bobs against his hanging body, falls forward, backward, forward again, and continuous this hyper motion for the next ten ... thirteen ... sixteen minutes, until my nemesis informs, "Stop, or I'll shoot. I can't keep my load in a moment longer."

I listen to him. If I don't, the man is going to spray his sticky fish-churn on my face, which will only cause my eyes to sting. What I have in mind is far better than a mouth to fish-cock blowjob, anyway. Superheroes like me always have gigs up their sleeves, which are mostly raunchy but fun — exactly what I want to share with my captive.

"Spread your legs, Panis. It's time for your ass-fuck."

He listens, and slides down the wall a touch. One leg is pulled up and over his right shoulder and his toes stick to the wall behind him. The fish-guy is like plastic: bendable, stretching, and flexible. Now, he carries this same action out with his left leg, which provides me with easy access to his rump, and whatever else I want to carry out with him.

A condom and some lube are applied to my eight-inch shaft; even superheroes can spread diseases. Within seconds, I step up to his waterhole, jam two inches of my spike inside his wishing well, wedge four more inches inside him, and practically watch him become semi-unconscious against the tank's wall, unprepared for my hefty size and our blending.

To my utter shock, Panis instantly surfaces from his immediate pool of pain. "More ... shove more of your dick inside me, Seale."

Again, I listen. What do I have to lose, since he is my prisoner for the time being, under my full care, touch, and spell? Six inches enter Panis ... seven inches ... ... and all eight inches. My stiff timber rests comfortably inside his bottom, settles here, grazes his fishy organs, and suffocates his ass.

"Fuck me," he demands, into our gig, desiring nothing less than my supervillian staff to pump his insides.

"You want it too badly."

"Shut up and do me."

My pounding begins. Six inches pull out of his hot core; four inches push inside. All eight inches slide out of his pit; all eight inches punch inside.

"Bang all the good out of me, Seale."

"You're naughty, Panis. Do all your superhero fans know this?"

"It's our little secret."

My thumping action continues for the next seven ... nine ... eleven minutes. We both grunt and groan as I bash his rear with all my weight. Our scaly chests touch, sliding together, connecting, blending with friction. We kiss like lovers, which we are surely not. Tongues meet and teeth click together. My hairy balls slap against the aquarium's wall because of my frantic motion. A hollow murmur of excitement exits my mouth, enjoying my fishy cock-ride.

I also cause Panis to bang against the tank's plastic wall. With every thrust, he lets out an intoxicating roar of contentment. One bang turns into dozens … until he turns his head away from my heavy kissing and warns, "I'm going to blow."

This is my cue to gently pull my hairy and rock-hard chest away from his, but leave my rod to continue with its fiery bottom-action. Now, I reach forward with my right palm, apply it to his ten inches of fun, firmly wrap my appendages around his tool, and begin to gyrate it up and down on his rough and plated muscle.

Friction is devised within a matter of seconds, which causes the superhero to close his eyes with pure delight. More moans of deep satisfaction tumble out of his wide but beautiful lips. A gurgle is heard, and … within heartbeats, mere digits of chaotic time, he sprays his pent wad against my merman-like chest, splashing my tight pecs, rigid abs, and my concave navel with his fishy churn. Here, he becomes spent against the wall, weak under my Poseidon-like spell, explosive and orgasmic at the same time. And here, he empties his tuna-like system of his white and sticky caviar, draining himself completely.

Our dirty and naughty act within the tank is not over as of yet. I tell the superhero, "I want to blow now."

"Bring it on. What are you waiting for?"

Following a number of jolts to his core, jacking my pole inside his center, yanking it free from his warm and cozy hole, I stand in front of Panis, rip off the condom and toss it to the aquarium's floor. Now, I apply both fists to the eight inches of upright stick between my steel-like plated legs and begin to rotate my palms up and down, breeching orgasm.

"Do it, Seale," the superhero in front of me coaches.

"Coming … soon." I yank on my goods with pure pleasure. My Swamp Thing-like hips thrush forward and backward. A string of masculine grunts fill the tank, echoing within our ears.

"Spray it, Seale. Stop fucking around."

"Right … now," I reply, and wash his sting ray-shaped chest, still-firm cock and balls down with my seed, covering his fishy texture with my white blow, and releasing every drop of the goo from my middle that I possibly can.

SWIM TALE 5 – SUPERHERO SPENT

We don't kiss following our sexual tryst within the tank. Instead, Panis slides off the wall, stands in front of me, and admits, "You took advantage of me."

"You wanted to be taken advantage of," I challenge. "You've always wanted my cock inside you; it's all you can think about."

He shakes his head. A scowl forms on his handsome face. "Everything about you is foul. You've always envied my goodness, even when we were children."

I reach out with three fingertips, graze his chin, and clarify, "I care for you deeply, Panis … this is my fatal error. I want you to be bad with me. Imagine what kind of damage we can accomplish together on this planet. Think about all the fun and sticky sex we can share as a couple. Wanderlust between us is just one step away for you. Be bad with me, Panis. Let's think about taking over this planet. Let's rule the world together, pal, what do you think?" Now, I drop my fingers from his chin and lower them to his cock. Here, I collect a few drops of my self-exploded caviar from his limp tube of meat, lick it away from my fingers with zeal, and consume it into my system.

Again, he shakes his head in a brisk manner, frowning. "Never. Goodness prevails over evil all the time. Read all the great novels of our worlds."

"Not in this case. I have you right where I want you. You're in no position to suggest such a thing."

"I wouldn't count on it, Seale." The words are barely out of his mouth when my three golden boys/pets/toys (Adam, Aaron, Alex) enter the extravagant bedroom; each are still beautiful with their bare chests and tight, white briefs. One carries a gas mask while the others handle plastic tubes of pink gas: Cellulite, of course. I watch Panis nod his head at the trio of blonds, who now react quickly, betraying my employment.

The gas mask is tossed into the aquarium, which Panis promptly slides over his head. The two other golden boys now toss the tubes of Cellulite into the plastic tank, which both break open and ...

"It's over for you, Seale," Panis mutters above me as I plummet to the tank's floor.

I begin to choke and collapse fingers around my throat. My scaly skin feels as if it is going to shrivel and fall off my bones and muscle. A throbbing sensation occurs between my temples. My dick begins to soften, and my ball-sack starts to feel empty.

Panis climbs out of the aquarium; the three golden boys/pets/toys assist him. In doing so, he feels my right palm reach up for his left foot, which I grasp. Quickly, he tugs his foot away and scowls down at me. "Over," exits his fish lips, which is accompanied with a childish grin.

Following his exit, water begins to fill the tank again. Cellulite, in a pink liquid form, is added to the aquarium by the three golden boys. I feel my eyes close with ease. I feel weak and exhausted. I feel ...

It's not over for me just yet. I won't die here. I can save myself, of course. The battle between Panis and me is not over. I will have him as my confidant, and soon. We will become lovers and mesh our powers together. Earth days are limited. A silly aquarium filling with liquid Cellulite cannot deter me ... especially when I have to continue my sexual adventures with Panis and bask in his lust again, our naked connection, fish-man to fish-man ... wholly.

HOT TO THE TOUCH By R. W. Clinger

1. Man-Hot

I know Frankie Temp's secret: the guy can start fires with his hands/mind ... something. He can light campfires, cigarettes, stoves, and candles with just the slightest touch, along with anything else that can combust with heat and flame. The guy is a walking flamer, and not the queer twink-kind that dangles wrists and speaks with a lisp. Frankie has a superhuman power that is totally unbelievable. Think a male pyromancer with abs of steel, a Zac Ephron grin, a Bieber haircut the color of cocoa beans, cerulean blue eyes with specks of red, muscled shoulders, narrow waist, 220 pounds, six-two frame, and a cock the size of the Empire State building. Frankie is not yet privy to the information that I know about his "special" ability. The twenty-four-year-old is pretty oblivious to the notebooks I keep on him; numerous entries regarding his conspicuous talent and incidents pertaining to his fiery accidents.

Facts: We went camping this past summer, and he heated up a can of soup without a campfire; he takes the coldest showers; I purposely ask him to retrieve a glass of iced tea from the fridge for me and when he delivers it to me, it's hot tea; I know he sleeps with the air conditioner on in his bedroom, even in the winter; he never has to wear a jacket in January; when he takes a walk in the rain, he stays completely dry, even when he's not protected by an umbrella; he avoids oil in the kitchen and never frequents gas stations; once, I bumped into him inside our shared kitchen, accidentally pressed my palm to his hulking chest, and practically seared my flesh; he boils water in a second at the stove. And, I'm pretty sure that he can start fires with his cock-juice, but I've never seen him accomplish this.

A personal fact, which isn't in my notes at the lab: Frankie is hooked on me, everything about me, and lusts for my skin and whatever else he can obtain.

Once, watching a lame Vin Diesel DVD, I question him about his fascinating talent. "You're different, aren't you?"

He gives me a boyish look that is completely irresistible and melts me like wax. Frankie winks at me, "I could be. You'll never know."

Truth is I want to reach out and graze two fingertips against his rounded chin, but I'm afraid of receiving a bad burn. I say to him, "Someday you're going to tell me your secret."

The cutie shrugs a shoulder, beams a pearl-white smile at me, and responds, "Cody, something tells me you already know my secret."

"I'll never admit to that even if I do."

"Just don't put my real name in those crazy science papers you write at the lab."

"And ruin my chance of becoming your boyfriend?"

"Or something."

His secret: He likes guys instead of girls. He likes me. All of me, Cody Edmund Shore. Every ounce of my jockish body. My curly blond hair and five-eleven frame, all 190 pounds, my pine green-colored eyes, and the eight-inch slammer between my firm thighs.

I analyze Frankie on a daily basis. He makes it so easy for me since he's been my roommate for the last year. I'm a scientist down at Bleaker-Patton University, and he's like an easy subject for me to write about, and … he's about as handsome as a movie star, which I don't mind concentrating on at all, almost always sporting a boner in his presence.

My lab notes: He sets accidental fires around the apartment; plastic is a no-no to keep around him; he lights the stove with his right index finger when the pilot light burns out; although we have a microwave, we really don't need one since he can cook anything with a single touch; Frankie can light candles in the apartment with one snap; burn marks are on the kitchen counter from a recent accident with a paper plate; ashes decorate the coffee table from a seared paperback novel he's been reading; I see his liquefied toothbrush in the garbage; and the shampoo bottle in the shower has a melted handprint from his recent use.

More lab notes: He doesn't work because he doesn't have to. His father and uncle invented a military fire-throwing device, which accumulated millions. Frankie was little and stood and watched the two. An unexpected accident/explosion occurred in making the device and affected my roommate, giving him his special superhuman fire ability. Frankie Temp doesn't really spend any of his millions. Instead, he reads a lot of books, paints with acrylics, drinks a ton of coffee, and spends most of his time exercising, which is why he's XXX built.

2. *Firestormer's Pyro-lust*

Reality: He's not a plumber or heating technician. When a January northeastern storm swoops over the city and twenty-seven inches of snow accumulates on the ground, and our furnace hits the shits, Frankie cannot fix the metal beast in the apartment building.

Since I like him a little too much, and since I'm freezing my gonads off, I find his bedroom in the middle of the night, enter without notice, and snuggle against his (not mildly warm, not even cozy warm) radiant-hot body for heat throughout the early morning hours.

He wakes up at my immediate spoon-position next to him and proclaims, "Be careful, Cody. You might get burned."

Does he mean this metaphorically, romantically, or literally? I'm not really sure. To clarify my confusion a little, I inquire, "Do you want me to go back to my own room?"

"Stay here. I know I can keep you warm. You'll freeze to death tonight if you decide to leave."

"How will I get burned if I stay?" I push the envelope a little more, dying to hear his confession that he's Firestormer and victoriously sports fire-lighting powers.

"Let's not get into that."

"Of course not. Whatever. Thanks for warming me up."

"Anytime, pal. You already know I like you."

"How much do you like me, Frankie?" I've always wanted to know the answer to this question. Maybe someday he'll share this tidbit of information with me, too. Then again, maybe not.

"Go to sleep," he urges, rolls onto his back, and …

Perhaps ultimately surprised, I realize he is naked in the bed. Positioned on my left side, facing him, having my legs wrapped around his legs, and my muscular torso against his right side, my right palm accidentally brushes the V-area between his legs and fingertips meet his soft tangles of superhero man-hair.

Investigating comes naturally for me, hence the reason why my palm travels down between his legs and discovers … his limp and uncut fire hose, which is about as hot and as thick as a summertime bratwurst on the grill. I decide to give his tube of fiery-hot meat a tug … two tugs … three tugs, and enjoy my closeness with the pyromancer.

"Cody," he whispers my name in the darkness, which is barely decipherable since the wind outside whips in nasty and brutal S&M movement.

"What?"

"You're making me hard."

"I think that's my intention."

Of course he will pull away from me and tell me to leave him alone; what roomie wouldn't? This doesn't transpire, though. Instead, his man-tool grows into nine thick and sturdy inches. Pre-leak drizzles out of its cap because of my handy motion. But, the ooze shockingly evaporates within seconds because of how much heat his cock produces. As a scientist of pyrogenics, I continue to stroke my sexy sidekick off, forcing more bubbles of his pre-leak to expel from his timber, and evaporate just as quickly.

"You're burning up," I tell Frankie. This is no lie. The guy feels like he is about 150 degrees Fahrenheit.

"Comes with the territory, I guess," he confesses in a whisper.

"What territory?" I ask, on the brink of learning his pyro-secret in full detail.

He pulls the bedspread and sheet away, and prattles, "Never mind … Just beat me off, but be careful about it."

I intend nothing less, of course. Jack after jack becomes rapid on his joint. Heat builds within my right palm: warmness that turns into what feels like a July suntan at Fire Island. Perspiration on his cock surfaces for just a few seconds and immediately turns into vapor, rising within the room.

He growls with satisfaction under my touch. The oddity finds heated pleasure by my hand. His hips thrust upward, into my fist. The man's right arm clamps onto my boxer-brief-covered eight inches between my legs. The mass is stiff and ready to burst by his single grip.

In truth it only takes a few more ample strokes to prompt the flame-thrower to burst his creamy load. Another gasp and groan is released from his nighttime mouth. Hip-bolts fly into my grasp, and he clarifies in a blunt tone, "I'm going to shoot ... Don't get burned."

I honestly have no idea what he's talking about as I continue to get his rocks off. His comment does come into vivid perspective when he finally fires his load. In doing so, gray-white steam rises within the bedroom from his cock. Furious heat builds on my palm, and it begins to burn. And, fiery spurt flies out of his erect stick and splashes against his solid and nicely developed chest within the dimly lit room, illuminating it with the goo's orange-gold flames.

One single drop of his blazing cream lands on my right index finger at the second knuckle and smolders my flesh. Immediately, I yelp like a girl, pull the hand away from his eruption, and wipe the digit on the bedspread, removing his acid-like spunk.

Of course, Frankie isn't done coming. Instantaneously, a sort of masculine giggle escapes his lips as he decides to thatch one of his own palms around his veined pole and finish himself off. After three hip gyrations and consecutive tugs with his left palm, more fire-goo flies out of his nine-inch wanker and splotches his chiseled chest, which evaporates into steam upon contact, rising within the room.

Honestly, it's too much to handle; any scientist of the modern world will agree with me. During his last bursts of goo, I quickly escape the bed, vanish from his room, and discover safety two doors away in our shared apartment. Here, within my own bedroom, I seek shelter, find it very difficult to sleep the night through, and rub the place on my right index finger where his man-ooze sizzled my skin.

3. Fire Frenzy

The furnace mysteriously works in the apartment again this morning. I half-wonder if Frankie didn't purposely sabotage it for the night, so my body could slip next to his with such ease. Is my roommate this sly, though?

"About last night, Cody ..."

We stand just a few feet away from each other in our tiny kitchen, preparing bowls of cereal with skim milk for breakfast. The time is shortly after eight o'clock in the morning. I'm dressed in a pair of sweats, wool socks, and a hoody to stay warm. My roommate sports a pair of cherry-red Rufskins on his sculpted body and nothing more. I take in his smooth and rippled chest, his firm pecs and nipples, the tiny strings of treasure trail beneath his navel, and his massive biceps and shoulders. Part of me wants to pass on my cereal and have him for breakfast instead.

"What about last night?" I inquire, placing the skim milk back into the Kenmore.

"How's your finger?"

I lift the digit and study it: a pencil-tip size wound stares at me, which stings with pain. "It will heal."

He finds my finger, lifts it to his mouth, applies a kiss and saliva to it and ... the wound vanishes, instantly.

Following this superhuman act, I rub the finger, realize it's completely healed, and ask, "How did you do that?"

"Do me a favor and try not ask any questions about what I can and cannot do. What do you say?"

Again, my eyes study his sexy-firm body. Every muscle, curve, and hair on it. I desire him with ultimate hunger and want to sexually feed on his luscious frame. Not only am I turned on by his XXX looks, but I also find his uncanny superpower a total dick-rising treat, which I want to learn more about.

He surprises me by applying a simple kiss to my cheek, which is boiling hot and intense. Speedily, he pulls away from me as my skin begins to warm, and Frankie says, "I need to control myself around you. I'm going to set the apartment on fire or accidentally burn you with my lust."

"Is this your secret?" I inquire, knowing that it is.

His shaft is semi-hard in his underwear, which I concentrate on with my intoxicated stare. My roomie grins from ear to ear, decides not to answer me, collects his bowl of cereal off the kitchen counter, and eats his breakfast.

The city is at a standstill from the blizzard. The lab where I work is shut down for the next two days. Streets, sidewalks, and buildings are nothing but a white mound of snow. Almost three feet have accumulated within hours. Schools are cancelled. Everyone is off from work ... except for Frankie.

"What are you doing?" I inquire in our paper box-size living room, sit on the Belgium sofa, and watch a local weather report by a cutie meteorologist who happens to resemble Taylor Lautner.

"I have some work do," he answers me, tying up his boots and eventually stuffing his arms into a wool jacket; not that he needs either, since he's fire-man.

My lab notes clearly indicate that he can wear clothes without setting them on fire. The reason Frankie Temp can start infernos is simple: if he becomes excited, if his body temperature severely rises, if his sexual desire increases, and if his blood pressure escalates, the guy can set flames to just about anything. Leave these factors out of the equation, and he's just about as normal as you and me.

"You're going to melt some snow around the city, aren't you, pal?"

He doesn't answer me. Why should he? It's his business what he does with his superhuman power. Hell, I'd probably be traipsing about the handicapped city, too, melting the blizzard's residue away, if I had his uncanny ability.

"I'll catch you in a few hours, Cody," he admits, wraps a scarf around his neck, and walks out of the apartment in search of good deeds.

Facts: He melts building ice and snow on the Hudson; the Brooklyn Bridge, JFK Airport, and La Guardia are all clear of snow; Rockefeller Center is accessible again to New Yorkers; Wall Street looks dry as a wheat field in a Kansas August; Greenwich Village doesn't have a snowflake in sight; Chinatown is snow- and ice-free.

Frankie shares a fire frenzy with the city and works his toasty ass off during the post-blizzard. Following his three hours of labor, things start to look better in the area, and the city is less handicapped.

When my roomie returns from his city task and adventure, I make him a cup of hot cocoa, can of vegetable soup, and a toasted cheese sandwich. He gobbles up the provisions as if they are his last meal, thanks me for the food, and implores across the two-person table in our anti-Martha Stewart kitchen, "Cody, tell me something."

I sip my own cup of hot cocoa, stare into his red-flecked and cerulean blue eyes, take in his handsome face, and reply, "What kind of something?"

"How long have you known about my … ability?"

I practically melt across from him because of the puppy dog gaze he shares with me: sad looking eyes, puckered lips, slightly dented cheeks. "Does it really matter, Frankie?"

"To me it does," he responds and nods his head.

I don't lie, ever. Why should I? There are surely better things to accomplish with my life. I clear my throat, take another warm sip of my hot cocoa, absorb the handsome guy in his seat, and confess, "I started putting it all together about six weeks after you moved in."

"What were some of the clues?"

The list was limitless according my lab notes. A few examples come to mind, and I jabber, "I found your melted Crocs by your bed. The pencils on your desk were covered in ash one day. You never wear a lot of clothes. Every time we accidentally bump into each other … I get burned. And, you never use the microwave to heat up leftovers when you're hungry."

He blushes, grins at me, practically slaps me in the face with his charm, and confesses, "I wasn't very careful, was I?"

"Trust me, Frankie, I like you for you, not what you can do with your fire-gig."

"I figured that. It's why I never moved out."

I consume his comment, mentally collect my notes and facts that are based on him, and find the courage to ask, "Frankie, if I decide to kiss you … will I catch on fire?"

He laughs at me: opened-mouth, high cheeks, wide eyes. He explains, "I'll try to control whatever this thing is I have."

"So I can kiss you?" I want to be sure he's not going to torch my eyebrows or set my clothes ablaze.

"I was hoping you would ask me this someday. Let's give it a try, guy."

4. Codymancer

We lean over the table and meet in the center. Our noses touch first, now our lips, and we connect the way gay guys do in the metropolitan area during the post-events of a blizzard.

Again, the kiss is heated and melting, and just about everything I have always wanted to share with him since the day he moved in. If he wants to light my body with flames, I'm all for it, since he has a severe crush on me.

The kiss ends just as quickly as it begins. To my surprise, my lips fail to melt off my face and drip to the table that separates us. Instead, Frankie pulls away from me, has a horny glint in both eyes, and says, "I want to try something hot with your cock. What do you think, Cody? You up for it … and me?"

"Try me," I chant, surprised by his willingness to bed me … or whatever intricate sex-gig he has in mind. I'm all his, as a human torch or not, anything he wants to accomplish with me, next to his muscled skin.

Less than five minutes later, we are in our shared living room, and he rips my clothes off. Frankie falls to his knees and rolls his hot hands up and down my muscular chest. Fingertips pinch my erect nipples. His steamy tongue drags around my navel and falls down and over my happy trail. Within seconds, his mouth consumes my solid shaft, and he begins to suck on its length in a rushed frenzy. Frankie squeezes my balls, grasping them in his left palm. On his best behavior, keeping his fire-starting skill under control, the man gives my balls a tug ... two tugs ... three tugs, and inevitably causes me to groan with delight.

My eight-inch pole is sucked, licked, lapped, and its cap is lightly bitten, which pivots me into a state of pure eroticism. Above my fiery seducer, I grunt and groan, waver to and fro, and almost shoot my pent load into his mouth. Again and again, his throat consumes my rod, breaks free, and consumes it yet another time. Without any inhibitions whatsoever, we meld together, lost in our twosome of intense fun.

Smoke rises from the apartment's carpet where he kneels. Hourglass-shaped spirals of the airy carbon lifts into my nostrils, which is now consumed into my healthy lungs. The apartment will surely catch on fire if I don't push the superhero away. The entire building will most likely burn to the ground if he doesn't stop his mouth-work. Inhabitants, including myself, are in severe danger. Hence, this is why I plant my palms on his volcanic-hot shoulders and reluctantly force him away from my skin and future danger.

On his knees, he peers up at me with concern locked into his eyes, wipes the back of his right hand across his mouth to remove some un-evaporated spittle, and questions, "Don't you like to get blown, Cody?"

I shake my head. "It's not that. You're catching the carpet on fire."

He rises from the floor. Two circular burn marks scar the taupe-colored faux Berber. The marks just happen to be where my model-like sidekick was resting on his sweltering knees. He looks at the dilemma and says, "My bad."

"Keep your fire-thing under control. I'm hoping to get your hose in my ass … just so you know."

"I'll do what I can," he admits, turns me around, pushes me over the Belgium sofa's cushioned back, and becomes frisky with my tight bottom.

Because I am greedy, willing for some tongue-action by the mysterious man, I half-expect him to use his face on my rump. This isn't the case, though. Instead, Frankie pivots his heated dagger at my pink crevice, ready for some man-inside-man friction.

How does his cock feel nestled in my backside? Like a molten steel sword is being pushed inside my core. Like a piece of flaming timber is being wedged against my intestines. Like a blazing kitchen utensil is shoved into my center and rocks my world. Like a hellish inferno brews between my kidneys and tickles my liver. Like …

"Deeper," I instruct, willing him to push all of his nine inches into my center. "Don't be a pansy."

It's the right thing to say at the right time because Frankie listens to me. He shoves all of his nine inches of rock into my middle, yanks the slab of meat out, compresses its mass into my bottom again, and continues this action for the next eight … eleven … nineteen minutes.

Bubbles of perspiration fly off his torso and sting my flesh. It feels like acid dropping against my spine, shoulder blades, and ass. Unyielding pain with pleasure mixes together as the superhero proceeds to connect our bodies by man-lust. My roommate becomes Codymancer behind me, throttling his weight forward, backward, and forward again. His hot palms char my hips. Spanks to my buttocks scorch its tender flesh. My skin blisters under every inch of his wanted touch, desire, and linking.

"Frankie," I moan in front of him, still hunched over the sofa. "Frankie, I'm going to burst. I can't hold my load in, guy."

"Do it," he coaches, plastering my backside with his weight again, manipulating my center with his firework shoved up my ass. "Spray it, Cody."

As if on cue, I reach between my stern legs with my left palm, grasp the eight inches of throbbing meat, and begin to rock it up and down in the most hyper motion, which inevitably sends me into orgasm, and no escape.

A ripple of lava-like heat rolls throughout my torso, between my temples, and eventually collects at my cock's cut head. Following a cadence of ten strokes, another ripple of euphoria, and my skin physically burning under my cohort's strange touch, white ooze flies out of my stick and sprays the floor, my feet, Frankie's feet, and part of the sofa's material-covered back.

Of course, the pyromaniac insists he has to blow; honestly, I expect nothing less. While yanking his orange-red-yellow hot poker out of my behind, he warns, "Step off to the side. I don't want you to get hurt. My cream will act like an accelerant similar to gasoline."

I listen to him; one can never be too careful to avoid a semen/fire spraying between lust-partners. Next to Frankie's upright body, I watch his two hands move wildly up and down on his shaft. To my utter surprise, sexual delight, and horror, his swinging balls, cock, and fists all turn into a ring of golden-bright fire. Sweat gleams on every ab that lines his torso. His biceps pulse with excessive work. The cords that line the fire-creator's neck tighten. Moans and grunts and baying escape my roomie's mouth and …

Within seconds after his hand-game, spirals of wet inferno-semen ejaculates from his sun-glowing rod. Arc after arc of his blazing ammunition flies over the back of the Belgium sofa and splats against its puffy cushions. The secondhand piece of furniture in the living room immediately catches on fire. Smoke and foot-high flames begin to engulf the piece of furniture. More combustible spew continues to shoot out of my superhero's pipe. And, the sofa is on fire in many places, turning into a torch.

There is no time to become spent and mesh together as fresh boyfriends or intoxicated lovers because our shared apartment begins to burn down around us. There is no kissing and intimate playful nicknames assigned. Instead, I rush to the kitchen and fetch a Kidde fire extinguisher. Now, I return to the human torch's side and the sofa engulfed in a firestorm. Here, I use the extinguisher on the sofa, putting out the fire. Once this is accomplished, I spray down Frankie Temp from head to toe, extinguishing the fire at his center, dousing his flat stomach, upright dick, sculpted thighs, and the pair of swinging balls between his athletic legs.

When both fires are out, laughter ensues between us. Now, we meet for a kiss, but separate quickly. The hallway smoke detectors begin to blare in the apartment building. City fire trucks sound in the distance. As Frankie kisses my burns away from our lust-fest, ridding my flesh of wounds with his healing saliva, I say, "I always thought you were hot."

"Hot to the touch," he admits between licking and remedying my wounds, again using his interesting superhuman power.

"It's just the way I want you, Frankie. Don't ever change."

"Not for you ... Not for anyone."

"Perfect," I whisper and decide to kiss him once again before we slip into clothes, evacuate the apartment building with the other tenants, and wait for the city fire trucks to arrive at our post-sex place, claiming the sofa fire in apartment H-12 a minor accident.

FELLOWSHIP OF SUPERHERO PATRIOTS
By Jay Starre

Endeavor One

You had to hand it to the Cloud Runner; he knew drama. He appeared out of a pristine blue sky, silver-slate wings flapping almost lazily as he swooped down head-first, then braked by rearing straight up with those glorious wings wide apart and full. The slash of orange on his face mask and his glowing golden hair added flair as he landed ever-so-softly on the crown of the hill above us. I couldn't help noticing the broad shoulders and tight waist either, or the prominent bulge in his crotch. I'd heard about the size and stamina of his dick, coaxing it out of his normally discrete right-hand man, Detective Dag Smith, who now stood beside me along with the other members of our little fellowship.

The Fellowship of Patriot Superheroes — I thought the name for our clan of misfits was pretty lame, but Dag, our President, defended his sweetheart's choice in that matter. Master Mind didn't say shit unless it was forced out of him, and his partner Nicolas Cyrnica was just as tight-lipped when he wanted to be. Of course there was the chatty and flamboyant Acrobat, irritating to a certain degree. I hoped I wouldn't be stuck with him as a partner for the upcoming Endeavor, as our President Dag had named the gig ahead.

Be careful what you don't wish for. You usually get it.

"Acrobat and Super-Slider will partner up for Endeavor One. That leaves Cloud Runner and Master Mind to take on Endeavor Two," Nicolas announced in his strong Armenian accent. Filthy rich and the money behind the madness, he was our Secretary and Treasurer. Dressed in expensive designer duds, his emerald shirt and cream slacks contrasted sharply with his rather brutish and somber looks.

I liked him. I'd heard about his exploits with Master Mind, too, and couldn't help imagining that beefy butt of his plugged with an emerald vibrator, or my own cock!

Acrobat's slender arm slipped over my shoulders. I cringed slightly, but managed to fake a suitably neutral expression.

He leaned in to whisper in my ear. "They're pairing up the bad boys, it seems, Slider. Well at least we won't have to suffer the company of that idiotically grinning Cloud Fucker, or that serious-as-death Master of the Asses."

I had to chuckle. I was starting to like Acrobat. Just a little.

Dag kissed his hero on the cheek briefly before going into his spiel. In meticulous detail, he explained the current threat and the plan to thwart it. I have to admit I spaced out a bit, my eye wandering toward the other pair, Master Mind and Nicolas, both tall, dark and deliciously sexy.

I got the gist of it, though. It was Dag and Master Mind, being the good detectives they were, who'd uncovered the despicable plot that now threatened the Free World. And here we were, at the doorstep of the Evil Scientist's Lair. Naturally, he was nowhere to be found, as Acrobat and I had already discovered. Fortunately for us, his ingenious Time Machine was present and accounted for.

Just inside the bunker's concrete gates, one of Lars Anderson's Henchmen was tied up and ready for Master Mind to interrogate. Then, if all went as planned, we were off to the past.

It was simple enough for the masked Master Mind to ferret out the necessary info from the squirming and whimpering Henchman. All the big superhero did was place his gloved hands on either side of the bound Henchman's head, and secrets spilled forth like water from a burst dam.

Skipping to the good part, we were ready for action within half an hour.

"The four of you have to get naked," Nicolas announced. A slight grin brightened his blunt features.

Now that sounded fun! I'd already been springing wood just contemplating Mr. Nice Guy Cloud Runner with his costume zipped down and his big juicy dick flopping out. Or that dark goodie-goodie Master Mind with his skin-tight rubber costume down around his knees and that muscular ass of his on view.

We lined up in front of the gleaming copper contraption that was to ferry us into the past. Now it was time for us Superheroes to get undressed!

Master Mind was first, a no-nonsense kind of guy if there was one. Dressed in dark emerald from head to toe, he quickly began to peel off the clinging latex while the rest of us paused to gawk. I'd heard he used to wear leather, but his side-kick Nicolas had conned him into this shiny latex outfit, which I admit suited his muscular frame to a T.

On view now were his flat stomach and narrow waist, broad shoulders, big round ass, and a fat pipe of a cock that swelled slightly as he noted the eyes on it. His mask was last, falling away to reveal his classically handsome face. He'd recently received a buzz cut, again due to the influence of his side-kick, and the short nap of auburn framed his perfect features magnificently. Bowed lips, dimpled chin, upturned nose, and those amazing pale-grey eyes. He was almost too good-looking.

Not to be outshone, Acrobat stepped up to the plate with his usual flourish. The contrast between the pair was sharp. Master Mind breathed muscular poise, cheetah-like and dangerous. Acrobat was all willowy slenderness, tricky rather than menacing. He hadn't changed his costume like Master Mind; skimpy and clinging shorts, boots and gloves and hood in contrasting red and green, it took mere seconds to shed them.

I was already half-hard, and now my dick stood at attention. I might find him annoying and hard-to-like, but Acrobat's vulgar aura appealed to me in a visceral way. His lean and limber frame was smooth, hairless and tanned to flawless perfection. He smiled, a big gash of a mouth that opened to reveal his pearly white teeth and pointed tongue.

I'd heard about that tongue from one with first-hand experience. Dag. He'd been probed to great depths by that lengthy appendage. The dark eyes under dark brows sparkled. The short curls of his raven-black hair were slightly unkempt.

He looked directly at Cloud Runner and smirked, then licked his lips.

The Cloud merely smiled. The dude was just too nice. With practiced ease, he slipped out of his more elaborate costume. His black body suit fell away to reveal the leather straps that served to attach his wings, criss-crossing his chest and shoulders. Although his help was not necessary, Dag stepped up to release the silver snaps for his super-lover and then reverently accept the slate-grey wings that Cloud shrugged off.

They gave each other such a sappy look of pure adoration. I just couldn't help rolling my eyes. I jerked as I felt a pinch on my ass and glanced to my left to see Acrobat winking and grinning.

Bad minds think alike!

It was my turn, but naturally I had to sneak a final glance at the entirely undressed Cloud Runner first. What a powerhouse! More muscular than even the tall Master Mind, with bulging shoulders and immense thighs. His cock matched the dark hero's in girth, but it was his balls that caught my attention. Enormous! I looked up to see him staring back at me. Soft blue eyes under blond brows, a face that could only be described as angelic. Yikes!

My keen sense of smell all at once went into overdrive. Three naked superheroes at my side. Cocks, balls and asses exposed. The stench of male sensuality had me reeling!

I shook it off. I had to get naked quick or delay our little endeavor to halt the destruction of the world as we knew it. I'd chosen to wear a cape on that day. Otherwise my superhero costume was even skimpier than Acrobat's.

The ankle-length cape was covered in a kaleidoscope of color, my trademark. Dragons and forest and waterfalls splashed across the shimmering surface, dazzling to the eye. I shed it with a shrug to reveal my equally dazzling body.

Tattooed images of dueling dragons and angels vied for attention with symmetrical bands of Greek and Arabic script. Nearly all my body boasted those colorful tattoos, except my butt, which was free of them and pale as milk. My platinum blond hair was buzzed short in a zigzag pattern. My costume, what there was of it, was all leather and striped with zigzags of alternating platinum and plum.

A band of thick leather encased my muscular neck, a strap ran down the middle of my broad back and into the deep crack between my plump but solid butt-cheeks. A jock-strap encased my cock and balls. A harness framed my chest. A dozen rings of mixed silver and copper and of various sizes glinted in each ear. A pair of copper hoops dangled from each pointed nipple. A thick silver ring hung from my wide-spaced nostrils. A silver and opal stud was planted in my navel.

As I shed that jockstrap, my cock reared out and up, the huge silver ring that pierced the head shiny with precum.

I wasn't the only one with a boner. Acrobat, not to be outdone in the vulgarity department, actually stroked his. Cloud Runner's fat one was half-hard, while Master Mind's was starting to twitch. The smell of those ripe cocks and naked butts assailed me. Always with a vivid imagination, I fantasized a sudden superhero free-for-all, with wild cock-sucking, rimming and some lusty ass-fucking.

"Into the Time Machine, you two! No time for fun and games," Dag announced severely.

Well, he could sure tell a tale or two about his precious superhero boyfriend, but he wasn't about to let someone else get their greedy hands on him. The smell was driving me half-crazy, and I was about to throw caution to the wind and test Cloud's goodie-goodie nature by lunging for his rising cock and offering him a royal tongue-bath, but Acrobat, bless his nasty heart, saved the day by jerking me forward and into the waiting Time Machine.

Built like some mid-eighteenth century prince's carriage, it had seats open to the air and high steps to ascend, all copper plate and polished to mirror-like perfection. We plopped down, butt-naked, on the cold polished seats and prepared for departure.

One glance at Acrobat to catch him smirking and still pumping his lengthy hard-on, and then a brilliant light flashed and blinded me. A lurching sensation threw me back into the seat, then it was broad daylight. We stood beside each other outside the Time Carriage, and a salty breeze wafted over us while tall palms reared on a ridge above.

The Time Carriage had transformed. It was now a copper and chrome 1935 Dodge sedan, the current stream-lined version that was becoming so popular then. Clothing was piled on the front hood. Our wardrobe.

Nicolas had obviously chosen those clothes. His coarse, stable-hand physique and features offered no hint of his flair for fashion. He and Acrobat shared that proclivity. The slender Superhero was all smiles as he donned his new costume, circa 1937.

Rust slacks and a cream dress shirt, suspenders and tie in matching gold, completed by a bone-beige coat and matching boater hat, not an outfit that most would wear, but actually current for the time period.

With my gear, Nicolas had outdone himself. He'd provided slacks, suspenders, vest, tie, dress shirt, double-breasted coat and sleek fedora, all the usual male get-up for the day. But ingeniously, he'd used color and pattern to create something that perfectly suited my personality, and my powers. Hues of blue, grey and beige combined and clashed with geometric patterns on my tie, the plaid of my coat and the stripes on my vest, shirt and slacks. Even my fedora was checkered in shades of blue. The effect was to dazzle and confuse the eye of those who might look at me. It was hard to tell where my coat ended, my shirt or slacks began. Just like my tattoos, this garb would allow me fade into the background.

Once dressed, we obviously didn't appear typical for the times, but then again, we didn't look like we were from Mars or the future!

"Sweet Jasper, there it is. The second house on the left. I see a trio of guards planted on the front porch. That's swell. All we have to do is get past them."

I stifled laughter at Acrobat's valiant attempt at the period lingo. Best he did so, as our sketchy plan included him getting in for a close interview with our targets while I stood by prepared for the final pounce.

"We'll leave the Time Machine here. It's close enough for the Time Cuffs to be effective, at least according to Master Mind."

It was broad daylight, around 2:00 pm I figured. We were somewhere a little north of Santa Monica and the California coast stretched away in both directions. Sunlight sparkled on the waves and glared off the sandy shore. A trail led down to the row of isolated beach houses. We scrambled down it between shrubs and wind-bent oaks, stealthily crouched so as not to catch the attention of those wary guards.

I wasn't worried much about being seen. I was usually invisible to most men's eyes unless I wished otherwise. Even if you looked directly at me, you wouldn't really see anything but the area surrounding me. If I spoke, though, all bets were off. Somehow that altered a person's perceptions and all at once, there I was.

Acrobat followed me closely. Very closely. I felt his nose in my butt as we made our way to the small road that fronted the homes. Even though the situation was tense, and I should have been focusing on the task, I couldn't help thinking of my partner's big tongue, so close to my crack, and how it would feel sliding up into that warm crevice, licking up and down, and finally slithering deep into my hole ...

We continued in a crouch as we sprinted around the side of our target house while the prowling guards looked right past us.

A large back porch faced the beach. Luckily the area was isolated, and since it was mid-week and the off-season, no one was anywhere around. I pulled Acrobat down and under the floor. There was room enough to almost stand. We huddled together as I pricked up my ears and concentrated on the rooms closest to us.

There was a radio playing, but I easily filtered that out. A moment later, I discerned two voices in deep conversation. The deepest voice spoke in clipped English that was too perfect. That had to be Akio Daichi, the Japanese General who was also the chief scientist in that Empire's military aeronautics research division. The other voice spoke in good old twenty-first century American. He would be Nathan Grant, the Evil Scientist's Evil Henchman. Master Mind had ferreted out that important info in his little mental chat with Lars Anderson's captured other Henchman.

Now it was up to us to prevent the pair from successfully collaborating. I listened while Acrobat fidgeted at my side. After about five minutes, I was alarmed enough to decide we better act.

I whispered in my Super-Partner's ear. "Japanese tanks are in the streets of Shanghai, right now. And this Henchman bastard wants to give them the A-bomb? I'm beginning to feel a little more enthusiastic about being a member of the Fellowship of the Superhero Patriots. We better act. They're still negotiating, but I can't tell if they've exchanged any vital info yet. Get in there and play your cards!"

"I'll make them wild about me, Kid," Acrobat drawled with a smirk, then planted a prim kiss on my neck before slipping away and heading toward the front door to confront that trio of armed guards.

I had every confidence in Acrobat's ability to do as he claimed. Not only was he a superbly gifted athlete, he was gorgeous to look at. His body was amazing while his big dark eyes were impossible to resist. He could be charming as hell, if he chose not to be irritating as hell. He was also the smoothest liar imaginable.

I waited and listened. It was less than five minutes before I heard my partner's voice in the nearby room above. Success! Now what, though? Acrobat's irresistible charm was about to be further tested. He'd convinced the guards he was an associate of the Henchman's. Now he had to convince the Henchman himself and then precipitate the nasty action that would hopefully place us in position to spring our trap.

I stifled laughter as I heard what Acrobat came up with. "Hello, Nathan. Lars has dispatched me here to sweeten the deal for our esteemed Japanese friend. Interested in a swell ass like this one?"

There was a moment of what I believed to be shocked silence. I waited breathlessly. Of course, Master Mind had alerted us to the fact our Jap General was a gay boy. The Evil Scientist, Anderson, had dispatched his gay Henchman to hopefully ensnare the lusty military scientist with the promise of sex — along with the promise of some rather astounding military secrets.

Finally, after a moment of that silence, laughter. Then, more silence. Then gasps and grunts and the sounds of smacking lips. That had to be good.

I needed to get closer. My ability to see through solid objects was barely a tenth of my ability to hear through them. I had to see what the heck was going on.

I could hear the guards chatting at the front door. The back porch was clear. I scrambled out and up, silent as a snake. A moment later, I plastered myself against the wall beside one of the tall back windows. Now, even if a guard came around on his patrol, he wouldn't see me there.

Hidden from view by the drawn curtains inside, I peered in through the porch window beside me. My big hound ears picked up every sound inside as if there was no wall or glass between us. I was glad for those freakish ears, having come to terms with my differences during the difficult adolescent years. I'd chosen to not only embrace my unique abilities and looks, but also to emphasize them with tattoos and pierced rings and studs and hoops.

Music played from a large mahogany floor radio, the dominant piece of furniture in the drawing room, much like a big flat screen television in modern days. An upbeat tempo, lots of brass and a crooning male voice, warbled in the room as background to the grunts, whimpers and gasps the trio on the couch emitted.

Acrobat was in the center, delectable ass in the air. Naked of course. On either side perched the pair we were after. A real live 1937 Jap General on one side, and one of the Evil Scientist's Henchmen on the other. They were half-naked, and they were taking turns eating out my super-partner's pouting pink hole!

Bent over with his knees on his shoulders and ankles splayed wide, his astounding flexibility was on full display. His smooth ass was wide open, and the hairless crack glistened with spit. The Jap and the Henchman were both naked from the waist down with hard-ons raging. The Jap, his dark face contrasting with the creamier tan of Acrobat's butt, was licking furiously up and down it, then pausing at the hole to delve deep with loud smacks I could hear right through the walls and even over the blaring music.

As interesting as I found the view, it was time to slide. Acrobat had done his part, enticing the pair into getting half-naked and occupying them with something that kept their attention focused on him, which was his amazing ass and hole.

I quickly discarded my suit. Not that I really needed to, since anything I wore close to my skin would slide with me. Clothing was simply no longer necessary. Our Endeavor would end in this room, and being naked just like Acrobat was all part of the plan.

We only had the one shot to return to the present. All three of us, Acrobat, me and the Henchman had to be together, flesh to flesh and wrists to wrists when I snapped on the Time Cuffs. Also, we had to decide if the Jap knew too much. If he did, we'd be forced to take him with us. But best not to take him along or we'd risk changing the future, which was our present. It was complicated and dangerous and without certainty.

So the hell what? That's life, as far as I'd experienced it.

I wrapped the Time Cuffs around my trim waist and hooked them together. We would need them. Then I slid. The sensual excitement of passing through a solid wall always got me hard, and I came out on the other side dripping stiff.

The trio on the couch did not see me, even though I was only a half dozen paces away. Acrobat's feet were hooked in his armpits, and he was staring up at the ceiling, so he wouldn't have noticed me anyway. Our pair of targets were intent on the slick ass they had their own faces buried in.

I slipped closer. I needed to join in; the closer I was the better. And distracting the two conspirators was our goal anyway. What better way to do that than to stimulate them into the raptures of sexual pleasure?

I was there. I reached out and pressed my hand down in the center of Acrobat's muscular back. I pressed twice, our pre-arranged signal.

"Why don't you sit on my face, Nathan? I've got a swell tongue I know you'll love!"

Acrobat's ploy was perfect. We needed to get the Henchman totally besotted with sex, so we could get him to blurt out what we needed to know, namely how much he'd revealed to the Jap. The Jap himself was secondary, but we still had to keep him distracted or he might smell a rat and call in his lurking bodyguards.

We didn't want that. If we got in a scuffle, there was no telling who might get hurt, or killed. Not likely Acrobat and I, we were both tough dudes and capable of taking care of ourselves. But if we killed someone back here in the past, how would that affect the future?

Nathan the Henchman played right into our hands. He was up and crouching over Acrobat's face in a flash. As he sat down on that handsome kisser, I was able to look him right in the face, although he was staring down at Acrobat's lush ass and was totally unaware of me.

The Evil Scientist had chosen well. What a cutie! Fair-haired and blue-eyed, with an upturned nose and a curved upper lip, and wide cheeks with a hint of peach fuzz that indicated his youth. Probably just out of his teens. A fool, most likely, but obviously a tempting morsel for the lusty Jap General.

I got a good look at his face as my Super-Partner began to drill into his asshole with that snaking tongue of his. He went nearly cross-eyed, and his bowed lips gaped wide open before he buried his face in Acrobat's ass and began to suck his juicy asshole inside out.

I had to stifle a gasp of sheer appreciation. It was imperative I make no sounds! I could maintain my invisibility only as long as the others were distracted, and as long as they didn't have any reason to focus on me. From experience, I'd learned that remaining as silent as possible was the key to my ability to keep up any visual subterfuge.

But there was no reason not to join in the fun. To further our goal, naturally. Our General's stiff cock reared up from his waist within easy grasp. I slid a hand around it and began to slowly pump. Although rather stubby, it was thick as a club and instantly responded by growing even fatter while jerking lustily in my fist.

He was riveted by the sight of the other two engaged in their nasty mutual ass-eating games. Kneeling on the couch beside them, his small dark hands roamed with intimate greed over both their bodies. He didn't care who had their hand on his dick and didn't bother even looking that way.

One of his hands came down over the back of the Henchman's head and pressed viciously. "Yes, you little American whore, eat that succulent ass while your own tender anus is eaten. Slobber over it! I want to hear you!"

A demanding, dominant and lusty Japanese General. Go figure!

He was handsome enough; I'll give him that. With big golden eyes in a broad face, delicate features and the smoothest walnut complexion, he looked healthy and exuberant. His lips were wet with drool, he himself had been chowing down on my partner's delectable hole only moments earlier, and his eyes were big with lust. His small nostrils flared as he snorted and gasped. He was having a great time.

Nathan was, too. His stocky body wriggled wildly over Acrobat's face. I could only imagine how far up his ass chute that devilish tongue burrowed. For good measure, I slipped my other hand between the pair's bellies and found the Henchman's cock. A big one, too, and very long. I squeezed and pumped it as he heaved and squirmed over the tongue twirling around in his wet asshole.

The demanding Jap Akio Daichi upped the ante. "I believe it is time to fuck this American slut of yours, Nathan Grant. Yes. Fuck him now."

Lube? I didn't trust this pair to be all that considerate so quickly released the dicks in hand and scampered quietly away to the nearby bathroom. I was in and out and back just in time to catch the trio before cock went in ass.

The cute blond Nathan was on his back on the couch with his legs up and wide apart. My Super-Partner straddled him, ass poised over that lengthy pink Henchman dick. I discretely placed the tin of Vaseline Camphor Ice in Acrobat's hand then stepped back behind Akio Daichi to watch and wait.

Acrobat was quick, too. He flipped off the tin's lid and scooped out a huge hand full of the gooey stuff. Arching his flexible back and reaching behind with both hands, he coated the rearing Henchman's cock liberally, then buried his hands in his own ass and layered it with the sticky-slippery substance. It was a treat to see his long and nimble fingers slithering deep into his puckered hole, then sliding out again.

Then, arching his back even further in a display of amazing agility, he reached right down between Nathan's splayed thighs and found his spit-wet hole. As the Henchman groaned, he shoved those same three fingers up the eaten-out slot and liberally lubricated it with that translucent Vaseline goo.

Both asses glistened with a sheen of the semi-clear lube. So did that stiff cock rising up from Nathan's lap. It was the impatient Jap General who seized Acrobat's firm round ass and shoved downward on it. The dark hands settled on the swell of round cheek just below that tight waist and remained there.

As Daichi pushed down, Acrobat aimed the Henchman's cock directly at his greased hole. The tapered head slammed inward and disappeared, followed by all ten inches of the glistening shank.

"Sweet Jasper! That's swell! Why don't you fuck him while he fucks me, Mr. General Sir?"

Acrobat could be pretty bossy, too, in his charming way, but for the moment, the Jap was too preoccupied with the amazing vision in front of him to react to the suggestion. And I couldn't blame him.

Acrobat squatted over Nathan, his bare feet planted on either side of the cute Henchman's lap. His body was a miracle of symmetry, from the broad shoulders down the V-shaped back to the slim waist, then curving outward at his firm ass cheeks and held up by his lean but solid thighs. He was already bouncing up and down over Nathan's cock at break-neck speed, hole swallowing all that meat, then disgorging it, then swallowing again. Grease glistened and oozed.

The radio, which had been blaring out that peppy big band music all at once, offered another tune. An operatic aria floated out over the room, a little tinny and a tad scratchy due to the present state of the art, but moving nonetheless.

My amazing super-partner immediately caught the haunting rhythm and translated it into a sensually writhing performance. Back arched and both hands down on his own round ass-cheeks, his head tossed back and the short black curls topping it in disarray, he grinned brazenly. Huge tongue out and licking at his lips with eyes half-closed, he rode that cock with a slower-paced but equally devouring lust.

Our Jap General moaned aloud and lunged. His fat cock rammed deep into Nathan's greased hole. The impaled Henchman howled, thrusting upward off the couch to drive his cock deep as that Jap dick torpedoed him good.

Akio Daichi went a little berserk, which was chilling to watch. Give that bastard and his countrymen the secret of the A-bomb? Definitely not a thing in the interests of humanity, I figured.

The first few vicious pumps went deep into the howling Henchman's tender asshole. But then, the General went for Acrobat's ass. Pulling out with a juicy smack, he drove up toward my super-partner's hole while pulling down with his hands on that solid ass. That dark blunt head slammed up into Acrobat beside the pink shaft already buried there.

"Oh yes! That's swell, Mr. General! Give it to me!"

Dark cock and pink cock slid in side-by-side as Acrobat arched his back and took it. A hell of a lot of dick was up his butt! I was amazed.

Daichi pulled out with equal brutality, then slammed his thick meat back into Nathan's greased hole. The Henchman shrieked and jerked, ramming his own cock balls-deep into Acrobat's juicy hole.

The Jap took turns brutalizing the pair of holes, sweat flying from his brow and big golden eyes concentrated on the two asses he fucked so violently. The aria on the radio swelled and soared.

I was sorely tempted to give the Evil General a taste of his own medicine. His bare ass, dark brown, smooth and sexily solid drove forward and upward in a crazed rhythm. Feet planted wide apart, I was offered a good view of his own puckered brown asshole.

I fisted my cock, a weapon to equal any of the others in the room. Especially with the big silver ring embedded in the knob. I'd scooped up some of the Vaseline Camphor Ice from the tin Acrobat had discarded on the couch, and the stuff tingled along the length of my cock, a kind of medicinal kick to the goo that was definitely stimulating. I could only imagine how the cold heat affected Acrobat and Nathan's battered holes.

And the smell! All that leaking cock and oozing ass, sweaty pits and lathered cracks, it was a stench so exciting I was light-headed and swaying on my feet.

I badly wanted to step forward and ram the Jap's ass. Give it to him good!

But that was not in our best interests at the moment. I had to think of something else or risk giving in to the nearly overwhelming need to teach that Evil Jap a lesson!

Something had been nagging at me and now seemed a good time to turn my thoughts to it — a puzzle to take my mind off the need to ram hole with my aching cock.

What, really, was Lars Anderson's goal in this crazed scheme? Master Mind and Dag had guessed the Evil Scientist planned on either returning to the past at the perfect time to take advantage of an Axis win in the war, or set himself up in the present to benefit somehow. According to his Henchman whom Master Mind had interrogated, Lars's supercomputers had calculated the future outcome of such a topsy-turvy win and what the Evil Scientist must do himself to take advantage of it. It sounded wildly risky to me. But scientists did tend to think with their heads up their asses a lot of the time.

When Acrobat and I had first breached the Time Machine Lair earlier in the day, we'd discovered a sizable stash of gold and silver bars hidden away there. Ready cash for any time period. It appeared Lars was practical to a certain extent.

If and when we returned to the present, I hoped we would have some answers. While Acrobat and I worked our asses off here and now to thwart the Evil Scientist and his Evil Henchmen, our Superhero Patriot buddies should be busy doing the same in Endeavor Two. Hopefully they'd have some success.

My ears pricked up. Acrobat had all at once curled forward, his face down close to Nathan's. What was he whispering?

"Have you given him the plans yet?"

Flushed bright pink, Nathan's face dripped sweat. Then, he shook his head. No!

I acted.

Whipping off the copper chain around my waist, I leaped forward to shove the now unimportant Jap General aside. Pressed against Acrobat's back, I reached around him and quickly snapped on the Time Cuffs. One on Acrobat's wrist, one on Nathan's and one on mine. I pressed the button on Acrobat's cuff.

It was instantaneous. All three of us were in the front seat of our waiting Dodge on the hill above, still entwined in a tangle of sweaty limbs. And all three of us were shooting wads of juicy cum all over the place. What a rush! Acrobat grinned in my face, his eyes glowing, while our cute Evil Henchman, Nathan, was beneath us thrashing about as our jizz squirted on his belly and chest. His cock sprayed like a fire hose while he emitted a half-shriek of shocked ecstasy.

Although it was a delicious moment, there was no time to waste. I pressed the button again.

We were back in Lars' Lair. Dag and Nicolas ran forward to greet us.

"Are the others back yet?" Acrobat was able to ask, much more composed than I.

"No. We can only wait. Good work, though, Boys. Nathan Grant will join his pal in a cell in the other room," Dag answered.

So, questions still loomed. And the fate of the world still remained up in the air.

Well, what was new about that?

I found myself facing a grinning Acrobat, still as naked as I. "You haven't been treated to the infamous Drilling Tongue yet, my friend. How about a quick round? I can see you're ready for action."

Dag had left the room with Nathan. Nicolas remained, and with a smirk plastered over his brooding features, he chimed in.

"I agree. We got nothing to do but wait now. Might as well pass the time doing something exciting."

What the hell? One quick orgasm was hardly enough when the fate of the world hung in the balance.

And I was really beginning to like both these guys!

Endeavor Two

The two Superheroes had discarded their costumes on the floor of the Evil Scientist Lars Anderson's lair only a few minutes earlier. They watched their partners, Acrobat and Super-Slider, enter the gleaming bronze Time Machine and disappear amidst a swirling kaleidoscope of light. In the aftermath, the machine was still there, but the naked superheroes were not.

Neither Master Mind nor Cloud Runner hesitated. They bounded up into the machine and took their seats. Detective Dag Smith flipped the appropriate switch while Nicolas Cyrnica looked on.

In the blink of an eye, they found themselves seated in another machine, a silver and gold Grand Luxe Renault, one of France's finest in the year 1937. Outside the vehicle, the sun was setting in a wash of magenta over the rolling slopes of a vast vineyard.

They were still naked, but their new costumes were on the seat beside them, courtesy of Nicolas, Master Mind's Armenian lover.

"Before we get dressed, there's one thing I need to try. If you're willing."

Master Mind stared into Cloud Runner's pale blue eyes as he spoke while his large hand settled between the muscular superhero's spread thighs and directly atop his semi-stiff cock.

"Uh, is there time for tomfoolery?"

"No," Master Mind replied with a rare chuckle. "I want to attempt a mind connect. I've only successfully accomplished it twice. And since, according to plan, we'll be separated, I'm hoping through this action we may be able to maintain a mental link between us. You'll be able to see, hear, smell and taste everything I experience. When the time is right, you can rescue me and apprehend our target, the Evil Henchman Ronald Trump."

Cloud Runner's lovely lashes fluttered rapidly, but he didn't look away, and his cock stiffened considerably. "Is that possible?"

"Yes, but difficult. And it can be traumatic. We'll share our thoughts and some of them will definitely not be pleasant."

"Let's try," Cloud replied immediately. He wasn't one to cringe in the face of mere unpleasantness.

"Ok. Lie back and spread your legs."

A slight smile played over Cloud's plump lips as he complied, but Master Mind remained poker-faced even with that somewhat ludicrous statement hanging in the air. Both were large men and bulging with muscle, although Cloud Runner was the bigger with his massive thighs and incredibly broad back. Both boasted gigantic cocks, which slid against each other as Master Mind settled in over the supine Cloud.

"Cock-to-cock, and bare skin against bare skin. This is the most effective way to achieve the proper result. I'm going to kiss you. Then, watch out. It could be quite a ride."

Cloud Runner was devoted to his partner, Detective Dag, and wasn't inclined to cheat on him. He told himself this act was in the line of duty, but there was no denying the sexual charisma of the dark Master Mind. He sensed this was a necessary emotion, and he neither opposed it nor allowed himself any guilt over it. Master Mind's next words proved him right.

"Don't resist. Let your thoughts run free. Let me in and let yourself out."

The two looked somewhat alike. Both handsome with full lips and pale eyes, and even with similar dimples in their chins. But Master Mind was classically handsome with perfect features while Cloud had more character in his face with broad cheekbones and a strong nose and that bright mop of blond hair. Master Mind's recent buzz cut only accentuated the perfection of his scalp and features.

If only he'd smile more, was Cloud's last thought before those surprisingly soft lips clamped over his and a tongue plunged into his mouth.

It was electric. His cock was mashed between their firm bellies with Master Mind's cock throbbing directly against it. As that tongue drove into his mouth, a vibrating, pulsing shock struck directly in the tip of his hard-on, then rocketed down the shank, into his balls, down his perineum, up his asshole and through his body back upward to meet the tongue inserted in his gaping mouth.

They were flying. Master Mind clung to him, sucking on his tongue, thrusting his pipe of a cock against his. They soared into the heavens, night, day, night and day blinking by in a cascade of weeks, months, years. Dark secrets, dark longings, powerful hedonistic urges, criminals' evil plots and evil fantasies; all these thoughts and emotions spilled into him from Master Mind's vast repertoire of experience exploring the depraved minds of the underworld.

Cloud offered no resistance. He let that cascade of horror in, opening wide to the tongue swabbing his mouth. Then he thrust his cock against Master Mind's and released what he had accepted. Sudden orgasm rocked the pair. Cum flew out of their cocks to spew between their naked torsos.

It was over. The tongue came out, and Master Mind rose to stare down at him. A sudden and disorienting vision had him looking down at himself. His pale eyes were half-glazed, his chest heaved, and cum smeared on his belly. He looked divinely lustful and utterly fucked, even though there had been no real sex to speak of. He blinked, and he was now looking up at Master Mind. The Superhero was also flushed with satiation.

"I think it worked. It's tricky though, and might take some time to control. Let's get dressed and to work. There's no time to lose."

As a glorious sunset bathed them in orange light, they donned the costumes Nicolas had picked out for them. His choices were inspired and suited the Superheroes perfectly. Shortly, Master Mind was dressed in a black suit and black dress shirt, with jade-green vest, tie and suspenders. A green bowler, green dress shoes, and of course green gloves completed the outfit. Cloud Runner was dressed similarly, only in different colors, slate-grey suit and rust-orange vest.

It was the south of France in 1937, and they looked the part. Now, time to work on thwarting Lars Anderson's plot to provide the secrets of the A-bomb to the Nazis and thus alter world history.

The vineyard was not only extensive, it bordered a number of others equally large. No one was in sight on the June evening, and they easily slipped through the rows of green vines without detection as twilight descended.

A chateau loomed out of the darkness. Their destination. Inside, the Evil Henchman would be in conference with the Nazi scientist Hans Anderson, Lars' own great-grandfather.

"Here, I can slip inside through the tunnels and cellars undetected while you wait for my signal. You know what to do then."

They had come to a low ditch that lined the south wall of the sprawling stone mansion. Cloud murmured his agreement then hunched down in the shrub-lined ditch to wait. It was the correct decision for him to be the one to wait. He had more patience than Master Mind, or any of the other Superhero Patriots in their recently formed Fellowship.

It was imperative that they disturb the past as little as possible. Both had considerable strength, agility and powers to rely on and were capable of forcing their way in through any number of armed guards, but that path was least desirable.

Stealth and subterfuge would be their initial weapons, followed by a swift and decisive strike when the time for that came.

The location of the gated tunnel entrance to the chateau was one of the facts Master Mind had sucked up out of the mind of the captured Henchman back at Lars's lair in the present. It was not extremely difficult for the pair of muscular heroes to force open the rusty chain and padlock. Combined, their strength was indeed heroic.

Master Mind slipped inside without a glance backwards and descended into darkness. In his breast pocket Nicolas had placed a powerful flashlight disguised as a pen. He used that to illuminate his way as he trotted down into the subterranean world of twisting tunnels, cobweb lined storage rooms and vast wine cellars.

He didn't know exactly where he was going as the Henchman he'd interrogated didn't have that information. But he had a super-human sense of direction. He did know where the pair he sought would be conducting their meeting. He just had to reach that particular room.

One false turn, a quick back-track, then success!

Several bare bulbs illuminated a corner of a large chamber. Wine bottles were stacked along the walls high up toward the gloomy ceiling. In the corner, several wooden cabinets stood behind a sturdy oak table. Two figures sat across from each other.

All along, he'd felt Cloud Runner's presence in the back of his mind. Their mental link had so far proved true. It had been a bit distracting, but he made no attempt to block it out. It was imperative he not risk severing the fragile connection. Cloud needed to know the exact path Master Mind took and needed to know when to strike.

At this particular moment, he felt the blond superhero's presence keenly. For a disconcerting moment, he felt as if he was staring at the scene in front of him out of Cloud's pale blue eyes instead of his own grey ones.

What they both saw were the two men in suits hunched over that table eye-to-eye and between them papers scattered over the dark oak surface. The Nazi himself looked much like his grandson, Lars, blond and lean and very Germanic. Ronald Trump was stocky and peach-complexioned with wavy black hair and bright golden eyes. He looked young and keen.

It was immediately apparent to Master Mind that Ronald Trump, regardless of his youth, was no push-over. It would not do to roughly seize him, press hands to temple, and force out his secrets as he'd done earlier with his fellow Henchman in Lars's Lair. That had been a cake walk, the frightened dupe spilling secrets in a cascade of lucrative details.

One of those details included the important fact that Ronald Trump was not only a member of the Freemasons, but an adept at Tarot, crystal reading, and even witchcraft. He was Lars' right hand man.

A mind scan was the surest way to discover what he'd revealed to the Nazi Hans, but not so simply accomplished. And so far as the Nazi was concerned, one glance assured him this creature was nearly as difficult to read.

The man's mind was so locked up with secrets it would take all of his powers, and a focus he couldn't afford, to crack it. The Nazi had come by his mental control not through diligent training like Ronald Trump, but through much hands-on practice at deceit in his climb through the ranks of Hitler's depraved friends and allies.

Difficult to get what he needed out of this pair. There was a way, though, and he had no choice but to risk it.

"Lars has dispatched me to sweeten the pot, Ronald. Is this sweet enough for your Nazi friend?"

He strode out of the gloom into the glare of the overhead light. His fly was unsnapped, and his cock was out. One big fist surrounded the thick shank while the blunt crown boasted a shiny smear of precum.

It was a stupendous cock, and Master Mind was a stupendous man. Tall, handsome and physically intimidating, any male would find him a daunting prospect. Any male with a lust for other male flesh would find him irresistible. Another important fact he'd ferreted out of their captured Henchman; both Ronald and this Nazi were of that oh-so-gay nature.

"Vell, vell, Ronald! I am quite astounded by your excellent taste! Come, handsome stranger, ve vill sample your vares! Now."

The Oberst, a Nazi Colonel, barked out his orders like the truly sadistic creature he was. Master Mind didn't require a mind scan to understand this man's nature. It was written all over his outwardly placid features, the cold blue eyes, the perfectly coiffed platinum hair, the erect, unbending posture, and the predatory flutter of his finely formed hands.

Ronald offered a beaming smile that outwardly appeared genuine, but the eyes told a different story. Calculating, suspicious, but willing to wait and see.

Master Mind would have to tread very carefully! Still, boldness at this moment was critical.

As he strode forward, almost bouncing with that particularly lithe grace he possessed, he discarded his clothing in a mesmerizing flurry. Coat and tie, suspenders, vest and dress shirt, shoes and socks, dress slacks and underwear, and finally gloves. Only his emerald green bowler remained.

What a specimen of manhood! Narrow waist, bulging shoulders, powerful chest, rippling muscles on arms and legs, he was the picture of proportion. His cock reared outward and upward, thick and solid.

"What is your pleasure, Oberst Anderson? Your wishes are my command."

His glorious nudity and pulsing cock were not the only formidable weapons at his disposal. His husky voice was pitched in a suggestive purr, meant to convince the one who heard it to believe his words were their desires.

The Nazi's cold blue orbs burned with intense focus. His smile was ear-to-ear. It was obvious he didn't require much convincing!

"Ronald, vould you be so kind as to open the top drawer in the left cabinet? Our host and my good friend Viscount Pierre Trudeau and I often come down here and entertain ourselves. He has left us some items ve vill find most useful."

The peachy-faced Henchman obeyed with alacrity, but Master Mind knew it wasn't because he was captivated by Master Mind's awesome appearance. It was because he would do anything to accomplish the job he'd been dispatched to do.

Master Mind arrived at the table and immediately dropped to his knees in front of the standing Nazi. His amazing body was poised in a position of submissive acquiescence, exactly how he believed the Evil Nazi would best appreciate it.

Ronald had done as he was told and placed the Viscount's nasty toys on the table out in plain view. A pail of pasty lubricant sat beside two midnight-black objects — a large butt plug and an even larger strap-on dildo!

Master Mind had no time to contemplate the uses of those obscene toys. The Nazi Colonel had reached down and cupped his strong chin. His icy blue orbs stared down into the handsome superhero's grey ones. As those fingers came into contact with his flesh, Master Mind experienced a shock of gut-churning emotion.

Cloud Runner, crouched in the ditch in the darkness outside the chateau, experienced the same shock of horrible sensation. The Evil Oberst's base nature flowed through those fingers into Master Mind like ice-cold water from a glacier-fed stream.

Cloud was rattled to the core. This mad creature was fully capable of fucking you, then murdering you, and with equal pleasure! By nature, the blond superhero saw the best in everyone, rather than the worse. Faced with this naked cruelty he almost lost the will to maintain the pair's vital mental link.

Master Mind was both strong and experienced enough not to quail. He rescued them both by allowing the barbarity to flow though him, displaying not the slightest tremor, but rather offering a smile instead.

"Yes! Ve vill enjoy subjugating this masculine morsel! But first, ve vill prepare you, Ronald to participate in this delightful task. Strip and place yourself on the table on your back."

The Nazi offered a sardonic smile as he reached over and turned up the dial of the radio atop the nearby cabinets. Piano played in the background as a husky French voice crooned a throaty love song. Master Mind understood the loud music was intended to mask any sounds they might make from the Nazi guards he was certain lurked outside the closed door on their left.

The Nazi's cold eyes gleamed and that smile grew broader as he watched Ronald obey his command. He snapped out a second order for the kneeling Master Mind.

"You vill sit on that sweet young face vile you ornament our friend with those lewd toys. Understand?"

He did. What would come afterward, he tried not to guess at. He would take it one step at a time, portraying the compliant slave to the Nazi's every whim, no matter how depraved. He leaped up onto the table in a single bound, then after a brief glance down into Ronald's intense golden eyes, turned and squatted over his pretty face. He sat down on it, as commanded.

Ronald played his part with equal enthusiasm. His hands came up to seize the muscular ass-cheeks and spread them. His nose drove up into the parted crack, followed by his lips, then his tongue. He began to suck and slurp, vying with the French singer in the background to be heard.

Master Mind settled over that mouth and tongue and allowed his asshole to open to it. The delicious sensation did nothing to deter him from the task at hand, not yet at least. With a furtive glance at the piled papers shoved to the edge of the table, he reached out and took up the first of the two toys — the strap-on dildo.

He laid the black cock on Ronald's creamy-pale thighs just below his cock and balls. He had a big cock, not exactly thick but very long with a wicked curve in it. It was already stiff and looked somewhat like a bow ready to be strung. He smiled as he gripped the base and leaned down to suck it into his mouth.

Ronald's sturdy body lurched upward as wet lips and warm mouth enveloped him. His tongue stabbed into Master Mind's tender asshole and his fingers squeezed the superhero's solid ass-cheeks. Master Mind buried his face in the squirming Henchman's lap, opening up his throat and taking that curved shank to the balls.

"Wery nice. But I am a little impatient. Move on, glorious stranger."

The barked order was followed by a sharp slap to the face that served to knock Master Mind's green bowler from his head. He obeyed immediately, unaffected by the stinging blow. He expected the possibility of much worse to come if he wasn't constantly alert and prepared to move swiftly when the time came.

He rose off the bobbing cock with a wet slurp and did as the Nazi Oberst ordered. With one hand, he scooped out a handful of the pasty grease from the open pail, some kind of thickened lotion redolent of linden flower. It melted into a slippery translucence as he applied it to Ronald's twitching cock with his fist. He pumped up and down the pink shaft, squeezing and tickling the head. Ronald reared upward, his tongue twirling farther up into the depths of Master Mind's asshole.

Then he slid the strap-on over that greased pole, the hollow interior a close fit but pliable enough to accept that lengthy curve and swallow it whole. Now, instead of a pink cock rearing from his crotch, the Henchman boasted a truly enormous black dick, with a blunt head and rippling with fake veins. The target for that big black weapon was pretty obvious.

He slid the greased fingers of one hand down between Ronald's squirming thighs. The Henchman immediately raised his legs and spread them, opening up his ass-crack. Master Mind's slippery fingers trailed downward and across the puckered hole he found there.

After tickling the hole only briefly, he finished off attaching the strap-on by securing the leather straps around Ronald's upper thighs and waist. There was a cavern in the base that accepted his balls so that by the time Master Mind was finished, the thing was firmly attached to his crotch, cock and balls now hidden from view behind that gross black dildo.

But there was more. One toy remained to be utilized. He picked it up and placed it down between Ronald's splayed thighs. Scooping out more of the pasty grease, he lathered up the Henchman's crack with it. He began to work some into Ronald's pouting pink hole.

The young Henchman raised his feet and reared upward. His hands, which had been clamped over Master Mind's firm ass, came out to grip his own toes. He pulled back and down, exposing the entire expanse of his luscious ass. Round and hairless, it was pale as milk and without a single blemish. It jiggled slightly as Master Mind rubbed the slippery paste all over it with one hand and used the fingers of the other to lubricate the youth's hole.

One finger slipped inside quite easily. He probed with it, feeling the warm interior churning as the grease melted. Ronald gurgled something unintelligible as he continued to suck and lick at Master Mind's asshole. When a second finger slid into him, he reared up and gurgled louder. When a third stretched his quivering butt-rim, he grunted and jerked wildly.

It was time for the plug. The thing was big, almost half the size of a clenched fist. The tip was tapered to easily fit between those greased ass-lips, but almost immediately it swelled outward into a fat center, then tapered back down to a narrow end just above the square base.

He was not gentle, but neither was he as brutal as he made it appear. After all, the Nazi was watching and expected no mercy. Ronald co-operated in their subterfuge splendidly.

He began by rapidly plunging the greased tip in and out, a touch deeper with every shove. Ronald squirmed enthusiastically and emitted histrionic though muffled squeals. Master Mind knew what he was doing. Not only was he experienced in asshole play, his keen senses allowed him to accurately read every nuance of Ronald's reactions.

"Yes, my Glorious Stranger. Plug that sveet vite ass! Soon enough it vill be yours feeling all that agony!"

Understanding the Nazi's cruel desires, he drove the plug home with what appeared to be a final violent shove. His timing, though, was impeccable. Ronald reared upward to slam his jiggling ass against the plunging plug at that precise moment, and together they drove the fat part of it past the Henchman's suddenly yawing sphincter. It slid inside him.

The square base protruded from the jiggling mounds, black and greasy. The Henchman was now plugged and strapped.

"Excellent. Now you vill bury that handsome face in my firm German ass. I trust you vill enjoy licking the ass of a superior man?"

"Yes, Oberst. I will enjoy licking your superior ass — while my own inferior one gets fucked."

The Nazi tossed back his head and let out a chortling laugh. He'd stripped off his own suit while the pair on the table had been engaged in obeying his orders. Naked, he was all lean muscle and as pale as Ronald. His body was taut and rigid, including his slender cock. There was no softness in that torso nor the wiry limbs. None at all.

As the Nazi clambered up onto the table, the other two came down from it. Ronald offered Master Mind a small smile and a conspiratorial wink, but his eyes were still guarded. He moved with his thighs wide apart, obviously feeling that plug buried up his ass and the weight of that enormous strap-on rearing out from his crotch.

They took their places. The Nazi Oberst crouched on the table top on his knees. His head was down over his folded arms. Rather than appearing like the cruel master, with his legs spread wide and his ass in the air, he looked more like the submissive bottom willing to take tongue and more up that smooth white butt.

Regardless of the fact his ass was obviously ready for use, submissiveness was not in his nature as he proved with his next words. "Now, you vill lick the Oberst's ass vile young Ronald fucks yours vith that big strap-on. And you vill squeal vith delight as every huge inch inwades your tender asshole!"

With little choice in the matter, the pair obeyed. Master Mind leaned against the edge of the table and reached out to grasp the Nazi's ass-cheeks. He spread them apart and bent in to bury his face in that parted crack. His first surprise was how full and soft those white mounds proved to be. The rest of the Nazi's body was so lean, he hadn't expected the lushness of that round ass.

His second surprise came as he stuck out his tongue and began to lick at the crinkled pink hole.

It pouted and yawned open, yielding like a blossoming flower to his lapping tongue. The Nazi seemed to have only one soft spot in his body, and that hole was it! Master Mind wasted no time. He slid his tongue as deep as it would go and twirled it around.

"Yes! Yes! Delightful! Now, young Ronald, prove your trustvorthiness. Fuck your accomplice. Fuck him hard!"

Fortunately for Master Mind, the peachy-faced youth had taken a moment to liberally grease up that gigantic strap-on. But that was about all he did to ease the brutal invasion. He stepped in between Master Mind's spread legs, grabbed hold of his stupendous ass-cheeks, and thrust up into the parted crack with that huge strap-on.

After sliding around momentarily, the blunt black head found hole. Master Mind had one split second to prepare himself. He knew what to do. Resistance was futile, and so he reared backwards, arched his back and relaxed his sphincter.

Still, when the gigantic head of that dildo rammed past his butt-rim, he let out a less than manly squeal. Partly to satisfy the cruel lusts of the Nazi Oberst, but partly due to the fact that big knob was straining his poor asshole to the limit as it pushed past the ring and into the tunnel beyond. It was like a fist was being jammed up him!

"Yes! Skveal like the American pig you are! Skveal vile your American friend fucks your gorgeous ass into submission! Skveal, little piggie!"

It actually helped, emitting those high-pitched shrieks while slobbering over the Nazi's pale round ass. Letting out those squeals somehow aided him in not only relaxing, but pouting outwards with his asshole to accept more of the enormous dildo pumping into him.

It worked, sort of. It felt as if he had an arm up his ass, but he realized only the head and a few inches of the thick shaft were inside him. The daunting prospect of all fourteen inches of the monster toy driving up his gut was more than a little challenging!

Back in the ditch in the darkness outside, Cloud was fully aware of what was happening. Not only could he feel and smell and taste everything Master Mind did, he could also hear his thoughts. The crouching superhero realized he needed to strengthen Master Mind's will power somehow. It was a crucial moment, and their enemy was armed to resist. There was only one thing to do.

He quickly stripped off his shoes, slacks and underwear. Naked from the waist down, his stiff cock reared up between his thighs. Crouching down, his hefty ass-cheeks were spread wide, his enormous balls dangling between them. The cool evening air wafted over his exposed butt valley and twitching hole.

Mentally, he threw himself back into Master Mind's head, while maintaining an alternate vision of his own semi-naked body. He felt the huge strap-on as it plowed deep into Master Mind's quivering ass channel, and at the same time he leaned over, arched his back and visualized that same strap-on ramming deep into his own tender hole.

Whispering aloud, he urged on his superhero accomplice, "Let it in! Welcome that huge toy like it's your lover's hot cock! You can do it!"

Cloud bit back a triumphant shout of he imagined he felt that huge greased toy drive far up his ass. They'd done it!

Master Mind heard Ronald's shocked gasp as that dildo drove home. The stuffed sensation in his gut was no longer unpleasant, due to Cloud's timely aid, but there was more required.

The Evil Henchman recovered from his shock almost immediately, proof of his mental strength. He pulled half way out, and slammed home. Master Mind took it without a hitch, which only spurred Ronald on to even more savagery.

He began to pummel the bent-over superhero with that monster black strap-on, slapping his ass and shouting out crude comments, which the Nazi Oberst certainly appreciated — and echoed.

"Yes! Fuck that American pig vile he licks my ass and skveals! Hard, yes, wery hard!"

And in the background, the radio played that crooning French ballad.

Master Mind was able to cope with the savage pummeling and those equally savage comments due to the heroic force of his will power. But in order to reach his goal, delving into Ronald's mind, he knew there was even more required. He must actually enjoy the brutal fuck, rather than merely pretend to. That was the secret of his power over others, not devious subterfuge, but his ability to speak or act honestly, even while manipulating others toward his eventual goal.

He willed his ass to open, to collapse inward, to suck in the huge strap-on, creating a well of slurping ass pit that was absolutely irresistible. He slammed his hefty ass back against Ronald's thighs, caterwauling between the Nazi's spit-wet ass-cheeks, groveling in the stink of hole and ass and male sweat. He ate that hole out, sucking the lips outward into swollen pink petals.

He thrust his tongue far up the Nazi's quivering slot, twisting, twirling, stabbing. The kneeling Oberst's nasty shouts degenerated into whimpering pleas as he felt his own hole becoming a sloppy pit of pleasure like never before.

It didn't happen exactly as he'd planned, but it happened. As Ronald shouted from behind and the Nazi whimpered in front, gigantic dildo burrowed its way home in his gut. His tongue stabbed viciously at Nazi prostate and all at once the mind bridge occurred.

He accomplished something he'd never even attempted before. The mind connect not only trapped the enthusiastically fucking Ronald, but yanked in the Nazi Hans Anderson as well, simultaneously, while Cloud Runner hovered in the background listening to it all.

The three-way mind connect occurred not through a temple-to-temple meeting, but through something deeper. That brutal hole invasion had become a trap for the Henchman's dildo-encased cock — and his evil soul! Ronald was drawn in, descending into a vortex where he could not pull out. And the Nazi, with that deliciously tantalizing tongue up his ass, was sucked in as well.

Thoughts spewed. Secrets, even those barricaded behind the cleverest of mind tricks, were revealed.

Cloud acted. Leaping up, he thrust himself airborne through the open gate into the stygian darkness. Wingless, true, but he didn't need his wings to fly. He certainly used them to increase his speed, along with his ability to twist and turn and brake, while of course adding drama to his costume and appearance. But flying was in his nature, and now when it was needed, he flew.

The darkness was no impediment either. He could see the exact path Master Mind had taken earlier in his mind's eye. It took less than a minute to reach the action.

He came flying in and took in the scene in one heart-pounding flash. It was crudely obscene. Ronald Trump's round white ass jiggled and heaved as he thrust forward with that ludicrously huge black dildo and impaled Master Mind from behind. The black straps outlined his heaving buttocks. The square base of the big plug buried in his ass protruded nastily from the center of his deep crack.

At the other end of the mass of heaving flesh, the Nazi Oberst knelt on the oak table with his lean thighs splayed wide apart and pale ass coated in sweat and spit as Master Mind's tongue impaled his pouting rosy-red butt-hole.

The two evil-doers shared the same glazed look of depraved ecstasy. It was apparent they had no idea Master Mind was sucking all their thoughts from their gaping minds!

Cloud Runner continued on, flying low to slam into the trio, scoop up both Ronald and Master Mind, swerve upwards to twist and slam his feet against the cellar wall and spin them around backwards toward the way he'd come in a moment earlier.

Leaving behind a grunting, bewildered Nazi with his wet hole pouting empty, Cloud managed to do three things at once. While cradling the pair beneath him in his powerful arms, he whispered into Master Mind's ear to let him know the all-important Time Cuffs were in his vest pocket, while he veered around the twisting walls of the cellar maze.

Master Mind, with dildo still planted deep in his ass, managed to act as swiftly. He reached up and back to snatch the cuffs, then snapped them onto all three of their wrists. While still flying, he pushed the button that instantaneously transported them back to the parked Grand Luxe Renault that was their doorway to the present.

They were suddenly inside the front seat in a pile of squirming flesh. Cloud had abandoned his slacks and underwear so was naked from the waist down. His cock had been stiff and dripping during the entire nasty interlude as he experienced all of Master Mind's most intimate sensations and feelings.

It was no wonder he shot a huge load into the heaving crack of the butt-plugged Henchman beneath him. And Master Mind, too, released a copious spew, his pipe-cock spraying the seat beneath them.

Ronald was trapped between the pair, bewildered, bemused, and foundering in the erotic miasma of Master Mind's skillful trap. His cock, encased in that strap-on and buried up Master Mind's exquisitely sucking asshole, could not escape the same fate at the other two. He shot.

It seemed there was something about the Time Cuffs that encouraged that type of rapturous response. The trio thrashed about in the front seat in the darkness sharing a mutual orgasm that was profound to say the least.

Even so, with that monster dildo rammed up his ass and unloading all over the seat, Master Mind maintained enough composure to push the button on the Time Cuffs for the second time.

The trio were back in Lars Anderson's lair, sprawled within the Time Machine and looking out at their compatriots.

"Did you succeed?" Cloud asked Super-Slider breathlessly as he helped the other two down from the machine.

Slider replied with a jaunty salute and a smirk. "Mission accomplished! And it looks like a juicy success on your part as well!"

Ronald Trump stood between the pair, still bewildered, and with that greased black strap-on protruding from his crotch. The cum-smeared dicks of both Master Mind and Cloud Runner told the tale.

Master Mind pushed their captive over to his brute lover's welcoming arms. "Lock him in with the others. I've milked him dry."

Nicolas grinned as he smacked the luscious young Henchman on the butt, then slid his hand between his round ass-cheeks and pressed against the buried plug. "We'll leave him like he is. His buddies can take advantage of his new endowments!"

The auburn-haired superhero smiled in return and nodded before he turned to the other members of The Fellowship of Superhero Patriots.

"When Ronald shot, the last of his secrets spewed with his wad. I got all we need to capture our final perp. Lars Anderson had planned on returning to the past with all his gold just after the Nazis and the Japs won the war. He would have joined forces with his grandfather, Hans, and together they would have re-invented all kinds of technological miracles from our present time and thus become not only fabulously wealthy, but the most powerful men on Earth. Not a happy prospect. But now, we merely have to hunt him down and capture him."

Super-Slider spoke up. "That's all? Where is he? And he seems kind of smart and tricky. I can't see this being such a snap of an endeavor."

Both he and Acrobat had donned their costumes again and Dag was busy helping Master Mind and Cloud Runner back into theirs. He turned to Slider and offered his take on the matter.

"Master Mind and I are good detectives. Lars won't be able to hide from us. And meanwhile, you and Acrobat can have the honors of destroying the Time Machine. It's not a good invention."

Acrobat grinned, his big tongue snaking out to flick at his full lips. "Awesome! A bit of delicious smashing to be done. Just up our bad boy alleys, eh Slider?"

The pair set about their destructive task with whooping enthusiasm as the other three huddled together to make plans.

Dag kissed his lover on the lips and gazed up into his eyes adoringly while Master Mind looked on. "Well, Endeavor Three is about to begin. Another adventure for The Fellowship of Super- Hero Patriots! I hope the last one wasn't too dangerous? You know I worry about you."

Cloud Runner's pale blue eyes met Master Mind's paler grey ones and they shared a look of mutual understanding before he answered. "Dangerous, of course. But illuminating. I'll fill you in later."

Master Mind had no doubt the blond superhero would be entirely honest with his devoted side-kick. It was his nature.

AUTUMN BLAZE By Jay Starre

Stephen felt safest when he was above the dancing crowds in his booth mixing music. The blaring beat drowned out conversation — or intimidation. Choosing a fresh sound and feeling it rock the dance club, then watching the reactions on the multitude of frenetically dancing men soothed his demons.

Even in the dim light of the dance club, he wore sunglasses. It was his disguise, not against others, but against himself. His control board radiated with intense directional lighting; he could see it perfectly even through the tinted lenses. The crowds outside his isolated tower glittered in their finery under pulsing overheads, yet were a blur of anonymity. That suited him.

He raked a hand through his bushy jet-black hair, pushing it back over his scalp and sighing. It would soon be time to go. He sensed the night outside, the warmth of the autumn day finally bleeding away under clear, cold skies.

Autumn. Yes, it had come again, and with it the strange alteration inside him. A night creature, Stephen worked at gay clubs and events throughout the city, nearly always after dark. He did dare the light of day on occasion, and yesterday he'd felt its call. He'd walked through the park and breathed in the heated air, a last vestige of a dying summer. He'd soaked up the autumn colors, vibrant reds, shimmering oranges, stark yellows. Dying leaves displayed all their gory finery.

Tonight he would don his costume, his autumn persona. The sight of those red-orange leaves had precipitated it; the crisp air had sealed it. Why did it happen, that change in him? He had no idea; he merely accepted it. He did wonder if it had something to do with his crazy psyche. He was crazy, pretty much.

His replacement came into the booth to disturb his reverie. Don grinned gratitude at the mood in the house Stephen had created with his inspired choices. The newly arrived DJ could play crap, and the crowd would eat it up. Already in a dancing frenzy, nothing would stop them now except exhaustion.

Stephen slipped out the back door into the dark alley. The potent urges swelled and throbbed inside his taut frame the moment he inhaled the chilled air of the autumn night. He rushed home to his downtown condo through back alleys, avoiding people as much as possible.

Inside, he quickly stripped, feeling aroused briefly in his nudity as he stared into the mirror. His lean body was smooth and well-muscled, amber-gold flesh nearly blemish-less, good-sized dick now swollen and jutting from his crotch, a well-formed and desirable butt curving out behind. He had lovers who enjoyed that body, but he himself mostly felt distanced from it. He shook off the usual doubts and slithered into the skin-tight body suit he'd sewn himself.

He was good with a thread and needle, he'd discovered, and not a bad fashion designer. He was gay, of course, and that must have been why he was a wardrobe freak. Most of his quirks and qualities he attributed to being gay.

A navy-blue hood concealed his head and face; a thigh-length cotton coat of the same color covered most of his body and flamboyant costume. The dark of night would shroud him until he reached his destination.

That destination was as yet unknown even to him. Once outside, breathing in that crisp fall air, his senses stirred. What new power would manifest this season? He picked up a distant sound, very distant. A mile away, in fact.

Ahhhhh. It would be his hearing this year.

Every autumn something would alter in him, some sense heightened to unbelievable acuity. He cocked his ears, like some kind of hunting animal, and listened. He heard it again. He took off at an easy lope. A disciplined jogger, he could run for hours.

It was in the park. Yes, the disturbance he craved was there. He knew the spot, the parked cars in the isolated dead-end. Trees leaned over to conceal whatever sweaty night groping occurred inside and outside of cars, pavement and bushes.

A gay cruising ground, it would be teeming with furtive and not-so-furtive men searching for satisfaction in the clear autumn evening. It was also a dangerous place, as on this night.

"Get on your fucking knees, fag, and pray to God for forgiveness for being a pervert before we beat your cock-sucking head in!"

The hate in those words resonated in Stephen's head like a hissing snake gone mad. He was there, close enough to see the gang of six surrounding their hapless prey. The far corner of the parking lot was deserted of cars, and the streetlight was broken. It was nearly dark there, with only the stars to illuminate the violent scene unfolding.

Stephen heard the choked sob of someone who had already been kicked and punched. Fear stunk in the air, exhaling out of both prey and attackers. Golf clubs hovered dangerously in the air, innocuous weapons but devastating when wielded with anger.

The surge of power rocked Stephen back on his heels, halting his headlong rush briefly. But nothing could stop him now. He leaped ahead and thrust his way through the menacing group to its center. In a lightning-swift move he shed his outer garment.

Light blazed in gaudy violence. Shimmering violet-red, sun-searing gold and mind-numbing orange pulsed in the air, emanating from Stephen's striped red and orange body-suit. The blaze blinded everyone nearby except Stephen himself.

In the midst of gasps and growls, Stephen felt time freeze as he surveyed the attackers. Young, from sixteen to twenty-two. Two were white, one black, two Asian. Racial harmony only achieved in their shared hate. Fools, idiots, overtaken by their own inner anger. He felt sorry for them, an emotion he only occasionally experienced. He snatched a moment out of the adrenalin-charged well of time to savor and taste that brief experience of humanity.

Then, he struck out. He whirled in the light that blinded all except him. His hands and feet, trained in martial arts from a young age, snapped out like coordinated whips. Golf clubs flew from upraised hands. Knees buckled, and youths went sprawling onto their backs.

The outcry resonated dread. "It's Autumn Blaze! Run, fuckers, run!"

"Yeah! Run, you little fuckers. Before I break your arms and legs," Autumn Blaze hissed out at them.

The light blazing from his body made it impossible for any of the group to see, but they managed to stumble away. On shaking legs and shielding their eyes, they sobbed like children. The only one remaining in Stephen's circle of shimmering light was the kneeling victim.

He sobbed, too. His eyes gaped wide open, drinking in that pulsing glow. His arms in the air where they'd been poised to protect, now reached for Autumn Blaze, his savior.

Stephen stepped in and took those hands in his. This was another moment of extreme inner confrontation. As he gazed down at this innocent victim, he hoped to feel a sympathy akin to what he'd felt for the attackers. He hoped to feel sorry for this innocent man.

But more than that, he hoped and prayed to feel guilty.

Their hands touched as Autumn Blaze's eerie light shimmered all around them like a sun in nova. The shield of pulsing color held the outside world at bay.

Stephen remembered.

He was just a teen then. Eighteen. His buddies, his gang, had chanced on a prancing youth from their own high school in a back alley late at night. "Faggot!" The ring leader shouted as Stephen and his pals surrounded the simpering teen.

They beat him to the ground with fists and feet, hurling insults and laughing crazily. Stephen's feet and hands did their dirty work as much as any of the others. They left him there, bloodied and crying. The next day it was in the papers, and a week later, the poor kid returned to school with his lurid bruises and stitches.

Stephen remembered.

He'd tried to feel sorry for the kid. But that wasn't what he'd felt at all. He'd felt glad, happy that it was this skinny kid pummeled, and not Stephen himself who'd been beaten. Stephen allowed himself to blame that fear on the fact he was Asian. A minority, easily picked out from the crowd for any kind of humiliation or assault.

He hadn't admitted he was gay, not yet, not then in the confused world of teen angst.

Later, after his first fumbling sexual encounter with another guy, and a stark realization that he liked it, really liked it, he shed a false masculinity like a snake sheds his skin. He became a DJ, danced with the other gay boys, wore tight clothes he designed himself, called his friends "dear," and couldn't care less what anyone thought.

Except, there were his own thoughts, and what he thought of himself. This was the difficult part. Always it came back to that gay-bashing when he was a teen, and his unforgivable lack of remorse.

Stephen had poured over psychiatric journals, wondering if he was a psychopath, or sociopath, or some kind of as yet unnamed bad-opath. He'd come to only one conclusion. He simply couldn't make himself feel something he didn't.

He wanted to fall in love. His first boyfriend, Jimmy, was white, tall, blond and full of life. They'd fucked each other like mad rabbits, tasted every part of each other from asshole to navel. It had been raunchy and uninhibited, and somehow Stephen had felt that made him more normal, less a psycho. He wasn't fucked-up about sex, it appeared.

It all fell apart when Jimmy admitted he was cheating and, worse yet, he was leaving Stephen for the other dude. The other dude was white, tall and blond, too. Stephen's reaction had been distinctly odd. He shrugged it off, his final words to his first lover nonchalant. "See you later, then. Oh, yeah, do you think I could keep that green jacket of yours? It looks good with my eyes."

Stephen had really, honestly felt almost nothing — except a nagging suspicion that something was wrong with him to feel that detached. Something very wrong.

Then, it had happened — his transformation.

Autumn came a week later, bursting over him in a blaze of incandescent orange-gold. The first change, a heightened sense of sight, had startled him when it abruptly struck. It was night, and coincidentally, he was cruising in this same wooded park.

Suddenly, Stephen could see all around. Not as if it was actually day, but like it was still night yet with a shimmering moonlight illuminating every little thing. Every branch, every bent-over ass-fucked, grunting man in the nearby bushes shocked with their detail of glowing radiance.

The light blazed out of him, freaking out his own sexual conquest, who had Stephen's hard dick up his ass. There was a moment of almost liquid coalescence as he felt their sweat melt together, the lube coating his stiff dick and the dude's seething asshole suddenly so moist and slippery he felt as if he was falling into that other human.

He was suddenly incensed and rammed his cock home. The dude squealed like a gored pig yet heaved backwards for more of the same. Hole and dick pulsed as one for a brief, incandescent moment. Then the light surrounding them and emanating from his own body grew too intense for his partner.

The dude fled, stumbling over his jeans around his knees, afraid of that glowing sun blinding him.

Autumn Blaze was born that night, in the midst of a loveless sexual tryst. He couldn't even recall the face of that anonymous stranger. Oddly, though, he remembered with perfect clarity the mop of blond hair, the length of the torso and thighs, the pale flesh. The stranger had been tall, blond, and white, Stephen's personal grail. The person himself hardly mattered. The shell had served Stephen's need, or at least he thought it had.

Autumn Blaze watched the blond stumble away in a daze of wonder and fear. What was happening to him? Had his lust finally made him mad? He was experiencing a schizophrenic episode! Yeah! That was it. Warnings from all those psychiatric journals he'd poured over throbbed in his head, in his loins, like a dire tidal wave about to overwhelm him. He was going nuts!

The outside world intervened. Perhaps the messiness of real life saved him from an inner explosion.

Someone nearby was being robbed.

Stephen witnessed it in perfect clarity through the maze of branches and shrubbery surrounding him. Some poor fucker was down on his back being forced to surrender his wallet at knife point.

Stephen crashed through the brush, his shimmering aura following like a second skin. The thief dropped his knife and screamed, terrified of the apparition barreling down on him. He ran off, and Stephen was left with the victim, a scenario repeated endlessly, it seemed, over the next five autumns.

That first victim Autumn Blaze rescued crawled up from the dirt and leaves of the forest floor to embrace Stephen's waist. The fool blabbered his gratitude while Stephen stood dumbfounded and wallowing in disbelief. What was this shit all about? He vaguely noticed the victim and his shell-shocked blubbering. With quiet determination, Stephen focused enough to raise the blinded victim to his feet. Stephen sent him on his way with a pat on the shoulder, a false display of a compassion this new Autumn Blaze seemed incapable of actually experiencing.

The nasty evil of the real world pulled Stephen back from inner turmoil. His brand new and amazingly keen eyesight followed the thief through his crashing flight, more intent and concerned with him and his feelings, than with the innocent victim. That disturbed him. He should have felt more for the victim. He should have felt something, at least.

Anger focused his actions. He bounded through the night, ablaze with furious illumination. He pounced on the frightened thief, prepared to pummel him into submission. His disciplined training in martial arts thankfully held that anger and fear at bay. Stephen merely twisted the hapless criminal into a face-down flop and tied his hands behind him with his own belt while the dude whimpered and begged.

For a moment, their eyes met in the dying light of Stephen's unearthly radiance. Stephen shuddered at the recognition of some shared failing. What urges compelled them both?

He had no answer, other than to kick the whimpering thug's legs wide apart as he knelt between them. Without consciously planning it, he whipped out his pocket knife and sliced open the back of his tight jeans. White, round ass-cheeks were revealed. Ivory pale and smooth, solid yet plump, exactly the kind of ass he loved to fuck.

"Are you going to fuck me? Please, don't hurt me! Just fuck me! I can take it. Fuck me as hard as you want!"

The begging whine only incensed him. Along with that trusty pocket knife, he had lube in his jeans, too. He'd come to the park prepared for sex, which had been interrupted by his strange transformation — and this creep trying to rob someone. Now he would get what he had been looking for.

"You bet I'm going to fuck your sorry ass," he hissed.

Light blazing around them in the darkness of the woods. He yanked down his own jeans and squirted lube on his cock and that lovely white ass. The firm mounds heaved upwards. The crack opened up as the thug spread his own legs wider. Hole, hairless and pink, was exposed. Stephen squirted more lube into that deep valley then thrust his stiff dick into it.

His cock, brown and thick, drove beyond the pink ass-lips. Deep within seething hole. The thug cried out.

"Yes! Fuck my sorry ass! I deserve it!"

It was the most exciting, depraved fuck of his life. He thrust and pumped and drove balls-deep. The tied-up criminal squirmed violently, but made no attempt to escape. He only begged for more cock.

Lube squished and spurted from the ravaged hole. The white butt turned bright pink with the exertions of its owner. He drove his lily-white butt upwards to meet every jab of brown bone forced on him.

Stephen's cock was on fire from all that friction. He pulled out with a grunt and shot. Cream sprayed over that heaving white butt.

"The cops will come for you soon. They'll find you on your belly with your ass exposed and my cum all over you. Don't move until they get here. Confess your crimes. Or else, I'll be back for you."

Stephen left the whimpering criminal there. He had no answer that night for why he acted as he did, or why he'd felt a kinship with the thug and not his victim. Yet Autumn Blaze was born, to appear out of the blue in back alleys of the gay district when crime was being perpetrated. In gay cruising areas, the parks or outside bars, or along the docks, Autumn Blaze burst onto the scene in time of need.

The name had been coined by someone that first season and stuck. Stephen rather liked it.

His flash of memory faded away. He was back in the present, the horrible present of relentless denial and self-recriminations.

The most recent victim of gay-bashing Autumn Blaze had saved wept piteously at his knees. "Thank you, Autumn Blaze. I could have been killed. I could have been killed," he repeated.

The light of his strange powers pulsed around them, a sexual undertone to it that had his cock stiffening under that skin-tight body suit. The hapless victim on his knees pressed into Stephen's crotch and felt the rising meat against his chest.

Sex. Lust. Maybe that was the answer to Stephen's need. Maybe that would absolve guilt and salve wounds.

In the moment of recognition, stiff cock pressing into vulnerable victim, sexual desire throbbing to the rhythm of Autumn Blaze's eerie radiance, he surrendered to their shared needs.

Autumn Blaze burned brighter than ever before. Anyone even close was forced back, blinded by that cold light and a little frightened of it, even though their superhero was known only to harm the criminals.

The pair were utterly alone in that glorious red-gold light. The face at his crotch mouthed his swollen meat then fingers found the cleverly disguised fly, and the hidden zipper. Fingers delved within, fished out plump cock, then moist lips surrounded it.

The kneeling victim, wallowing in his rescue, sucked like a champ. Tongue lathered the broad cap of his cock then dug into the piss slit with greed to slurp in a sudden gusher of precum. It was as if he was coming but without the release, instead experiencing only a wildly ecstatic pleasure of surging juice and throbbing cock.

That mouth gulped him to the root, taking the oozing knob deep into tight throat. There was no sensation of gagging as the kneeling victim gurgled and suckled. It seemed he needed to suck in every ounce of nut-cream possible.

Autumn Blaze continued to vibrate in golden Technicolor as that amazing suck-job continued. Fingers stroked his nads, as if milking them for all the superhero juice possible. The mouth began to pump up and down. Slobber coated his thick brown rod. Slobber coated the kneeling victim's chin and cheeks and lips as he worshipped the cock in his mouth.

He didn't exactly experience orgasm. Instead that constant oozing of his seed into that ravenous mouth was a welcome release of its own. He accepted gratitude, if that was what motivated the sucking dude at his knees and allowed himself to feel more pleasure, more emotion, than he had in a very, very long time.

Something forced Stephen's eyes down toward the man kneeling at his feet.

Good God! It was his old boyfriend, Jimmy!

Those same blue eyes he recalled so well, that mop of blond hair, that pale face. Gratitude shone out of those sky-blue eyes. Relief from fear plus a lust for physical reassurance vibrated in the kneeling form and the arms wrapped around Stephen's thighs. Cock in his mouth, Jimmy gazed up with eyes filled with awe and reverence, and a form of love mingled with desire.

Stephen felt something churn and turn over inside him. Here was a victim he could relate to, for the first time in his life. Here was someone whom he had once loved. Only moments before Jimmy had nearly been beaten or killed, but saved in the nick of time by the superhero Autumn Blaze.

Jimmy was so happy to have been rescued; there was only room for gratitude and joy in his shocked consciousness. It was clear he had no idea who Autumn Blaze really was.

Stephen felt himself disengaging, as he always did when emotion threatened to overwhelm. Yet those blue eyes, welling with confused gratitude, awe and desire, pulled him back from the brink.

Stephen remembered now.

A welling bubble of pain tore at his chest. His heart beat with rhythmic, crushing loss. Jimmy had loved him. He had loved Jimmy.

It wasn't the memory of sex that Stephen dredged up. It was a more poignant moment.

Another crisp autumn day, when they were still together, he and Jimmy. They raced across a soccer field muddied from a fall night's recent showers. Soccer was the one sport Stephen easily played the jock for. He was good at it, had been since his little legs could pump him across the greens as a child.

He wove in and out of running opponents, Jimmy just ahead with the ball. Jimmy's blond head turned, his blue eyes met Stephen's. They shared a moment of utter understanding. Jimmy kicked the ball across the grass toward Stephen. Like a message of mutual trust, the soccer ball approached and sped neatly into place for Stephen's powerful kick. Past the leaping goalie, into the net.

Jimmy raced across the field into Stephen's arms. They burst into wild mutual laughter as they danced their victory together. Stephen recalled with total clarity that instant on that amazing afternoon. Against the field's edge a wall of autumn oaks behind Jimmy framed his blond head like a blazing fire. The world was on fire.

That had been love.

And Stephen had lost it when Jimmy walked out the door.

Now, aching with pain long denied release, he shot his load deep into Jimmy's gullet. Swallowing every drop, Jimmy continued to gaze upwards with adoration.

His heart pounding and gasping for air, Stephen pulled his cock from the wet mouth. He pulled Jimmy to his feet and embraced him. Jimmy, unaware of his rescuer's inner turmoil, merely felt the strength of those arms around him. He sensed something in that crushing embrace though, a kind of emotion that possibly equaled his own sense of escape from near death.

They clung to each other. Stephen almost, almost could not let go. Jimmy himself was content to bask in the safety of the superhero's embrace as long as it was allowed.

But it had to end.

Jimmy dared more. He pulled back from the embrace and stared into Autumn Blaze's golden eyes. Tentatively, he reached up and took hold of the edges of the superhero's navy blue mask. The silken material fit snugly across scalp and face, tidy holes for eyes, nostrils and lips.

Both men held their breath. Then with a groan, Autumn Blaze nodded. Jimmy slid off the mask.

A look of disbelief was followed by a wan smile and then a nod of obvious approval.

"I won't tell anyone."

Heart-broken, but shuddering with an unexpected balm of self-awareness, Stephen relinquished his hold on Jimmy's shoulders.

Without a word uttered aloud, Autumn Blaze stepped away. With tears in his eyes, he took a deep, shuddering breath and said goodbye in his heart.

Autumn Blaze turned and ran off, his light diminishing as he entered the woods, then blinking out into a mere memory as he made his way home.

Tears came, but so did a shaky smile. He had not only been unmasked by his former lover, but also the mask on his soul had also come off.

It was still true; he couldn't make himself feel something he didn't. He couldn't feel guilty for something he'd done years earlier, as bad as it had been. He could make up for it, perhaps.

He was still a mystery to himself, but on that night, recalling Jimmy's grateful, sky-blue eyes, Stephen realized he was not alone. Others were a mystery to themselves, too.

Autumn Blaze would make his rounds, make his amends for a few more seasons. How long the superhero would exist, would need to save gays from the world's cold treatment was unknown.

In the meantime, Autumn Blaze was the disguise Stephen still required in his search for himself. One day, he would shed that radiant skin, perhaps reluctantly, as he'd shed his love for Jimmy.

Perhaps he'd find a new skin. Perhaps he'd find a new love.

SOUNDER By Logan Zachary

"Stop, or I'll shoot." He jacked his cock, and the tip of a metal sound poked out of the end.

The man froze in his footsteps and held his hands up over his head. He slowly turned around and saw his captor holding his huge penis. A smile broke out across his face, and he lowered his hands. "What are you going to do? Fuck me to death?" He turned his back to him and started down the back alley of the First National Bank.

"ZING!" The metal sound shot out of his cock and embedded itself into the brick wall, trapping the sleeve of the robber.

The masked man jacked his dick again and sent another sound zinging into the wall. The metal vibrated in a high tone as it captured his other arm. He stepped behind the robber and ran his thick cock up his butt crease.

The man's whole body tensed. "I surrender. Don't shoot again, not there." His butt cheeks clenched together so tightly the muscle mass shrunk down to half the size.

Red and blue lights flashed around the corner, and the masked man was gone.

A policeman jumped out of the squad car and tapped him on his shoulder.

The robber freaked. "Don't shoot! I give, I surrender. Don't shoot!"

It took the cops ten minutes to calm the robber down and get him into the car.

"Who is this masked man running around town capturing people?" Sam Turcheck said, throwing the newspaper down on the table. He looked out the floor to ceiling windows that overlooked the skyscrapers of the city.

"You're the reporter. I figured you would have the contacts needed to find out." Pedro Sanchez stepped behind him and wrapped his hairy arms around him. Pedro's robe had opened up, allowing his hard cock to slip easily between the muscular gluts.

Sam squeezed his cheeks together, catching his lover's dick. He looked down at the headline. He leaned forward and rested his palms on the cool surface. "I thought you were running late?"

Pedro pulled back and spun Sam around, kissing him deeply. He pushed forward and pressed Sam's body against the table. He guided his naked body down and lifted his long hairy legs up. "I can't get dressed with his raging hard-on. My dick has your name written on it."

Sam's cock slapped his hairy torso as he lay back. His legs rode up Pedro's body, and his ankles circled his ears.

Pedro grabbed the bottle of lube and applied a coating to his cock and poured more across Sam's hairy hole. He inserted his finger to apply more inside and circled around and around, relaxing the tight muscle.

Sam closed his eyes and took a deep breath.

Pedro guided his massive uncut cock to Sam's hungry opening, inch by inch, he feed him his thick Hispanic sausage. As his bush tickled Sam's balls, Pedro grabbed his pulsating cock and started to jack it slowly, running up and down the length with a gentle hand.

Sam looked out the window, wondering how many could see their breakfast bang. He brought his hands up to his hairy chest and pinched his nipples. He pushed his ass down on Pedro, encouraging him to go faster, deeper, harder.

With Sam's encouraging and the hot, moist opening, Pedro increased his speed. He pumped into Sam's butt and pulled on his penis.

Precum flowed out of him and down his shaft, adding to the lube. Pedro's hand increased its speed as his dick increased its.

Sam moaned with pleasure, the sensation taking over his body. He could feel the pressure building in his balls as Pedro's cock drilled his prostate. Each blow milking out more precum, as his skin turning more and more sensitive, all his nerve fibers firing at once.

Pedro slammed into him one more time, and his cock exploded. White hot cum flowed like lava, spilling deep inside Sam and forcing his balls to release.

A huge load sprayed over Sam's hairy body, glistening in the sunshine.

Lube and lust poured out of Sam's ass onto the table, pooling as Pedro collapsed on his cum covered body and slowly withdrew his over-sensitive cock. They lay together, gasping for breath.

Pedro slowly stood and grabbed a napkin to clean up. He tossed the used cloth onto Sam's belly and kissed his throbbing cock. "I'm off to get dressed. See you at supper."

Sam watched Pedro's brown smooth ass as it disappeared into the bedroom. He felt the man cream flow over his body and down his sides. He sat up and looked out the window. Heading over to a chair, he stepped into a pair of loose shorts and pulled a T-shirt over his head. His dick, still hard and oozing, formed a wet spot in the cotton. He picked up his gym bag as he stepped into his tennis shoes.

He poked his head into the bedroom. "I'm off to the gym. See you later." He blew a kiss at Pedro's bare ass as he bent over to pull up his underwear.

Water ran over his nude body in the shower. His thick hair was matted down over his whole body, showing his muscular form. He caught a glimpse of his physique in a mirror and knew why the bodybuilders shaved for definition, but not him.

A skinny, smooth, pale guy stepped into the shower room and turned on the water a few stalls away. He looked over at Sam's great body and turned the water to cold to avoid embarrassment.

Sam turned his back to him. His hairy ass flexing as he did.

The skinny guy dropped his shampoo bottle and had to chase it across the wet tiled floor.

Sam watched the man's skinny butt bend over to pick it up. He stuck his head under the hot spray of water for a final rinse and turned off the water. His feet splashed in the puddles as he walked over to his towel. He wiped off quickly and wrapped the white towel around his narrow waist.

He stepped into the steam room and inhaled the eucalyptus. In one of the far corners, he heard a muffled gasp. He squinted into the thick fog and saw a large shape hulking over a struggling smaller one.

The big form held the other one between his legs.

Sam slipped his hand between the towel's opening and jacked his cock once.

"ZING!" a sound shot out and embedded itself into a fleshy butt cheek.

A scream of pain came as the hulking form lost his hold and reached for his ass.

The smaller man scrambled away and out the door. He looked up at Sam, tears running down his face. "Thanks," was all that escaped from his mouth. A trail of blood ran down his leg and across the floor as he escaped.

Sam waited for the door to swing shut before he bolted forward and slammed the man against the wall. He jacked his cock and pinned both hands to the tiled walls and kicked the man's legs apart before he nailed his ankles to the wall. One last stroke and a sound secured the man's low hangers to the wall.

Officer Morgan Thomas sat in his car in the police station's parking lot when his partner approached and opened the passenger's door. "Pedro, there was another man found nailed to the wall. This one was at a health club."

"What? Which one?" Pedro jumped in, buckled his seat belt, and opened his notebook.

"The Sweat Factory."

"My partner works out there."

"Call him and see if he saw or noticed anything?" Morgan said. He flipped on the lights and sirens and took off to the warehouse district.

Pedro took out his cell phone and pressed Sam's button.

"Hello," Sam answered on the second ring.

"Where are you?"

"I'm sitting in the parking lot of the health club."

"Stay there."

"Why?"

"There was another attack."

"An attack? Where?"

"In the steam room."

"Shut the fuck up; I was just in there."

"Did you see anything?"

"No, nothing." Sam looked into his own lying eyes in the rearview mirror.

"I'll need you to interview everyone you see."

Sam pulled the keys out of the ignition and opened the car door. He grabbed his notebook and camera. "I'm heading back in right now."

"We'll be there in fifteen." The siren wailed.

"Did you want me to wait for you?"

"Hell no. Get in there. The guy may still be there. You probably showered next to his bare ass."

"If only I could be so lucky."

"I'm the lucky one with your ass." Pedro said. "Thanks for this morning."

His partner coughed. "Hello. I'm still here."

"Then don't eavesdrop ... Sam, we'll be there soon, get busy."

A few minutes later, Sam had his press pass out and had lined up the men in the locker room. Two men sat naked on the bench and one stood with a towel wrapped around his waist. He took down their names and asked if they noticed anyone.

Pedro and Morgan walked into the locker room.

Sam looked up from his notebook, shaking his head. "No one saw anything. The guy was raping someone in the steam room and ended up being nailed to the wall, but he escaped, only the metal spikes and smears of blood were left."

Morgan tapped Pedro on the shoulder. "I'll go check the surveillance tapes."

"They don't have any cameras in here, or so they've said, but maybe you'll find out more." Sam swallowed hard, worried that there may have been a hidden cam, but felt the steam room would have been safe. "Maybe I should go check …"

"Morgan can take care of that." Pedro waved him away. "I need you to get everyone's name, address and phone number." He pointed to the hot man with the huge penis.

Sam nodded and tapped his notebook. "I'm already ahead of you."

Pedro moved over to the naked man on the bench and scooted him over.

The man stood, and his huge penis flopped between his legs.

Pedro didn't see the naked man exit the shower room and head to his locker, but Sam did. He was the man who had blood all over after the attack in the steam room.

Sam followed him to his locker. Red marks and bruises were rising on his pale body. Red fingers marks were seen around his neck and despite the shower, a small trail of blood still oozed out of his butt as he bent over to pull up his underwear.

"Are you okay?" Sam asked.

The man jumped and tripped as he tried to insert his leg into the briefs. His naked body fell into Sam's arms.

Sam felt his warm, naked body and held him close. One hand slipped between his legs and cupped his balls. One finger touched his hairy hole and felt the warm trickle of blood. "He won't hurt you again."

The man's body tensed. He looked around frantically with his eyes. Panic threatening to overtake him.

"Shhh, it's alright. You're safe. He'll never do that to you again." Sam spoke quietly.

"But you …you …"

"I didn't do anything. I just stopped him from hurting you."

The man calmed slowly and finally pulled up his underwear. "I woo … won't say anything."

"All I want to do is help."

"You have. Thanks," he said.

"Pedro is my partner at home," Sam said. "Don't tell him anything."

"I won't. I promise." The man quickly dressed. "He did say one thing that I thought was odd."

"What was that?" Sam pulled out his notebook.

"He said that he had enjoyed watching my ass and was finally happy that he could tap it today."

"Where do you live?"

"The Skyline Condos."

"We live there." Sam closed his notebook.

"Watch your ass," he said and left.

Sam headed back to Pedro and shook his head. "Nothing, not a clue."

Pedro had his Billy club between the hung man's legs and pulled his hairy low hanging balls up. "Are you sure he didn't shoot at you, too? You don't have any pain?"

Sam frowned at him. "He looks fine to me. Unless he was doing something wrong. I doubt our man would attack him."

"Excuse me, sir, but could you turn around and bend over. I want to make sure that the serial rapist didn't get you."

The naked man looked concerned as he stood up and turned around slowly. He spread his legs. A deep hairy crack opened up to reveal a tender pink bud.

Pedro slipped his Billy club into his crease and explored his hole. "Does that hurt?"

The man moved his legs further apart. "A little."

Pedro slipped the club into the loop on his utility belt and brought his hand between the furry cheeks. His finger traced down the crack and circled the tender hole. He pressed his tip to the pucker.

The man moaned.

His finger slid in about an inch, sucking on his digit.

Sam's cock swelled as he watched his partner finger fuck the witness. He adjusted himself and licked his lips. He didn't approve, but what could he do?

"Sam, you had two years of medical school, did you want to check him out to make sure he's all right?" Pedro pulled his finger out of the man and caressed his ass. The hair crackled with static.

The naked man's eyes opened wide. "Did you find something wrong? Am I okay?" Worry entered the man's voice.

"Sam, check him out. Reassure him that he is fine. Make him feel better, the only way you know how to."

"Please, make sure I'm okay." The naked man waved his perfect ass at him.

"Don't make him beg. Help him out."

Sam glared at Pedro.

Pedro knew that look. It said, "Wait until I get you home."

Sam stepped between his long hairy legs and watched as his low hanger swung back and forth, full heavy balls. He ran his hand over his butt and slid down to the crease. His finger entered and explored the warm, wet trail. He found the opening and tenderly examined it, over each crease and bump, down to the hole. His tip pressed into the tight pucker and slowly entered. He pushed in and out as he went in. The tightness felt amazing on his finger. He imagined what his cock would feel like going deep into him. He pushed harder into him and slowly his finger entered and found his prostate gland.

Precum flowed out of his dick and pooled on the bench, and the naked man moaned.

"It looks like everything is fine," Sam said, as he slowly withdrew his finger.

"Oh yes, it sure did feel fine." The naked man sat down on the wet spot on the bench. His thick throbbing dick was fully erect and dripping.

Pedro reached over and ran his finger over the thick mushroom head and removed some of the clear liquid. He brought it to his mouth and tasted the salty sweet. "You are so fine. Don't leave town; we may need to debrief you again." He licked his finger one more time and snapped his notebook closed.

Sam wiped his finger off and followed Pedro out of the locker room. "I think the victim lives in our building, and his attacker has been watching him."

Pedro stopped so fast, Sam ran into him. His hard-on slammed into Pedro tight ass.

"If he's been watching him ..." Pedro started.

"He could have been watching us ..." Sam finished.

"I have a plan," Pedro said.

"Why was I afraid you'd say that?"

"You know me too well." Pedro kissed him.

Sam lay on the bed, naked and bare assed. His muscular cheeks glowed in the moonlight that shone through the window. The golden brown hair took on a deep rich thickness. "Why do we have to use my ass as bait?"

"Your butt is primo, why wouldn't it be the perfect one to lure in this maniac? I'm sure he's been watching me tap your ass, so why wouldn't he want his turn?" Pedro said from his hiding place on the balcony.

The sliding door was wide open, the sheer curtains blew in the breeze, and moonbeams reflected off his ass. All he had to do was write 'Welcome' across his butt cheeks.

A dark shadow slid down the side of the condo and gently landed on its feet. It tip-toed to the open door and disappeared between the curtains.

Sam sensed more than heard his footfalls on the thick carpet on the floor. He flexed his ass, making it wink at him as he shifted his body in the bed. His cock swelled to full length as his balls rolled underneath him.

The heat of a hand hovered up his hairy leg and stopped above his ass. The other hand joined above his butt.

Sam arched his back, spreading his cheeks as wide as he could to allow for his pink pucker to tease him. He felt two hands open him wider and a thick cock slid along his crack. He let a low moan out and continued to pretend to sleep.

The fat slick cock started to enter him, when Pedro jumped out of his hiding place. "FREEZE!"

The cock slammed into Sam all the way, and he wasn't able to move.

Pedro took a step toward the door and pushed the curtain out of the way.

Sam felt the thick cock retracted from his butt, and the weight of the body left the bed.

The man sprang and dove at Pedro.

Pedro tensed as he saw him pounce, but he wasn't expecting so much force. The impact pushed him against the railing and both men flipped over.

"PEDRO!" Sam yelled, as he flung himself off the bed and crawled to the railing.

Pedro started to slip off the edge of the building. He tried to grab onto the edge or the railing, but his hands slipped, and his body seemed to fall in slow motion.

Sam jacked his cock rapidly six times. Six sounds flew out of his dick and caught Pedro's sleeves and pant legs, pinning him to the metal awning.

Pedro didn't see what Sam had done as he blindly looked for a hand hold, but the sounds found him and nailed him to the awning. His clothing ripped from the fall's force, but the fabric held. He hung against the awning, his face pressed against the metal flashing. He clawed at the slippery metal, trying to obtain a grasp.

The intruder slid over Pedro's body and grabbed onto his ankle as he went over the end. He swung suspended over the twelve story drop and pulled harder to fling his body onto the patio below.

Pedro pulled on his arms ripping the fabric that held him to the awning and freed his arms from the sounds. He worked his legs free as Sam scrambled down the metal fire escape and scanned the alley below.

Muffled cries came through the open door from the man in the apartment below theirs.

Pedro pulled the last sound out and slid over to the fire escape where naked Sam caught him. He didn't wait before running to the condo. His gun had flown over the edge and was gone.

Sam followed close behind, cock still erect as he ran bare-assed and barefooted.

The man from the steam room was held by his neck as the man tried to enter him. He fought with all his might, making it difficult for the assault to take place. When he saw Pedro and Sam, he paused for a second. Just long enough for the rapists cock to slip into him. His whole body tensed as it was drilled.

"Freeze!" Pedro said, picking up a fire iron from the hearth.

Sam stayed behind him with his hand on his cock.

The skinny man recognized the men and knew he had to help. He leaned forward, bent his knees and then pushed back with all his might.

The man flew off his back.

Pedro raced forward and swung the poker, which connected with the side of the rapist's head.

Sam jacked his cock once and sent a sound sailing across the room. It entered the hole at the end of the rapist's penis.

The man flew back against the door. His body hit with a hollow thump and slowly sank to the floor.

The skinny man ran out of the room and brought back two sets of handcuffs.

Pedro quickly secured his wrists and feet, as Sam wrapped a blanket around his waist.

The skinny man called 9-1-1 and returned. "Thank you so much for helping me."

"It was your clue of living in this building that helped us set a trap. I wish we would have caught him before he came here." Sam said.

The man's eyes scanned Sam's body and nodded.

"We'll have him out of here ASAP," Pedro said.

Sam moved over to stand by him and wrapped the blanket around both of them. "You're safe now and thanks for your help."

Sam felt the man's hand wrap around his waist and hang on.

Pedro rolled over in the bed and licked along Sam's crack. His tongue explored the pink pucker and kissed it. "I hope he didn't hurt you."

"Not at all." Sam pushed his butt into his face and held it there.

When Pedro came up for air, he rested his chin on Sam's butt. "I do have a favor to ask you."

"Anything for my hero."

"I want you to top my ass tonight."

Sam rolled on his side to look into Pedro's eyes. "Why?"

"I want to have you inside me."

Sam narrowed his eyes, but didn't argue. Pedro's smooth brown butt was tight and so sweet. He would enjoy this.

Pedro lubed up Sam's cock and had him roll onto his back. He straddled his pelvis and guided his butt over the thick cock. "Slow, I'm tight."

"And oh how I know this. Did you want me to lick it and loosen it up for you? It would be my pleasure."

Pedro was all business. He pressed down on Sam and rode him. Inch by inch, he descended onto Sam's lap. He threw his head back and waited for his ass to stop spasming.

Sam grabbed Pedro's cock and started to stroke it.

Pedro's butt relaxed, and he started to move again, slowly at first, but as Sam's hand worked his magic, Pedro's legs started to hump his own ass harder and faster. His hands rested on Sam's chest to stabilize him as he rode.

Sam rocked his hips and drove into him as Pedro sat down. His hand worked harder and faster. He felt precum flow out of Pedro and help lube his cock.

Pedro's ass was so tight, Sam held back as long as he could, counting backwards, biting his tongue. Anything. But his balls pulled up and blew their load out of his cock.

Pedro's prostate gland felt Sam's gush of cum and sent its own load out of his dick. His orgasm sprayed over Sam's hairy chest and glistened in the moonlight. He pinched Sam's nipples and fell forward to lie on his cum covered chest.

Both men held onto each other and savored the warmth and wetness.

Pedro moved slowly as Sam's cock popped out of him and rolled over onto his back and stared up at the ceiling next to Sam. He reached over and jacked Sam's cock a few times and watched. Cum flowed out of the tip and dripped down the shaft, and he looked disappointed.

"What's wrong?" Sam asked.

"Nothing."

"Tell me."

"I thought you were Sounder."

"What?" Sam asked rolling onto his side to face Pedro. "Who's Sounder?"

"The guy running around town stopping crimes with his cock. He shoots metal sounds out of his dick."

"Why did you think I did that?"

Pedro jacked Sam's dick again. "Every time someone was captured you were close by is all."

"Bad timing?" Sam suggested.

Pedro got out of bed and padded to the bathroom.

Sam watched his bare ass walk to the can. He lay on his back and stroked his cock.

"ZING." A sound shot out of his cock and embedded itself in the ceiling.

"Shit," Sam said.

"What?" Pedro called from the bathroom as he peed into the toilet.

"Oh nothing, Dear, just wanted you to hurry back into bed," he said and prayed he didn't look up until Sam could pull the evidence out of the ceiling.

Pedro jumped back under the covers.

Sam pulled his lover's face to his and kissed him, and thought, I can do this all night ...

THE ORIGINS OF FORGET-ME-NOT
By Logan Zachary

15th Century Germany

Sir Carlton Koenig bent in his suit of amour and picked a small bouquet of delicate blue flowers. The small centers glowed yellow like the sun and the long hair of his lady love. His brigade was moving out tomorrow, and this would be the last time he would see her in months.

"Flowers for Milady," he said, as he offered them to her, bowing slightly. "Tis said that the wearer of this flower will not be forgotten by his lover. So, do I offer these to you? Or do I wear them myself?"

The fair maiden pulled her long flaxen hair away from her face and smiled. "My love, I feel that we should both wear said flowers."

"Ah, such a smart, fair lass, I should pick more, so we both can wear them." Sir Carlton stepped closer to the river bank, but as he bent over to pick another sprig, his foot slipped. His heavy amour made it impossible to catch himself. As his body splashed into the water, he threw the bouquet to his love and shouted, "Forget-me-not."

And the water washed over him, pulling him down into the depths to his death.

The fair maid dropped the flowers and ran, screaming for help, which she never found, flowers forgotten.

Present

Carl Koenig awoke, gasping for breath. His drowning dream had returned.

"Are you okay?" Detective Vance asked. He rolled over in their bed and pulled Carl's body next to his. He felt Carl's hairy body mold to his and wrapped his arms around him. His hand brushed his erection and gently stroked it.

Carl's breathing slowly returned to normal. "Thanks for holding me."

"Even superheroes need saving sometimes." Detective Vance kissed his neck and inhaled the sexy masculine scent mixed with an earthy loam and floral aroma.

Carl snuggled against Vance and felt his man's morning wood slide between his cheeks. "I see you are fully awake this morning."

Detective Vance pumped his hips a few times and worked along Carl's crease. "I'm helping you with some plowing."

"The Arboretum could use you."

"I think the head gardener could use me, and I know which head I'm wanting."

"Such a horny boy." Detective Vance grabbed Carl's cock and stroked it a few times as his cock explored his hairy furrow.

"What would you like to plant today?" Carl laughed. "Feels like a tree trunk to me."

"You're so kind."

"Just hold me for a few more minutes before the alarm ..." And Carl drifted back to sleep.

15th Century Germany

The cold water filled his suit of amour and pulled his body deeper into the river. He struggled to break the surface and get another breath, but he was too far down, his armor too heavy.

As he struggled, he thought he saw a huge splash and worried it was his fair lady jumping into the water to rescue him. But as he looked through the slits on his helmet, he saw a flash of short blond hair, not long and flowing. The skin was deeply tan from the sun, not pale as ivory.

The next thing he knew, he felt strong hands pulling off his metal pieces. First, the helmet, and then the gloves. His hands were suddenly free to help. Sir Carlton kicked as the blond dove deeper to remove his boots. One by one, his legs freed and grew lighter, almost able to float. He kicked his legs as his breast plate came off. His vision was going dark as he tried to hold his breath.

Water seeped into his mouth and into his nose. As the hands pulled the final steel plates from his legs, he kicked as his chainmail pants slipped down his legs. His legs were free, but he couldn't move, his arms were so heavy, so ...

The blond water nymph pulled the chainmail shirt off his chest and grabbed his naked torso. He kicked and pulled. The light seemed to get brighter and brighter.

Sir Carlton's head broke the water's surface, and he felt his limp body slowly being dragged to shore and out of the river. He coughed and spat out water as his naked body lay on the grass.

The bronzed body tipped his head back and blew into his mouth, thick fleshy lips found his and lightning shot out of them. He kissed instead of breathed, sticking his tongue into the helping mouth. This was a bold kiss, a manly kiss, not a timid virgin peck.

He felt a hand work down his body, caressing his chest, down his ribs, to his flat stomach and lower, where the hair grew thicker. His fingers combed through the bush and ran down his thick shaft.

Present

Carl woke with Vance's hand working his hard-on. Their mouths were sealed together.

Vance's cock slipped between Carl's cheeks and nestled there, precum oozed out and mixed with the sweat to lubricate his crease. He broke the kiss and said, "Best way to wake up sleepyhead."

Carl pushed back and moaned. He usually was the top. It was how his special powers worked. He sent his bad memory seeking semen into the victim's body and sucked it back out once it had captured the sadness, the loss, and he would swallow it, gone for good.

Vance's horrible heartache and break-up were gone. Vance smiled to himself, knowing how lucky he was to have such a superhero in bed with him. He knew he helped fight crime in his own unique way, but always for good, a modern day Robin Hood.

15th Century Germany

"Let me help you into my cart, and I'll bring you home." The bronzed, blond god said to the semi-conscience knight.

Sir Carlton couldn't catch his breath and still felt as if he were drowning.

The naked man lifted his body without difficulty and swung him into the back of his cart. The bed was filled with flowers of every shape, size, and color.

The floral scent smothered him. As he was having trouble breathing before, this was so much worse. He struggled to inhale air, but none would come. He felt his body strain and struggle. The little blue flowers with the yellow center seemed to surge over him, covering him, filling him, overpowering him. The memory of the flowers overcame him, and he felt as if he was back underwater, drowning.

The naked man slipped a loin cloth around his narrow hips and started to pull the cart to his home. Before he went far, he heard Sir Carlton's gasp and stopped. He jumped into the back of the cart and kissed him, breathing the life back into him. "Forget the bad, remember the good. Forget the bad, remember the good."

Sir Carlton welcomed his mouth and the kiss of life. His breathing improved, and he no longer struggled; he felt as if he were breathing normal again. The scents of the flowers intoxicated him; his body started to warm up, and his manhood rose.

"I'm glad you are back with us brave knight." The golden man moved to straddle his loins. His loin cloth did little to cover him as he sat on his arousal. Their bodies were still wet and slid against each other easily. He caressed his muscular hairy chest as his butt slid along Sir Carlton's member.

A moan escaped from Sir Carlton, and he started to thrust his hips up and forward.

The savior rode his shaft and clenched his cheeks together. "What wild steed have I unleashed?" But he didn't slow his pace, the steady rub turned into a trot. "May I be so bold as to ask for more?"

Sir Carlton heard the words, but did not understand what he meant. "Yes," he gasped between kisses and thrusts.

A small vial of oil appeared as if by magic and was applied to his manhood. "Sir Knight, may I be the sheath for your mighty dagger?"

Sir Carlton understood and nodded.

The golden man rose over his erection and descended onto it. His muscles were tight, but slowly swallowed him whole. The loincloth fell away to reveal his own throbbing erection. He stroked himself as he rode Sir Carlton. Their trot quickly became a gallop.

Sir Carlton reached up to touch the bronzed skin. His pale white flesh had never seen the sun, unlike this man's. His skin was warm and soft, it covered powerful muscles underneath, which rippled with each motion. Heat radiated from his body like the sun.

A fine sheen of sweat broke out of the rescuer's body aiding in the lubrication and sliding of their bodies. His furry, heavy balls danced over Sir Carlton's torso.

Sir Carlton's hand worked down and cupped the balls. He squeezed and milked them, rolling them in his palm, feeling the weight and the heat.

"Oh yes, Sir Knight, hang onto my family jewels."

Sir Carlton had never felt anything like this before, his fair maiden long forgotten. He switched his hand position and took over stroking his rider's shaft. He pulled down the foreskin to cover the tip, only to pull it back, releasing the creamy pearls it held. He squeezed hard and faster.

The rescuer stiffened, and his cock released its contents between his fingers and across his chest. His whole body spasmed and transferred the pleasure into Sir Carlton's body.

Sir Carlton's balls exploded into the tight sheath, time and time again. He bucked into the willing body that rode him, the gallop turning into a jerky ride.

The man leaned forward and said into his ear, "Forget the bad, remember the good, forget the bad ..."

Present

The scent of flowers hung in the air, as Detective Vance's hot mouth kissed him deeply. Their tongues touched, and he tasted paradise. Forget the bad, remember the good, and then he shot his load into Carl. He pounded into him, expelling all he had.

Carl's cock exploded across the sheets and sent wave after wave of cum into Vance's hand, emptying his balls.

"That's starting the day off right." Vance kissed Carl deeply and held him close as his body returned to normal. "Shower with me." He slapped Carl's fleshy ass and rubbed its muscles. He withdrew from Carl and slipped from the bed. He rounded the end and reached down to help him up.

Carl took his hand and swung his legs over the edge of the bed. "Maybe you could drop the soap ..."

Detective Vance smiled. "You know how clumsy I can be." And he trotted off to the bathroom, his magnificent ass flexing all the way.

15th Century Germany

Sir Carlton's heart sank as he remembered his love. Did she think he was dead?

The golden man looked down at the knight and asked, "What's wrong?"

"My fair maid is gone."

"The flowers are there to help you remember, but they can also be used to forget."

"How?"

"Roll over and let me show you." He waited until Sir Carlton lay on his stomach. He moved between his muscular butt cheeks and spread them wide. He licked the tender pink bud he found.

Sir Carlton's whole body tensed.

"Relax. Let me in." His tongue worked his opening and sought out the seed he had just planted. "Think of her. Remember everything." His mouth sucked on him.

Images of her flooded Sir Carlton's mind, walking by the river, riding a horse, walking in a flower filled field ... her long blonde hair blowing in the breeze ...

The golden man's tongue entered him and found his seed. He started to suck and swallow it. Tendrils of cum grabbed the knight's memories and drew them out of his mind, his body, his soul, just like venom from a snake bite. He swallowed memory after memory until all traces of her were gone.

Sir Carlton's only golden memory was of this amazing naked man, bronzed from the sun and scented from the flowers and rich earth. A sense of peace settled over him, and he fell into a deep sleep, warmed by the sun and intoxicated by the flowers.

Present

Detective Vance toweled off from the shower and slung the towel around his narrow hips. He walked into their living room and flipped on the television.

"Another victim of the Backdoor Burglar was found last night. Police are baffled ..."

Carl rubbed his head with his towel and stepped next to Vance. He watched as the images of the big blond man appeared on the screen. He wondered why he looked familiar. "Isn't that one of your cases?"

Detective Vance nodded. "There still haven't been any leads."

"I've seen that man before, but where?"

"Really? Why do you say that?"

"He looks ..."

Their back door burst open, and a muscular blond man came in. "Looks like me?" he finished for Carl. He pulled out a huge gun and aimed it at Detective Vance.

Carl stepped in front of his lover. The towel he wore slipped from his hips and pooled around his ankles.

The Backdoor Burglar looked down at his huge penis, it was semi-hard and still damp from the shower. "Prepare ..."

15th Century Germany

"Prepare the flowers like this and that will help you absorb the memories."

Present

Backdoor forced Detective Vance to the bedroom. He secured his hands to the top of the headboard of the bed and spread his legs wide, forcing him to kneel and making for easy access to his amazing ass. He admired the bubble butt that waited for him. He aimed the gun at Carl. "I saved your life a long time ago, and I'm not afraid to take it back today." He motioned for Carl to sit in the chair. "Secure your legs to the chair, and then I'll get your arms. I want you to watch what I do to your lover."

Carl sat down on the chair and tied his legs to the chair.

"Hands behind you and hold very still." Backdoor moved behind him and took the rope he brought with him and wrapped it around Carl's criss-crossed wrists. "That should hold you, until I need you."

Detective Vance pulled on his restraints to no avail. His ass flexed as his balls swung between his legs.

Carl started to get hard at the sight of his lover.

Backdoor pulled off his clothes and jacked his cock to full erection. "I'll make you forget him and me and everything else." He crawled onto the bed and positioned himself behind Vance's ass. He caressed it lovingly and rose up onto his knees. He guided his huge cock between the spread cheeks and stuck it into his opening.

Detective Vance gasped as the thick member entered him. He smelled flowers as the sweat broke out over his clean body.

Carl pulled on his restraints, but they only seemed to tighten on his limbs. The chair rocked back and forth, much in the same rhythm of Backdoor's cock into Vance. His cock started to ooze as he pulled on the ropes and watched his lover's assault.

"I'll make you forget the best fuck of your life." Backdoor increased his speed on Vance. He set the gun down on the bed and reached around to grab his cock. He plunged in deeper, all the way to the hilt, his balls slammed into the bubble butt, skin slapping skin.

Vance's dick swelled under his touch, and the pain became pleasure. He started to match his pelvis's speed with Backdoor's.

"Tell me I'm better, tell me." Backdoor slammed into him.

Carl rocked the chair back and forth, the wood creaking as he did.

Backdoor didn't notice and didn't care. He had what he wanted. Faster, faster, harder.

Carl tipped the chair over, cracking the frame apart. He pulled on the ropes and worked them free from the splinters. He crawled across the floor and up onto the bed. He brought his tied hands in front of him and wrapped them around Backdoor's neck. He plowed his erection into Backdoor's backdoor.

Backdoor knew what was happening, but he couldn't stop now. He surged into Vance, harder, faster.

Carl drilled Backdoor's ass.

All three men pistoned into each other. Moans and groans of pleasure and pain filled the air as the scent of flowers slowly became masked by sweat and sex.

Vance's balls released and splattered across the headboard. His semen flowed over Backdoor's hands and set off a chain reaction.

Backdoor's balls blasted into Vance's ass.

Carl came in Backdoor, pounding his load in as deep as it would go.

Their hips thrust in and out of each other, sending electricity through the room.

As soon as Carl's last spasm hit, he pulled out of Backdoor and brought his mouth down to his hole.

Backdoor withdrew from Vance's ass with a pop and sucked down on his opening.

Strands of semen grabbed memories and feelings, images and ideas, love and lust. Both men drew on their partner's butt, trying to empty them of their memories. A cosmic semen filled tug of war raged between the men.

Vance tried to resist. He clenched his butt cheeks together as tight as his restraints allowed, and he pushed his cock to the headboard, trying to make it as hard for Backdoor to suck everything out of him.

Carl lay across the bed and swallowed Backdoor's mind. He had the head start and worked hard. He pulled back on the strands of semen and pulled with all his might.

Backdoor paused for a second, what was he doing? What? Memories flowed back into Vance, as his memories poured out of his ass.

Carl sucked and drew all he could.

Backdoor lost his grip on Vance's hip and dropped to the bed.

Vance pulled forward, out of his reach.

Carl swallowed Backdoor. Empty.

Backdoor curled into a ball at the foot of the bed.

Carl wiped his hand across his mouth and struggled to free Vance. His fingers pulled on the restraints, and soon his lover was free and flopped onto the bed.

"Vance, Vance? Are you okay?" He held his lover's head in his hands and willed him to open his eyes.

"Remember the good, forget the bad, remember me." He brought his mouth down to his lips and blew into him, sending what memories he could into him.

Vance's eyes flipped open and stared at him.

"Vance?"

A blank look was in his beautiful, bluest eyes. "Come back to me."

Vance reached up and pulled Carl's face to his. He kissed and held him close.

15th Century Germany

The blond knight wore a white surcoat with a black cross as he assumed his knight's uniform. A small sprig of forget-me-nots wrapped around the cross. He looked at Sir Carlton and said, "Our motto is '*Helfen, Wehren, Heilen*', Help, Defend, Heal," as he caressed his lover's face.

Present

Detective Vance pulled Carl close and hugged him tightly. "We did our job, serve, protect, and help."

Carl looked into his eyes and said, "I love you."

WEAKNESSES By Mark Apoapsis

Cliff finished lashing the stocky blond thief to the lamppost with the last of his rope. Then he took a loop of heavy-gauge wire — he'd salvaged it weeks ago from an old chain-link fence and carried it hanging from his belt — and wrapped it around his captive's thick wrists, already bound securely behind his back with rope. The police would need pliers when they collected him, but Cliff was taking no chances. When they'd traded blows, he'd hit the thief as hard as he'd dared, to no apparent effect, whereas his foe had come close to knocking Cliff out. His jaw still throbbed.

"You're making a big mistake," the perp repeated sullenly. "I can explain."

By now the elderly victim had hobbled up. Cliff scooped up the old woman's purse, which clinked with what sounded like perfume bottles. "Here you go, ma'am."

"Thank you, dearie." She sighed theatrically. "I can still remember a time when it was safe to walk the streets of this city at night."

"I'm hoping, with my help, it will be again. The police will want a statement from you, ma'am. I've already called them."

"Oh, my! Look, he's getting away!"

Cliff whirled around to find the thief bounding away. He pounded after him, caught up five blocks away, and tackled him. Landing on concrete is no picnic — it knocked the wind out of Cliff even though the man under him took the brunt of the impact — but the guy didn't so much as grunt. He wriggled out in the seconds it took Cliff to recover, and damn near got away. Cliff grabbed his ankle at the last minute, yanked him onto his belly, and dragged him back. Standing up, he lifted the struggling man overhead bodily and threw him to the sidewalk. He regretted his impulsive act while his foe was still in midair, realizing the guy might break his neck or snap his spine.

Instead of landing in a heap as Cliff had expected, the body bounced several inches in the air, and rolled into the street.

Before Cliff could react, a passing car ran over it, to Cliff's horror. Incredibly, the thief leaped to his feet. Recklessly running through the busy street to the sound of screeching tires, he ran into a building. Cliff followed more cautiously, and caught up just in time to see the door to the stairs slowly swinging shut. He pounded up the stairs, taking them five at a time, and caught the man on the 17th floor. Three more and he would have been on the roof.

"What were you planning to do?" Cliff panted, flapping his half-buttoned shirt to cool off with the hand that wasn't holding the perp's shoulder. "Jump off the roof as soon as I caught up?"

"You're not as dumb as you look," he said. As Cliff slammed him angrily against the wall, he added nonchalantly, "Stronger than you look, though. And that's saying a lot."

"Well, you're tougher than you look," Cliff retorted. The guy looked like a sturdy fellow, but no normal man would still be standing after the pounding he'd taken from Cliff, let alone from the car. His shirt was ripped to shreds, maybe from being dragged across the sidewalk on his belly, but there wasn't a single scratch on the smooth muscular chest underneath. Just tire tracks, on both his skin and his shirt, continuing down one leg of his jeans, which were ripped at the knees. Cliff had to wonder if ... no, it was better not to ask. He didn't want to give away his own secret only to find out he'd guessed wrong. Silently, he began hauling the cocky purse-snatcher downstairs.

"You think I'm a crook, don't you?" his prisoner said.

"I'll leave that to the judge to decide," Cliff said virtuously.

"That could take weeks!"

"You should have thought of that before you decided to steal an old lady's purse. Hey!"

His thickset prisoner had hooked an elbow around the banister and now had a firm grip on the bracket that connected it to the brick wall.

"Let go!" Cliff gave a warning tug. "Let go, or I'll break your arm!"

"Just try it, buddy!"

Cliff pulled harder. Hard enough to dislocate a normal man's shoulder. Wrapping his arms around the man's chest, he dragged him bodily away from the wall of the stairwell, inch by inch. It was like dragging an overturned car: his feet kept slipping. He'd gained maybe half a yard, yet somehow his foe was still holding onto the banister. He saw the man's forearm actually bending around the metal, and expected the bone to snap. Instead, the banister suddenly pulled loose, and they slammed into the opposite wall. He cracked his head on the wall just as the banister bounced off his prisoner and grazed Cliff's jaw.

# # # # #

I carried my unconscious foe up to the next landing. Setting him down with a grunt — he weighed at least 250 pounds and felt like solid muscle in my arms — I laid him out on his back to examine him. His hairy, muscular chest was still rising and falling. I reached for his throat. His pulse was strong. He'd probably be okay, I decided, but it would be best to call the paramedics once I got a safe distance away. For all his strength, he was obviously vulnerable to injury. His knees and elbows all had scabs in various stages of healing, the way mine had always been when I was a boy, before my parents died and I was sent to the H.E.N. House. I'd never met a grown man who could get into so many scrapes, and he had to be around thirty, like me. No scars, but a few bruises, half hidden in the fine black hairs that densely covered his arms and legs. He had the softest body hair of any guy I'd seen this close up — and I'd seen a lot of guys this close up, sometimes under much friendlier circumstances. His chest hair, revealed by his half-unbuttoned shirt, looked just as soft, and even more abundant. My hand brushed it as I reached into his shirt to check his ribs. Yeah, warm and soft, not at all wiry like the chests of most guys.

He moaned softly. A reassuring sign, but it meant he could wake up at any moment. I didn't dare stick around. I fled upstairs to the roof. But when I looked over the edge and saw the street far below lined with the flashing blue lights of police cars, I suddenly felt weak in the knees and experienced a sinking sensation in my stomach. I dropped to all fours. I wasn't usually afraid of heights, but every instinct in my body was telling me not to jump. I was quivering like a taut string.

A booted foot appeared next to my hand. "Finally had enough?" His face, less handsome with blue light bathing it eerily from below, grinned triumphantly down at me.

He hauled me to my feet and threw my now-limp arm around his broad, solid shoulders. We took the elevator down.

# # # # #

Whatever was wrong with me, it didn't get better. Normally I can get out of handcuffs by simply pulling really hard until my hands slip through. I'd tried that in the back of the cop car. It hurt! What did that guy do to me, to make me able to hurt again? I wondered if he was a fellow experimental subject from the H.E.N. House and whether he'd escaped before or after it was destroyed in the bombing that had killed all my friends.

I could barely drag myself out of the cell's bunk in the morning. My knees and upper body still felt weak. I was crawling across my cell toward the basin, feeling chilly in my boxers but lacking the strength to get dressed, when suddenly my right arm started feeling normal again. A sunbeam from the window had fallen upon it as I crawled. That couldn't be a coincidence. I crawled into the sunbeam, and the warm sunlight on my back instantly cured whatever weakness had been afflicting me. Laughing in relief, I rolled over and let sunlight play over my bare chest.

It took me many hours of patient pulling to bend one of the bars in the window enough to remove it. That gave me just enough space to squeeze my head through. Then I waited until dark. It just took a few minutes of wriggling to get the rest of my body through. It was easier when I stripped back down to my boxers, especially once I'd worked up a good sweat. After dropping a few stories to the ground, I clambered over the fence, careful not to snag my boxers on the barbed wire. The jail was close to downtown, but I still nearly froze by the time I found a clothing store that had closed for the night. The male mannequin in the window looked rather fetching in this season's fashions, although thinner and taller than I. I pretended he was the big hairy lunk who'd gotten me into this mess, as I was stripping him. I tried to brush the splinters of glass off my skin and shake them out of my shorts before I got dressed, but it was like those hair clippings that always seem to get under your shirt no matter what the barber does to prevent it: I was still picking splinters of glass out of my ill-fitting new clothes when I finally reached home.

I allowed myself just a quick hot shower and a change of clothes before I reluctantly went out again. I had less than 48 hours now, thanks to that muscle bound do-gooder. Then I passed a newsstand, and the headlines screamed out at me:

37 Dead, Hundreds Sick After Bioterrorism Attack
Guard Found Dead from Ice Pick to Back of Neck

I was too late. The old bitch had moved up her schedule.

# # # # #

After months of trying to get back onto the trail of the bioterrorist ring, patiently casing nursing homes and retirement communities, a string of clues suddenly presented themselves to me. They led to an apartment in the low-rent district. The entrance would be guarded, but the window was only a few stories up and could be reached by climbing a fire escape and edging my way along a narrow ledge. I was pretty sure I wouldn't fall.

But when I entered the alley that night, I was slammed into the brick wall by a mugger. Young guy, built like a football player. Normally I'd have enjoyed teaching him a lesson, but under the circumstances, I decided to just knock him out and get on with my mission.

Then I saw he had friends. My first thought was that the bioterrorists had ambushed me, but these guys didn't fit the profile. They all looked around twenty. One scrawny guy in the back might have been forty, almost old enough to be one of the grandchildren the terrorists used as henchmen, but no, he wasn't wearing a sweater. Muggers, then. And three hefty guys is usually my limit. To beat up, I mean.

I could fight my way past them, but I wondered if it would be quieter to just let them pound on me awhile and take my wallet, so I could get on with my plan. I'd sacrifice my wallet sooner than lose the trail.

Three of the big bruisers grabbed me, one on each arm and one in a head-lock. They were strong, and it would be difficult to break away, and very noisy.

Two of the youths who weren't holding me turned on flashlights, the kind that use bright LEDs. These were blue. The remaining young thug unzipped my jacket, lifted up my T-shirt in his left fist, and punched me in the bare stomach with his right. I would have doubled up from the unexpected pain, but his buddies held me upright.

"It works," the eldest man said. "Strip him."

Letting go of my shirt, the young guy unbuckled my belt, unbuttoned my jeans, and yanked them down to my ankles. I sagged helplessly in the arms of my attackers as my legs seemed to turn to rubber. Then they stuck their flashlights up the sleeves of my jacket. I found I could barely lift my arms when they released them to pull off my jacket and peel off my T-shirt. Then one guy grabbed me from behind and wrapped his arms around my chest while another lifted up my legs and unlaced my shoes.

Soon I was shivering in my boxer shorts as the thugs played their blue flashlights over every part of my body. They even pulled out the waistband, stretching the elastic to its limit, to shine it into my crotch and over my ass. I couldn't do a thing about it. I would have crumpled to the ground if not for the hands roughly gripping my armpits.

\# \# \# \# \#

Cliff was walking down a deserted street the next morning when he saw a young construction worker standing by his truck and peering anxiously down into an open manhole. The man swore softly and shouted down, "Troy! Are you okay, buddy?"

"Is something wrong, sir?" Cliff asked, rushing to the construction worker's side.

"My coworker just suddenly collapsed down there. I'm going down after him. Call 911 or something." He put one foot on the ladder.

"Whoa!" Cliff protested, lifting the burly man out by his suspenders. "A lot of would-be rescuers die that way, buddy. There's probably no oxygen down there."

"I can't just leave him to die!" the man protested as Cliff set him on his feet.

Cliff glanced down the hole. The unconscious man looked about the same size as his coworker — 200 pounds, tops, even assuming he was all muscle. "I'll get him."

"But how will you breathe?"

"I'll make it quick," Cliff explained, taking a last deep breath and starting down. At the bottom, he grabbed the man's arm and tried to yank him to his feet. To his momentary horror, the arm came off — he hadn't pulled that hard! Then he saw the arm was stuffed with straw. He ripped open the shirt and found nothing but more straw.

Lungs burning, he scrambled back up the ladder. At least both hands were free, since he wasn't carrying a limp body under one arm as he'd planned. But as he climbed, he saw the manhole cover eclipsing the circle of sunlight. When he neared the top, he heard the sound of a truck being parked on top of it.

# # # # #

Someone threw cold water in his face. His found he was chained spread-eagle to a wall. He was wrapped in aluminum foil, from his manacled wrists to his bare ankles, which were shackled and chained to the floor. The water ran down his chest under the foil, finally dripping down his leg and off of his toes. He felt it trickle down his belly, crotch, and leg. Apparently it had nothing to soak into. Where were his clothes?

Two men were looking him over as though inspecting a side of beef. One was setting down a bucket. He looked about twenty-five. The other, about forty, held a clipboard. Cliff struggled to break free and heard metal creaking in protest, but then he sagged against the chains, exhausted.

His younger captor stepped close to him and examined something at chest level. "You were right, Dr. Baker. The altered mitochondria cut out as soon as his skin temperature reached 38 Celsius."

"It makes sense as a safety feature, although I wonder if they intended to be that conservative. What about his radiating surfaces?"

"They heated up first, like you predicted."

"Excellent. Now let me show you the other subject."

The younger man lingered long enough to grip Cliff by the wrist, just above the foil, and twist his arm savagely. Cliff resisted weakly, and his captor laughed at him, as if relishing the fact that he could overpower a bigger man.

"Come along, Kurt. We'll have months to experiment on him."

As Kurt moved out of his line of sight, Cliff saw that they had a second captive, an extremely tall and thin blond man, stretched out stark naked on a long table. There was some kind of contraption with gears near his bare feet. His ankles were secured by metal bands bolted to the table, holding his thin legs spread slightly apart, their stringy muscles stretched taut. Cliff ran his eyes along those surprisingly long legs, lightly dusted with blond hair, up to where they met in a nest of light-colored pubic hair. The prisoner's uncircumcised penis lay draped flaccidly against his thigh. The pubic hair trailed up to his navel and ended there. The hairless skin of his long torso was stretched tightly over his widely-spaced ribs. His skinny arms were stretched over his head, exposing swirls of auburn hair in his armpits. Then Cliff took a good look at the blond captive's face. He recognized him as the self-assured thief he'd caught stealing that little old lady's purse, the one who'd been hard to capture and impossible to hurt. Stocky no longer, the poor guy's body had been stretched out — much further than humanly possible.

"The undergrads and I captured this one last night. From what little we've learned so far about the Human Experimental Nanotech facility's research, they designed his flexibility to switch off in response to light with a wavelength of 450 nanometers, like these commercially available blue LEDs. The scientist pushed a button, and the naked figure was bathed in blue light for a few seconds. "That freezes him in his current shape, so we can do as we please with him. It's the only way to draw blood samples. We can reactivate his flexibility at any time with 590-nanometer light. That's this button here." Yellow light illuminated the prisoner. "In this mode, we can stretch the subject out further. You turn that crank by his feet while I turn the one by his arms."

The naked captive whimpered as the two men labored to turn the cranks. "Can I get the jocks to do this for me?" Kurt grunted.

"Certainly. That's the sort of thing I hired them for. And given how little discomfort the subject is exhibiting so far, I predict it will take weeks of careful tightening before we determine his breaking point. Save your back."

"Amazing," Kurt marveled, stroking a quivering naked thigh no thicker than his own arm. "Do the bones themselves stretch, or just the ligaments between them?"

"That'll be part of your research project. I've already taken the baseline X-ray."

"Can we start the next experiment on the other subject?"

"Aren't you forgetting something?" Dr. Baker pressed the button that turned on the blue LEDs.

"Always disable his flexibility before turning your back on him."

"Sorry, sir. It won't happen again. Now can we unwrap the other subject?"

"I was going to suggest we break for lunch first, but since you're so eager ..."

# # # # #

I watched helplessly as they tore a hole in the foil inside my fellow prisoner's elbow and injected him with something. Soon he was slumped limply in his chains again. The grad student, Kurt, began stripping the aluminum foil from his brawny arms. An armpit was exposed; I realized they'd taken off his shirt. He struggled weakly in his chains as his hairy chest was laid bare, then his furry abs. One more sheet of foil gone, and I saw pubic hair sticking out. Clearly they'd removed more than his shirt. When Kurt had finished, the big man was as naked as I was.

"His chest hair feels almost fuzzy," the grad student commented. "I guess I should have expected that, after seeing the sample under the microscope."

"It has hundreds of times the surface area of normal chest hair," the researcher replied. "That's why I wasn't surprised that it got hot faster than his skin. H.E.N. must have designed it as the fastest way to get rid of the heat his muscles generate."

"His arms and legs are covered with the same stuff. And his armpit hair feels just as soft." The half-conscious beefy man squirmed under Kurt's probing. "And his pubic hair, too."

"I know. I examined all the samples you collected while he was unconscious. We'll shave his entire body, just to be sure."

The captive superhero protested groggily when he heard that, squirming in his chains. The grad student ignored him and started shaking up a can of shaving cream. He slathered it all over the prisoner's chest, then took a straight razor out of his pocket and opened it. "Hold still," he ordered. "You wouldn't want this to slip, would you? Especially not while I'm shaving down here." He bent over and did something at the big man's crotch. I think he had his balls resting on the flat of the razor blade.

He behaved himself after that, as the blade was scraped down his chest, following the curve of his pectoral muscles, leaving smooth hairless skin in its wake.

# # # # #

"Hey, buddy," the big man called softly, after our captors had left. His muscles looked even more impressive now, denuded of hair, but I knew the strength was gone from them. He was utterly helpless now. We both were.

"Since when are we buddies?" I muttered miserably.

"Since we wound up in the same dungeon."

"Lab," I corrected. "The diagnostic equipment should be a clue. Also that emergency shower in the corner, for washing off chemical spills. Even bigger clue."

"Dude, they've got us both naked and in chains. I'm strung up by my wrists, and they're torturing you. I'd say we're prisoners in a dungeon together. What's a little purse-snatching compared to that? Maybe if we work together ..."

I interrupted, "You know those bioterrorists they never caught?"

"Uh, yeah. They think it's the same organization that broke into that bioweapons site earlier. Both places, the guard was killed with an ice pick to the back of the neck."

"Wrong! It wasn't an ice pick. It was a knitting needle."

"You mean ... that sweet old lady, with her purse full of little clinking glass bottles?"

"The ring-leader."

He hung there silently for a long time, looking more vulnerable than ever with his skin naked even of hair. Finally he said quietly, "You should have killed me when you had the chance. All those people!"

"It wasn't your fault, buddy," I said gently, suddenly ashamed. He didn't deserve what they'd done to him any more than I did, and now I was laying this on him when he was down. "You thought you were doing the right thing. My name's Rod."

"I'm Cliff. How are you holding up, buddy?"

"I hate being out of shape," I quipped lamely.

# # # # #

"Man, it's like a sauna in here," one of the beefy undergraduates complained. I recognized him as the one who'd punched me in the stomach when they'd ambushed me. His muscle shirt was already damp, and the hair under his arms was matted down.

"Dr. Baker's orders," Kurt explained. The grad student was now also dressed in shorts and a tank top. He was the scrawniest one in the room, not counting me with my currently stretched-thin muscles, but I could discern his deltoids and biceps as he and the jocks helped Cliff limp across the lab. "Turns out this dude has more trouble with it than we do. Keeps him weak as a kitten."

They eased their big prisoner into a chair and strapped his arms and legs down, leaving his wrists bound in front of him with rope. I watched as Kurt took some of his blood, made him pee into a cup, and started a physical examination.

"How long will this take?" The second jock, one of the ones who'd held my arms in that alley, mopped his brow with his shirt hem, revealing impressive abs.

"Go upstairs and get some cold beers," Kurt sighed. "And bring me one, too."

He continued poking and prodding the defeated hero, then finally put the test tubes in a centrifuge. "Where are those stupid jocks? I meant for them to bring the beer down here." He walked over to me and flashed the blue lights — an unnecessary redundancy; I was already powerless — before releasing my wrists and ankles. My limbs didn't snap back; they were like limp noodles. Flopping one arm around his sweaty neck, he muscled me over to the X-ray machine, letting my legs trail behind us. He flopped my upper body onto the table and paused to catch his breath before bending to pick up my feet and throw my legs onto it. My knees spilled over the edge until he gathered them up.

After an eternity of wrestling my unresisting naked body into humiliating positions and snapping X-rays, he dragged me back to the rack and clamped down my ankles again. But pull as he might, he couldn't quite get my wrists to reach the clamps.

"Guess I'll have to wait for the jocks to help," he admitted reluctantly. "But at least the other one can walk." He went over and released the straps on Cliff. He guided him back across the lab, with the naked prisoner leaning heavily on his shoulder.

As the sweaty grad student reached up to open the manacles, Cliff knocked him down and dashed to the emergency shower.

Reaching up with his bound hands, he pulled the chain. Water sluiced over his shaved armpits and sheeted down his smooth chest. Snapping the ropes that bound his wrists, my erstwhile foe hurried over to where I lay helpless.

# # # # #

The grad student scrambled to his feet. Once the shower water had steamed off his shaved muscular body, it was a fairly even match: an unathletic young student versus the natural strength of a big brawny guy who'd been chained to a wall all day. I watched them wrestle as I massaged kinks out of my limbs. The smaller man put up a good fight before he was overpowered. And he wasn't all that small. His shirt proved to be just a little tight on me, once I'd recovered my thickset shape, and his knee-length pants came down to my mid-shins.

We were still arguing over whether to risk looking for Cliff's clothes when the two jocks settled it for us by finally coming back to work, half drunk. We surprised them, allowing Cliff to pin the arms of one of them behind his back while I beat the other to his knees. The larger jock — the one who'd pulled my pants down during the ambush — was built like a linebacker and wore clothes that fit Cliff perfectly. As for the smaller one — the quarterback-sized one who'd wrapped his arms around my bare chest while his buddies took off my shoes, socks, and pants — we tore his clothes into strips and used them to bind and gag them both. The grad student was already hanging from the wall manacles, watching helplessly, gagged with his own briefs.

# # # # #

The life of a superhero is not one of constant excitement, the way you see it in movies and comic books. Sure, there's crime in the city all the time, but we don't hear about most of it until it's too late. Interrupting evildoers takes patient detective work, street contacts, police contacts, and mostly a whole lot of good old-fashioned stakeouts.

I used to find those boring when I didn't have a partner. Many things in life are more interesting with a partner. Not that I hadn't had plenty of men before, but none of them had had any

ambitions but getting rich or getting laid. Cliff was the first guy
I'd ever met besides myself who had actually devoted his life to
making the world a better place.

"I'm glad we teamed up," I told him as we lay together on a
roof overlooking a seedy neighborhood where there'd been
reports of gang activity. It was a third day of our stakeout. He
was lying on his back with his shirt open, enjoying the sun while
the daylight lasted. His washboard abs were once again hidden
under a carpet of wispy black hairs, but still felt rock hard when
I reached over to tickle him.

"Me, too," he murmured. "I always wanted a sidekick."

"Sidekick? Who you calling a sidekick?" I rolled on top of
him and tried to pin his arms over his head. It was our favorite
game: anytime either of us of felt like tussling, he'd call the other
one his "sidekick" to goad him into attacking. For the first
month, I'd consistently trounced him, taking shameless
advantage of his weakened state that had left him no stronger
than any other brawny guy. Not today. In seconds, he was
standing, hoisting me in the air by my shirtfront while my feet
dangled. With the hand that wasn't gripping my twisted shirt,
he undid my fly, which was conveniently at his mouth level.

"You really are recovering your strength," I gasped as he
fished around with his fingers until he found what he was
looking for. "You used to need both hands."

This was my favorite position, and once he started sucking
and chewing, I forgot to keep struggling. Which is a good thing,
because it allowed us to hear the sounds of a real struggle
beginning on the street below. He dropped me. I zipped up as
we rushed to the edge of the roof. In the alley below, two young
white men in gang colors were holding a terrified young Latino
wearing the rival gang's colors, while a third slashed his shirt
open with a switchblade. "This is like *West Side Story*, only
uglier," I muttered.

"Actually," Cliff started to say, "I think they're kind of ..."
But I had already jumped.

My partner was already in the air when I landed on my feet. I adjusted my stance and caught him in my arms. His own arm slapped my shoulders, and I crumpled like an accordion beneath his massive, hurtling body. Just like we'd practiced. We were both on our feet before the gang members had recovered from their surprise.

# # # # #

I called 9-1-1 while Cliff tied the three white gang members back to back with their own belts. In case the rest of their gang was in shouting distance, he also gagged them with their own shirts. Suddenly, the Latino, who had been sitting against the wall I had helped him to — using a strip from his ruined shirt to stop the blood from welling up from a shallow cut across his chest — sprang up and ran away before we could stop him.

We'd been planning to keep an eye on our prisoners from a safe distance until the police arrived. Now we had to stay here and guard them in case their victim brought his own gang back first. That's exactly what happened. A dozen Latinos, armed with switchblades, tried to push past us to get at their rivals we had rendered helpless. Outnumbered as we were, we couldn't afford to be gentle. Cliff had to break one guy's arm to avoid getting stabbed in the gut, and I had to knock out several to protect his back.

The cops still hadn't shown up when, several minutes later, the rest of the white gang attacked us, and we had to defend the trussed-up Latinos. One of them pulled a gun on Cliff. I jumped in front of my vulnerable buddy, and a bullet bounced off one of my ribs, then two passed through my chest. I felt them exit through my back and heard them clatter, momentum spent, on the ground behind me.

As the gunman reloaded, another white gang member drew a gun. Cliff prudently rolled between two parked cars. I waded in, managing to knock out three of my opponents before five more piled on top of me and pinned me to ground. One of them stabbed me in the chest. He looked surprised when I failed to scream in agony and the knife came out clean. Good thing I'd already ordered a new case of T-shirts online.

Then I heard bullets bouncing off metal, followed by the sound of metal being gently rapped against a skull. My opponents were yanked off me one by one, each landing with a grunt. The last two, Cliff lifted gently by their collars, one in each hand, and held out to his sides, struggling.

There was a car door on the ground beside him. "Oh," I said, "so taking an old lady's purse is unforgivable, but now ripping up some innocent guy's car is okay?"

"Actually, it's from an SUV," he said.

"Oh. I guess that's okay, then."

# # # # #

In the weeks that followed, neither gang completely disbanded, but they did agree to make the disputed neighborhood a buffer zone and steer clear. One of the more respectable neighborhood businesses, a health club, was so grateful that they offered Cliff and me free use of their facilities. They even gave us a key, so we could use it after hours, when we would have it all to ourselves.

"Let's try the basketball court," Cliff said after he finished a set of wrist curls with more weight than I was bench-pressing. He stripped off his T-shirt, tossing it in my face.

"I should have guessed what your warped idea of 'basketball' is," I complained ten minutes later, my voice muffled on account of my mouth being wedged firmly in my own musky-tasting armpit. "I won't fit through the hoop, you know."

"Maybe I'll make you fit. Consider this payback. You were merciless for those few weeks you were stronger than I. You knew this would happen."

I shut up. Talking tickled. Anyway, he was right. He'd made plenty of colorful threats as he'd writhed under me, including this one: to knot me into a ball and dribble me, spinning helplessly, feeling his palm and the court's smooth wooden floor contacting unpredictable parts of my bare skin.

Finally, after one hard bounce that took me near the ceiling, he caught me against his bare chest and unraveled me. Flopping beside me on the floor, he laughed at my dizzy attempts to stand up. "All the knots out?" he asked, kneading my shoulders.

"I don't know," I groaned. "Maybe the steam room would help."

It was an excuse, of course. Once he'd taken off his shorts and joined me, I let my hands wander all over his body while I my mouth explored the soft nest of chest hair between his hard pecs. I loved the feel of it on my tongue. Better yet ... I laid him flat on his back on the tiles and straddled his chest, careful not let him roll of the tiled shelf.

Rubbing the underside of my cock against his silky chest hair, I murmured fondly, "You're the best sidekick a guy would possibly want."

"Oh, buddy, now you're really asking for it!" He tried to push me off. I pinned his wrists above his head. He looked surprised, then his eyes narrowed. "You tricked me."

"Who's the sidekick? Say it!" I lowered my head, still keeping his arms pinned above his head, and rubbed my unshaven cheek against his chest, just as I'd done so often in the good old weeks when it was smooth and defenseless.

He moaned. "I'm gonna stretch you between four of the weight stacks and pluck you like a string! Then I'm gonna buy an ice cold can of soda ..."

"Say it!" I ground my jaw against his nipple.

A whimper escaped his gritted teeth before he said, "How about 'partner'?"

"Good enough," I said. "Truce?"

"Never!" He bare feet scrabbled uselessly against the slick tiles.

"Have it your way, then," I said, determined to take advantage of his weakness while I still could, knowing he'd probably get me back as soon as we got into the shower.

VULNERABILITY By Mark Apoapsis

I can't be hurt. Not physically. You could subject me to torments that would make an ordinary man writhe in agony, if they didn't kill him outright, without causing me the slightest pain or injury. Not that I feel nothing when someone, just for instance, stirs up my insides by passing a few bullets through my chest. Just that the sensation I feel isn't anything like pain. The only thing I can compare it to is that it's like when you take an ordinary man and tickle his balls with a feather. His nerves won't register pain, but they'll sure register something. Likely, he'll either want desperately to get away, or he'll be turned on by it — maybe both at the same time. At least, I think that's how an ordinary man reacts to having his balls tickled. I'm judging by a small sample size, due to the lamentable scarcity of volunteers to experiment on.

Sometimes I think I went into the wrong line of work; I could have been a super-villain and not worried so much about informed consent.

I may be impervious to damage and to pain, but I am exquisitely sensitive to humiliation. I like being in control. Just at the moment, I was feeling a certain lack of control, because my legs were pinned under the tires of a car parked in an alley, with a huge guy standing on each of my arms, one foot planted on the forearm and one on the palm. Their leader, now squatting beside me, could do anything he wanted with me. The fact that it wouldn't hurt was beside the point.

"Man!" he marveled. "Doesn't anything kill you?" He grabbed my chin and roughly turned my head from side to side, then forced my mouth open, looking amazed that all my teeth were still in place.

"Apparently not," I said, blinking the grit from my eyes. "But driving across my face is a new one on me; I'll give you that."

"I'd like to wipe that smirk off your face. But the tire tracks might come off with it, and I kind of like the way those look on you." He patted my cheek. "Well, let's see if you laugh when I'm cutting you." He thrust his fingers into the bullet holes in my T-shirt and began to pull.

"Go ahead," I said as he ripped the fabric wide open. "Saves me from doing laundry. I buy shirts at a bulk discount."

"You don't fool me. You're scared. I can tell by how hard you're breathing." He ran his finger down the hollow of my rising and falling, and now bare, stomach, right where the invisible wisps of blond hair lead down to my navel. I squirmed, trying in vain to throw one of the guys on my wrists off balance. But I wasn't scared. Not for myself.

At least I could still hear the sounds of battle from the other side of the alley: the worrisome sound of gunfire alternating with the reassuring thuds and grunts and skidding noises of men being tossed around bodily.

The gang leader stood up. "Which of you guys has the longest knife?" The thugs standing on my hands, and two others, grinned and drew their blades, holding them out side by side for a size comparison.

It was just too good to resist. "You guys must really have a lot to compensate ..." I started to say, before the leader kicked the wind out of me. He followed through with several more viscous kicks, aimed at my exposed ribs, that would have put any other man in the hospital.

"Is that all you've got?" I taunted. Cliff often kicked me in the ribs a lot harder than that as foreplay, although I didn't feel like sharing that intimate detail with these guys.

"No," he said, squatting beside me again. "I've also got this." He showed me a long and wickedly serrated knife. If he expected my eyes to widen in horror, he was disappointed.

He started by drawing it lightly, almost tenderly, down the center of my bare chest, trying to make a shallow cut. I tried not to react but involuntarily drew in a sharp breath. Not because it hurt, but because the barely-sensed tickle of my flesh parting before the knife edge and closing behind it was sending shivers down my spine.

"Not a scratch," he marveled, running his fingertips down my sternum. "I'll have to go deeper."

"I'll bet you were one of those kids who cut frogs apart in your backyard even before they made you do it in biology," I said, to try to keep my mind off all this unwanted intimacy.

He plunged the knife deep into my chest, directly below a nipple. I felt it slip between the fibers of my muscles, which gradually relaxed around it, adjusting to its presence.

"Still alive?" he whispered, his face an inch from mine, watching me intently.

"Do your worst," I whispered back. Just as well we were whispering, since the knife was squashing one of my lungs, forcing me to breath shallowly.

With an effort, he cut sideways, slicing through muscle fibers that resisted, stretched, finally snapped, and then reassembled in its wake. It was just on the edge of being painful, like a deep tissue massage by a masseur with really strong thumbs. I allowed a moan to escape my lips. I hated giving them the satisfaction of any reaction, but the longer I could keep these guys busy with me, the longer Cliff had to finish off the rest of the gang.

He pulled out, and stopped to stroke the unbroken skin it left behind as if not believing his eyes. Then he inserted his blade higher and closer to the center of my chest, probing until the point touched my heart. He must have felt it beating against his hand, the vibrations being transmitted through the knife. He prodded, probing around the surface of my heart. I felt the blade find its way into the cleft between my ventricles. Or was it atria? My only clear memory from my own Biology 101 class was how good my handsome lab partner had looked in goggles.

Whatever those chambers were called, my captor was trying his best to work the point of the blade between them, to tease apart the tough muscle fibers of my heart. Then his cell phone rang.

"Don't you hate it when that happens?" I murmured.

A little to my surprise, he withdrew his knife and took the call. "Hello? ... Who? Really? Uh, sure, I'll hold ... Yeah, at least one of them, anyway ... Yeah, amazingly enough, he is, despite my best efforts ... Shit! How much?! ... Sure, that, um, that definitely makes it worthwhile ... We'll be here."

# # # # #

I never wear a watch, since they tend to either slip off or get smashed during my daily activities. Not that I'd have been able to check it under the circumstances anyway. But I'd estimate about a zillion hours passed as I worried at the sudden silence that fell moments after the gang leader had left my side. Enough time, anyway, that the thugs looming over me had to take turns standing on my wrists when one or another of them needed to take a leak against the alley wall — not without some jokes about how it would be less trouble to just piss right where they stood. I hoped they just had Cliff holed up somewhere in a standoff, or that for once in his life he's been sensible enough to run away and let me fend for myself. He hadn't won the battle, that much was obvious, or he'd be at my side by now, lifting the parked car off my legs and swinging my tormenters by the ankles until they passed out. Still, I allowed myself to hope. I passed the time trying to decide which of the thugs had the cleanest-looking shirt, in case we needed it to bind Cliff's wounds.

Then I saw Cliff's limp body being carried over, one big guy holding him by the legs while the other, walking backwards, held him under the armpits. The good news was I didn't see a trail of blood in their wake, or blood stains on his clothing, and his chin was resting on his chest at a natural angle, with no sign his neck might be broken. The bad news was that he was completely unconscious, his shirt bunching up under the hands of the guy walking backwards. My heart sank at the sight of my strong partner so completely helpless, with his hairy and very vulnerable belly exposed, being carried closer to the guys with all the knives. That's the thing that really sucks about having a partner. I used to have only one secret weakness. Now I have two.

A new guy walked up, holding a syringe. Kneeling beside my outstretched arm, he swabbed the inside of my elbow with an alcohol wipe. I almost laughed at that precaution: if I could get infections, I was already doomed, having just endured a knife blade exploring every cubic inch of my chest cavity.

He injected me with whatever was in the syringe, then took my pulse and peered into my eyes. He seemed puzzled. He waited a few more minutes, took my pulse again, then went and got another syringe and swabbed my neck. "What, not my ass?" I joked weakly.

Sometime later, after giving me a third injection, he told the gang leader, "I don't get it. Just one of these doses knocked his buddy out cold, and his buddy must outweigh him by a hundred pounds. This guy's not even yawning."

"If I do, it's your sparkling conversation, not the drug."

Ignoring me, he said, "Let me try something else."

He came back with a bottle and a sweet-smelling rag, which he placed over my nose and mouth. "Now that's more like it," was the last thing I heard before I passed out.

# # # # #

I woke up in some kind of military compound. Paramilitary, actually. I knew exactly who they were; Cliff and I had foiled their planned attack on the state capitol building a few months before. Even if the all-male, all-white army hadn't clued me in, I would have recognized their uniforms immediately. After all, Cliff and I had claimed a dozen of them as spoils of war, and we still had some of them in our trophy collection. We'd even found one shirt big enough for Cliff, and one pair of pants short enough to fit me without rolling them up or stretching me out, and a shirt that fit my stocky build, and set them aside for our private use when we were in the mood for that kind of thing. Apparently, the organization was still well-financed enough to afford a vast tract of land somewhere in the desert and to purchase us from the street punks who had captured us. I wondered how high a price we'd fetched.

It turns out that it's hard to think straight or to get a good night's sleep, when one has a Jeep parked on top of one's chest. I knew my ribcage would spring back when they finally moved it off me, but meanwhile, it was an effort to get enough air into my lungs to remain conscious. Before the breeze had even turned unpleasantly cool against the skin exposed by my torn-open shirt, I had lapsed into semi-consciousness.

# # # # #

The wind whipping in my face woke me up the next morning. They were giving me a ride with the Jeep to the perimeter of the compound to show me how they'd put Cliff to work. I say with the Jeep, not in the Jeep, because technically I wasn't in the passenger seat, but bouncing along behind, my wrists chained to the back fender. Within moments after I woke, we left the shreds of my pants behind in the gravel, and then my boxers didn't stand a chance. What was left of my shirt came loose from one shoulder as my twisting and turning caused it graze the ground, and finally it fell away entirely when the other shoulder made brief contact. My sneakers also quickly fell apart, toes wearing away first, then the rest.

They'd put Cliff to work ripping apart old cars with his bare hands and assembling an eight-foot barricade out of the junk. I'd never seen my brawny partner physically exhausted from overexertion before. Sweat ran down his bare chest, turning streaks of the dust caked in his chest hair into mud. He'd been stripped to the waist. I might have assumed he'd taken off his shirt off voluntarily because he was overheated, if not for the soldier standing nearby with the bullwhip. Cliff had two or three red stripes on his back already. He looked completely defeated and looked even more miserable when he spotted me meekly walking behind the soldiers leading me, naked and dusty, by my chains. I had no choice but to follow meekly; everyone around us carried side-arms, and we wouldn't stand a chance; Cliff would have been shot before we could take out more than a couple of them. This was all my fault. I'd been the one who'd figured out the plan to attack on the capitol and made us these new enemies. I was supposed to be the brains of this partnership; I should have been aware of how much power these guys still had, and that there had been a price on our heads.

As soon as they'd given us a good look at each other, they dragged me back to the Jeep, denying me even the small comfort of a conversation or embrace with my enslaved lover.

# # # # #

"All day stretched out naked in the sun, and not even pink," the paramilitary sergeant who seemed to be in charge of my torment observed that afternoon.

"The secret is a good base tan," I retorted.

I'd heard of men being stretched out in the sun, but in my case it was more literal than usual. Four Jeeps were attached by chains to my shackled wrists and ankles, their parking brakes set after being driven as far as they would go. Periodically they were started up to strain again in four directions until their wheels spun in the dust. Nothing like a good old-fashioned drawing and quartering. Except the quartering part wasn't going to work on me. It felt like they'd managed to stretch my normally stocky torso to a shape befitting an undernourished basketball player in the first hour, and the Jeeps had been getting a little further apart on each run ever since. My tautly-pulled, quivering limbs were stretched several times their relaxed length.

"Can't say as much for your, um, partner," the sergeant replied. "He's going to look like a boiled crawfish by sundown."

"You bastards! You're going to kill him!"

"Not for a few weeks. Don't worry; we'll make sure you're there to watch it."

With that, he left me alone with my dark thoughts, except for the corporal assigned to guard me. Like I could get away. The corporal didn't just take up a stationary post, but chose to smart about-face each time he reached the chain shackled to my wrists or ankles. He kept his face impassive, but I suspected he was enjoying the sight of a nude superhero rendered utterly helpless and stretched out for his inspection.

Late in the afternoon, the corporal suddenly tripped, his arms flailing. I glanced over in time to see his head snap up so that the point of his chin hit the ground. He was out cold.

"So someone finally caught you guys," said a voice beside me. "I wondered how long it would take before your heroics caught up with you."

Startled, I turned my head to find a man in a tank top and shorts, with a runner's compact muscles, standing calmly at my side.

"Where did you come from?" He wasn't working with my captors, that much was sure. His skin was a nice shade of light brown, and his features hinted at some kind of mixed ethnicity. I couldn't identify his race, but my captors would never have done business with anyone who wasn't lily-white. For once, the color of a man's skin was of some use in judging whether to trust him.

"I squeezed past one of their patrols when they opened the front gate for them," he answered. "Need some help? It's gonna cost you, though."

"Who the hell are you?"

"Let's just say that you and your partner aren't the only ones who have some amazing abilities. They call me Stat. I thought I'd offer to help you out. But you have to make it worth my while. I don't wade into battles out of the goodness of my heart, like you two. Man, you look really fragile when you're stretched think like this. You're normally so sturdily built. Does it hurt?"

"Please, could you get Cliff out of this place?"

"What about you?"

"Don't worry about me. They can't do anything to me."

Stat pointedly ran his eyes up and down my stretched-out body, surveying what they had in fact done to me. "Yeah," he said, "I see you've got everything under control." Mischievously, he stroked the hairs of my wide-open armpits.

"Cut that out!" I said, choking back a laugh.

"For a guy they say is impervious to pain, you're surprisingly ticklish."

And completely vulnerable and helpless at the moment, it went without saying. I almost wished the guard would wake up.

"I see you're also sweating," he added.

"It's hot, in case you haven't noticed." I'd noticed that his bare shoulders and face had been shiny with sweat when I'd first seen him, but had dried in less than a minute.

"I just find it interesting that your body does some things just like any other man's. Do you produce the full range of body fluids?"

"Look, are you going to help Cliff or not?"

"What about you? What makes you so sure they can't hurt you?"

"They've done their best. Nothing can hurt me."

"Oh, really? What if they decide to try chopping pieces off of you?" He glanced down the length of my body, then up at my hands. "If you're real lucky, they'll start with your fingers. What if they use a cleaver wider than my hand?" He mimed chopping at my upper arm, which was stretched thinner than the width of his hand. A frightening thought. "What happens then? Do your pieces crawl back together?"

"I ... I don't know," I said, suddenly not so sure of myself. With a few words, the bastard had stripped me of my sense of invulnerability.

"What about fire, Scarecrow?" he asked, stroking my now long and thin flank between two of my widely-spaced ribs.

My skin was exquisitely sensitive to his light touch; something about my nerves being stretched so thin. I had to concentrate to remember his question. "I burned my arm on the oven once, but it didn't turn red, and it felt fine after a minute."

"Burns can be a lot worse than that. I should know. My day job is in a clinic. Just because you have no inflammation response and don't feel pain doesn't mean you can't burn up. Imagine that you'd left your arm touching the oven. What if they — shit, he's waking up."

I glanced over at the prone corporal, who was moaning softly. By the time I glanced back, my would-be rescuer was gone. After a moment, my guard got to his knees, rubbing his jaw.

"Have a nice trip?" I asked.

He glared at me. "If you tell anyone I tripped over my own feet ..."

"Tell you what. Give me some water from your canteen, and I swear I won't tell anyone."

The guard looked doubtfully at his canteen, then shrugged. "Well, I reckon no one specifically ordered me not to give you water."

When he held it to my lips, I discovered that I'd been much thirstier than I'd thought. He supported my head with his free hand as I sucked gratefully at the canteen. For the first time, it occurred to me that it was possible my captors could kill me just by denying me water. I was feeling less sure of my invulnerability by the minute.

# # # # #

After they parked the Jeep on my chest again that night, just as my head was starting to spin and my vision was getting blurry, I heard a voice whisper in my ear, "Here's what I want, in exchange for getting you and your partner out of this. I want you. I get to do whatever I want with you, whenever I want, for, let's say, a year. I know you can't talk. Think about it. I'll be back tomorrow."

When I groggily turned my head, through the dark spots swimming before my eyes I thought I saw Stat lying beside me on his belly, under the Jeep. But when I blinked, there was no one there.

# # # # #

They used me for target practice the next morning, still naked. At one point, while they had paused to let the smoke clear, Stat appeared behind me and said, "Time's up. Quick, give me your answer, now."

"Anything. Whatever you want," I said. But he was gone.

# # # # #

After lunch — theirs, not mine — they gave me a pair of boxers and camo pants and used me as a training opponent for hand-to-hand unarmed combat, with Cliff held hostage on the bottom bench of the bleachers, shirtless and sunburned, with at least one welt visible through the hair on his chest. I was ordered to defend myself but not strike my opponents hard enough to do any real harm, while they practiced strikes that would be lethal to an ordinary man. Since they had several soldiers at the top of the bleachers with rifles drawn and a clear shot at my partner's completely exposed back, I had no choice but to obey.

In the middle of my fifth or sixth round as human punching bag, there was an uproar in the bleachers. I looked up and saw Cliff on his feet, with his red-striped and sunburned back to me, bending down to grab the bench he'd been sitting on. Two or three soldiers above were aiming at him, but apparently they were discovering that none of their weapons were loaded.

Cliff picked up the entire stand of bleachers and tilted it, spilling soldiers from all sides as they toppled or dove or leaped free. Several of the occupants of the lower benches tried to club him with their rifles. He shoved three of them away, grabbed the rifles of the next two and sent them spinning through the air to land two hundred yards away. But meanwhile, another soldier snuck up behind him. I was just starting to shout a warning when the man cried out and staggered back, yanking his shirt and his T-shirt out of his belt. He had a moderately hairy belly, but a patch of the hair was missing. He was still staring at his plucked belly when Cliff turned and shoved him hard. and he skidded a dozen yards on his back.

My current opponent had abandoned his training match to run toward the fray, leaving me alone in the makeshift arena. So I was startled when someone asked from right behind me, "What size shoe do you take?"

I whirled around to find Stat standing there. "What?!"

"What size shoe do you wear?"

"What difference does that make?"

"Because with shoes, you can run faster, on this hot gravely ground, than a bunch of guys in bare feet. Should be fun to watch."

I turned back and saw that every single solider was either sprawled on the ground or still in the middle of going sprawling. And not a shoe or a sock was in sight. Cliff was the only one still wearing shoes. He started running.

"Eight and a half," I said, and no sooner was the last syllable out of my mouth than I found myself slammed down onto my back. I was wearing boots. I now noticed an array of nearly identical boots neatly lined up a short distance away.

"Found a pair," my rescuer said. "Now run. Follow your buddy to the nearest Jeep."

I got up and ran, and in mid-stride I found myself wearing a uniform shirt, exactly like the one I had at home for when Cliff and I were in the mood for uniforms. It fit me moderately well, and I had a T-shirt on underneath, both neatly tucked into my pants. I was even wearing a belt. I had the strange lingering sensation that someone's hands had been all over me. I noticed that Cliff was suddenly fully dressed, too.

I looked back. We had a little bit of a lead on our barefoot pursuers. Two of them were now also bare-chested, I noticed: one short and stocky and one big and beefy, with the sun and shadow throwing the muscles of the latter's smooth chest into fascinating relief as his arms pumped. I forced my mind back to business. Our lead would be wider by the time we reached the Jeep, still a long distance off. I just hoped it would be enough for us to climb inside and get it started.

As that thought crossed my mind, something slammed me from behind, and I ran into something hard and solid. No, not into Cliff: a metal door. I was confused for a second, then saw Cliff running toward me in the distance with the soldiers in pursuit, and realized I was somehow at the Jeep I'd been running toward, with no memory of covering the distance. I got inside, finding that the keys were in the ignition and the motor already running.

# # # # #

The marks on Cliff's torso had long since healed, and his sunburn had peeled off. He looked none the worse for wear. I suppose in our line of work, living long enough to get skin cancer is not exactly on the list of our top-priority worries. Any more than cholesterol.

The doorbell rang.

"That'll be the pizza," Cliff said. "I'll get it."

"You always get it. You just want to see that cute delivery guy again."

Cliff grinned over his shoulder as he walked out of the spare bedroom we used as our office, trophy room, map room, and all-around secret headquarters. His broad shoulders had barely cleared the doorframe when something slammed into me, and I felt air rushing past me, as if I'd stood up in a convertible at highway speeds. If I'd been wearing a shirt — which, a split second ago, I had been — it would no doubt have been ripped at the seams, the way I'd discovered my stolen uniform shirt had been after we'd made our escape from the compound in the stolen Jeep. My bare back slammed into a wall, and I slid down until the manacles on my wrists stopped me. I was chained up naked.

"Not again," I moaned.

"Get used to it," said Stat. "You've still got most of the year left."

"Why me?"

"Because you're the only man on the planet I can haul around at those speeds without turning him to jelly," Stat said, walking slowly toward me, running his eyes up and down my body, savoring his power over me and anticipating what was coming. As before, we were in some kind of abandoned warehouse, probably one of the ones a few blocks away from where Cliff and I lived, and he'd chained me so that my bare feet dangled well above the concrete floor and my crotch was conveniently at mouth level.

149

"There are plenty of guys who'd let you suck their cock without you having to, you know, kidnap them and chain them up."

"Aw, what would be the fun of that? Uh, just a sec." He flickered for a split second, reappearing in almost the same spot. I thought I might have glimpsed his blurred figure running out the door and back, but that was probably just because I expected to. I wondered how he kept his tank top and running shorts from ripping off. Did he have some kind of personal force field, or did he just take them off and run with them balled in his fist the way I'd seen some joggers do with their shirts? They didn't seem as sweaty as his skin was.

"We don't have much time," he said. "Cliff had his hand on the doorknob."

I'd be lying if I said my cock was still completely soft by the time Stat put it in his mouth. "You're not much for foreplay, are you?" I said, breathing hard.

He stopped and grinned up at me, and suddenly every inch of my naked body was slick with warm saliva.

"Dude, that's gross!"

"Yeah, okay. Next time I'll take my time, so you can savor the feeling and I can enjoy every little involuntary whimper I force out of you. Or maybe I'll bring ice cubes. I know those drive you nuts. I came in the other day and saw you and Cliff in one of your one-sided wrestling matches in the living room. He had your shirt off ..."

"How the hell did you get into our apartment?"

"Oh, I've had a duplicate key ever since the day Cliff surprised you with that 65-inch plasma screen. I came in behind him as soon as he was clear of the door, and hid until his was busy mounting it on the wall. Then I unlocked a window. Then I just checked back every ten minutes, and while you guys were in the shower, I borrowed your key long enough to get a new one made. Anyway, that one time, he had your shirt off, your arm twisted behind your back, and your other arm stretched out over your head ..."

"You pervert! If we ever get our hands on you ..." But I literally never had. In all this time, Stat hadn't once let me touch him. He was probably afraid I'd try to grab him. He was right.

"It looked like you were in the middle of a scream. I assume it was because of the ice he was sticking into your armpit." He reached up and stroked the fine hairs in my open armpit, currently slicked down with his saliva.

"Someday we're going to teach you a ..." I started to say, but I lost my train of thought as my cock was again imprisoned in his warm mouth. Slowly and patiently, for him, he brought me closer and closer to climax.

He was really good at this. Even better than Cliff, at least the times Cliff chose to suck me off as if I was normal guy and skip the chewing. Stat wasn't as good as I, of course, but then no one is as good at blow jobs as I because I knew exactly how it felt — thanks to countless times Cliff had forced me to practice on myself. Which is not as much fun as you'd think. Turns out it's only slightly more satisfying than tickling yourself. The only thing that had made it hot was Cliff's iron grip on my bare shoulders, holding me in that folded position until I came in my own mouth. Remembering that now brought me right to the edge ...

Stat pulled away and said again, "Just a sec."

He really was gone almost a whole second this time, a maddening interruption under the circumstances.

"I made the pizza boy drop his change. That'll buy us a few minutes."

"Why don't you just make him drop his pants? Hell, steal all his clothes, while you're at it, and strip Cliff, too. That'll buy you a lot of time, especially if the kid is into big hairy musclemen."

"Shame on you. Is the guy even eighteen?" He disappeared for another split second. "OK, he's nineteen according to his real ID and twenty-one according to his fake one. But still. That wouldn't be nice."

"And this is?" I asked, squirming in my chains as he started sucking me off again. At least he'd never fucked me. Well, not as far as I knew.

I added, "Do you have any idea what Cliff will do to you if he finds out?" Actually, I was bluffing. I wasn't at all sure Cliff cared if he was putting his mouth where another man's had been, especially a good-looking one who had saved his life. We'd never really discussed it; somehow our idea of a trusting, committed partnership had always revolved around more practical matters than sexual exclusiveness.

"He'd have to catch me first," Stat paused long enough to say.

But I savored the mental image of Cliff holding Stat still, with one meaty hand wrapped firmly around his biceps, while I took my time finding out what kind of muscles were hidden under that tank top and just what he had in those running shorts. Between that fantasy, my bound and helpless reality, and the inescapable stimulation of Stat's tongue on my cock, I quickly felt myself on the edge of climaxing.

Stat chose just that moment to vanish again, and the next thing I knew, I was sitting down hard in the chair I had been snatched from a couple of minutes before. I was fully clothed, my raging hard-on tucked carefully into my pants, my shirt starting to stick to my tongue-moistened chest.

Cliff stuck his head in the room literally two seconds later. "Pizza's on the table."

"Be there in a minute," I said, concentrating on not creaming my pants.

Cliff ducked back out, and a blurred instant later, I found myself once again naked and strung up by the wrists, swinging slightly from the chains.

"Now, where were we?" said Stat.

I DON'T — ANTIMATTER MATT'S
SUPERHERO VOWS By Derrick Della Giorgia

"I don't believe in love because it is something that changes every second. I don't believe in marriage because those who invented it were not thinking of our happiness. I don't believe in religion because I don't feel anything in front of Jesus Christ. I don't believe in violence because those who use it will never see the truth. I don't believe in gender because I don't know anybody that doesn't feel like a man and a woman at the same time. I don't believe in everything people say or think because if I did I couldn't be myself. But I do believe in you because I don't know of anything similar. I do believe in you because sometimes I don't distinguish you from myself. I do believe in you because you are part of me being myself. I do believe in you because if you ask the world there would only be reasons for us not to be together, but we still are!" Antimatter Matt concluded his intense and slow speech, finally allowing the guests to bring the flute to their lips. He knew those words were like stones fallen on a glass roof, but a real man speaks the truth when it's needed.

Ten years after his first shower with Connor, Matt was unstoppable when it came to his relationship. Not that Connor's family didn't love him to death, — the whole village of Peschici and the three Tremiti islands were his biggest supporters — but the free thinker he had grown into didn't easily blend with the more traditional points of view of these people. One day, life is fishing, raising babies and celebrating everything in church. One decade of superpowers later, the Amalfi coast of Puglia is all over the news every other day and the main characters of every happening are two guys madly in love.

"You are crazy," Connor commented, pushing back an avalanche of tears of emotions and fears. "And I love you, my AntiMatt. Let's eat now!" The *Zoo Gargano della Regione Puglia* director's son could read the swollen happiness on his mother's face but didn't miss the uneasiness of the situation either. Relatives, politicians, friends and other more rigid people were sitting at the table where vows were being exchanged in a ceremony that didn't want to be a marriage nor a contract, but simply feelings made public: augmented feelings, like the couple liked to joke.

"I love you, Connor!" To the couple's disbelief, everybody applauded, and some old ladies even wet their napkins with tears. Everything was perfect. Until Matt, in one of his clumsiness moments, rubbed his lucky fibroma against his chair. His power button didn't fail to function. As it had happened since his adolescence, antimatter oozed out and immediately turned into pure energy, which activated every kind of instrument in the adjacent kitchen.

"Not again, Matt!" Antonio Rizzello in person, the same overweight but agile man that had requested Matt's help when dealing with the rising temperatures in the Northern Trail at the zoo, commented on the superpowers guy. Nothing had changed in ten years. Luckily, the only loss was the red pepper sauce that was still in the open blender. If anybody wanted to use it for their chicken, they had to scrape it off the surface of the cabinets.

"Please, be careful," Connor whispered into his boyfriend's ear. He was still taller than Matt, constantly more tanned, definitely more buffed and still a master at exposing his body in public. He now flew his father's helicopter and accompanied Matt on his emergency calls.

After the opulent dinner, the same shower that had been the witness to their first physical encounter was the set of more of Connor and Matt's desires. As soon as Antimatter man uncovered his milky white skin and his carrot freckles, the Mediterranean pilot's abs contracted in impatience following the rhythm of his groans. His briefs were already swollen, weakly fighting against the massive package.

"Come here. I have an emergency for you …" Connor pinned him to the white tiles like the first time and worked his fingers into is pants.

"You know how to push my button …" They both smiled at the dangerous double meaning of that sentence and went back to more serious affairs. "Yeah, push it ..." Soon, fingers were not enough, and they resorted to lube to step up to the next level. With his legs around Connor's waist, Matt grabbed the little bottle hidden behind the shower gel and squirted the shiny transparent liquid into his lover's robust hands anticipating the sensations they were about to give him.

"Turn around." The spanking echoed in the little shower cabin. The redness spread on Matt's ass for the pain and on his face for the excitement. They symbiotically moved to the sink, where it was easier to accommodate the position they were going for. The antimatter hero grabbed the faucet as Connor slowly made his way in. He plunged into his boyfriend and then flexed his biceps knowing the little trick turned the other one crazy. The lube was much appreciated after thirty minutes of that position, when every pause was carefully studied to prolong the pleasure. Connor could fuck Matt for almost an hour straight without coming.

Unfortunately, this was not the case. Matt's Blackberry beeped, and both knew it wasn't a call they could just ignore. Only emergency calls reached that number.

"Yes?" Still with his man inside, Matt limited the number of words uttered to catch his breath. "I understand. I'll be there as soon as I can!"

"Where is 'there as soon as I can'?" Connor asked, a little disappointed their stupendous orgasm was interrupted.

"Offshore." He licked his pilot's lips and smiled. "I'll finish you later."

Shirtless Connor was concentrating on flying the helicopter to the exact latitude where they were needed, but his virile arms operating the machine kept distracting the still unsatisfied superhero. It was hard to work together, especially considering the pilot's proneness to being naked all the time. One journalist had once written: "Which is the superhero? The ever naked muscular man or the freckled skinny guy?"

"How are you going to fix it?" For some reason, the marine biology researchers exploring the Tremiti islands' sea depths had lost power. They were short of oxygen and risked dying trapped in the submarine alimented by the Queen of Gargano. The ship's captain — how he'd introduced himself over the phone — was Connor's father's childhood friend and one of the researchers who was trapped, his daughter.

"I have no idea. I just hope that some antimatter will be enough to restart the generator onboard." The doubt left unspoken was that the power wasn't getting down to them because the problem lay with the cable that connected the underwater lab to the ship. In which case, pumping in more energy would have been useless. "It will." Matt added as the big old lady of the Gargano appeared in the distance. Once used to travel to Greece, now it was merely at the service of science: short trips back and forth from the islands carrying the scientists and their instruments, including the submarine from which the SOS call had departed.

"I want you to be careful. I know you will do anything in your power to save those people. But I don't want you to do stupid things. Please." Considering Connor was never scared, that plea added more austerity to the situation.

"There they are." Captain Oronzo was already waving at the helicopter, probably hoping that would have sped up things even more.

"How much oxygen do they have left?" Matt yelled to the old man, trying to overcome the unbearable noise caused by the propellers still in motion.

"Seven minutes, son."

"Take me to the generator." In a scene that reminded him of his first mission behind the man whom he now called father in law, Antimatter Matt reached the steamy room where the machines had decided to stop working. The silence was improper for that environment, somehow foreshadowing something bleak. It didn't take long to understand the problem didn't come from there. What seemed to have caused the tragedy was the interminable cable. The worst scenario.

"What do you think broke?" The grimace on the captain's face revealed his pain and terror.

"I need to go down." Contrary to what lovers think when the phone doesn't ring, four minutes is not a long time — especially when it is the last four minutes of oxygen.

Matt jumped into the water ignoring Connor's questions. His lithe body penetrated the immobile sea, giving everybody — but most of all, the captain, — hope again. Two minutes left.

"Tell them we'll fix it!" His last message to the people who watched him in awe. He took a deep breath and vanished in the underwater world, closer to the researchers than the worried sailors. Isolated in the blue liquid, the special guy from Maglie overcame his fears and abandoned his body to the slow currents of the Tremiti islands. The ship above looked like a giant black cloud from which a broken umbilical cord hung lifelessly. The cable went down, more than Matt could see, to a point where it entered another blackness, where the submarine unable to breathe rested. It didn't take a physicist to understand his superhero lungs were not enough to swim to end of the cable. He climbed more of it, slowly feeling the pressure in his ears reaching a painful level. Frustrated by the helplessness of the situation and the hunger for air, he punched the cable that kept him from floating back up.

"Matt." Connor mumbled under his breath, careful not to be heard. Although serious, his concern couldn't be compared to that of a father about to lose his daughter. How does one feel when they only have two minutes to save the world? The pilot stepped away from the other spectators to conceal his terror.

"Damn!" The superhero was powerless, completely under the control of his need of oxygen. He punched the cable again, causing it to writhe like a long heavy snake. In the belly of one of those curves, he noticed the erosion that had uncovered the vital wires packed together. Instead of swimming back up, he contracted his thighs and pushed to slide down to the problem. At that point, he hardly managed to keep his mouth shut avoiding to succumb to his physiological desire to breathe in; his vision started to fade. His only consolation was that if everything went well, the few seconds left were just enough to revive the machines that could save the researchers. He rubbed his fibroma and directed the flux of energy onto the colored wires as an explosion of green sparks immediately surrounded him, making him lose his senses.

"Something's wrong." Eaten up by his unanswered questions, Connor jumped into the water after Matt, digging into that bottomless mass of water until his hands were on his boyfriend's body again.

"Hello beautiful!" As soon as Matt opened his eyes, he was covered with kisses of a different nature than the last ones he'd gotten on his neck not much earlier. In the last hours, the situation had completely reversed. Now, it was the submarine crew waiting outside the captain cabin who worried about their savior's life. "You made us worry."

"How's everybody?"

"Don't talk. Everybody is fine. They got oxygen as soon as you reached the erosion. They only want to thank you now."

"What happened?"

"You lost your senses. I had to bring your superhero ass back up."

"Antimatter Matt saved by his HOT boyfriend!" Matt felt the hard-on growing in front of his eyes in the pilot's white shorts.

"You think you have enough strength now for me?" Peeling the sheets off the resuscitated hero, Connor started kissing his chest.

"I'm very weak. You have to do all the work ..." Matt whispered and turned on his side, offering his back. But before he could finish the sentence, Connor resumed the shower scene. In a hurry dictated by the long interruption and the people outside, the couple satisfied their carnal needs in a position that soon became an addition to their book of love.

"Take control of me. Make me fly." Matt whispered when the pilot moved his body, positioning him in a way only his ass was off the mattress.

"Bend more!" Exactly perpendicular to his boyfriend, Connor demanded a more acute angle to reach deeper. His uncut erection consumed the little lube left inside Matt, causing the friction to get incandescent again. Only this time, he had to come! He grabbed the little body he was fucking and pressed it against his contracted abdomen and thighs. Matt moaned in pain, receiving a flux of energy that was surely more powerful than his antimatter in that moment. The peak of the orgasm was only shortened by the scream outside when the couple accidentally caused more antimatter to spill out.

"The anchor!" They heard as soon as they were finished.

DISTRICT SUPERTEAM By Thoby Musgrave

It may seem rather strange that I am the one to relate the exploits of District D's newest superheroes — and not one of the region's more qualified correspondents such as the famous Simon Smudge of *The District Blatt*, but as you will see, I am singularly eligible for this journalistic purpose. Notwithstanding, this document will remain unread and secret until such a time that DARKSTAR and KID BUCK are no longer performing their public services.

The names are provided here in upper case. This is not merely the habit acquired by me in imitation of the reporters over at the offices of *The Blatt*, but like them, I depict the characters in their third-hand persons in capital. They stand in superhuman contrast with the mortals of the District who are familiar with them to varying degrees. Thus, I give you DARKSTAR and KID BUCK. In addition to the mighty fighters of evil themselves, only two other persons know of their true identities, their back stories, and their intimacies. These things must remain secret, for District D is awash with the criminal elements, which would use the information to destroy them — and also gleefully extinguish the last remnants of civil society here.

So only we four know. To the grateful citizenry, the Dark One and his sprightly sidekick are represented by their singular costumes and disguised, masked visages — and by the powerful force of law they bring. Two figures in the night, appearing from nowhere and surging into action. This is how the crime-busting Superteam are perceived by surprised witnesses, related to eager reporters, and described the next morning in the crumpled dailies.

Hardly anyone knows of their foibles, loves, or fears. Only I and a couple of others.

My name is Sylvester Wipplesmart, and many will know of me already as the elderly proprietor of District Steam and Bath, and indeed, that is what I am. Many will also know me as the curmudgeonly and grizzled local businessman who complains with much energy of the modern direction taken by so many facets of life in the District today, and this, too, bears an element of truth. You will likely have heard me muttering denouncements of society as I stalked toward my long-standing establishment on Bent Street or as I bent to fetch a towel from behind the counter. My walking-stick is renowned for its accuracy in sweeping some item of confounded litter to the gutter and clearing a path. In earlier days, small children would form a line behind me, skipping and merrily singing some brainless shanty. These days, of course, they are all indoors turning their minds to custard with infernal video-games.

But that talk is merely of your somewhat learned narrator. This document is supposed to be about DARKSTAR and KID BUCK, the two vigorous superheroes. Certainly Simon Smudge of *The District Blatt* could have done a better job — and that well-worded correspondent also shows sufficient interest in the powerhouse pair, following them around at the Mayor's office hoping for a deeply intoned quote about something from the Dark One, and showing up at crime scenes, alerted by his police scanner — but the young Mr. Smudge is not conversant with their lives to the extent that I am, so the job falls to me.

I have hesitated, delayed, and filibustered, and now my hand trembles as I commit the life-and-death secret to the parchment.

A Mr. Blake Starr operates the video shop, which attaches to my building on Bent Street — an establishment that caters to popular tastes in District D, as mine does — and thusly, we are neighbors, although his concern is not as sizeable or as long-standing as mine. Nevertheless, we are both happily successful. This is despite the unfortunate levels of crime, which have risen and which threaten to engulf District D. Blake Starr's business suffered a robbery by armed stick-up men, an event, which was dutifully reported in *The District Blatt*:

BENT STREET HOLD-UP UPS SECURITY

Byline: Simon Smudge.

A broad-daylight robbery at a video-rental store in Bent Street yesterday has caused the manager to promise an upgrade to security measures. Blake Starr of Starr Vid and Peepshow said he would install new, stronger grilles and replace his security system.

"This robbery has highlighted the out-datedness of my CCTV and remote callout system," said Mr. Starr. "F*** it, I've got to get newer gear," he continued. Mr. Starr then went on to say that replacing his security equipment would not be all. "There will be other measures taken, too," the video-store proprietor mysteriously commented as he ominously slapped his fist into his opposing palm.

This reporter then hurried off to an appointment with Betty Bonke of the District D Drag-Queen Mafia before being able to establish just what Mr. Starr meant with his enigmatic, deeply intoned pledge.

So you see, the useful Mr. Simon Smudge can do part of my job after all. In fact, he and I share a few interests and preoccupations, and these will also be seen to relate to the story of DARKSTAR and KID BUCK.

As far as many of us were aware, after the emptying of the till and the rummaging of the attractive shelves at Starr Vid and Peepshow, Blake Starr employed a nineteen-year-old lad named Ky Buckfield as an assistant, his job seeming to consist of slouching behind the counter whilst eating popcorn and watching copies of *Zap Man* and *Pow Boy* on the elevated monitors. Now, Zap Man and Pow Boy are two characters popular for their crime-fighting and general do-gooding exploits, and young Ky Buckfield should be complimented on his attentiveness to their activities, but they exist within the realm of fiction, and here, we are dealing with the gritty reality of modern urban life.

Unbeknownst to the populace at large, other things had been planned and undertaken behind the scenes, as it were, and Blake Starr's unfortunate encounter with robbers and his subsequent engagement of a shop assistant were not the full extent of his actions.

"I'm thinking seriously about it," Blake said to me one night after his closing time as we shared a bottle of fine blend (one of mine) in my office within District Steam and Bath.

I knew what he was talking about, for he often disclosed his thoughts and concerns to me in that private chamber.

"Bah!" I said in my regrettable way. "The days for that sort of thing are long gone! These crooks belong to well-organized, well-connected gangs! And they're everywhere! Put some bars in the windows and get a guard-dog, and give that young chap a baseball-bat to keep under the counter. What's his name again?"

"Ky. Ky Buckfield."

"What an idiotic name. How do they think these things up? But he does seem a very ... erm ... nice young lad ..."

"No, really. I'm serious about this, Sylvester. And Ky would join me."

"Hmmm," I said thoughtfully. And in truth, I had really only just started to think seriously of the proposals Blake had been making.

"Look at me," he said. "Two hours a day at Steele's Gym, Judo and Tai-Kwon-Do at Kim Too's School of Ass-Busting, rappelling on the weekends, boxing champion, I've got a rope with a hook on the end of it ..."

My friend Blake Starr — forty years old — appeared freshly to me at that moment. The hard, squared jaw and the steely blue eyes like sparks from flint, and the massive protruding chest were suddenly apparent in new, as yet only imagined conditions. But still, I persisted with my habitual naysaying.

"All that rumpus-humpus belongs in the good old days!" I said. "Why, in the good old days there were Steam-Combustion Man and Puff Urchin, but all they had to worry about were pickpockets and clock-forgers. Nowadays, you have video piracy, ram-raids, drugs, extortion ..."

"Dammit, Sylvester!" the largely built Blake Starr said, his fist thumping upon my teak table with a resounding clout, making the whisky glasses rattle. "That's exactly my point! District D needs cleaning up!"

Momentarily, I was silenced. And I suppose silence is an unusual condition for me, as my reputation runs to being one of considerable verbal output, and in a short time, I had regained the use of my mouth.

"Now, you mentioned that that young fellow would join in with this enterprise. In what capacity?"

"As my sidekick, of course."

"Fiddlesticks!" I responded. "The youth of today are in no form for public service! The only things they're interested in are tagging their wretched graffiti all over honest business premises and otherwise turning their brains to sand with drugs and their infernal video games! Damn things! And twocking DVD players! Not that I have one of those, mind, but all the same ..."

"Sylvester," my friend interjected in a somewhat gentle but nevertheless deep intonation. "Ky is a very fine young man. I was lucky to snag such a respectable and hard-working employee. Although he should spend more time straightening out the foreign film's and less time in the porn section ..."

"See!" I said.

At this point, the reader may well be wondering what could possibly have sparked this friendship between me — a grizzled landlord dating back to the good old days of District D — and Blake Starr — a younger, and positively more masculine member of society. Reader, the answer is a simple one. The District D Chamber of Commerce is a closely-knit arrangement, and one blinkered shopkeeper will likely find many points of same-mindedness with another. Add to that, the fact that our respective businesses were next door to each other.

Further, I found Blake Starr to be a very upright and knowledgeable character — one who, if you will forgive my constant harking, really belonged in the District D of yore, when it was safe to traverse the streets and one could purchase a penny-bomb at Firework Frenzy without having to produce ID as if one were planning to blow up Mrs. Keneally's letter-box. Similarly, Blake must have found some solace in his conversations with me, for he often liked to come over to my office and share a quality blend.

The inner-city enclave of District D had been my home for many years — since, in fact, the days of public piddle-posts and dog waterers. I am still fond of the quarter — something which very few have heard me admit — and continue to operate my moderately successful District Steam and Bath — a local institution, if I may say. The village contains a host of noise some and colorful characters, as it always has done, but at the time of which I speak — when this particular conversation took place between me and Blake Starr, many evil things were afoot in the District. Of course Mayor Volte endured much of the blame for the crime-wave, but in truth, the good Mayor was largely helpless in the face of the onslaught. The organized gangs operated from their filthy nests, away from an underfunded Police Department, which was unable to uproot the illegal cells behind the ATM rip-offs and street-front bombings. Audacious crimes were typical, but to serve as an example, I recount the infamous occasion whereby the "Pilfer Posse" commandeered a passing ambulance, ejected the crew and poor Mr. Clegg — victim of a heart-attack — and attached the powerful vehicle by way of a strong chain to an ATM mounted within the brickwork of District Bank. The machine was wrenched from those dignified premises in a shower of mortar-fragments and loaded into the orifice formerly occupied by Mr. Clegg. No one has seen the ATM, the cash, or the ambulance since.

Such outrages were becoming more common, and as I looked upon the stern, squared face of Blake Starr that night in my Steam Bath office, I knew within myself that here was the man to don the outfit of some type of savior.

Citizens were forming temperance groups, law and order lobbies, and morals campaigns. The police were wringing their hands inside their armored stations, and at City Hall, the Mayor fretted on the telephone to numerous officials, agencies, and old Mrs. Dorothy Jadenshaw who had had her handbag snatched at Spend 'n' Consume Mall. But no one, it seemed, was taking the decisive and required action to combat the degeneration of our decaying neighborhood.

I thought of the possibility. Blake Starr as superhero?

"But listen here, Sylvester," he said. "No one must know! There are many details I haven't thought through yet, but you are the only person I'm trusting so far! And Ky, of course."

"Just what about that young fellow?" I asked. "Is he ... exactly ... up for something like this?"

"He's a stout lad ..."

"Yes, he is."

"But stout as in strong. Slim around the waist."

"Yes. Very."

"And supple ..."

"Hmm ..."

"Very quick and agile."

"I'll bet he is."

"Ass cheeks as tight as knotted rope."

"No wider than the span of my hand," I agreed.

"And you should see his cock, Sylvester!"

"Yes. I rather think I should."

In my visual examinations of the young Mr. Ky Buckfield, I had noticed not only the typical delinquent in sagger-jeans and baseball-cap, but also the whip-thin younker of attractive proportions, with a long, slender neck and a moronically bobbing head topped with a ridiculous mop of bright orange hair. Not naturally red hair, mind, but a collapsed flop-cut sprayed with some disgusting colored substance from a can.

Our discussion went further and included deliberations on the attributes and abilities of Mr. Buckfield, and Blake formed the outline of a plan, whereby he and his young sidekick would form a team — a "Superteam" he called it — to do battle with the forces of bad in District D.

Now, the reader will no doubt harbor a number of reservations as to the viability and likeliness of such a scheme, and I would be remiss if I did not also mention that uncertainties were similarly entertained by me. Not the least of which were connected with a certain Ky Buckfield.

However, you should understand that District D embodies a fantastical and unique character that lends itself somehow to fanciful exploits. We had seen this kind of thing before. Yes, superheroes. They had, at various times, dashed to and fro collaring wrongdoers with fluctuating degrees of success. I will refrain from describing their individual powers and feats and their colorful outfits, but if one were to visit a local newsagent and explore those racks carrying brightly inked periodicals illustrated for the enlightenment of the younger set, one will read of typical acts of crook-catching. And also, Zap Man and Pow Boy appear regularly on the television providing inspiration. These eloquent dramas and literary narratives — some are very well known — will serve to inform the interested researcher of the standard template. A powerful, justice-driven figure of serious intent with public well-being in mind will be accompanied by a young accomplice, and it is upon this pattern that District D acquired its latest heroes. But my doubts were both strongly held and well intentioned.

"I know you well enough, Blake," I said. "I think you have the fortitude and stamina for any assignment. Now that you're talking about all this, I think it's time all that training at Kim Too's School of Ass Busting is put to some useful purpose. But what about this teenaged whip-snap? How long have you known him? How do you know he won't turn to glue-sniffing next week?"

At that, Blake's eyes sharpened in their steely blueness.

"I know enough about Ky," he said, intoning deeply. "And I know he's solid! He's as fast as a gazelle and as fit as a cheetah! He won't let me down!"

I paused, considering the dark inflection of my friend's voice. The daylight attack on his store had hardened his resolve. I was convinced, and with a moment's consideration, I trusted his judgment regarding any aspect of his intended actions.

"Fiddle-diddle-dee!" I said. "Blake Starr, I believe you! And if you take up the mantle of superhero in District D, then you shall never want for assistance from this useless, curmudgeonly old business-keeper on Bent Street, whatever that assistance might be!"

A tough but warm smile came across the lips of Blake Starr, the corners of that hard-set mouth spreading and turning. He held out his hand, and mine was firmly engulfed in his mighty fist as we shook.

"Thanks Sylvester," he said simply and firmly.

There were many details to be sorted out, obviously, and at this juncture, your narrator is faced with a difficulty, which concerns matters of privacy. Perhaps, the reader can, himself, imagine a small hole bored in the brick wall between the premises of District Steam and Bath and Starr Vid and Peepshow, and a surreptitious voyeuristic eye peering through and bringing to the reader the very secluded moments between the huge, muscular superhero and his virile, nineteen-year-old sidekick. I think that these things comprise at least some of what the reader wants to hear about. But these difficult questions can be forestalled for the moment.

The building within which District Steam and Bath resides is a sturdy one, built in the days when things were done properly and an edifice of dignity was deemed to have an expansive basement as a necessary part of its architecture. The basement was out of use, although I had considered having it refitted as a dungeon-themed adjunct to my Steam and Bath club — for clients of the "steam-and-bath" persuasion tended toward that sort of thing. The underground structure was made of solid cement, its walls, floors, and ceilings echoing coldly the footsteps of any explorer who might visit those lower parts. There were corridors dimly lit with aging, exposed electric bulbs — steel doors — collections of old rubbish belonging to me and other piles originating in quarters escaping my memory. In short, the catacombs were literally unknown to all except an intimate few, and they suited the purposes of Blake Starr. He had already identified them for their usefulness and proposed a "Headquarters." For this, my basement seemed ideal. Heavily protected, secret, and serviced by the Waterworks and Electric-Company, these concrete rooms were perfect for the operational base of a local superhero crew.

One entrance was a heavy cement hatch, which existed in the tiled floor of my Roman Bathroom. The tiles were good quality pink ceramic — for my facilities are fitted for the discerning user — and the bare feet of my towel-wrapped customers passed unknowingly over this door as they made their way to the cream-marble sulfur pool with tickle-jets installed in the seats. This would be a handy exit if ever the vibrant superheroes needed to emerge suddenly into the midst of a crowd of wet, naked men, but ideally, it was decided that Blake needed an entrance, which led directly from his own business premises next door. Some small excavations would be required.

So, the underground site later to be known as "HQ Superteam" was fitted out in the style befitting a top-line costumed duo, and a door was punched-through from the back-room in Blake's peepshow section. It was during the undertaking of these works that I met and became familiar with the vital sidekick.

Ky exhibited many of the usual characteristics of the current generation. His tongue often lolled idiotically between his supple, dry lips, indicating a total lack of cognitive functions within his rounded, lollipop-haired head. His big, vacant, mud-pie brown eyes rolled in watery blankness from beneath the drooping fringe of bright orange as some concept requiring thought was presented to him. Rounded shoulders slouched and loose, swinging limbs carried the tall, shuffling figure from one place of daft amusement to another, and at first being introduced to the lad and for a short time after, I wondered what on Earth had made Blake think that this was a suitable specimen for any kind of useful activity — never mind that of a superhero. But when Blake stiffened his imposing presence and intoned in sharp proclamations, the youngster whipped the silly fringe sideways with a flick of his neck and squared his shoulders. Little pinpricks of light appeared in those big doe-eyes, and very suddenly, the boy was snapping to the orders of his superior. And that was not all that impressed me.

An underground channel was dug between the peepshow section to my basement, and for this work, Ky demonstrated an exemplary willingness with pick-and-shovel and a shirtless, sweat-slick form all too easily considered. Pert, upright breasts were mounted high and jutted with understated erectness. They peaked with proudly-pouting, brown little nipples and were laterally separated with cuts of hard muscle where sweat trickled in rivulets. Artistic tucks of muscle made ridges on the flanks and around the ribs, forming a slender, underdone 'V' which tapered down to willfully narrow waist. Here, there were the obligatory columns of belly muscles under soft skin — fluttering and swirling about the twitching navel. There was no fat, and that torso twisted and stretched from side to side in fluid, bending movements as the pickaxe was hefted. Veins stood out on the elegantly proportioned upper arms, and it was obvious to me that the lad owned the strength and grace for superhero sidekick duties. I still had my doubts about the intelligence.

"Pray, young Mr. Buckfield. I've been meaning to ask you something," I said to the lad one day as he prepared the cement floor of "HQ Superteam" with pavement paint.

"I would, Mr. Wipplestorm, and I'm sure I should but me and my friend Joey burnt down the vestry when we were eleven and Father O'Tooley said we would burn in Hell and don't darken the doorstep of the church ever again."

"What?"

"We nearly burnt the whole church."

Disregarding this puzzling soliloquy from the lad, I continued my enquiry. "Look. Just how keen is a fine youngster such as yourself on this superhero business. How much convincing did Blake actually do?"

"Oh well. I look great in a swim-brief, and the nylon feels nice, but I said I don't want anything too gay. Have you seen Titan Man? He's got a kind of black brassier, and I don't want anything like that. Horny, but not gay. I was thinking about these white leather shorts I saw in the window of Fabric Wholesale and Fetish. They had lace-ups right across the front, and my bulge would look great in that but really, a swim-brief would show-off my cock best ..."

"No. What I was asking about was ... A swim-brief? Well. Now that you mention it, I suppose that's what many superheroes wear. I wonder how that tradition started."

From the floor, Ky's posterior wiggled in tight jeans from side to side as he applied the brush-strokes on hands and knees. Blake had selected a dark green for the floor of the HQ, and the paint was being slathered on in generous quantities. More of it had decorated the silky skin of the bare-chested youth who smeared it. Streaks and flashes of green paint made attractive embellishments on the finely muscled colt, and more and more, I became thoroughly convinced that the boy would serve extremely well in the colorful attire of a superhero.

I left him to his labor, his speech on swim-briefs and fabrics and the bodily parts they contain being partially interesting and partially mysterious to my mind.

And here, we will embark upon another fascinating discourse concerning the preparation of the two superheroes. The names DARKSTAR and KID BUCK had been decided upon by Blake in isolation, and when these monikers were mentioned to me, the two alter-egos — at that stage only conceptual — began to seem real. Not yet embodied, the characters nevertheless became fondly regarded and entirely suited to the super-fit pair.

The underground HQ Superteam became a training ground. On occasion, I was to hear the inviolable, sharply-barked commands and see the straining bodies. One of my tasks, eventually, was to make a careful, discreet approach to Miss Amanda Spang, member of the District D Chamber of Commerce and owner of Fabric Wholesale and Fetish.

Miss Spang was well known to me — and still is — but caution needed to be employed. The costumes of superheroes bear their public identity, and the dressing room is the place where the transformation takes place. That is to say; it is the moment when the secret is most vulnerable. Fabric Wholesale and Fetish is a long-standing concern in the District, and Miss Spang is a long-standing public figure. I knew she could be trusted but ...

"I'm sure it'll be alright, Sylvester. I know Amanda well enough, and you've known her longer than me. If you agree that she can be let in on our identities then ... let's approach her,"

Blake said to me as the problem was discussed. "Anyway, I don't see what choice we have. It's the only way we can have all the right fabrics supplied and the fitting done, and I don't think any of we three know anything about color coordination or costume design."

"Amanda Spang's scary!" Ky said. "She's always in black PVC, and she chased me out of her shop for trying on a blue g-string. 'Non-returnable item,' she said. Yeow! She was mad!"

"I'm sure she has a sign that says 'For hygiene reasons, some items cannot be tried on,'" said Blake in an explanatory fashion. The boy's eyes were blank.

Amanda Spang welcomed us to a private fitting, wearing the aforementioned tight, shining black PVC, heels on towers, and makeup to frighten gargoyles. I will refrain from repeating, word for word, her every acid-laced comment about the "do-goody superheroes" and "the saviors of District D."

"Honestly," she said. "Does this neighborhood really need a couple more hair-brained muscle-bosons running around? I thought we'd seen the last of that sort of thing. But come on through to the spandex section. Now that you're here, it might be fun to dress up a couple of fine examples like you. Usually it's middle-aged drag-queens with fetishes for nets."

Amanda Spang's vocally expressed estimations as to the merits of superheroes notwithstanding, she seemed eager in some small degree to outfit our selfless bringers of law and order. And I was sure she was up to the creative assignment.

Much time was spent away from my view, and occasionally, I heard the weak, whine some protestations of Ky Buckfield as some "gay" garment was trialed, followed by the stern remonstrations of the soon-to-be DARKSTAR. Eventually the new champions emerged from the fitting area, and reader, I will slow my beating heart and dampen my quick breaths in order to describe the scene coherently. I saw two freshly created superhuman persons of striking design. Amanda Spang had excelled.

DARKSTAR was a tightly clad, sinewy man-mountain in metallic midnight-blue. He appeared mightier and larger than any normal hominid. The silver-flecked blue was a neck-to-toe spandex skin. It rippled, flexed, and clung to every flowing contour. The mammoth chest was a horizontal projection with two big, protruding nipples. The heavy high-gloss boots were in black leather, ringed at the soles in an inch of polished chrome. Big black leather gauntlets matched.

Shining black latex pants were strapped with a leather equipment belt and an ample, rounded chrome codpiece. More polished leather formed a heavy four-way harness which reached over the wide shoulders and around the powerfully muscled flanks. The ring at the center of the breast was covered with a bright chrome star the size of a plate, which indicated the nipples with two of its points. A black rubber cowl enveloped the head, ears, eyes, and nose of DARKSTAR, leaving the nostrils and no-nonsense jaw exposed. Verily, when that stern-fixed mouth spoke, it was the voice of command and authority, visually backed by impossibly severe points of blue flint in the small rectangular eye-slits.

On the forehead of the cowl was another, smaller chrome star, and the cape was a streaming sea of warm velvet in deep red with grey underneath. The vision of DARKSTAR was more than surprising. It was frightening, especially at the first encounter, and I could hardly believe that beneath this professionally inspired suit of potency, there existed one Blake Starr — my friend of five years. It simply wasn't Blake at all. It was DARKSTAR — the Dark Predator. I was speechless.

But the monumental figure visually competed with an eye-catching rival. KID BUCK was a shockingly lurid counterpoint in Day-Glo hot orange and electric violet — narrow, svelte, and trembling with coiled energy.

Sharp-pointed boots of glowing orange PVC were split at the top, almost to the toes, and flared expansively at the heels. Same-colored gauntlets reached almost to the elbows and fluttered with plastic streamers. A tiny, tiny bathing-suit of glowing orange nylon stretched about those reed-slender loins, worn low and in a slim line cut. The indecent packet was hefted to the left, reaching to the hip and throbbing visibly — a fulsome torpedo, its ridged underside pressing firmly at the sheer fabric.

A short sleeveless vest of glossy electric violet latex was laced tightly down the front. It exposed a swiveling tree of bared belly underneath and was cinched high to the neck where it met with a bright-yellow leather collar. That collar formed part of a simple harness. Linked by a chromed buckle, a single yellow leather belt went down, over the laces of the vest — down further — across the vertical plain of constantly contracting tummy muscles and navel — terminating at a silver shackle snapped around the base of the genitals. The shining fixture could be seen just above the drawstring of the meager, low-worn bikini-brief — along with a snatch of wafting blonde hair. The Day-Glo orange matched the dyed hair and the electric violet matched an inked-on eye-mask. The silk cape was yellow to match the harness.

"Virile and authoritative, boys. Very nice. Here, let me jerk this snappy little number for you," Amanda said as she hooked the waistband of KID BUCK's bikini brief with a long, painted fingernail. She curled the twisted nylon into a little loop around the adroit digit and hiked the garment gently upwards. The elastic and stretched fabric quickly coiled and slipped like a binding thong of rope into the rearward crack, as if sucked. The tensed rump was neatly muscled and ever so small, and the left cheek bore a flashy ink-stamp proclaiming "K.B." in yellow, violet, and orange. My eyes popped from their sockets, and my mouth watered as I saw the bloated male-meat at the front wrestle with the nylon, rubbing its underside against the fabric. The corners of KID BUCK's mouth widened with concern, and those rounded brown eyes sharpened.

"Waddaya say, Kid? Ain't we the modern crime-busters of District D?" DARKSTAR playfully slapped the Kid's shoulder-blade with one of those massive, gauntleted hands, and the Kid responded with a petite little whimper, half sulk and half genuine distress. A Day-Glo hot orange PVC gauntlet gently cradled the heavy front-load encased in shifting nylon.

"Blake! I mean DARKSTAR! All the kids will laugh at me!"

"No they won't! And anyway, no one knows the secret identity of KID BUCK! You look flash! They'll be envious! And you vetoed the hot pink! How's that nut shackle?"

"It feels OK I guess. But don't talk about it in front of Miss Spang!"

"Nonsense, boy! She's the one who fitted it!"

"I've fitted weirder things, believe me," Amanda said. "And I must say I'm very happy with how you look! I've never seen such a fearsome superhero and such a pretty sidekick! I couldn't find anyone who wanted that shipment of silver-flecked metallic midnight-blue spandex, and I couldn't fit a smaller short-pants suit to an elf. Congratulations on that backside, Mr. KID BUCK. And also for those thighs. They would win prizes. How do you get them like that? Cycling?"

"Ky ... I mean KID BUCK ... does twenty miles a day," said the towering Dark One.

Blake — or I should say DARKSTAR was positively animated at the conclusion of the costume-fitting and its spectacular results. KID BUCK, less so. The boy sniffled, wiggled his hips slightly in discomfort, and adjusted the tightly-wrapped parcel binding his haunch and folding into his clenched hindquarters.

"I don't see how I can appear in public in this," he sniveled. A spread hand in hot orange PVC continued to obscure in conspicuous fashion the loaded pouch at his front.

"Blake ... I mean DARKSTAR!" he whined later, when those pointed orange boots were shuffling awkwardly on the dark-green painted floor of HQ Superteam. "This swimming-racer is winding up into my ass! I should've gone for the leather shorts!"

"Rubbish, boy! That's a mighty fine stamp applied to your butt, and the public should see it! Now quit your fucking bellyaching and get that car washed!" The newly created DARKSTAR betrayed a distinct lack of patience, his voice edged with menace. The briefly attired sidekick shuffled to obey, silenced and scrabbling with a plastic bucket and sponge.

A long, low black Jaguar had been acquired at a second-hand car yard at the edge of District D, and it was parked in the cement enclosure of the Steam and Bath car park. Verily, reader, I was slightly surprised at the efficiency with which young Ky Buckfield ... nay ... KID BUCK engaged with the task, yellow cape fluttering and bared hips swiveling. In ten minutes flat, the black vehicle was a deep, shining probe of gleaming wax, polish, and the odd, stray soap-bubble.

"Good job, Kid," the Dark One stood with enormous arms folded above that colossal breast — black-booted feet widely planted.

"The water's c-cold!" said the wetted sidekick. Soaked and transparent, the filmy textiles ran with sliding suds and restrained the pink sausage of retreating manhood.

Dear reader, if DARKSTAR had commanded this elderly shopkeeper with the same frightening peril, then I, too, would have made utmost effort. And I actually shuddered at the prospects for the habitual criminals of District D in their soon-to-be confrontations with the Dark One. Already I had formed a sharp distinction between the alternating identities of the mammoth superhero and the Blake Starr I knew from next door. It really was as if they were two different people. And as for the KID BUCK, well, those twin, finely-tweaked bare buttocks — as tight as two nuts and working like alternating pistons, one stamped with the undulating mark of "K.B." — seemed to belong not to the slouching youth who verged on delinquency, but to someone else entirely.

Later still, I am ashamed to say, I made use of the miniscule peephole after I had diplomatically retired to my own quarters. With trepidation, I relate what I saw.

The suited Dark One grasped two wrists in Day-Glo hot orange from behind with a single hand, and the longest digit of the other fist made an effective, querying probe. The boy panted and gasped and emitted pitiful squeaks as the finger found its mark deep between the taut, smooth rump-cheeks. The orange bikini was hopeless to contain the lurching member, and in very quick time there was a hot gush of dripping glue. The release was manly and efficient. A gasping nineteen-year-old superhero of firm muscle and graceful limb sank to the green-painted floor, pitching and heaving and whimpering pitifully, discharging in powerful, youthful spasms. With elbows bent and on hands and knees, the KID BUCK turned his ass to the ceiling and softly moaned in abject exhaustion. Over him stood the black, towering shape of DARKSTAR.

I knew, really, that I should have withdrawn from the small, secretly-bored hole and departed the cavity beneath the Steam and Bath Roman Room, but reader, where would this leave you now? Uninformed of the private actions of the heroic twosome, that's where. The freshly-minted DARKSTAR unbuckled his newly fitted equipment-belt and produced an upraised prong befitting a superhero. One of those mighty gauntlets dug into a large tin of commercial-grade lubricant and slapped the greasy stuff generously over the mighty weapon of male meat. It gleamed and strained, and nosed its way into the dark crevice previously described, bypassing the paltry cord of the twisted briefs. It seemed to me at that time that an ass as tight and as compact as the athletic Kid's would be unable to accommodate the formidable appendage, but it was apparent that Blake Starr and Ky Buckfield had prior skill to guide them. There was a rhythmic series of open-mouthed "Ahh's" from the Kid, echoing closely in the hard confines of the underground bunker. Other noises included panting, grunting, and the scraping on the floor of DARKSTAR's chrome-rimmed soles. The big, black-gauntleted hands gripped the smooth bare limbs and maneuvered the twisting young body with some measure of practice, and the shafting gained momentum until it was a flesh-slapping, piston-driven pounding.

Don't ask me how or when the arrangement was consummated, but if proposing a guess, I would say that it was at the juncture when Blake Starr first interviewed a strapping young lad called Ky Buckfield for the position of video-store assistant. Simon Smudge, however, is unlikely to report on such things. You will remember him as the diligent correspondent for The District Blatt, and for superhero-related occurrences in other contexts, we should turn to him now.

SUPERHEROES SEIZE SPRAYCANS, THWART THEIVERY, DIRECT SKATERS TO HALF-PIPE

Mini Crime-Wave Undone by Brand-New Superheroes on Scene!

Byline: Simon Smudge

A group of bemused teenagers are firmly advised to carry — not ride — their skateboards to the District D Half-Pipe, the facility built for that purpose and inaugurated by Mayor Volte late last year.

A large spray-can of white paint is confiscated from a long-haired lout, no doubt intended for tagging-mischief.

And most spectacularly, carjackers are collared and marched directly to Police Headquarters — by COSTUMED SUPERHEROES!

That was the scene yesterday on Droop Street during what is probably the first appearance of District D's latest Superheroes! Amazed bystanders were agog as a whole section of the street was "cleaned-up," — as one witness put it — by a huge, black-and-blue clad muscle-man in cape and tights, and his garishly-clad young sidekick! This reporter can announce that the names of the two superheroes are DARKSTAR and KID BUCK! And this dual crime-fighting powerhouse intends to stay!

A shit-brown brown transit van with louvered windows and a decorative rubber dinosaur stuck on the tow-ball was in the process of being 'jacked at the intersection of Droop and Main yesterday at 9:01 am, when DARKSTAR and KID BUCK dashed onto the scene! DARKSTAR went around one side of the van and KID BUCK went around the other, and in concert, two law-breaking carjackers were hauled from the vehicle! But that wasn't the end of the show for surprised passers-by! The hardened crooks proceeded to fight with the imposing heroes. One tried a karate-kick to DARKSTAR, but DARKSTAR grabbed his ankle and flicked him over. The other would-be bandit sent a flying, haymaking fist toward KID BUCK, but the speedy sidekick swiftly ducked, and caught the crook with a jabbing uppercut. Stunned, the villains were soon apprehended.

Earlier, a graffiti crime and possible skateboard misadventures were averted by the crusading superheroes. DARKSTAR spoke briefly.

"I'm DARKSTAR and this is KID BUCK," he intoned warningly. "And we're going to patrol District D, protecting its citizens and catching wrongdoers!"

DARKSTAR wears a spandex bodysuit of metallic dark-blue, black boots, gloves, and cowl which disguises his identity. His cape is red. KID BUCK is more briefly attired in Day-Glo hot orange swim-briefs, boots, gloves, and mask, and a cute little purple vest. Both superheroes also wear harnesses.

The last time District D was in tenure of protective superheroes was ten years ago, when Mayhem and Maul Rat patrolled the streets. The District Blatt undertakes to report solemnly on any further exploits of DARKSTAR and KID BUCK!

# # # # #

Reader, the correspondent Simon Smudge is a very accurate one, and I can just imagine these events unfolding on Droop Street exactly as he describes. But the adventures of DARKSTAR and KID BUCK will no doubt include more than the garden variety of law-breaking such as car-jacking and wayward skater-kids. After the arrival of the two superheroes in District D, the dominion of crime must inevitably turn to more imaginative and elaborate schemes, and it is these dastardly exploits, which, I fear, will challenge and confront our brave maintainers of justice in times to come.

Epilogue

Dr Werner Wertham clasped his hands together, his white knuckles betraying an otherwise suppressed agitation. He leaned forward in the leather chair, speaking nasally, his spectacles pushed down and to the end of his nose.

"Mayor, it's not my intention to expose District D to any other dangers than those with which it currently has to deal. In fact, quite the opposite. That is why I must air my concerns with you."

"I've no doubt you have the District's welfare at heart, Doctor Wertham," said the Mayor. "And you've expressed your concerns admirably."

"You see," Dr Wertham continued. "I have very extensive knowledge of the insidious effects of this sort of thing, and the current situation is most worrying. It seemed that District D had seen the last of the superheroes something like ten years ago, but now, seemingly out of the blue, they're back. You do understand my apprehension. I gave many speeches and lectures on the degradation of core moral values caused by these colorfully-suited creatures, and these latest ones are causing quite a stir."

"Yes, they are, Doctor Wertham. And that's one of the points I wish to make. People are happy about it. There's been almost universal approval in the letters pages, the opinion columnists are endorsing the situation, everybody I speak to is enthusiastic, and the Police Chief was on the news the other night saying how effective the superheroes are — he's said the same to me personally. As well as all that, there is a difference. Every couple of days there's a crime thwarted. Now, it may not always be the worst kind of offense, but the troublemakers are being driven down. It's fear. You can sense a more law-abiding community here. Maybe these superheroes aren't all they're cracked up to be in the press, but golly, it's enough to make the next hold-up crew think twice."

"Many people I've spoken to are questioning whether vigilantes – unidentified vigilantes – should be usurping the role of the police, however strikingly those vigilantes might be dressed," the Doctor responded.

"I agree that's a valid issue, Doctor Wertham, but right now they seem to be doing a lot of good, and the Police think so, too."

"Mayor Volte, the Police are riddled with vice and corruption. Perhaps they're happy for some attention-seeking self-styled crusaders to divert public attention by swooping on minor felonies while they continue to participate in the real fraudulent activities, which plague our district."

"I'm not saying we still don't have problems, Doctor Wertham. But we're making headway."

The Doctor sighed. "Mayor," he said. "That's all a matter for valid debate. But what I'm most worried about is the flashy image these outlandish heroes project to the District's impressionable youth. While crook-catching is an exciting and virile activity, at the same time they're casting about the idea that it is altogether acceptable to not only dash about in contravention of the law, but also to do so in an extravagant and gaudy manner – very publically – and with costumes which defy common decency. DARKSTAR's prominent loins are emphasized with shining chrome, implying ... nay, flaunting a palpable sexuality ..."

"Yes, Doctor Wertham ..."

"And KID BUCK! The smallness of his tights is not something for innocent eyes to behold. Why, it's nothing more than a meager string, more suited to the beaches of some depraved European resort than for ..."

"Yes I know, Doctor Wertham!"

"Quite often he exhibits the most profound state of erect ..."

"Yes Doctor. I know."

"And not only that. Many people are starting to comment on the doubtful moral standing of ... a very large and masculine ... mature gentleman apparently in co-habitational coupling with a virile youth ... also obviously mature ..."

"Doctor Wertham, let me assure you I've taken all your points solidly on board. Now if you'll excuse me, I have a great many appointments to which I must attend."

The Mayor took up a stack of papers from the large, oak desk and shuffled them into alignment. It was clear the meeting was over. When the Doctor had departed, Mayor Victoria Volte picked up the phone with delicate fingers, her long, lilac-painted nails clicking against the brittle Bakelite.

"Michael," she purred into the mouthpiece with feline authority. "That quote *The District Blatt* wants. Tell them the Mayor not only fully supports the Chief of Police in his co-operation with DARKSTAR and KID BUCK, but would like to add that it is most reassuring and comforting to once again have costumed superheroes protecting the law-abiding and largely civilized residents of District D. Got that? Smudge is the one who contacted my office. Oh, and Michael? Can you please pick up those statistics from the District D Casualty Hospital Rectal Foreign Objects Ward? And tell them not to add any x-ray images as an annex this time."

# # # # #

"Bah!" said Dr Wertham as he descended the stairs at City Hall, slapping the manila file he carried and squinting in the bright sunlight. Inside that folder were a number of newspaper clippings, including the most recent one by Simon Smudge — with picture — detailing the arrest by DARKSTAR and KID BUCK of a gang of video-game pirates.

"Bah!" he said again as he stalked along the sidewalk. "And fiddle-dee-dee!"

One half hour later, Dr Werner Wertham sat in his darkened dressing-room, high up in District Regis Towers. He leered with growing delight into an ornately-framed mirror as ugly red and green makeup was applied, altering his features into an unrecognizable rictus. He sneered at himself, winking and grinning. His whitened knuckles reached for a small video-camera where a red light blinked.

"Citizens! Residents of District D!" he giggled horridly into the lens. "I know not when this message will be passed to you. But heed it when you hear it — your perverted 'Superheroes' — and the corruption they have caused you — will be an imminent riddance! For I am DOCTOR WARP! And I am soon to be the vehicle by which your filthy morals will be reformed and your psychological transferences to ridiculous heroes in costume purged from the collective and clinging infantilism you harbor! HA! Do you hear? I am DOCTOR WARP, and I am here to rescue you from your own dim-witted fantasies! HA! ... And HA HA! ...And HA HA HA HA HAAA!"

The Doctor cackled maniacally, throwing back his green and red face and thrusting his chin to the ceiling.

THE WRONG GUY By A.J. Damian

So I'm a hundred feet up in the air above New York, fighting for my life, and the lives of the citizens of this fine city, the wind whipping through my hair, my shirt and pants billowing around me. I had to be brave against the cruel might of the Dominator while my other half, Sonic Man had to fight Turmoil, the Dominator's ruthless partner, so in essence we had this hero versus villain combo thing going on. The Dominator's got his hand on the seat of his helicopter, while I'm still half way up the rope, clinging to it as he's stood there looking smug, giving me an ultimatum.

This is pretty intense, so I suppose I better start at the beginning. I find myself at a corporate dinner with Michael Knave in a suit trying to look as comfortable as he can, despite the fact he's Sonic Man and I'm Jake Neil, also trying to look as if I belong here even though I'm Hypno Boy when this handsome, tall man comes my way wanting me to follow him. He turns out to be the owner of the mansion and offers to show me around his private gallery, which houses some of the most famous artistic works (read into that boring) from the past three or four hundred years. I'm not an arty type, but I go just to humor him. It's Lars Henning, also owner of Henning Pharmaceuticals who, it happens me and Mike are investigating. At first I wasn't impressed at the paintings, but there were some of the biggest I had ever seen, even though I wasn't cultured enough to know them by name.

"Don't tell me this is your first time." Lars said with a wry smile.

"Err ... no, I've seen paintings before, just not that big." Henning placed his arm around my shoulder.

"I suppose they are big, but look at that one." I could smell his cologne, manly and enticing. "That's Caravaggio's composition of Bacchus. Look at the way he holds the drinking vessel, the drape of his robes, his sensual body. Isn't he lovely?" I must admit I liked the way it had been painted. I could see that some hard work had gone into making it appear real. It looked a lot better than that abstract crap that tended to go for millions at auction.

I went with him to the next painting. It was huge and loomed over me. "This one's the *Mona Lisa* by Leonardo Da Vinci. Rumor has it this painting is a self portrait of the artist." With his arm around me, somehow I felt comfortable around him. My personal space did not feel invaded. I hated to say it, but I wanted his closeness even though he was someone we were investigating, he was one of many, and I felt attracted to him, and my cock felt the same way.

"What about this one?" Lars led me to another painting, I assumed it was by another old master, but said nothing; my interest wasn't in the art around here. I couldn't stop looking at Lars, his blond hair, sky blue eyes, and his tall strong physique made me hot under the collar. I imagined him naked, it doesn't take much. Noticing my interest, he came closer, our faces moments away from touching.

"I know I've seen you around, Jake. You remind me of someone."

Rule number one of being a superheroes' side-kick — never let anyone you are investigating know your true identity; or the identity of your partner. Lars Henning was one of many suspects, and I was not sure of his intentions with Henning Pharmaceuticals. We had a tip off that one of our suspects might be planning world domination — they always are; and neither me nor my partner would let that happen. "I can't think of anywhere you might have seen me." There was something about him, his demeanor, his strength, his cologne that enticed me.

"You're that reporter from the New York News." he kissed me on the cheek, curling his arm around me as I got comfy with him. "You produce some good stories, Jake. I'm sure that's where I've seen you."

It seemed possible Lars could be the one who planned the destruction of the city, but there is one problem, though. I would hate to think that Lars might be corrupt and dangerous enough, let alone the one we are looking to take down. I do have a confession to make, and it's not a good one. There is something you have to understand about me. I never fall for nice guys. I go for the bad guys, always have. The ones who have a dark ruthless side, I find them sexier, just as I find Lars irresistible. There is a good chance he is the one we are looking for, but I don't care. The good guys take you to dinner, the bad guys demand sex, rampant, hot and fast; I can deal with that. He brings me to a couch in the center of the gallery, I know instantly what he wants, and it has nothing to do with the art on these walls; he senses my need and his own, nothing more.

"I try my best, Lars."

"Then why don't you just lay back and let me explore."

How could I refuse him when I am already at his place, his breath on my neck, his lips running kisses down my chest, continuing his exploration, stroking my pecs and thumbing my nipples. He delves lower to my stomach, and all I can think of is me hoping he likes the look of my abs — I worked on them at the gym for ages trying to get them to look like Brandon Routh's. When he removes my shirt, then his own, he shows me his muscular frame and tight pecs, but I am also drawn to his chin, and the strange scar marring his skin. Lars notices this and kisses me with a savage intensity.

"You like being teased?" he asks.

"You like to tease, I can see that ... alright, yes I do, but." My cock's straining in my pants, and I can't afford to get the crotch wet — they are new on. I meant to get them off, but his hands stop me.

"Don't move, Jake." Within seconds, he had them off my legs, though his hands never once touched the hardness between. I knew I would be one of many men he brought here, but I did not care. When my eyes wandered, his cock was huge even inside his pants, and I needed it. By my side, he kissed me; his full lips made me shudder at his forceful touch. As he kept kissing me, he tugged at my bottom lip, playful, his eyes closed, hands stroked further down to my abs. Did I say he had offered to show me his private gym, too?

"Fuck me, please." I moaned.

"Not yet, Jake, not yet," I guess he wanted to play for a while. "I've had plenty of men but you're different. There aren't many out there who are willing to submit."

I closed my eyes, soaking up the control he had over me. It's then I felt he is naked, as his cock slammed against mine, my legs under his. With one hand he stroked both our cocks together, the sensation of his pulsing member against mine made it harder still. His hand increased its speed; holding me at the very edge then making me wait. He was lucky I had control of my urges, even with a man like him.

I loved being with this guy. He enjoyed sex, not just as an end product, but for the raging orgasm he seemed to build up to the act. When I think of all the wham bam, thank you, man types out there, I thank my lucky balls there are men like Lars with enough stamina and drive, not to mention patience. While he stroked both our cocks, I leaned forward, hugging him, his other hand cupped my butt, squeezing it, slapping its taut mounds. My cock rubbed against his, the veins engorged. I felt my body pulse from the movements, eager, and passionate. His tongue explored me, while I felt his hand leave my cock and ass and heard the sound of a top being flipped open, and the feel of his finger pressing inside me with something slick, and wet. It was as if his finger was attuned to my whole body; he knew how far to delve, what to press, and more important to me anyway, he didn't have nails. I hate nails on guys — they rake where you don't want them to. Lars's fingers were smooth, his nails well manicured and stroked every inch of my hole with expert ease. He took every care to make sure I enjoyed what he did, from the gentle prodding in my sensitive areas, then further inside, then out. Another finger slid in with the lube, but I couldn't take it, the pleasure as I squirmed over him, my erection becoming too much for me to handle.

"Can't you fuck me now? I'm desperate." I panted, his fingers pressed harder inside.

"I want your lips around my cock — we'll have to compromise." he joked.

I moved from his grasp once he removed his fingers. I knelt between his legs; my lips teased his cockhead, getting my own back on him for not wanting to fuck me earlier. I smiled as I licked the tip, watching it juice, his cock reared in response to my touches, then when I knew he could not take it anymore, I took it all down, not thinking about his size, the uber cock that made me gasp when I released it to see how Lars looked mid moan.

"Now you've earned that fuck."

Lars got me onto my side, stroking more lube over his length, before pressing it against my ass. I moaned into my hand as he eased it further in.

"Just push it in, fuck me, please. I need it so bad!" I had been patient, my hard-on weeping in my palm as I jerked along with his hard thrusts. I felt pain when he rammed it inside in one go, but the sensation gave me the feelings I relished the most. As his cock swelled inside me, he moved with calculated thrusts rather than satisfying himself. I got the impression he wanted to make me happy instead. I never had a considerate lover before. His big arms and bulging biceps above me, plunging in and out of my arsehole with a steady rhythm I loved. Lars licked my neck, I felt him give me a few play bites and as my neck was a sensitive part of me, I moaned into the couch, Lars increasing the speed of his thrusts. I felt his meaty balls slap against my ass as he repeated his thrusts. I could say with conviction that I had not been fucked like this in a very long time. His self-confidence extended to the bedroom, or in my case, the gallery — his cock plundered my insides, and I stuck my ass out for more. I needed him to deepen his thrusts even though he steadied, knowing I desired more from him than he was willing to give. His strokes plus the slick lube sent a few shivers up my spine.

Lars acted different from the other guys I had slept with. He took his time to give all he could to his date for the night. I wondered how many more surprises he had in store for me. Picking up speed, I could sense everything from him, his smell, his sweat as he made me feel good, and the sheer pleasure I got from him. I turned my head around, licked his lips, and then kissed them. This made the stroking I gave my cock more frantic in my need for release until I begged for his cock juice to burst inside me before I came, but I held back my own need, realizing I wanted more satisfaction later. Lars lifted his hips further up, plunging deeper, and faster inside me.

"Are you ready for my cum?" he snarled, planting a deliberate, harsh thrust into my ass for good measure.

"Oh yes, I need it, fuck me!" For the first time what I said during sex weren't empty words; they had meaning for once and as Lars kept the speed up, I felt his body slam into my own with a power I had not experienced before. And as I felt the surge of warmth inside, and the rush of his juice burst within my walls, my hand drew down to the base of my cock in one jarring movement, shooting three spurts of my own cum into my hand.

We both lay panting on the couch. He had given it his all, bless him.

"You were amazing — the best." Was all I could say mid gasp, but I saw the way he looked at me when I laid back into his arms, his strong body comforting me when I expected to be already dressed and tossed out the door.

For a suspected bad guy he was doing rather well, yet something in my mind started to bother me. Michael would be looking for me at some point. That was obvious. He had a keen sense I might be in trouble if I was away for more than forty minutes. He had no other reason for his concern than professional — we were both a team, and as I well knew there's no I in it. Sooner or later I knew he would come, and I thought I had better get moving.

"Going somewhere?" As I was starting to get up, I felt his hand on my shoulder.

"I have to go, my partner Michael — he'll be waiting for me." I hoped he didn't get that bit of my hesitation. It was important I did not give any information that might make us targets. With his overbearing presence, around me, I fell back into his arms.

"Tonight was no mistake, Jake, believe me. I never make mistakes where men are concerned."

"I meant to ask you a few questions, as a reporter I mean, but I got carried away." I said as he held me there, not letting me go. Fear mingled with excitement as my pulse rose just as his cock did once more.

"You're not going anywhere."

"I have to, or it'll look suspicious."

"Why?" Lars had me now. What could I come up with to satisfy his curiosity?

"What is so important that it takes you from my side?"

"My friend — err, he's really my partner. I work for him at the New York News."

"And you wanted to ask some questions, too?"

"Yes."

He lifted my body over his, his cock straining at my ass, my legs spread, he stroked mine while I asked away. I have to admit it was starting to be the weirdest interview I ever had. "Alright, Henning Pharmaceuticals, the rumor is it's a cover for a huge weapons making factory."

Lars slowed down his stroking of my cock for a moment. "You'll have to excuse me; I'm not used to being pumped for information, but my company has made weapons in the past, not now, of course, as I have to create a better future with the drugs we make."

I asked him the rest of the questions I needed to hear answered, and he did do a good job of making sense of the rumors. I had one last question. The clincher, either way I would know the identity of the Dominator. "The two gold pendants you wear around your neck — the letter D, what is its significance?" He turned his eyes from my cock, to the lengthy chain, a smile on his face that told me he expected me to ask about it.

"Oh, these," Lars thumbed the pendants, as if remembering. "The letter E is for Evan. a former lover who died in a drive by shooting. The D, well, that is my pet name he gave me, Dom, as he spoke of my dominance in bed." I should not have been surprised to hear of his lover. It would be strange for him not to have any one else as he was so handsome and self-confident. He looked the sort of man other men fancied.

His confidence oozed from every pore, his whole look, dress sense said it all, he had money, influence and expensive taste, but for all that, he still pissed and crapped like the rest of us. His hand still stroked me, and I could still feel the throb of his organ press against my ass. I still needed to feel him deep inside me again, but I had to leave. I leaned forward again, ready to go, and he knew this time he couldn't stop me.

"You can come with me, then if there are other questions the two of you want me to answer, I'm already available." I could see where that would be useful for us as Mike wouldn't get the wrong idea from us coming out of the gallery together, getting back into my clothes seemed alien to me after spending so much time with him naked.

"Mr. Henning, I wondered when I'd finally meet you. You've been evasive these past few hours." Michael looked impatient, I could tell. He loathed these kinds of gatherings, and being the son of an already wealthy businessman after taking over Knave Corp ten years ago, he grew to hate them even more. Lars saw the both of us stood together, but I'm glad to say he neglected to notice that we had any special bond, or even knew what we had been up to ten minutes ago.

"Ahh, so you're Jake's reporter friend, nice to meet you."

Mike stared at me, unsure at first, then played along once he realized. "Michael Knave, likewise."

Lars smiled at Jake. "Jake's told me hardly anything about you while I was showing him around my gallery. I had hoped to learn more about you."

Mike gave him a stern look. "It was you who I hoped to learn more about, Mr. Henning."

"Please call me Lars. I loathe formality."

Looking at Lars's shirt open the way it was made the heat rise up my face remembering what we had done, but the chain around his neck convinced me, I could tell there was something between the two initials on it that started to fascinate me; it looked like another initial but I couldn't quite make it out until now. It was a small initial A that hung between the E and D, but what could it mean to him? It seemed the more I tried to find out about him, the more of an enigma he became. Was Lars so used to offering so little of him to others, or did it come as naturally as breathing?

After the party, I never saw him again, but I did receive texts from him saying how much he had enjoyed our night together. My heart sank at not being with him, Lars said at some point we would meet again, though the months passed, and Mike, in his wisdom came to the conclusion that Lars must be the Dominator of local legend, and unfortunately, I had no evidence to say otherwise. The fiend was still at large, and Mike had told me of several times this month where the Dominator had made an appearance, and from the descriptions of him being six-four and well-built, Lars could well be him. Even though I have a thing for bad guys, I hoped deep in my heart that he was not the suspect. When I lay on his couch that night, we were one entity, one soul. Both our hearts beat within the same chamber. I never knew what love was, but in my mind, it started at the heart and grew once we got to know each other. I did have other feelings for him, though, most guys don't admit to, the ones that give you a lump in the throat and a fluttering in the heart. That is how I felt around Lars, and the only thing that stuck in my mind was the pendants around his neck. I could never replace Evan, and I would not even try. I had an attraction to him that had me thinking of no other guys around me — I didn't even want to date another guy in-between being with him, and that's unusual for me. I was a fool who held out for a man who might not even show up again, but I hoped, fumbling through copies of porn mags in order to take my mind off of the aching in my crotch.

I'm not that shallow all the time, honest. I get a guy who's a real dish, and I get urges when I'm away from him. It's rare, but it happens when I feel I've got a special bond with someone.

Contrary to popular opinion, we superheroes don't have cases all the time, help the cops and kick bad guy ass — sometimes we have quiet days, and for me this happened to be one of them. I sat waiting for a call from Mike about another sighting of the Dominator. This time, he had not tangled with him, but his side-kick and it was only brief, Mike had been slammed into a building off lower Manhattan, tumbled off it and lived to tell the tale. I felt his brush with Turmoil was enough, but the Dominator had the upper hand if you'll pardon the pun, and I couldn't help but remember how possessive Lars had acted at the party. He didn't want me to leave, and now it seemed I did fall for the bad guys after all. Where was my control when it came to my private life? My skill, my special ability as Hypno Boy was to persuade others to do my bidding through talking to them. My voice had a soothing quality that brought others around to my way of thinking, and I used special keywords that helped with the hypnotism thing. It could work on anyone, anyone at all but that night, it hadn't worked on Lars. He might have been strong to be able to ignore and counter my power, and as much as I hated to say it, I started to believe Lars might be the Dominator. He could have been using me to break down my resistance, my strength, make me fall for him, so I looked weak as part of the team with Mike.

I wasn't always the great kid who helped the crime rate drop. When Mike first asked me to join him as his side-kick, I had doubts about my ability. When he saw me use my hypnotic voice on the card sharps in a downtown gambling den, he said I could use my ability for good instead of greed. At first, I thought him nothing more than a do-gooder, but it took real balls to believe in him. Mike got his man whether or not it was dangerous trying. Danger, I found became part of the job whether it involved gang warfare, serial killers, or all too powerful drug syndicates — he'd be there, and I felt proud to be a part of that. Though when I fucked-up, it took even more cojones to admit I'd failed, and I wasn't just failing myself, I'd failed him, too. From then on, I had to be on the alert, ready for action no matter who it was. Mike had been waiting for the big one to come along, the criminal mastermind whom we could net, and that my friend's wish had come true, all that work had paid off.

I only hoped I could be as useful at defeating him, or his faithful assistant, Turmoil. Mike had sustained a lot of damage the last time he'd fought him; he'd come away with concussion, broken bones and bruises for his trouble, so Christ only knows what the Dominator could do given the chance.

The phone call came through, and I clad in my white rubber outfit with gold H in the center of my chest, gold boots, and essential equipment at my belt dashed out to meet him. There was a reason I chose white for the outfit — it had a statement, a sort of does my cock look big in this quality.

"Remember what I told you, Hypno Boy, about the Dominator," His voice told me how pissed he was he had not caught him until now. "Leave him to me — you deal with Turmoil and use that voice of yours on him. He'll soon be under your power."

"Don't be so sure, Sonic Man. It didn't work on Henning that time I talked with him at the party." I didn't go into details. We both liked guys, but it wouldn't look professional on my part if I told him that I'd let him fuck me the first time I met him. That would make me sound like some kind of man-slut.

"Whatever happens, you let me deal with him, while you keep Turmoil busy. You know his weakness." His eyes looked determined even behind the mask.

"Yeah, I know. His overconfidence is his weakness." I knew his weakness, but I also knew mine.

"You can get him; I've every faith in you." He slapped me on the back, and I joined him in the Sonic Mobile hearing the engine purr as I watched the glass shield move over our heads.

"Remember Soames," he whispered to his butler. "Drop us off at the city center — you've got one of these on," He pointed to his specially designed watch, Soames showed him his matched. "Come pick us up when I tell you, okay?" Soames nodded and drove us to our destination.

Commissioner Norman had received a garish purple and scarlet envelope with a note inside that told him the Dominator and Turmoil would destroy several landmark buildings; hinting that Sonic Man and me were weak and ineffective at tackling crime and helping to bring criminals like them to justice. I could understand that he was annoyed — we have always been there and beaten other enemies they might have looked to as role models. This letter turned out to be his calling card, a challenge to us, and our usefulness to the NYPD. If we fucked this up, lots of people would die, and our faces would be plastered all over the morning newspapers for all to see, and being a reporter, I knew how bad that could look. As a superheroes' side-kick I felt on borrowed time already, and this single assignment would test me to the very limit of my ability, or until I got another coffee down me; skinny Cappuccino — I've got a super-figure to watch, you know!

I heard a thundering noise, looked up and saw a helicopter in the distance, tear gassing its way above, while in another direction, a purple light and a scarlet one was near it, knowing the Dominator and Turmoil had appeared right on time. Sonic Man turned to me. "You know what to do." I nodded, and we got out, leaving Soames to get out of the way. It would be a dangerous night, and my reputation was on the line. I had to find and confront Turmoil, but I felt curious about the helicopter — it had a familiar logo on it I recognized. I had seen it at Henning's party. So he thought he'd throw us by having two we thought might be the culprits, and a third who might be the real one, crafty, eh? Well, if he was as crafty as he was cunning, then I'd be in for a good night, and maybe a grudge fuck later.

As I got closer to the helicopter, I saw three men inside. One was the pilot, and there were two I couldn't quite make out. A ladder suspended from the helicopter moved in the wind, I reached for it and climbed, remembering my small arsenal of weapons at my belt, which would be put to good use in the coming battle. If I was being deceived, the Dominator had to get up a lot earlier in the morning to outwit me even under these circumstances. Looking ahead, I saw a huge man lean out the window. He had on an outfit, but was it for a superhero or a super villain? Whoever it was, he had the same scar Henning bore when I first met him. My heart skipped a beat, and then sank. Just thinking about him clad in his outfit gave me a hard-on, and I shouldn't have felt that way for someone who got his kicks out of destroying the city and its people. I had a mike taped to me and hoped he had, too, or with this level of noise, I wouldn't have been able to hear him.

"I thought you would come, eventually." He said. Good, he had one on after all. The man moved his hand, urging me to climb higher. "I knew you would be curious enough to find out who it was up here." I didn't know what to think, but I recognized the logo, and had an idea it could be Henning.

"I think you're the Dominator — you're the bastard we're after, and you used me as a pawn so Sonic Man would be alone." The realization I'd gone after the wrong guy annoyed me, as he was wrong in so many ways.

"You think so, huh?" He moved back a bit at that, but it was too late, I felt the anger grow inside me.

"Yeah, I think you're him and you're Lars Henning, too, aren't you?" Silence, I saw him give the pilot a signal to carry us away from the city, the whirring blades loud and imposing to my ears made me shout much louder than I wanted to.

"What makes you think that?" So he was out to tease me in a different way this time. "I've met less troublesome boys." He pulled off his mask, a huge smile on his face. I hated guys like that, that he could smile at a time like this. It was Henning. "Are you satisfied that you've exposed me?"

"What, as the Dominator?" I said, but inside I still felt mad at him, but what else could I feel — I couldn't love a man like him — could I?

"So you still think that huh?" The helicopter took us around the water's edge, I could see people all around, they started to resemble ants below, and suddenly, I felt more vulnerable at this height.

"Okay, if you're not the Dominator, then what's the meaning of that letter A on the chain around your neck?" I saw the bastard laugh, and I didn't like it one bit. I wanted to punch him right in his scarred jaw, but I was too far away from him for that. I climbed higher, so I was only a few feet away from him. I wondered if he would evade this question, or if he'd evade it at all. It could be that I'd not be any closer to finding the truth, yet his silence told me he might offer up some kind of an answer.

"Ahh, Jake," The realization struck him as to who I was. "You remember I told you about Evan's death in the drive-by shooting — well, after he died I couldn't stand the thought of the low life that killed him still living and breathing when he had destroyed the only love I had in my life," From the look of him, he wasn't lying. Why would he when I could see the passion in his eyes. "The A stands for Avenger, and it's my name, the one persona I use when I hunt the streets, removing them of the sort of scum that don't deserve to live their lives like the innocent citizens of New York do." I thought he was going to say that he killed them, but I hoped he didn't stoop to their level. "Come on, Hypno Boy, Jake. I'll prove to you I'm not the Dominator." I wanted to climb further until he pulled me into the back, but I still didn't believe him. "I've been monitoring the Dominator for a while now, his actions, his targets," He gave me a cocky smile; it was just like him to act this way when faced with a tricky situation. "So don't go thinking you're the only superheroes out there trying to keep order on the streets."

"How do I believe you're not the Dominator?" Okay, I was going to put my career on the line for this — I had to, and still the wind whipped around me.

"You'll have to trust me, Jake. I'm not the bad guy, the bad guys are still out there — so are you coming or not?" I loved it when he acted forceful.

I climbed the rest of the way, accepting his hand. He was right. I had to prove myself in the heat of battle and prove to Sonic Man I could be as strong as him. There would be a battle out here I couldn't afford to lose.

"Alright, I'll do it; we'll go out there as a team. Avenger, Sonic Man, and Hypno Boy — just how it should be!"

Lars turned to me, the helicopter swerved over to land again, where Sonic Man was busy fighting. "Alright, Jake let's go kick some ass!"

THE PIPER AND THE PALADIN
By Joshua Skye

As I sit here with the Green Goddess in hand, a rare mistress indeed, I find myself turning my attention from all of you down to her and her swirling emerald promises. I could get lost there, I should think … swim in her warmth and drink of her to chase my demons away. But they really wouldn't be gone would they? They'd come back. And they'd laugh at my silly, silly naïveté. Oh, let me not dwell on such inevitable things. Demons never leave us. So let me stand and offer first a toast! To all of you fine and distinguished gentlemen all of whom I can sincerely call my friends and some of whom I can honorably call profoundly more, I thank you for your company, your witticisms and most especially your coveted acceptance. We're much rarer than our Goddess here, aren't we? We certainly know darker things. Now, let me burrow back down into the worn comfort of this tufted eyesore and tell you my tale as the candles flicker and the fire crackles and you all share with me the comforts of our patron Goddess.

I'm getting old. I can feel and hear my bones crack in their wearisome, sometimes painful ways. The passage of years has knotted my fingers, turned my knees into splintering hinges and made a painful twist of my back. I wasn't always like this, an old man with a map for a face and a sagging willow tree for flesh. I was once beautiful, lithe and quite the devilish saucebox, if I do say so myself. My closer friends here would agree, of that I am sure.

The city streets were not fit for the more fainthearted among us to roam at night as anyone can attest, but I did. With my trusty barker in one pocket, a shiner in my stocking and my trademark secret weapon I had the means to equalize any situation in which I found myself either outnumbered or out-girthed, shall we say. I found that if I walked with a certain stride and a particular nonchalance in my gaze very few offered trouble, not that I didn't see my share of it. Dandies, as you know, often happen across it even if we're purposely over-cautious in our attempts to avoid it. That's how the world works, you see. They, those fine and eminently dreary hostiles, favor themselves above all others and forever search for physical ways to prove it to themselves. I cannot claim that I've never stuck my shiner in one of them, and likewise it would be untrue to state that I hadn't found gratification in delivering to them what they had been so willing to deliver upon me. In fact, as one bible-browed porter had held his lower insides in the cups of his hands after attempting to violate me with a broken whiskey bottle, I'd laughed in his pinched, fat face. And I had seen that he'd realized at that moment that he'd deserved it if not for what he'd intended with me than for what he'd already done to anyone else he'd felt the need to prove his masculinity with. I hate tomcats.

One day in mid-December as the city streets piled high with snow, I'd found myself without a bed to sleep on and a meal to warm my belly. I won't go into the sordid details of exactly why my previously gracious host had decided to give me my walking-papers, suffice it to say that he wasn't too keen on the idea of sharing my succulent affections. So, cold and wet and hungry, I found myself in need of a swift romance that might grant me at least a little time to catch my bearings. With all the lost souls that haunt our fine city, it's surprisingly easier whispered than accomplished especially so on a night when I seemed unaided in my gutter crawl. Even businesses that catered to the night and her children were dark and vacant. The only sound was the rushing breath of the icy breeze. The sky was heavily overcast, and no hint of the moon or her sister stars was visible. Though I was more than aware of the countless hordes that dwelled here with me, I felt utterly alone. As a child, I might have found some imaginative play to occupy myself with as I wandered but as one on the cusp of adulthood indeed by some standards a full-fledged adult, nineteen and never been, I saw only melancholy in my surroundings. I wanted to be warm and sated. I wanted to be safe and satisfied.

I sat down on a frozen, pitiless curb and laughed as I realized that it was such a nice metaphor for veracity. I was what anyone, those just like me, mocked and ridiculed. Oh yes, they did it in whispers but were no less guilty. The street, void of all traffic, was a slide of white before me. I could feel my extremities cramping from the cold, my genitals were a tight knot in my crotch. I would have to get out of the weather soon before something quite horrible happened to me. I was a handsome young man, and I wanted to keep it that way. I'd seen what frostbite could do to noses, lips and eyelids. It wasn't pretty. Just as I was relinquishing myself to the idea that I would have to resort to picking up some trashy john down by the harbor there was a sound behind me. I gazed over my shoulder and saw a figure waking toward me through the gloom. Heavily bundled, the man had his shoulders hunched up to the sides of his head and his hands shoved into his coat pockets. I plastered on a coy grin, one that would speak to the proper target without arousing suspicion in some bigoted adversary. I waited until he emerged from the shadows and saw me. He was a handsome older man with salt and pepper hair just visible beneath the rim of his black fedora. His emerald eyes fell upon me, and he paused in mid-stride as he considered me. After several moments, his thin lips curled upward into an engaging smile.

I stood and dusted myself off. I said, "Hello."

"Hello."

I sighed in an attempt to seem nonchalant. "It's cold out here."

"Then let's get you warmed up," he said invitingly.

I joined him as he walked down the street; the only sound was the swirling breeze. I took note of his peculiar little limp, observed, too, that he fought to conceal it. Faint streetlights flickered strangely as we hurried by them. He either didn't notice or didn't care. We passed wealth-filled buildings where the curious doormen stared at us from behind thick glass, their faces distorted. And we continued beyond them to the buildings with no doormen where candlelight flickered in apartment windows. And still we walked through neighborhoods where there were no lights in windows at all. We made our swift way to a street so dark that I was forced to trust his instincts in navigating it. Beginning my seduction, I used the blinded opportunity to my advantage and casually pressed myself up against him. He made a sound, something akin to surprise and amusement. After a few moments, I felt his hand gently take a hold of my upper arm as he guided me through a shadowy doorway.

The foyer of the building was brightly lit, and I had to stand still until my eyes adjusted to it. The door closed out the swirling snow and freezing cold behind us. It was quite warm. The man turned to face me and moved his eyes across my features admiringly. I could tell that I was blushing. I imagined that my cheeks were a splattering of crimson. I offered him a perfected smile that suggested that I was shy. I wasn't sure if he bought the act but there was a hint of a grin there and a yearning in his gaze. "This way," he said, and he led me through a labyrinthine series of corridors that twisted, turned, inclined, declined and even forked. It was all so tremendously confusing. I'd have been utterly lost in that maze without the company of my handsome host.

After what seemed an incongruously long amount of time, we arrived at an ancient door that was sculpted intricately with archaic symbols and splashed in a crimson wash that revealed much of the primeval striations of the wood's grain underneath. For some inexplicable reason, I was reminded of something perhaps poisonous yet extraordinarily enthralling. I could not help but run my fingertips over it as I entered the ominous, beautifully decorated abode beyond. And as it closed behind me with an echoing chorus I was, for a moment, stranded in complete darkness. My heart fluttered, my crotch tightened and my thoughts raced with dark, dangerous scenarios until my host turned on a faint, faraway light. He removed his coat and hat.

Of no doubt, he was a man of refinement and taste. Everything was of ancient design, antiques from across the globe that had been tenderly cared for throughout the years. The place smelled of dust, wood, oils and polishes with perhaps exotic origins. As I strolled leisurely among the gorgeous objects, I removed my layers of warmth and protection with a slow, deliberate objective. Though I did not see, I could feel his gaze upon me soaking in my youthful exquisiteness and beguiling lure. Oh, I turned on my seductive charms … yes, oh yes indeed. And it was working.

"What's your name?" he asked with genuine curiosity.

I answered, "Maurice. And your name is …"

"Frederick," he replied stepping close to me. I could smell the remnants of a long-ago used cologne. It was unmistakably masculine but with an oddly floral nuance. I liked it and told him so. "Thank you," he said. His voice was low and modest. He reached out sheepishly and touched my tummy with the backside of his knuckles, his fingers tucked into a loose curl that seemed to quiver.

I raised my shirt and exposed just a sliver of my tight pale belly. His light caress tickled as he moved over my flesh, Goosebumps rising to the occasion. I coyly bit my lower lip as I watched his touch reticently move along the steam of my sparse, curly treasure trail. He unfurled his fingers, and the tips lingered around my coiled cave of a navel. He let out a soft sigh, the low sound of exultation. His gaze was resolutely focused on my swirly little button, his brow a windswept expression as his mouth hung open lips trembling. So long it seemed that he was frozen there, an unmoving statue ogling my stomach in a subtlety aberrant, unusually sensuous way. He very much liked what he was seeing. And I liked that he liked it. "May I?" he asked.

Not completely sure of what exactly he was asking I chanced a consenting reply. With an eager hiss spilling out of him, he hurried to his knees and pressed his face to me. His tongue entered me as a warm, wet thing exploring my navel enthusiastically. His moans started quite modestly, just noises oozing from a delighted man, but they quickly became thunderous grunts as his hands pulled me impatiently to him. I could feel rivulets of drool seep down my tummy where it doubtlessly soaked the waistband of my khakis. Soon my pubes would be drenched. Soon I, myself, would be oozing and saturating myself with my thick, warm fluids. Closing my eyes, I envisioned it … the whirls of my crotch hair steeped in the salty dissemination of my preliminary juices. I liked the thought of it, liked the thought of running my fingers through it and feeling the cream there between them. Would I bring my slippery hand to my lips and taste the brackish emulsions? Would I stuff his mouth with my fingers and make him have an indulgent taste? Would he groan for more? I could clearly picture him salivating over my strings of milky dew just as he'd drooled over my navel. I'd move my fingers over his tongue until it was all gone … until he'd licked me clean.

My sordid reverie was interrupted by a sudden jerking sensation. I opened my emerald eyes and glared down at Frederick as he fumbled awkwardly with the front of my pants. I was forced to suppress a nearly disobedient giggle, chewed on my lip and watched as he ripped the fabric of my khakis before releasing me. My rigidness slapped him across the face just before he excitedly sucked me into his mouth. Warm, wet, tight and intoxicating, his mouth enveloped me with a gradually swelling bliss. I rotated my hips in tandem with his rhythmic nods. I wanted to flood his mouth.

After a while, he gripped the base of my dick with one hand, cupped my balls in the other and gave my piss slit the same fervent attention he'd given my belly button. It was an exciting, delightful feeling, but it also tickled, and I found myself squirming as I stood before him. I could not contain the low, silly laughter that spilled out of me. Instead of finding it odious in some self-conscious way, he started to laugh, too. Before I knew it, we were both laughing quite loudly as we quickly and clumsily undressed. He pulled me to the cold floor and crawled on top of me. I liked the feel of his weight and the ribbed caress of his hard, washboard abdominals. His clothes had betrayed his amazingly beautiful physique, hiding it from admiring eyes. His chest was mouthwateringly hairy, just the way I liked it. His nipples were pearls enmeshed in the dark tresses. We gazed longingly into each other's eyes until slowly, so very slowly, our laughter subsided, and we were lying there ... the handsome older man comfortable on top of me, me the rosy-cheeked youth submissive beneath him ... silent and still. Then he kissed me.

In a proficiently accomplished move, he positioned himself between my legs spreading them until they settled efficiently into the hook of his powerful hips. It was his turn to rotate. His wildly throbbing cock rolled into the sensitive space between my genitals and my leg where it inched down, down, down until the slippery head of it fell along my left swell just barely missing my all-too willing dale. I was ready for him, excited to take him agonizingly inside where the bulge of the invading sting would progressively transform into all-encompassing gratification. I wanted him to take me in a way that I had never really allowed myself to be taken before. I didn't know why and though it confused me, angered me and roused a resentment inside of me I still swayed under him invitingly. And the next thing I knew, I was screaming while he was thrusting!

Long spent, my handsome host snored lowly in a near fetal curl beside me on the cold floor. I couldn't sleep; the thought of snooping around his cavernous home was too tempting. Slightly sore, and certainly loosened, I groaned to my feet. Freshly fucked holes have an odd sensation, not so much of a gaping sort but of a pleasantly parted seam that slid like wetted lips over one another as you walked. I rather liked it. It was an enjoyable departure from the stressed knot of the usual daily routine.

Every drawer and door was an incitement to poke around. And there were so many of them throughout his collection of fine, elaborately designed antiques. Most harbored no interesting secrets; in fact the vast majority of the drawers and cabinets were peculiarly and frustratingly empty. Some held papers that clearly didn't belong to Frederick as they bore bizarre foreign names that I could barely pronounce. There was even a drawer full of military identifications ... different faces, outlandish names, anomalous job titles. A gothic armoire in a deeply stained oak had a gaggle of carved faces gawking from a knot of twisted vines. And when I looked very closely, I could see that entangled in the wooden creepers were veiny cocks in various stages of salute. Some of them were shoved into frozen mouths, and at least three sprouted from the very faces that fellated them. There was something arousing through the nightmarish imagery, something that brought me to mast again. I pressed myself to the faces, closed my eyes and focused my senses on each one as I jerked off.

It smelled of fragrant incenses from the Middle East, tasted of bitters, and the more I relaxed into it, the more the wood felt alive and malleable. My mind dreamed as I masturbated. It wasn't my hand that moved over my pulsating dick, but a wooden orifice swallowing me, suckling me, milking me with a vicious zeal. And the other faces whispered in alien tongues that creaked like rusted hinges, bellowed like bowing floorboards and splintered like desiccated steps left long ago to decay. When I came, I mumbled perverse promises to the gargoyle visage that I'd been kissing. It didn't bother to respond. So rude! So I growled at it disapprovingly.

Feeling like a man emerging from a long, hot bath, heavy and tranquil, I walked away from the gaudy piece of furniture leaving my seed to drip, drip, drip down its twisted facade. There was more to explore! The kitchen was an unused thing, void of life and bathed in dull colors. The room just felt depressed, fallow. Plates and glasses were covered in a thick film of dust and the cupboards were bare. I did not linger long in that cheerless place. The bathroom stunk of antiseptic and soap. I stood above the toilet and pissed, the yellow stream splashing about with lackadaisical abandon. I wasn't particularly concerned that my little golden drops speckled the blindingly white seat or the matching tile floor. I flushed; the sound of it was annoyingly loud. I didn't bother to wash my hands but did admire myself in the huge framed mirror above the sink. Ah so young, so beautiful, so vain. I liked myself, what can I say. Feeling a little spirited, I turned around, bent over, pried my lily cheeks apart and looked at my pleasantly sore asshole. It wasn't a pinched little bloom as it normally was; instead it was a blushing line. There was something fascinating about it. I liked looking at it. I consciously made it oblige to a cute little pucker for me, imagined that it was blowing me a kiss, and teased it with the tips of my fingers. It felt good. Resisting the urge to slip my fingers inside and wriggle them around a bit, I stood upright and left the bathroom.

There were bedrooms, all of them flamboyant and decorated with an artist's touch, but most of them were long unemployed. When, at last, I found one that didn't have an old musty stench or a covering of dust, I knew immediately it had to be the one he actually slept in. In fact, the smell was musky, a light enduring aroma of body odor.

I crawled into the massive canopied bed. I sank several inches into a luxurious, cottony mattress. The jacquard spread covered a lush padding of linen so soft that I felt as though I were lounging upon a cloud. I rolled in it and then sprawled out over it as I gazed at the gloomy ceiling where the shadows of lanky insects fluttered about the light fixture. I wondered how they had gotten in … the room had no windows. Curiosity rising, I spun over to one of the ornately carved nightstands and opened the drawer. Papers, a bible and variously flavored pieces of chewing gum filled it. The door beneath opened to a stack of pulp novels with worn spines. The other nightstand was empty. I forced myself to get out of the bed's serene comfort and searched the drawers of the massive dresser, a behemoth that came to nearly the height of my shoulders. I found nothing but clothes there neatly folded and tucked away in what appeared to be an overly complex order system. I fought the childish urge to mess it all up. Feeling a little impish I started to hum a tune and danced with silly abandon over to the towering armoire and threw open the colossal double doors …

I was shocked silent and stepped instinctively back away from what my eyes were seeing. For a moment, I couldn't comprehend exactly what it was I just knew that it wasn't particularly normal. Autumn colors in severely muted tones, padded and bulletproof as everyone all across the city well knew, the thing hung there from thick wooden hangers above piles of newspaper clippings. And there on the inside of the right-hand door was the mask that matched the suit in all of its tangled glory, the dried woven spirals of woodland branches, vines and thorny stems.

"Curiosity killed the cat."

I flinched away from the low, threatening voice as I turned to face my handsome host. He stood there naked and beautiful in the bedroom doorway, his thick arms crossed at his tightening chest. His jaw muscles flexed with no small amount of irritation, and his eyes burned with equal ferocity. I backed away from him until I bumped into the behemoth that was his dresser. The jagged corner jabbed into my back painfully. I controlled the squeak that wanted to rush out of me.

"I knew it would be a mistake bringing you here," he said and moved slowly over to the armoire. He considered the contents but for a moment before closing the doors. "I was just so lonely. It's so lonesome being ..."

"The Paladin," I finished his sentence.

He froze; his feet planted firmly, his hands still on the soaring piece of furniture and his face down. Like a statue he just stood there for a very long time. I wondered what he was thinking, what he was plotting. He had to be plotting something. "Yeah, The Paladin," he confirmed with a grumbling snarl.

Our city's resident superhero, the midnight phantom himself in all of his famous grandeur was but a forlorn gentleman trapped among a suffocating collection of antiques with his secret life ... and everyone knows that secrets are best kept by a single breathing being. What was he plotting? Would the hero resort to villainy to keep his precious clandestine self unknown to the world? Were there not alliances out there in the dark desperately seeking The Paladin's elusive true identity and planning his gruesome demise in order to fulfill their various wrongdoings? He had to protect himself, didn't he? It was, after all, not just his own fate that he had to consider but the greater good of everyone, all the poor souls he protected from the raging hordes of bad guys that called the city their home. Sometimes committing an obligatory evil is the right thing to do. We know that all too well do we not my friends?

When he finally looked over at me I could tell from the dullness of his eyes and the resolute determination in his gaze that he had made up his mind. I was to be a necessary casualty in his war on crime and the masterminds behind it. He was not only very much bigger and stronger than I was in a traditional sense, he was also a superhero with feats of strength most of us couldn't even begin to imagine. With my barker and my shiner wrapped up in the tangle of my clothes far, far away I felt naked beyond the obvious. As he faced me and began to walk my way I had only one last resort … I had to sing for him. That, you see, if my trademark secret weapon.

My voice is beautiful, a siren's refrain, and none are immune to my deadly melody … sweet, profound, a preternatural resonance, a gift from the abyss itself. When I sing I control all that hears me, and I earn my moniker well … The Piper. I am The Piper! And so I sang to The Paladin his bittersweet swan song, enrapturing him, enslaving him, making him mine. Through all of his girth, I was able to throw him easily down upon the bed. I commanded him to open the nightstand drawer, and then I shoved his face into his bible and scattered pieces of gum while I fucked him. I fucked him hard; he grunted and buckled like a barnyard thing.

And so my friends, my fellow villains, assembled here in what was once the covert lair of our arch-nemesis The Paladin, now that you've listened to my tale please gather round. Watch him crawl to me as I summon him with but a whispered hum. No need to applaud, just enjoy the splendor on his hands and knees before you. See that though I met him when I was a much younger man and he seemingly older, while in my possession he has remained quite the same. Beautiful, alluring and through my piper's song only too willing to do as he is told. Our fair city's long lost hero is but now the plaything of its archenemies. See how he loves me and kisses my feet. See how he obeys me. Crawl, my lost little dove, into the center of our lounge. Yes, yes ... I love to watch you crawl. Show my friends your exquisiteness and your charms; do unto them as you would do unto me. That's it, my precious Paladin do as you are told ... for you see sometimes, though not nearly often enough, sometimes the bad guys win.

I win!

Raise your glasses, hoist the Green Goddess high. Cheers, my brothers! Remember who we are. We are the things that go bump in the night, the shadows that make people quiver, the animal in everyone unafraid to surrender to our natural instincts. No, no, no, no ... there's no need to go easy on him. He can take it as hard as you can give it; he's a superhero after all.

SHRINKY DINK AND BLOW PART ONE: GETTING TO BLOW YOU By David Connor

With one final hateful slice of the scissors and a villainous cackle, the tattered man-size pantyhose were stuffed down the garbage disposal. As the device ground stretchy nylon into tatters, the vindictive tights-shredder imagined doing the same thing to Blow, the despicable superhero to whom they belonged.

Thirty-year-old nude Caleb Little, dark, Mediterranean, sinewy and hairy, stretched out on the king-size bed in the opulently appointed boudoir. A flat screen TV hung directly opposite and off to the side, two younger, oiled-up twinks flip fucked on a drive-in-movie-size screen on mute because volume would have blown out Little's little eardrums. A baby grand piano took up an entire corner. There was another downstairs in the living room. Caleb didn't play, but he liked the way they looked. The three-story home he had picked up cheap from a previous owner had windows on every side. Parked right outside, where he could see, was a tricked-out repainted Corvette and a vintage motorcycle he often jerked off on. Caleb's russet-toned, muscle etched body was covered with sweat. The damn dream house needed a way better cooling system. A custodian at Killingham University, Caleb had the skill to do it; he just kept putting it off. As he imagined grad student and Teacher's Assistant Norbert Goode with each yank of his rock-hard uncut cock, the delectable eight incher got harder and hotter as his free hand played in his damp, thick bush, then teased his hair-feathered crack. He imagined Bert's fingers up inside him instead of his own and wondered what his cock would feel like — what it would look like. He could find out the later quite easily, without the object of his affection even knowing.

The much taller, dark blonde, blue-eyed, Ivy-League-looking stud with the tiny waist and incongruous but attractive broad shoulders and muscular pecs had asked him out once, mistaking younger-looking Caleb for a fellow student. Once Goode discovered what Caleb really was, though, the big jerk canceled. "Arrogant prick!"

But it was probably for the best. It wasn't just the class difference — Norbert was super-rich, lived in a mansion; while poor Caleb Little barely made ends meet with what he made mopping floors and changing fluorescent light bulbs — there were other obstacles — insurmountable ones.

Caleb imagined the precum on his finger was Bert's boy butter. He licked it. The taste and the fantasy sent an electric tingle straight to his hooded, swollen dome that made him leap from the bed. Barely holding back, he took the elevator quickly down, letting cum fly the moment his feet touched cheap, scratched wood. Caleb gasped as strings of warm white crisscrossed the top of his secondhand bureau, barely missing the laptop where a hairless boy swallowed his fuck-mate's simultaneous jizz fire. He shuddered uncontrollably for several minutes, just like always, then stepped down to the floor and fell back onto his too soft bed. He fingered the cream coated ring through his still thick, sticky dick tip before pulling up the threadbare polyester sheet. "I guess I'll always be alone, now," he sighed. "Good thing I enjoy whacking off."

The Killingham Kougars were finishing up their last lap around the field — perspiring college jocks in their delicious belly baring half-shirt jerseys and tight football pants — hairy legs and smooth, tight six-pack tummies on some, others fur coated and round on display, as Coach Guy Wood scribbled on his clip board and pretended not to look and Caleb Little, mowing the grass, definitely didn't.

"Vagina ... vagina ... vagina ..."

Coach Wood blew the whistle. "Hit the showers, boys," he screeched. "Except you." He grabbed Justin Hotly; adorable raven-haired, green-eyed A-plus student and place kicker — number 69 — by the waist of his pants. Lowering them a bit, he took a moment to admire the pitch black pubes. Forcibly turning him, he took in the lines of Justin's boy ass — and those of his jock strap, through perspiration transparent white fabric. "You see those uprights, ya dumb fuck?" Coach brought himself back. "You get the ball between them fifty times — fifty! — only then do you get to shower!"

The sky was a menacing gray. The wind warned it would soon be bending a heavy downpour over the bleachers and fucking it and anyone dumb enough to be outside up the ass.

Like that's a bad thing.

Justin felt the first heavy, huge drop on his forehead as he readied for punt number eighteen. "Fuck!" Suddenly, a huge gust. A loud metallic groan. Before he knew what was happening, the huge, weighty, yellow goal post upright was headed right for him. Justin closed his eyes. The brief second he had for his brain to say, "Run asshole!" was too brief; the thought never occurred. His life flashed before his eyes in an instant. Within another, a second strong gust, more like a vacuum, had him hurtling backwards, out of harm's way.

Disoriented, he opened his eyes, knowing time had passed. He was in the arms of a masked, muscled savior dressed in gray with a letter "B" on his chest. Justin grabbed him around the neck, bringing their faces even closer, one's breath entering the other. "Blow me again," he whispered. "Oh God! Blow me again!"

He had gotten his super power — the ability to blow and suck as hard as a thousand-miles-per-hour gale force wind, when storm chasing a violent twister with his stepdad. Amazed by the power of nature, he had stood in the field with his mouth agape as the vortex approached. It went right down his throat! Blow could use it to propel himself, like flying, as well as blowing — moving other people and objects. Under certain circumstances, it was a valuable tool.

As a crowd gathered from inside, Blow, like any good superhero, knowing someone would tend to Justin who was merely stunned, not actually hurt, fled the scene. When the boy came to a second time, rain soaking his handsomeness, making his almost see-through uniform cling to his delicious young body, Coach Guy Wood was cradling him in his arms. "You," Justin said. "Are you Blow?"

Though he heard whispers of "Blow" all around him, no one even noticed the other superhero scurrying, like a rodent, through wet grass. It tugged at his soul that he was easy to miss in a crowd of three, let alone dozens, no matter which form he took.

The next morning, as he sat in class waiting for Meteorology Professor Franklin Storm to start his lecture, Justin Hotly recalled the euphoric feel of being blown. Coach Wood denied doing the blowing. School policy mandated he always did. Whoever he was, Justin wanted Blow down his throat, just like the tornado that gave him his powers. He'd been researching him for months already, never dreaming he'd have an actual encounter. Finally, he had something concrete to go on — not a face, but a cock. He'd swear Blow got bone as he lay against him. Justin would never forget how it felt. All he had to do was feel that hardness again — in his fist first, then in his mouth and up his boy hole — and he'd know Blow's true identity.

Just outside the classroom door, Professor Storm; TA Goode; campus librarian, Nasturtium Ophelia Goode, Norbert's mom; and Sissy Wood, drama department head, also Coach Wood's sister, stood and chatted.

"I can't believe Blow was on our campus," Sissy beamed. "They claim his mouth works wonders. I'd love to feel it on my ..."

"That's enough! We need things to get back to normal here!"

A shiver played Norbert's spine like a xylophone. His mother's shrill voice had that effect. He hated her being at the school. The woman certainly didn't need to work. She had enough money to lounge about and eat bonbons all day in the manse they shared, but good old Nasturtium liked being in the thick of things — including her son Norbert's love life.

"Sissy dear, I'm sorry I snapped." Mrs. Goode said.

Killingham headmaster, Peter Smalley, sauntered by, smiling at the group, until he got to Nasturtium; she got a heavy scowl.

He stopped to look over janitor Caleb Little — sizing him up, it seemed, before continuing on.

"Come for dinner." Norbert's mom put an apologetic hand on Sissy's shoulder. "Bert would love to have you." She spoke the words with not-so-gentle innuendo.

"M-o-om ..." her son whined like a child.

"Hush Norbert!" Like nails on a chalkboard. "Say seven-ish, Sis?"

"I'd love to," female Wood said shyly. She had always liked Bert, but her secret identity kept her closed off from getting close to him — to anyone. Maybe he could be the first person she confessed to, the one who would accept her for what she was.

Justin spent the whole lecture staring at Franklin Storm's crotch. The old guy — almost sixty! — managed to stay hot by running and smoking two packs a day. But hot wasn't all there was to it — "Storm ... Blow ..." After class, he set up a plan to be alone with him, later that night, in the weather simulator in the back room. His experiment wouldn't be the scientific kind, more like a sexual one.

Villainous No Goode stood in the hallway listening. Blow had shown up at Justin's first "accident" — the goal post had been tampered with — but there was no way to trap him when the gawkers showed. "This time," the evil one sneered, "when rotten little teen stud Justin Hotly finds himself in peril, the campus will be empty. And sleazy Franklin Storm, he'll get his, too! Two birds, one very wet stone." No Goode wondered if Storm was Blow, too. "Doesn't matter, really," it was decided. "If he's not, the heinous hero will show, and I'll take out all three."

Justin was surprised — though not disappointed, when he arrived at the lab after dark to see Bert there, as well. He'd made out with the teacher's assistant before, during a private tutoring session at the manse. Dude sucked face like a master!

The "hot ass threesome," as Justin thought of them, entered the 8x8' Plexiglass cube. There was a single vent that sealed, making the space airtight for barometric pressure tests and a skylight above with an automatic shade, the same kind as between all the exterior walls, to block ambient light if needed. Justin left them open. He did not require dark. The boy wanted to see hot older guy and hot way less older guy nakedness in all its well hung glory. "Oh no!" he overdramatically wailed, placing the back of his hand to his forehead. "I forgot my notes! The experiment can't proceed, and I set the automatic door timer for two hours! Now what'll we do?"

"Two hours!" Bert tried the door. The lock was electronic and would not open until it counted down. "Shit! I have a stupid dinner date tonight!"

"Ok, relax," Franklin Storm soothed. "The janitor shows up every night at precisely 7:15." Storm had tried to seduce him not long ago, sitting buck naked at his desk, waiting.

"Vagina … vagina … vagina …"

"He can override the system. Meanwhile," Franklin winked, "I can ride one or both of you." He reached for Justin's belt loop. He'd been hoping for Hotly sex all along and invited Bert, who he'd already been with because the idea of doing the two together was positively too precum inducingly scorching to pass up.

It had been pouring buckets for over twenty-four hours by then, and the gutters on the science building were clogged, causing leaks in the roof. As Caleb Little approached the skylight over the weather simulation cube, he glanced down. Franklin Storm was on his knees in front of Hot Hotly, swallowing freshman dick.

"Vagina … vagina … vagina …"

When Storm shifted slightly, turning Justin with him, Caleb saw Bert in a similar position, going whole-hog at the boy's white, firm ass. The janitor no longer needed his "calm down" mantra. Horny was replaced by heartbreak — maybe anger.

"Norbert Goode is …" When Justin Hotly bent further over, exposing his, Caleb agreed. "Yeah, no doubt hot, but a real asshole!"

The three inside jumped in unison, startled as a warm rain started pouring down on them.

"This part of your experiment?" Bert asked.

Hotly blushed. "There was no experiment."

The minor nuisance soon turned aphrodisiac — like shower sex, as Bert and Franklin stripped off and Justin stepped out of his off-white jeans and striped boxer briefs. Tall, blond, lightly furred half-hard Bert; tan-lined-porcelain in all his special places, slightly shorter in stature, longer, thinner in erection, neck-down smooth to a thin, dark trail reaching inky pubes and wild, matching armpit hair Justin; and quite diminutive, buzzed gray on top, hairy everywhere else, with a fat, short, cut dick, Franklin Storm grappled for each other's wet body parts, fondling nuts, squeezing butt cheeks, kissing on wet faces.

"Fuck me!" Justin ordered, to no one in particular, as he bent over again, one palm against the see-through wall, the other hand rubbing his waiting, pink hole. "Fuck me hard!" He licked at the white running down the window — white that shot out of him from just being jerked and rimmed. "Make me come again!" he squealed with youthful, lust-filled exuberance. "Make me come again!"

"Wait," Bert gasped. "The water ..." It was pouring in way too hard and accumulating way too fast, already up to their ankles. "The drain," he said, his throat closing up from near panic, "it's been stopped up somehow. If we can't get out of here for two hours, we'll drown!"

Suddenly, an even heavier torrent and an explosion of glass fell upon them. The skylight above shattered and outside rain runoff combined with the manmade downpour inside, making the water rise even faster.

"Do something!' Justin pleaded.

"Like what?" Professor Storm asked.

"You're a superhero, for Christ's sake!" Justin was admittedly uncertain about the supposed telltale stiffy, but the way the old dude worked the cum out of him, he certainly possessed stellar blowing skills! "Blow the fucking walls down, Prof Storm — or should I say Blow?!"

Outside the door, No Goode stood watching. Unable to hear words, the look of dread on two naked men's faces was pleasurable — until the look on a third's made it frightening. "Oh my God! What's Norbert doing in there?"

No Goode's motives were pure jealousy. The tights, stiff with who knows what — well, everyone knows — were a tip off to a sexual encounter between Bert and Blow, one that set the evil plan to destroy him in motion. And there they were, naked together again! "Do something, Storm!" It had to be him, the disgusting seductive pervert! "Transform!" No Goode whispered. "Save my Norbert!"

"Who are you talking to?"

Face to face, bitter exes, Dean Peter Smalley and Nasturtium Goode eyed each other with hate until one remembered, and one discovered, someone they loved was trapped inside.

Sissy Wood sat at the end of a very long table as a butler refilled her water glass for the fourth time. Dinner with the Goodes had turned into a romantic dinner for two, which turned into a waiting game and an unstoppable urge to pee. "Something must be wrong." She doubted probably gay Bert was into her, despite what his mother hoped, but he was too nice to stand her up. She had to find him — to make sure he was ok. Sissy excused herself to the ladies' room. By the time she came out, she was no longer a lady.

The water had quickly reached chest-height. Justin, Bert and Franklin Storm pounded in vain on unbreakable glass. Peter Smalley had taken off without a word. Nasturtium had run off in search of Caleb Little and a master key to open the Meteorology Lab Justin had surreptitiously locked. Behind that door, Hotly, who regretted the whole set up, was still waiting for Storm to do something — anything! Finally the professor did. He made a gurgling sound. Then sank into the flood. Bert went under, too, buoying the old man, performing CPR. Storm, who was apparently not a superhero, at all, had had a heart attack!

A second gurgling noise, moments later, not from Storm — he was turning blue, but from the drain, filled Justin Hotly with relief. Slowly, but surely, the water began to recede as Shrinky Dink, like vermin, hid in the vent, holding on for dear life once he struggled to get away from the outlet he'd unclogged from the inside. "Yuck!" The powerful force of water sucked out by a pump with whirring fan blades at the end and a tiny, naked man with a one-point-four inch hard-on would not mix well.

Shrinky Dink wasn't one of those superhero types who dons a cape and a mask, like Clark Kent becoming Superman, or way more famous, at least in Killingham Heights, Blow. Dink was the transforming type, like The Hulk, or The Thing. His entire appearance changed. Anyone who knew him as his alter ego would never recognize him as SD. Unlike The Thing, though, Shrinky Dink changed back and forth once the adventure was done — by "Oh shit! Oh shit! Yeah!" — ejaculating. At least he could control returning to his real-life form. Changing into Shrinky Dink, which happened with increased adrenaline due to quickened blood flow, including when horny, not so much.

Tiny Shrinky managed to sneak his way through the vent system, out into the Meteorology classroom to climb up and reset the timer. The electronic door opened. Just as Nasturtium arrived, sans Caleb, still bare ass, Justin and Bert exited the cube. Poor Franklin Storm lay dead.

Bert and his mom, after talking to the police, returned home with Peter Smalley in tow. The pending divorce between Peter and Nasturtium was more contemptuous than their six-year marriage had been. Nasty, as he called her, was born into money and inherited even more when her first husband croaked. She was fifty by then; with a five-year-old son she had late in life and was way too obsessive about. Peter should have never married the bat, but once he got close to Bert, when the boy was a teenager, becoming his stepdad seemed the only way to stay that way.

The old crow had refused to take Peter's name and people often referred to him as Mr. Goode. He hated it. Though his own name might be a bit unfortunate to any male, he insisted, to anyone who would listen, "I ain't no damned Goode!"

The two of them were going at it again. Bert listened upstairs, as he used to in the past. He loved Peter in a way no one could ever understand. He loved his mom, too, though she drove him nuts. Unable to take one more moment, Norbert stomped down the stairs. "I'm outta here!" he yelled, and he slammed right out the front door.

"Now look what you did!" both supposed elders screeched in unison.

Shrinky Dink was still on the scene. He hadn't yet rubbed one out to grow back to normal. He was, instead, secretly surveying the scene for clues while eavesdropping on the cops who did the same. "It's obvious the skylight was booby-trapped to break once enough rain accumulated around it. The gutter system was also rigged, the flow pointed right in its direction. Someone knew the three men would be in the module thing and wanted to drown them."

"Who?" Cop two asked.

"Several people were witness to a custodian, Caleb Little," the hefty officer said checking his notebook, "on the roof just before, maybe during the incident. A co-worker said he had a crush on Norbert Goode. Jealousy is always a prime motive. I say we have enough to place Little under arrest for the murder of Franklin Storm."

"Then do it."

"Can't find him — just his uniform and underpants, left behind on the roof."

"What the fuck?" the other cop marveled.

Blow had the same idea as Shrinky Dink. He entered the simulator, once the cops had left, to check for evidence. His super sense of sight was not an actual power, but something he honed at the foot of his mentor, when, without choice, really, he became a crime fighter. He noticed Shrinky's subversive movement right off. Sensing a tiny human, he kept an eye on it. Maybe it was someone like him — destined for a life he hadn't chosen, hopefully geared toward good, not evil.

Realizing he had been spotted, hot little blue stippled Shrinky Dink tried to escape through the vent.

"Got ya!" Blow bragged. He held him by one leg, like a mouse by its tail.

"And I got you!" No Good cackled, slamming the door. "I knew you'd show up where Norbert was almost killed. Better late than never."

Just as before, the sound of his mother's voice, like kryptonite to Superman, left Blow suddenly and completely impotent.

"You will not steal my son from me!" Nasturtium Ophelia Good would be shocked to learn Blow was her son. "I've destroyed every man who ever tried! Franklin Storm is dead; Justin Hotly's brakes will go out on him next time he drives; Peter Smalley is trapped in my wine cellar to starve to death, and soon, Blow, with your disgusting, disgusting name, you will drift off to sleep never to awaken."

The rich bitch had lost her marbles!

"Norbert will be with that sweet Sissy Wood. He'll go straight and they will live with me forever. Forever!"

N. O. Goode — No Goode, twisted the knob on a canister just outside the simulator, like an oxygen tank, only filled with poison she'd connected to the ventilation system. With one last look of satisfaction, and another evil laugh, she exited the lab leaving our heroes, Blow and Shrinky Dink to die!

To be continued ...

Just kidding.

Blow immediately shut the vent. Nasturtium had no way of knowing it was airtight when closed. The poison could not get in. Unfortunately, though, blocking Shrinky Dink's easiest escape route thwarted his premiere rescue plan. As he tried to conjure another, a hideous sound over the P.A. system — torturous, really, broke into his thoughts.

"Feelings ... Whoa, whoa, whoa, feelings ... I'm going to sing to you until you're out," Nasturtium Goode cooed, momentarily ceasing what was apparently supposed to be a soothing melody. "I am not a hateful person ..."

Blow sank to the floor, hands over his ears. "Then don't sing!" he begged his mom, though he knew the P.A. was one way.

"I will lull you gently into death, like I lulled my baby boy to sleep as a child." Her caterwauling picked up again.

"Shut up! I can't do anything with your voice around me like that," Blow squealed helplessly.

"Hey!" Shrinky Dink, having first climbed up it, now hung from a lock of Blow's hair. He tugged on his ear.

"Ow!" Blow hollered.

"Shit, dude! You can't be that loud when I'm this small! Whisper, man. Whisper!"

"Sorry." Much lower.

"Better. Listen," Dink said. "Maybe I can go down the drain and get help — turn off the gas ... something."

"Jump on my hand."

"What?"

"I want to see who — what you are, up close." Norbert was captivated by what he swore was tiny azure wood in his masked peripheral vision.

"I'm like you ... only different."

"A good guy?"

"Yes."

"Just do it, then."

With a huff of frustration, SD climbed onto the gray, gloved hand. Blow brought him close for a zoomed-in gander. "Whoa! Nice blue bone!"

"I'd blush, but I'd turn purple." In his superhero form, for some reason, Shrinky Dink changed color and his skin became like a soft, bumpy shell.

Blow found the mini-hunk with uncut cobalt cock frigging hot! "How do you ...? Who do you ...? That little hard-on, there, do you have a little tiny wife to stick it in?"

"I'm into dudes, dude. And, sadly, no. I'm the only person I know this size." Shrinky went on to explain his situation, including the come to grow part. "I haven't had sex with a person since this first started happening to me!"

Blow laughed. It pissed Shrinky off. He jumped from the hand, running down Blow/Bert's muscular spandex covered, "B" emblazoned chest. When the laughing ass-hat sat up, Shrinky tripped, falling face-first into huge, half-stiff superhero junk in tights.

"Oh! That felt good." Blow sighed. "Do it again."

"You're thinking about sex at a time like this?"

"What? I can't hear ya that far from my ear."

"You're just like Bert Goode! Cock over any other organ! While I pine away for one guy, he's fucking anyone who'll bend over for him!"

"What?" Shrinky pacing back and forth over his package restricted only by thin nylon was turning Blow on. He couldn't hear the little fellow, but he could certainly feel him. When his thick bulge turned to a hard point, a disgusted Shrinky kicked it. "Ow, dammit!"

"Fuck!" Shrinky ran up Blow's arm, leapt up, latched onto his lobe and screeched as loud as he could in his ear. "Don't yell like that!"

"Don't kick my cock!"

Silence followed — except for Nasturtium's squawking — as two stubborn hotties wondered, "What now?"

"I'm sorry," Blow finally said, softly. "Look. We can't get outta here until the canister — the poison — runs out and the fat lady sings her last, butchered note. I could think of something, maybe, if I had a distraction, from the noise. So, can I … if it means saving us both, suck on your tiny dick? Please, Shrinky Cock?"

"Shrinky Dink. And no, you can't. You'd probably swallow me whole!"

"I can control my … suckage — like settings on a vacuum. I'd let you suck mine, but, obviously, you can't satisfy a man like that."

"You'd be surprised, oh arrogant one. I may not be able to suck you off, but I guarantee I can make you come in less than five minutes."

"I accept the challenge."

"Wait. Speaking of blow jobs, why can't you just huff and puff ...?"

"The chamber is pressure sensitive. If I blow hard, so to speak, all that's gonna manage to do is freak us out. The place is structured to house a tornado simulation, so ... We might implode, with the vent sealed up. In other words, whatever I can do won't do us any good."

"Makes sense ... I guess. That's why I should go down the drain ..."

"Go down on me."

"You're a pig!"

Blow snatched up Shrinky again.

"Hey!"

He licked his finger and gently rubbed just the very tip of it over the tiny ring through the itty bitty dick. "This is nice."

"Don't touch that." Shrinky squirmed. "I think that's where the shrink power comes from."

"Say what?"

"It's some thousands of years old, or something. My great, great grandfather allegedly found it in Morocco. I got it in a package from some ancient relative I never heard of who said it was in the family for generations and she wanted me to have it."

"And you stuck it through your cock head?"

"Seemed like a good idea at the time. I shrank the first time, afterwards, when I got wood, and now I'm kind of afraid to take it out. Maybe it was coincidence, I don't know. One time I opened the microwave and I'd have sworn it didn't shut off right away. Maybe that did it."

"Unlikely. How long have you been ... pierced?"

"Two weeks."

Blow laughed again. "No wonder you don't know what you're doing, then."

"How long have you been blowing?"

Bert grinned at the innuendo. "A few years." He turned Dink to gander at his ass.

"Easy. I get dizzy, ya know," the indigo peckered one whined.

Gently bending the Dink at the waist, paying no mind to his protests, Bert pulled his tiny legs apart. "Everything looks good back here, too."

"You're violating me!"

Blow ignored the scolding, still. He stuck his tongue out through his mouth opening and ran the tip between the tiniest of cracks, teasing it open to show an even tinier hole.

"Cut that …" A sound, a rather pleasurable one, replaced the last word. "At least take your mask off."

"I can't."

"You can. All you do is dress. I transform."

"Well, be that as it may, Tiny Testes, I can't risk someone seeing me out of disguise."

"Yeah. I know that feeling."

"If that groan was permission to proceed, though, I'll show you mine since you showed me yours. No harm in taking my pants off."

"We're both in the same boat! Why are you being so …"

"Do ya wanna see me naked, or not?"

Neither Shrinky, nor his alter ego, got to touch a hot, naked guy nearly as often as desired. Therefore, "Fine. Get naked," he acquiesced, "even if you have to leave the mask on."

Blow stripped down. Shrinky gasped — Caleb Little did, actually. He didn't need to see Norbert Goode's face. His body, which he had finally seen uncovered earlier, was ingrained in his mind forever! He went right for the erection — he couldn't help himself. Padding through the neatly trimmed triangle of golden curls around it, the texture against itty bitty bare feet threatened to make him come without even touching himself.

"Vagina … vagina … vagina …"

When Blow lay back, Shrinky did the same, on top of the cock, a couple of inches longer than he was — near 11 versus 8! He slid his whole body up and down it. Blow shivered and flexed, taking Dink for an unexpected ride — like lying naked on a mechanical bull. "Keep doing that!" the bigger one commanded. "Keep doing that," the smaller one thought.

And they did, at least for a while. Wanting to try something new, playing it by ear having never seen porn between an elf and a giant, Dink made his way up the shaft. When he reached the apex, looking down on the huge, pink glans damp with arousal fluid, he had a thought. With his arms wrapped around, as if hugging a tree trunk, he bent forward and lapped at the slit with his tiny tongue.

Blow moaned a long note, drowning out his mother's lullaby which was all but forgotten. "Forget the other thing," he said, dreamily. "Keep doing that!"

The taste of Bert's cock sent Caleb Little over the edge. He started yanking his puny pecker.

"Vagina ... vagina ... vagina ..." he said out loud, torn between the feeling and the fear of coming too fast.

"Did you say something?" Bert asked.

Caleb thought of a new position. He climbed the rest of the way up Bert's Johnson, positioned his pelvis against the round, tender tip, and stuck tiny wood in cum cannon's slit.

"Holy fuck!"

Dink started humping hard. He was soon close to coming. "True identity reveal be damned!" he cried. "I'm gonna shoo ..." Before he could finish the sentence or the act, Bert grabbed his own cock, stroking hard, sending Dink falling back, onto his gut, where he was soon covered in a bath of Norbert Goode goo!

"Holy mother!"

Bad choice of words as Nasturtiums off-key serenade continued.

Dink, literally swimming in jizz, stroked his slimy, Smurf-y schlong, soon firing a man-size load of white all over blue that outdid even Bert's.

"What the hell?!" The still masked Blow was astonished as Caleb Little, in his regular form, color, and height, was suddenly straddling his cum coated middle.

"It's me."

"Caleb?"

"I'm Shrinky Dink. Disappointed."

"Only if I can't suck you off." Bert grabbed him, pressing their sweaty, jizzy torsos together. "My God I have always wanted you. My frigging mother, when I told her I asked you out …" Norbert stopped, realizing he had said too much.

Caleb pulled off Blow's mask. "It's ok, Norbert. I already knew."

The two kissed passionately. "I'd love to make love to you."

"Me, too," Caleb said.

"Ya got a second load in there?" Bert asked.

Caleb fiddled with his dick adornment, taking it out. "I wanna stay big, so you can fuck me in the ass — or me, you! I hope I don't shrivel up or die or something — without this in me."

"So far, so good," Norbert said, embracing cute Caleb again.

The two fell back into a second passionate kiss — literally fell — maybe a little too hard.

"Oh, God. Stick that cock in me, Blow," Caleb sighed. "Blow? Bert?"

There was no response. Worse yet, Mama Goode had stopped singing. "You must be dead by now," she said over the speaker. "I'm coming to get you, Blow."

"Shit." Caleb checked to make sure Bert was OK. His breathing was good, and his pulse; he was just out. He knew he had to shrink again, to save his man his mental mama. He put his Prince Albert back in and dropped to his knees, bending forward to take Bert's fat dick in his mouth — "Vagina … vagina … vagina …" He couldn't help himself. He selfishly wanted a second or two to enjoy the sensation from the neck up while holding back things from waist down. "Mmm." Finally, "Ok, go," he said aloud, pulling back, licking cum from his lips. His cock popped straight up, and his size shot right down. Once again blue, tiny Shrinky Dink went down the drain. He managed, between little Little and full-size Little — knowing all he had to do was remove the ring from his dick head made things a bit easier — to get out, open the door and hide Blow's suit and mask. He could have tried to drag Norbert off, but that would have been pretty hard in the time allowed. He knew leaving him in naked "Bert form" was the safest bet. Nasturtium would never hurt her own son, but the crazy bat's reaction to the tidbit that Blow and Bert were one and the same was hard to predict. With one last peak at the naked, blond, grad school hottie who was coming around, anxious to flee before it was too late, Caleb made a decision. Though he would miss hanging out in Barbie's dream house, soaking in her hot tub, riding around nude in the once pink car, after conjuring the idea of a one superhero relationship — himself as the dutiful spouse once the bonkers mother-in-law was in a maximum security psych ward, he decided to give up his shrink power forever.

"Maybe, Blow can use it," he thought. As Nasturtium approached, humming loudly, Caleb folded the earring into his groggy future same-size lover's palm.

"Mom?" But when Bert Goode awoke he was clueless. "What happened? How did I get here?"

"Ma'am." A police officer entered. "We've apprehended the sexy, stubbled, swarthy, sweaty suspect." He kept a firm grip on the wrist sticking out from under a nudity concealing blanket. Caleb, not used to sneaking about in 6'2" form, had been easily trapped. "We know the janitor has killed before. He probably tried to hurt your son."

"I'd never hurt Bert! Never!"

The superheroes locked eyes. Struck by amnesia, Norbert Goode had no memory of what just occurred or why the janitor was looking at him the way he was. When he opened his hand, and looked at the genie's earring, in his palm that had once been in Caleb's dick, Norbert wondered what it was, where it had come from, he when he sniffed it, why it smelled like sex.

"Mmm!"

"Tell them I'm innocent, man," Caleb pleaded over his shoulder as he was dragged off to spend the rest of his life in prison. "Please, Bert. I love you. I need you to tell them I'm innocent."

Will Nasturtium Goode be punished for her crimes? Will Justin Hotly drive off a cliff to his death? What is Peter Smalley's secret connection to Bert and Caleb Little? Will he ever get out of the Goode wine cellar? Will Caleb be prosecuted for a crime he didn't commit? Will people ever notice Guy and Sissy Wood are never in the same room at the same time? Will Norbert Goode get his memory back? Will he fight crime? Will he and Caleb get to fuck?

Tune in next time, or turn the page to "Shrinky Dink and Blow Part Two: Tranny Get Your Gun" for answers to these and other sexy questions

To be continued ...

SHRINKY DINK AND BLOW PART TWO: TRANY GET YOUR GUN By David Connor

When last we checked in with our dick tasting duo, Drama Professor Sissy pined for hunky grad student Norbert Goode, who, unbeknownst to all, is really superhero Blow. Caleb Little, the Killingham custodian who uncontrollably morphs into Shrinky Dink, gave up his shrink power by removing his magic Prince Albert, placing it in Norbert's hand after the two discovered each other's true identities, and professed mutual affection. Unable to truly make love, since Caleb was in shrunken Shrinky form, they swapped cum as best they could and vowed to be together again soon. A passionate "sealed with a kiss" lead to Norbert banging his head, causing amnesia. Caleb, meanwhile, immediately afterwards, was arrested for a murder committed by Norbert's mother, aka No Goode, who also locked ex-husband Dean Peter Smalley in the cellar to starve, and, determined to kill all of her son's homosexual lovers, cut the brake line on college freshman Justin Hotly's car.

Will Caleb rot in prison? Will he ever get to have sex as a regular size man? Will hot Justin die? Who will win Norbert's heart? Will he remember he likes dick? Will the last page of this story be stuck to the first page of the next one by the end? Keep reading and find out.

# # # # #

The car careened out of control, heading for the guardrail. Three college jocks, off to Monday class, who'd been singing along with the Biebs, suddenly screamed like little girls.

Smash!

They hit the unyielding metal barricade, fishtailed across the opposite lane, one-eightied, and finally breathed a sigh of relief, one with wet pants, as they came to a stop in the middle of the street. "Holy fuck!" Joran Tinkler exclaimed.

"What the hell?!" Luke Warm accused. "Where'd you learn how to drive, Hotly?!"

"Eat va-jay-jay, Luke!" Justin shot back. "I got no brakes. I didn't do it on purp ..."

Bang!

Before Justin could finish his retort, the little lavender sports car that sat idle all weekend, every drop of its brake fluid draining onto the cement garage floor, was hit broadside by an eighteen wheeler, taking it back across the yellow line, ramming it through the guardrail, sending it plummeting over a cliff.

She yanked the stocking mask down over her face and swung open the door, waving her gun. "Everyone on the floor!" The people inside took a brief moment to stare at the tall, thin woman in just a green bra and panties, then did as instructed, except a rather ancient security guard who pulled his weapon a holster on his hip.

Bang!

She shot the fogey in the leg. "Anyone else feeling brave?" she twanged.

Minutes later, her bagful of cash in one hand, she grabbed some unsuspecting, scruffy, blue-eyed, dreadlocked stoner stud in a fringed leather jacket with the other, planted a wet smooch on his soft, magenta lips, and slid her palm down the front of his tattered, baggy jeans, groping beatnik bush, balls and boy bat.

"Whoa!" Peter Pothead gasped as the bandit suddenly disappeared — like magic! "Maybe I'm hallucinating!"

It was the robber's third heist in several weeks, and a newly discovered escape plan made her latest getaway the easiest one by far

"Thanks, Norbert!"

Peter Smalley listened to the robbery report on the radio, and, trapped a floor below, to the creak of the bed springs overhead, as his favorite protégé, Norbert Goode, finally rid of his bride, Sissy Wood, and his mother, Nasturtium Ophelia, after forty-eight hours of weekend that felt like a week, rubbed one out. It was Smalley who molded Blow after Norbert swallowed the twister that gave him his super blowing powers. Having once been stuck with special abilities himself that he didn't always understand, Smalley was now in charge of creating and grooming a new group of crime fighters. Sometimes they came into their powers accidentally, like Blow. Sometimes Smalley chose them, like hunky janitor Caleb Little whom he supplied with the magical alleged family jewel to stick in his in order to give Blow a sexy shrinking sidekick. He was hoping Shrinky would note his absence and come save him. So far, though, no go. After the report on the bank robbery, he knew why, as the newsman spoke of Caleb's arrest and all the evidence against him in the death of Professor Franklin Storm — "Damn you, Nasturtium!" Hearing about the college cuties car wreck next — "Not Justin Hotly! — Smalley knew he had to figure a way out, to stop that wretched No Goode, and fast! He noticed, in the corner, the breaker panel for the whole house. Electricity was a powerful weapon; surely he could use it to his advantage.

Coach Guy Wood had had a rather active morning. The lithe, cute, nerdy looking mid-thirty-something stood at his washing machine, naked, smooth all the way down his front, all pale and dark pink. He adjusted his glasses and ran a hand through his disheveled out-of-control white boy brown fro, as he loaded the washer with underwear — boxers, boxer briefs and panties — one pair that looked like they had been dragged through the street — where he found them. He wondered what in hell his sister did with her underpants and why they were left in a ditch!

He had come to leaning against his truck off the road — far off the road, in the woods, actually, for the third time in as many weeks with a cum puddle in his navel and spooge splatter all up and down his emaciated-looking bare chest and concave tummy. "I really gotta stop popping those pills to sleep at night!" he had thought. "Nude, public sleep-sturbating is gonna get me in trouble!" Back inside his silver pickup, thankfully, as before, a pair of jeans and his favorite redneck-style plaid flannel shirt lay waiting on the seat. This time, though, there was a note. Sissy, apparently aware of her brother's nocturnal naughtiness, took credit for the clothes, then demanded a favor. Pick up a gift for

Norby I hid in the bushes by Killingham Bridge, ASAP. Take it back to the Goode's and hide it under my marital bed."

The brother had huffed. She had spent two whole nights in her marital bed with amnesiac Norby after crazy Nasturtium managed to convince the lad he and Sissy were husband and wife! "I should just tell him the truth," Guy Wood thought. "One blow job from me, Norby'd remember he was a connoisseur of cock in no time!"

On his way to the old bridge, Guy had come upon the accident moments after it occurred, before a single cop or EMT.

"Oh my God! My hot boys are in trouble!"

He rushed down the embankment after setting off some flares, dragged lifeless Justin Hotly from the mangled car, ripped open his shirt, and his pants, just because, and performed CPR, working his palms between his place kicker's boyish pecs, blowing into his beautiful mouth hole. Once Hotly started breathing on his own, Wood checked on Tinkler. The QB was breathing fine. Wood gave him mouth-to-mouth anyway, just in case. Noticing the third passenger was unattractive stats recorder Luke Warm, the coach headed back to his truck. The ambulance was approaching. Someone else could blow into the ugly boy.

An hour later, after starting his wash, saving the boys, running his sister's stupid errand and stashing the bag he found under the bed Norbert Goode slept in — a triangular point in his 700 thread count bedclothes indicating a good dream, Guy Wood wrung out a washcloth. He swiped it across the supposed infirmed-one's well-developed chest, thoroughly washing each nip.

"Hey!"

The would be Florence Nightingale put a calming hand on the startled kid's wet torso, using his other to work a wild, wooly underarm bush into a mound of suds he massaged at with his fingers.

"Mr. Wood," the fully awake, twenty-three-year-old grad student protested, "this really isn't necessary. I can take a shower. I ... I'm fine, other than not remembering any ... Whoa!"

Guy had thrown back the covers and pulled off Norbert's pajama pants. He licked the tip off Norbert's still thick penis. "Cum residue?"

"Coach!" Norbert locked his knees and covered his junk. It took both hands and some still showed.

Forcibly parting Goode's legs, Guy Wood attacked smooth balls and the top of perfectly shaved crack with his washcloth, instead. "Like I tell my boys when I'm bathing them after practice, cleanliness is very important." Back at the basin, he wrung out the cloth to rinse. "Damn it!" He had accidentally dropped it. "It's ruined now!" The Wood siblings had a bit of OCD when it came to germs. "Stupid! Stupid! Stupid!"

"Our floors are very clean," Norbert pledged, hoping to soothe Wood's histrionics. "Your sister was on her hands and knees half the night working over everything but me. Whoa!" Norbert sat up. "You probably shouldn't be doing that."

"It's OK." Guy looked up from licking ass-crevice. "I'll bathe you like a cat. I'm your brother-in-law." A sneer became a contented purr. "Family does for family."

It felt right, having a man's face in his asshole. "But I'm hetero," Bert thought. "And married!" It felt great, though when Guy Wood took guy wood in his mouth — something wife Sissy had refused to do the night before when Norbert felt horny. Making things more confusing, naked Norbert found himself turned on by the outline of a long, skinny hard-on in denim mere inches from his face. He imagined swallowing it — all of it — which soon rendered his cat bath an effort in futility as cum residue returned not only to his cock's tip, but all over it, and also on Guy Wood's stubbled cheek.

"Oh my," Wood lamented, finger-scooping a couple of rogue white globs off Norbert's fuzz dusted, tight, sweaty gut as it moved quickly up and down. "Now we have to start all over."

In the ER wing, Black Irish Justin Hotly, lying on top of the covers, his short hospital gown and lack of underwear thrilling every female and certain male admirers of unshaven boy taint who purposely found reason to walk by, was hooked up to all kinds of machines, but was doing remarkably well. Studly Joran Tinkler, of Swedish descent, all shirtless and buff, his platinum blond thin body pelt set off by utilitarian fluorescent lighting, had two broken arms that stuck straight out in their casts. He leaned over slightly, watching the yellow fluid run through the catheter in his cock into the clear Foley bag. "How in hell am I gonna jerk off?" he wondered. Across the hall, Luke Warm pouted alone, as well-wishers — players from the football team, friends, and faculty — gathered around the other two as he lay in bed abandoned — not a single flower or card adorning his tray table.

Nasturtium Goode entered her son's room to find obviously aroused Guy Wood kneeling over her nude, goo covered son. "No homosexual activity!" she bellowed, ending in a gasp as the room suddenly went dark. Just below, Peter Smalley had thrown the main breaker to Off, preparing to make the last connection. He knew he'd receive a shock — hopefully minor, reasonably sure the necklace he was using as a conductor, one he obtained the same time as the earring he gave Caleb Little, didn't have magical powers. He was wrong, though. Throwing the switch back on, he was tossed backwards, a dozen feet or more, from the powerful jolt. Upstairs, light returned, brighter than the sun it seemed. Switches buzzed. Outlets popped — one igniting the drapes at the window. "Oh my God!" Nasty Good wailed. A spark jumped, lighting her over-sprayed head. Her flaming red locks became literally so.

The electrical surge at the Goode house affected the grid all over town. At the hospital, machines beeped. A current shot through the wires attached to Justin Hotly's body. Even the tube stuck in the end of Joran Tinkler's tinkle tool tingled, sending a shiver up the boy's spine and a few thousand volts through his inside boy plumbing. At the prison, where wrongly accused tall, dark and handsome Caleb Little showered among a group of burly, tatted-up baddies, alarms sounded and electronic doors slid back and forth, their locks and timers totally fucked up. When Caleb saw most of the other clothes-less criminals taking the opportunity to flee, he did the same, the one guard present, a-wood, as usual, watching the bad boys, bad boys whatcha gonna do soaping up big dicks and tight assholes, too, caught off his to stop them.

Back at the manse, Guy Wood had subdued the blazing bat's bun using the comforter from Norbert's bed before ripping the curtains from the window and tossing them outside, into the pool. Instead of showing gratitude, bad Goode lashed out, delivering, with all the force her deceptively over-the-hill, flabby-looking body could muster, a backhand upside Guy Wood's head, connecting with his temple, ripping the thick, silver earring from his lobe.

"Ow, you crazy bitch!"

"Get out of my home, you filthy homo! I'm telling your sister you molested my son!"

Norbert, slipping on his pj pants, tried to calm his mother as Guy Wood fled. "Mom, he was just bathing me. Now, we should really get you to the hospital."

Before Nasturtium could respond, Peter Smalley, smoking, not a cigarette, hair on end like Albert Einstein's, tackled her to the floor. "Run, Norbert!" He had managed to crawl out a small window between the wine cellar and garage and then out the malfunctioning automatic door. "Your mother has gone mad. She's a murderous bitch!"

"He's lying, Norbert!" Nasturtium wriggled away, "Get off me, you old fool!" kicking Smalley in his frank and beans.

"Do something, Blow," sore Peter gasped in agony. "Caleb is rotting in jail for things your mother did. Why aren't you saving him?"

"He's barely been incarcerated a weekend!' the villain objected. "I doubt any rotting has started! Although you look like hell. Wait!" She stood. "Why did you call Norbert Blow?"

"Because he is!" Smalley grunted holding his sack.

"I am?" Norbert asked dumbfounded. "The superhero? They were talking about Blow on the news this morning," he marveled. "No one knows who he is. He's me? I'm him?"

"Yes."

Norbert scrunched his handsome face. "The artist's rendering didn't much look like me."

"Trust me," Smalley said. "And you ..." He grabbed No Goode around her varicose vein coated ankle, easily bringing her down to the floor as she stood too stunned by the revelation to fight back — or so Smalley thought. "You'll be sorry, now!"

"No, you will." Surprisingly strong and nimble, Nasturtium flipped him like a WWE fighter. She grabbed a gun from under the bed and rose to her feet, pointing her weapon at her ex, pulling back the hammer. "Prepare to die!"

Approaching sirens startled them all.

"Ha! The automatic alarm must have one of. You're trapped. It's all over, now," Smalley vowed triumphantly.

Nasturtium put her son in a choke hold. "Not if I take Blow hostage," she said.

Meanwhile, back at the hospital, the boys were being released. Justin and Joran both felt a bit odd from the electrical shock, but were otherwise good as new. "I have to piss," Joran Tinkler announced.

"I'll help!" Pudgy, acne coated Luke Warm offered a bit too enthusiastically.

Without the catheter, with two broken arms, Joran was gonna need a hand.

"Eww. No," Joran scowled. "Justin can hold it for me."

The two sexy students went into the bathroom as Luke Warm cried outside. Justin swallowed hard, then unzipped Joran's wrinkled, olive cargo shorts, lifting his striped gray and white tee out of the way. The stud felt a charge in his own groin that had nothing to do with a power surge as he pulled back the fly of Joran's black, skintight skivvies, and reached in for his dick. "Damn!"

"Fat, yah?"

"Uh huh," Justin marveled at the thick piece of Swedish meat. He unfastened the button at Joran's waist and pulled his pants down all the way, working the briefs down rock-hard thighs after. "I don't wanna get any on them," he reasoned.

Joran stepped out of them and shoved them to the side with his foot. "Good idea."

Hotly moved behind Joran and reached around with his right hand. He pressed his pelvis into Joran's bare backside and inhaled the spicy scent of cologne from his team leader's neck. "Let 'er rip."

"That a hard-on in your skinny jeans or are you just happy to touch me?" Joran teased.

"Oh my!" Justin blushed. "Stop thinking," he advised. "You're boning, and, um, that'll make it hard to piss."

"Right." Joran concentrated — but on the wrong thing. Pretty quickly, his thick dong was even thicker — stiff as a rod in Hotly's hot grip, and the first shot of piss that fired out ricocheted off porcelain like a bullet.

"Oh my," Justin said again.

"Maybe you better take off my shirt, as well," the tinkler suggested. "And all of your clothes. This could get quite messy."

Hotly agreed. He worked out of his super-tight pants and rolled his argyle knit boxers over his pert pecker, letting it flick back up when released. He moved back into position, resting his scorching stud missile against hairless Scandinavian crack. "Ok. Ready?" He aimed is bud's erection at the commode.

"It's coming," Joran announced.

And it did, sporadic, at first, then in a rush so hard Justin had to grab on with his left hand, too.

"Ohgrm!" Joran made a sound.

"What's wrong?"

"I dunno. It feels ..."

Suddenly, the piss flow hit fire hose velocity. Justin lost his grip and Joran, his horniness and urination out of control, started turning in circles, shooting piss everywhere, pinging against tile, metal, and tall tan, raven haired, blue-eyed naked college boy flesh. Justin backed against the wall. Joran approached him, straddling his hairy leg, rubbing his piss soaked dick against piss soaked leg, humping like a Chihuahua in heat on an expensive, silk throw pillow.

"What is going on in here?" The African American male nurse with a queeny lilt in his voice put a large hand on each hip. "Oh my!" His assessment matched Justin Hotly's.

"Cup my nuts," Tinkler begged.

Justin put his right hand between Joran's legs.

"The other one."

"Huh?"

"Lefty," the quarterback said, shortly.

Justin palmed pouch, letting his long middle finger wander into unchartered anal Norse territory as he moved forward, rubbing against Joran as Joran grinded against him. The sexy Swede shuddered with ecstasy. "I'm gonna come," he said, breathlessly, just before his first jizz shot creamed the crevice where Hotly thigh met black masses of pube fur. The force knocked both teen dreams on their athletic asses, taking the nurse along, too, lathering all three with out of control pure white man meat meringue.

"Oh my!" Justin and Nurse Ned said in unison, one licking tasty Tinkler tool juice from his lips, the other off the supplier's shaft. "The power surge through your piss pipe," Justin muttered. "It made you ..."

"Was it me? Or was it your finger?" Joran asked. "The thing is electrified! I'd love to feel it in my ass," he added. "Maybe more than one."

The idea was put on hold, thanks to a cell phone call from Peter Smalley desperately summoning his soon-to-be new recruits, Tinkler and The Finger, to the college campus. When Luke Warm, gawking at the bathroom threesome with an erection in his Lee's and a wet spot on the front of his A&F shorts asked to tag along, he was rebuffed, left stranded at the hospital, hurt, and with no ride home.

Guy Wood's temple throbbed. The abrasion on his cheek was raw and his torn ear hurt like hell. He had just folded his sister's ivy green panties — the ones he found that morning, the ones she got from eBay, originally owned by a female super-villain from yesteryear — when the phone rang.

"Wood! I need you," Peter Smalley said. "Nasturtium has taken Blow — Norbert. Look. Norbert is Blow and my other go-to-guy is kind of tied up right now." Smalley wondered if Caleb/Shrinky was one of the dozen prisoners that escaped. "Anyway," he said, "I found a bagful of money under Norbert's bed — and there was a gun there. I think Nasturtium is the bank robber, too."

Always a do-gooder, despite his fear of No Goode's wrath, Guy agreed to help. Unfortunately, he decided to change clothes first. Giving into his fetish, he slipped on his sister's lacies, the ones he had just laid on top of the basket, still warm from the dryer, and then took time to shave.

Justin, Joran and Peter Smalley headed over to the college. Nasturtium was already there, planning on taking advantage of the crowd gathered for Satellite Information Network News Anchor Cooper Van Andersonbilt's lecture in the auditorium.

"What are we doing here, mother?" Norbert asked.

"I am going to take 2,000 people and another celebrity hostage. When Van Andersonbilt's private jet arrives, we'll hijack it to an island with no extradition policy. We'll send for Sissy later and the three of us will live happily ever after with no one else — especially no gays — to ever bother us again."

It was a gruesome thought — a gruesome future. Norbert, desperate for escape, thought about what Peter Smalley had said. If he was really Blow, he could escape from his wack-adoo mother quite easily. "There's no harm in trying," he decided. He inhaled deeply. "Worst case scenario, it doesn't work." Exhaling as hard as he could, Norbert flew from his mother's grip, sending her flailing across the vestibule just beyond the packed auditorium.

Meanwhile, right outside the window, Caleb Little poked his head out of a manhole. "Mmm, manhole" He knew the Killingham sewer system well and had traversed the underground maze with ease, making his way to the school. He spotted Norbert inside. "I must get to him," he thought. "But how?" He regretted ever giving up that earring, wishing he were little blue Shrinky Dink right then.

Norbert ran down the hallway, flashing lots of superhero ass he had to constantly yank up sagging pj pants to hide. When he heard voices behind him, he ducked into the dressing room just off the main stage, running into Cooper Van Andersonbilt. "It's about time you got here," the ambiguously gay SIN-ful newsy said with lust, staring at low sitting fleece and everything revealed.

Checking doors, searching for her son, with a totally crazed look in her eyes, reeking of burnt hair smell, and a scar from the fire on her cheek, Nasturtium came across Justin Hotly and Joran Tinkler in flagrante. Overcome with horny while waiting for Peter Smalley, the duo was buck naked. Having progressed from oral and fingering — "Pull it out! Pull it out!" Joran begged after only a few seconds. "I don't wanna come yet!" — Justin was bent over a stack of hay bales backstage — Sissy was mounting a production of Oklahoma — while a lubed and protected Joran prepared to mount him. Moments later, they found themselves being dragged across the stage in the surrey with the fringe on top while the gathered audience gasped and giggled. No Goode had positioned them almost as she found them, Justin leaning over, Joran ready to stick his substantial stiffy in Hotly's ready rosy rectum.

"We will learn today," the old lady said, "about the evils of homosexuality. Please enter your lover's anus," she instructed, putting the barrel of her gun in Joran's to bring the point home and get him to obey.

More audience oohs and awws erupted — some shocked, some lustful, as the never-far-from-horny frat guys and sorority chicks marveled at the live gay sex show that had come to their college stage.

"Fuck Rogers and Hammerstein," a particularly stimulated student stud thought, "I'd sign up to perform in this show!"

"Watch these boys closely," Mad Mama Goode went on. "One will soon be making a 'cum face'. When he does," she warned, "before he reaches full orgasm, I shall blow his head off, teaching you all that gay is not OK!"

Justin and Joran held as still as could be. The spectators, however, many of them — some surreptitiously, some not — too turned on by the sight and, oh yeah, the scent of boy sex to forgo self-pleasure, reached down pants and up skirts, through flies and leg openings. No guns were fucking pointed at them; they could masturbate — they could come — all they wanted.

Peter Smalley pushed on the locked auditorium door from outside. He had driven by Coach Wood's to pick him up, but Guy had already gone. Smalley wished he could find him. Coach Wood had a super-strong foot that could not only, in his day, kick a field goal or punt from hundreds of feet with only a feather touch, but, using a bit more force, it could take down a fucking wall. He had had it since conception. His mother, who artificially inseminated farm animals, accidentally mixed a donkey's sperm with that of Guy's donor dad. When her fetus first kicked from inside, she knew something was awry. Anyway, without Guy's help, Smalley would have to come up with another plan. He turned the corner, sneakily walking backwards, and bumped into a chick in a flowing, western-style frock with several layers of petticoats. "Excuse me, ma'am," he demurred. "Oh! Wait!" Sudden recognition. "It's you!"

Just a few doors down, in the kitchenette where food for the concession stand was prepared, highly flammable vapor accumulated that a single spark would ignite into an explosive inferno. The gas line from which it flowed had been purposely disconnected, the person responsible eagerly waiting for the BOOM!

In Cooper Van Andersonbilt's dressing room, the white-haired hottie was stripping down to his tighty whities. The designer's name on the waistband was not his mommy's. He turned to Norbert. "What the hell, dude? Get 'em off. My rider says I get a man whore. I ain't got time to waste with pajama pants."

"I …"

"Or talkin'." Cooper Van Andersonbilt did a three hundred-sixty, yanking down his undies. "Nice, huh?" He flexed his flaccid phallus and grabbed Norbert by the arm and pulled him to his knees. "Suck it, whore!" he said, smooshing his pasty penis into Norbert's lips. "And did I mention," he smacked Goode upside the head, "I like it rough?"

"I'm gonna come," Joran whispered.

"How? I haven't moved," Justin said fretfully.

"Your magic electric hand keeps touching me places."

"Shit!' Hotly tried to move his arms which Nasturtium had tied at his sides, putting his digits, when the two went doggy-style, between Tinkler's legs, the left one dangerously close to Tinkler's boy toy.

"You're making it worse. I'm gonna come! I'm gonna come! We're gonna die! We're gonna die!"

"Yeah! Yeah! Suck my cock, you stupid bitch!"

Whap!

Norbert lapped at anchor head, swallowing Dutch dick, slurping and gurgling talk show host precum, enjoying an experience his mama said he shouldn't. Someone who wasn't enjoying it; jealous Shrinky Dink, who had snuck into the auditorium through the hole in the box office window.

Flashback to moments earlier …

"Caleb!"

"Dean Smalley!"

"Why are you in a dress. Is that something you …?"

"No. Not usually. Made a good disguise, though."

Smalley explained to Caleb everything that was going on. "I need you" he implored.

"I don't know how I can help," Caleb said, sadly.

"Maybe you can't. But Shrinky Dink can." He held up the earring Nasturtium had ripped from Guy Wood's ear. "Will you ..."

Caleb took the earring. He fiddled with his skirt, trying to get to his cock. "Damned petticoats! How in hell did Ado Annie play with herself?!"

"Let me," Smalley offered.

He took the magical ring and crawled under Caleb's skirt-tent. "Kinda dark under here. Will Parker must-a needed a flashlight for a booty call!"

"Ooh!"

"Sorry," Peter offered. "Talking too close to your junk — it got caught in my mouth. Glad you forwent the bloomers. Lift your skirt. I need light."

Caleb did as requested. When campus security walked by, he dropped the dress back over Peter's head.

"When this hostage thing is all over," the straight cop said to the Little Woman, "I'll take my turn under there."

Caleb giggled demurely. "Hurry up," he muttered afterwards, "I can't wait to get out of this thing!"

He lifted the skirts again. Smalley snapped the Prince Albert into place. "Why aren't you shrinking?" he asked.

"She's taking her big ol' bra off," Justin whispered. "Her giant old lady breasts look like fried ostrich eggs hanging from a nail. She's gonna take off her girdle and granny panties next and make you stick your nose right in her smelly, scratchy, hairy granny snatch!"

"Yuck!'

"That slowing things down, Tinkler?"

More flashback ...

"I don't know," Caleb had said. "I guess I'm too scared for Norbert ... to be horny."

"Well, maybe I can remedy that." Smalley took Caleb Little's not so little penis in his mouth.

"No! Stop that! I love Norbert and he loves me!"

"Desperate times ..." Smalley had said.

Despite his objections and his nerves, Peter Smalley's peter-working talents got Caleb excited enough to start to grow, and therefore shrink.

Back to the present ...

"Hey! Cut that out!"

Caleb's Shrinky voice was too tiny to be heard over raucous sex noises, so he reached for his piercing, taking it out, growing to his normal size in an instant. "Guess that will work from now on," he thought.

"What the hell?!" News Scoop Coop exclaimed! "How did you get in ...?" He studied Caleb's buff, deep bronzed-colored body and equally tinted dick with its wet, pink head. "Never mind," he decided. "Feed me your dark meat while I beat off this chicken."

"Fuck that," Caleb said. "Get off my boyfriend, you talking head-getter or I'll fucking beat you!" He shoved Van Andersonbilt hard. Mr. Snow-on-the-roof-fire-down-below fell back, landing flat on his white-as-paper ass, stiff cock straight up, like a sexy most trusted newsman in the U.S. sundial.

Caleb ran to Norbert, throwing his arms around him, kissing him deep. "If we had more time," he said, "I'd make love to you right here."

"Do I know you," Norbert asked.

"It's not working anymore," Joran fretted. "I'm gonna milk."

Several audience members already had. It was a near orgy! Cum ran down the backs of seats and onto the already sticky carpet, not to mention coed skin. Gay sex, straight sex, three-ways, boy, boy, girl, boy, girl, boy, boy, boy I chains — students and professors grunting, moaning, squealing, the sounds and odors of wet flesh against wet flesh, of hot parts sliding in and out other hot parts egged on even those too afraid or Christian to touch themselves in such devilish ways! A high-heeled BAM against the auditorium's rear entrance got everyone's attention just as the most prim Amish boy on campus, Samuel Yoder, was about to probe his virginal one, his finger reaching down sturdy

Christian underwear for the space damp with perspiration and sinful arousal. "Drat!" It burst open — the auditorium's entrance, not the boy's.

"Give me my money and my gun!" The chick in green lingerie and matching shoes demanded. She ran up on the stage, charging Nasturtium. "And what have you done with my Norby?"

"Norbert, it's me, Caleb."

"I don't ..."

"You told me, just days ago, you had feelings for me." He brought Norbert's face close to his own and looked into his eyes, searching for any spark of familiarity.

"Caleb?"

"Yes. Yes. Caleb."

"I ... You're hot." Norbert's dick grew even harder at the sight of his alleged nude true love, "but, someone mentioned I have amnesia. I ... I have no idea who you are."

"Amnesia? Ok, then. Sorry about this."

"About what?"

SMACK!

Caleb's forehead cracked into Norbert's, hoping a knock on the noggin would bring Bert back to him.

Though the girl-on-girl action and ambient chaos temporarily stopped Joran from blowing his load as Sissy Goode tackled Nasturtium, wresting her for the gun, seeing Caleb and Norbert naked as the day they were born — only hairier, more hung, and erect, suddenly rolling around the stage — his favorite TA's wide open A and the hot custodian's thick-as-a-broom-handle cock rubbing all over it — sent Joran Tinkler over the edge.

"I'M COMING!" he bellowed!

The boy cream blast inside Justin's insides — thankfully the condom Joran used could have stopped a bullet — sent the wheeled cart they fucked on sailing across the stage, mowing down evil No Goode and Sissy Wood on the way.

Peter Smalley had followed the smell of gas to the food prep area. He turned off the main valve, but there was still a lot of it in the air. He ran through the now open dressing room door, onto the stage. "Everyone out," he squealed, working his way to Joran and Justin to untie them. "The place is gonna blow!"

"Look! We caught the bad guy," Justin said proudly as Smalley freed his hands. "We'd make pretty good superheroes, huh?"

"You will make good additions to my team," Smalley beamed.

"Your team?"

"Caleb! Norbert! Stop that!" Smalley chastised as his veteran and his second continued to play naked grope and tickle.

"I'm trying to French kiss his memory back," Caleb said.

"I'm not remembering, but I sure ain't hating."

"You disgusting janitor man!" Nasturtium got to her feet, kicked Sissy in the teeth, and lunged for Caleb.

"We don't have time for this!" Smalley fretted. "We have to evacuate the building before it blows."

Caleb grabbed No Goode, threw her to the ground and fell against her, pressing his hard, janitorial junk into her nether regions from behind.

"Ooooh!" she panted, "maybe you homos are on to something.

Norbert went for Sissy, who, distraught she had just had a dirty shoe in her mouth was easy to subdue.

"Hmm," Goode thought to himself. "My old lady seems to be packing something extra in her drawers!"

"Norbert!" Smalley turned his volume down to secret level. "Forget Sissy. I need you to blow ..."

"Him?" He pointed, all hopeful, at Caleb.

"No. I need you to create a ventilation cortex so the gas will dissipate. Replace it with fresh, outdoor air. Go over to the fire exit Nasturtium blocked. Blow it open. Then ..."

Before Smalley could finish the sentence, poor Justin, crawling off the surrey, cramped from the bud fucking bottom position he had been in so long, fell against the light panel that worked the overhead theatre lights. His left had sent a charge through the fixture, blowing a green light, a pink one, and then a large spot, causing a spark that set off a violent and eardrum shattering BOOM!

Luke Warm, who heard it all the way down the street, grinned, happy that the students and faculty that ignored him, along with that closeted-afraid-to-come-out-because-of-loons-like-Nasturtium-Goode-news-anchor, probably just shit their pants in fear. Within a moment, though, the homely-and-ignored one, more heroic than Justin Hotly, who ran screaming, leaving his armless, helpless like-a-turtle-on-its-back friend behind, fought his way into the school as many others — muscular dudes covered in sex fluids, chubby, spent and sticky, fought to get out, made his way to trampled over Joran Tinkler.

"Help me," Joran said, all sad puppy eyes.

Luke had received an invitation, just that morning, Fuck being a hero, it said, the real fun is in villainy. Join my team, instead; your first mission, destroy anyone connected to Peter Smalley. He thought about the words as he stepped over the Swede, moving instead to Norbert Goode's side, bending for the gun his mother, then Sissy Wood had dropped as more pandemonium ensued. He took a moment to admire Goode's exposed goods close-up, at face level, before zeroing in on his target as smoke and bedlam surrounded them all.

"Hand me the gun," Norbert demanded.

BANG!

Luke Warm fired, hitting his target right in the heart. The dead body collapsed to the floor.

Who did Luke shoot? Will Caleb and Bert fuck? Which one will bottom? Who will Caleb fuck if Bert is dead? Has Sissy gone bad for good? Will Samuel Yoder ever finger his butthole? For answers to these questions and a delectable Amish banana bread recipe, look for Shrinky Dink and Blow Part Three: Guys and Balls coming soon.

A HAZARD OF HENCHMEN By Edward Arcott

In the year of our Lord, 1887, the great coastal metropolis of Clevington was beset by *fin de siècle* anxiety ... and periodic incursions by deadly mechanical monsters. As part of his job, Eustace McGovern — a dark-skinned, well-set-up gentleman of twenty summers — was among those given the task of observing the automated attackers from an unobtrusive vantage point to ensure the giant metal war machines were wreaking suitable levels of chaos, panic and destruction. He was to report to his employer, the malevolent Dr. Raze, if the villain's steam-powered destructors were performing below par. Dr. Raze's latest assault had been timed to occur at sundown, when the streets of Clevington were sure to be filled with citizens leaving work. McGovern waited and watched from the top of the labor exchange building some distance away, using his binoculars to view swarthy, solidly-built dock workers perform their end-of-the-day routines (which were about to be violently disrupted).

As planned, the Doctor's devilish devices, looking very much like enormous motorized pot-bellied stoves, exploded from the water near the docks, rocketed through the air, and landed amidst the portside buildings. A battalion's worth of phallic weapons emerged from the machines and began the job of unleashing steel-jacketed mayhem. Bomb launchers launched and pile drivers smashed as the wheeled and walking robotic engines of death dealt dreadful blows to the structures of the port. Many a hat was lost as terrified citizens fled, or cowered in any available alcove, praying for salvation from mechanized iron doom. McGovern was shocked to witness their prayers being answered.

Raze's broad-shouldered lackey saw the stranger arrive, dropping from the sky like a blazing comet and landing atop a squat cinder block storage structure in the path of the metal beasts. When the stranger's aura faded, McGovern saw that the man was wearing a dark mask, a flowing pale cloak and a white bodysuit — not unlike that of a trapeze artist — along with leather boots and gloves. The strapping stranger raised his left fist toward the automatons and then the impossible happened: Licks of blue-white lightning issued from his outstretched hand! The destructors, one after another, exploded even as gale-force winds, doubtless summoned by the mystery man, ripped through the port and fetched up fragments of robot, blowing them away from the city and over the water.

McGovern wondered if this "hero" quite knew what he was doing. Not only was he challenging the will of the formidable Dr. Raze, the fantastic energies he brought to bear had fully stripped the lightning-wielder of his cloak and bodysuit, burning them away like kindling in a fireplace. It was only by using his right hand to shield his eyes that the wondrous figure had managed to retain his mask, thus maintaining his anonymity as he continued to devastate the monstrous machines in epic fashion.

As the remains of the last assault device fell, the champion relented and lowered his still-gloved hands. Citizens cautiously came out of hiding to be greeted by the sight of their rescuer, standing above them. The glow of gas-lit streetlamps reflected off the sweat that covered the smooth and solid contours of the man-god's body. Ladies, and more than a few men, fainted at the sight of their hero's impressive, unsheathed, dangling magnificence.

Breathing heavily, the nameless hero looked over the port and at the smoldering death machines, shattered by his force of will. Satisfied by the completeness of the job he had done, a hint of a smile came across the hero's half-hidden face. He seemed heedless of the gaping crowd and untroubled by his own nakedness. The mysterious champion of Clevington raised a fist toward the sky and streaked upward as a living, dazzling flash of light. Once the bright man had flown out of sight, McGovern lowered his binoculars. "This is no ordinary fellow," thought the young man who was instantly and truly besotted. And powerfully erect.

Unbeknownst to McGovern and his fellow observers, their dark-haired, goateed employer was hovering near the port in his dirigible, some 500 feet above. It was a last minute decision: The wicked doctor felt the thrill of seeing his plans come to fruition superseded any risk of being spotted in the area. As the villain's airship settled into a position from which he might observe the carnage, he was delighted to discover that Fergus, the craft's burly, red-headed pilot, would be happy to orally service his veiny wing-wang while the criminal mastermind sipped champagne and watched his glorious machines play their symphony of destruction. It was to be a semen-drenched, orgasmic feast for the ego immediately followed by a carefully worded extortion letter promising future attacks if the city leaders did not relinquish obscene quantities of gold bullion to him forthwith.

But it was not to be. The doctor watched aghast as his devices were demolished by the naked, beefy, burning man even as the moist mouth of a muscular Irishman massaged his man meat. The doctor was, to say the least, unnerved. "Fergus!" he cried, "Unclench my dangler and land this vessel at once!"

A short time later ...

Mr. McGovern was sitting upon a velocipede (a "bicycle" to you moderns) dressed in his finest clothes, pedaling toward his doom. Or so he thought. Delivering "interesting" news to Dr. Raze was not without peril, as former assistants would attest if one were to employ the services of a spirit medium and contact them. It was one of the reasons why the hired heavy had paused long enough to have a decent wank before leaving his rooftop perch — visions of glowing, square-jawed musclemen with sexy come-hither grins filling his thoughts ... his thick, lightly lubricated fingers wrapped around his manhood, vigorously coaxing a passionate and creamy release. It seemed the only way to finally relax his dark-n-chubby for a more comfortable ride back to the lair.

The lightly bronzed skin and chiseled shape of the brilliant champion of Clevington had left an undeniable impression, one that seemed to fortify Mr. McGovern as he approached the headquarters of his evil employer. As fantastic as Dr. Raze's science was, he would be no match for the energies of the "bright man." A pity, McGovern thought. For all of its moral improbity, his time with the doctor's gang had been a most comfortable and profitable engagement. Better than his time as a sailor, an occupation for which he was grateful in that, while arduous, it had nonetheless delivered him to shores more friendly to those of his particular hue. So atypically liberal were the local citizens on this matter that, had he wished it, he would even have been permitted to court a woman of a paler tone (within his social class, of course) without controversy. But McGovern had never been terribly attracted to the fair frails and his time on a merchant vessel had completely clarified his preference. As is well known, men confined to a ship at sea, even the ones who generally favored the comforts of breasts and vaginas, were often easily persuaded to subject themselves to exploration by a talented man's tongue or a stiff and ready penis. Equally, the philosophy of "any port in a storm" applied to a crew member's member and any bodily orifice someone like Mr. McGovern cared to make available.

The henchman wheeled through the gates of the Puckleby Tool & Die metalworking facility, the respectable façade, which served as a masque for the doctor's nefarious weapons factory and headquarters. Eustace parked his bicycle next to several others, an indication that his fellow observers had returned to the lair ahead of him. He felt slightly uncomfortable being the last to arrive.

McGovern removed his derby hat and frock coat as he made his way through the excessively warm factory, where men hammered raw, hot metal into parts for the factory's customers ... as well as parts for the doctor's destructive devices. Eustace hoped this would not be the last time he would see the shirtless, sooty workers flexing their sweaty torsos in service to the boss. Accessing the hidden elevator at the rear of the factory, Mr.

McGovern descended into the paneled, gas-lit hallways of the secret subterranean lair.

Passing by the hideout's laboratory, McGovern noticed Professor Chatsworth, one of Raze's exceptional lab gurus, standing with his back to the door. Chatsworth was older, balding, and his rugged face was lined by decades of toil, but he was one of McGovern's favorite partners for naked after-hours amusements. Slim and energetic with an agreeable distribution of chest hair, Chatsworth was also experienced, inventive and unbelievably responsive in all carnal matters. He had a smell to him that McGovern found irresistible — almost like cinnamon and sawdust with a hint of mint. The well-built youngster entered the lab and, as he had done so many times before, took Chatsworth from behind and buried his nose in the gentleman's neck, just below his ear, breathing in deeply. McGovern thanked him for permitting the intrusion by grabbing him tightly around his narrow waist and slowly moving his hand up the scientist's chest and back down to his crotch, giving Chatsworth's stiffening privates a playful squeeze. It was all such sinful play (they were the villains, after all). McGovern released the lab worker and turned to leave without a word. On his way out, he surreptitiously swiped several tubes of the professor's highly effective synthetic greasing agent, having used up the last of his own personal supply of the miraculous lubricant while gratifying himself on a Clevington rooftop.

McGovern breathed a sigh of relief when he saw that Dr. Raze hadn't arrived at the main office before him. He took his place in front of the doctor's desk standing next to Holyhead who stood next to Marmadon who stood next to Fotheringay who stood next to Buckwood.

The doctor stormed into the office, beside himself with anger ... and the pilot, Fergus. Dr. Raze was wearing his finest suit coat and a pair of shiny leather shoes, but apparently, he had been so busy dealing with the aftermath of the truncated port attack that he had neglected to put his pants back on. Endeavoring to quell his rage, he and his exposed dangly bits began pacing back and forth behind his desk as he addressed his men. "I've sent a message to the city fathers — or rather, my goody-two-shoes alter ego, Linus Puckleby, has sent a message — expressing his concern and offering the resources of the tool and dye factory to assist in any way we can with repairing the damage. At a modest discount."

"So, we'll make some money! At least it's not a total loss, right boss?" said tall, mad-eyed Marmadon. Dr. Raze threw a lead paper weight at him, hitting him in the head. Finesse and Victorian reserve were not the doctor's style.

The Janus-faced arch villain smoothed his hair, straightened his cravat and adjusted his testicles. The random act of violence had relieved some of his tension and allowed him to think more clearly. "Here is what we're going to do: I am going to personally prepare... the Razer II Master Mech!"

"NOT THE RAZER II?!?!" the boys cried. Even Marmadon, on the ground and thoroughly dazed, stood up and took notice.

"Oh, yes," said the doctor as he took seven shot glasses from an adjacent cabinet and lined them up on his desk. "But before the Master Mech is deployed, we must deal with that masked and meddlesome mass of menacing muscle!"

"You saw him? I couldn't believe what that fellow did! It was incredible!" said Fotheringay, a hairless giant of a man with a pointy head and large ears.

"It was as if he controlled the very forces of nature!" said Holyhead, a nondescript, sandy-haired gentlemen with a gift for blending into crowds unnoticed. "He dispatched the mechs without even breaking a sweat!"

"Oh, he broke a sweat," said McGovern before he could re-think the wisdom of making such a remark.

"And he could fly! And toss around lightning with his hands," said Buckwood — short, dark haired and vaguely simian with a dense handlebar mustache — who mimed flinging imaginary lightning bolts in his employer's direction. "He was like that guy in London who can turn invisible ... or that guy with the wings in New York who flies around rescuing people from burning buildings!"

"So, Clevington now has its very own hero," Dr. Raze said thoughtfully. He filled six glasses from a crystal decanter and distributed them to his lackeys. "Know this, my boys: In every difficult challenge, there lies the seed of an opportunity. The details of my revised plans are still forming, and I will reveal them to you all in due course ... but for now, a toast: To changing fortunes and shiny new possibilities. Cheers!"

Six measures of drink were thrown down six gullets. The whiskey tasted particularly cheap and harsh, but none of the doctor's underlings dared to say anything.

Later that night, in the lair's living quarters ...

McGovern was leaving the showers, toweling between his legs as he walked toward his cubby, when he heard the unmistakable sounds of the weekly orgy getting under way. The young man's fears that the afternoon's disappointments might cast a pall on the evening's regularly scheduled debaucheries had already abated. He had just left Holyhead who was still in the showers after having pinned young Gaviston against the far wall. Holyhead was holding Gaviston's wrists above his head and pressing him, face first, into the wall tiles while loudly and indelicately humping the metal worker's ass with his ridiculously long boner. From the exit twenty feet away, McGovern could see Holyhead's broad back and hear the fervent grunts that accompanied each forceful, furious hip thrust. From a distance, the pair looked like a large undulating "X" against the white wall. When Eustace finally tore himself away, the echoes of breathless groans were bouncing off the bathroom tiles with ever increasing volume.

Mr. McGovern passed the lair's small gymnasium, a room with a padded floor that was illuminated, like a few other areas, by newfangled electric lights (stolen from some chap named Edison). Mr. Mately, the factory's pale, blond bookkeeper, lay naked on the gym floor between two deeply tan, muscle-bound and bearded henchmen who were having their way with the lean office worker. But that was Mately's role: He was there to be used, a slender, lightly hairy instrument of flesh and muscle receptive to his coworkers' every indecent whim — to be tasted and probed, every inch of his skin caressed and explored while he, in return, stroked a shaft or offered his fuzzy bottom as a welcoming port of call. There he was, between two beefy brutes, his eyes closed, not breathing so much as panting, at the mercy of two hot mounds of tan muscle and two fiery, hard dicks about to shag him silly.

The lair's "bedrooms" were merely large partitioned stalls off of the main hall with bunks or daybeds, some with curtains that could be drawn for privacy. McGovern, still naked and a little bit wet from his shower, reached his stall to find Mr. Buckwood loitering nearby wearing only a pair of loose trousers. McGovern moved close to Buckwood and leaned over expectantly. Unlike some of the other boys — generally the ones who would have preferred to have young vaginas readily available, but who were, nonetheless, willing to adapt to circumstances — Buckwood liked to kiss. The stout, hairy *shtupper* was a mustachioed master of tongue-fu. One imagined him spending hours conditioning his lips and otherwise training himself to be an expert kisser. Buckwood became familiar enough with his fellow henchmen to know exactly where to place his hands and how hard to squeeze so that their bodies would instantly yield and expel all tension, freeing that barrel of a man to demand almost anything of his pliant new conquests. Always starting with a kiss.

Eustace dropped his towel, put a hand on Buckwood's chest and gently pushed him onto his bed. He unbuttoned the gentleman's trousers liberating the little man's big erection. McGovern pushed back the foreskin and took the shaft into his mouth, swirling his tongue around Buckwood's salty cockhead.

Rising up on his elbows, Buckwood noticed Professor Chatsworth standing next to the partition. The professor had been watching them, his shirt open, his lab coat in one hand, his other hand sliding over, down and around his hairy chest. The scientist undid his trouser buttons and a semi-erect penis flopped out into his hand. It was soon manipulated into a solid sex rod pointing insistently at the couple on the bed. The professor's chest was quickly rising and falling with his short, sharp breaths as he continued to stroke his manhood. He stopped, startled momentarily by the naked presence of airship pilot, Fergus Argyle-Gotham, behind his back.

"McGovern," said Fergus, "man the rear for a 'show stopper.'" This was a request that, as dictated by custom, was not to be ignored; giving head to the hirsute and watching scientists masturbate would have to wait.

The dark-skinned henchman got up, grabbed a tube of lubricant from his nightstand and followed Fergus to the dining area. Lying prone on one of the long wooden tables was Mr. Mately wearing only a thin coat of sweat, his legs dangling over the table's end. He was orally servicing Fotheringay's hard, straight-as-an-arrow stalk of man meat. Fergus leaned over and licked the bookkeeper's lightly hairy nipples and stroked the man's wanker. After applying some of the Professor's wondrous lubricant to his cock, McGovern lifted the legs of their blond sex toy and plunged his meat wand into the darkness beneath where it was enveloped by the warmth and gentle pressure of Mr. Mately's amazingly receptive ass.

It was a standard "show stopper": A three-man team taking extreme liberties with Mately while the other henchmen gathered to watch, most with cock in hand. Oblivious to the audience, McGovern was momentarily mesmerized by the up-and-down motion of Fergus' head. The Irishman enjoyed the feel of hard cockflesh in his mouth while eagerly running a hand over his subject's wispy carpet of chest hair. Eustace took a lusting glance at Fotheringay's sweat-drenched form, from his curiously large ears to his magnificently shaped, perfectly smooth pectorals. The dark henchman looked down and watched his own thick and swift chocolate rod gliding in and out of Mately's backside, exciting the tender regions of their writhing plaything.

Fergus the Red suddenly stood up straight, pumping his tool and breathing heavily. His body shook with ecstatic tremors as hot jets of cum erupted from his cock and landed on Mately's abs. But the Irishman wasn't finished: Fergus' powerful arms pinned the subject to the table allowing the pilot to further investigate the contours of his captive's torso with his lips and tongue.

Mately's stifled cries of approval were encouraging ever more aggressive manhandling. Held fast by the thickly muscled Irishman while getting fucked at both ends, the bookkeeper thrashed and strained to arch his back, stretching every sinew and driving the onlookers wild with his bucking and moaning, his entirely disingenuous protests muffled by a mouthful of fat British cock on the verge of an explosive discharge.

Just then, Mr. Holyhead blew up in the bathroom destroying two of the shower stalls and causing great distraction.

Later, the next week ...

Dr. Raze was sparing no effort in order to rapidly upgrade his doomsday weapon and could frequently be seen trotting about the lair carrying piles of cogs and belts and assorted mechanical thingamajigs from the Razer II Master Mech. On one occasion, he was seen in the shower, naked but for a tool belt. Before any of his henchmen could query the doctor about this curious behavior, the criminal mastermind froze, cried, "Damn! I knew it!" and immediately left the bathroom to make yet another adjustment to his steam-driven, mechanical trump card.

All of the showers in the bathroom were functioning again, but evidence of the extensive damage and its recent repair remained. As it turned out, the explosion of Mr. Holyhead (and the blowing-to-bits of his carnal companion, Mr. Gaviston) was merely an allergic reaction. Had Raze's team of observers been more observant that day in their leader's office, they would have noticed that their scheming superior was toasting to "changing fortunes and new possibilities" with an empty glass. Only the six assembled lackeys were given Professor Chatsworth's experimental mutagen, and only the luckless Mr. Holyhead suffered any ill effects from the concoction (Mr. Gaviston's messy demise notwithstanding). For the others, the strange tonic performed beyond all expectations as the five survivors soon acquired astonishing gains in strength, musculature and resistance to injury in addition to other unique gifts. The lads also enjoyed a heightened level of potency so dangerous that, until they grew completely accustomed to their newfound power, they were forced to limit themselves to intimate encounters with each other in order to avoid ugly accidents.

Ogden Fotheringay and Mr. McGovern were behind a stack of iron ingots amongst the maze of materials kept in the storage yard behind the tool and dye factory. They had been training with their compatriots moments earlier, consequently their clothing was limited to black flannel shorts, wrist bands, black wrestler boots, and a leather belt with a number of pouches attached, each containing all manner of useful accoutrements and inventions to assist them in their new mission: the eventual capture of Lord Brightman (as the hero of Clevington had come to be called).

While tossing ten-ton metal ingots back and forth, Fotheringay became fixated on the bulge in Mr. McGovern's shorts and grew determined to investigate it further. After persuading Eustace to join him in a more secluded area, the big-eared brute had only to suggest that the young man, "Turn around."

McGovern put his hands against the wall of molded metal for balance. Ogden liberated the henchman's unit from its cloth encumbrance; one hand manipulated the freed member while the other felt McGovern's groin and abs before pausing on its upward journey to clutch a well-formed round brown pectoral.

All McGovern could feel was the stone-solid body of Mr. Fotheringay pressing against him from the back ... an erect cock grinding into his ass crack, a pair of hard pecs against his shoulder blades. He felt the big Brit's hot breath on his neck while meaty fingers glided over his dick, now slick with precum. Eustace was getting weak-kneed and ready to burst. But something felt different. The orgasm wasn't just welling up from his cock ... it was all over, as if his entire body were one big jizz cannon about to go off ... as if he might do a Holyhead! But he was too close to stop — he was held fast by the eighteen-inch biceps of the world's best-built henchman who was saying directly into his ear, in a breathy British whisper, "Lemme see you shoot!"

Impatient to get his plans underway, the diabolical Dr. Raze had stepped into the storage yard hoping to gather his crew of merrily mutated delinquents. He was just in time to witness a shocking release of force mighty enough to send Mr. Fotheringay flying through the air. Racing to its source, the doctor found McGovern, still crackling with electromagnetic energy, looking slightly dazed with his dripping giant tally-whacker still hanging out of his shorts.

"Come with me," said the doctor.

An afternoon's worth of tests in the underground lair's laboratory revealed that Mr. McGovern had reacted to the mutagenic tonic in a surprisingly fortuitous way that the others hadn't. This was cold comfort to the young henchmen who remained locked into a strange machine of the doctor's design, one that resembled an odd, modernistic version of some sadomasochistic device inspired by the Spanish Inquisition. It was almost like a reverse chair, one that kept McGovern leaning forward and bent over as if he were about to be spanked. His feet and hands were spread apart and bound in aluminum metal sleeves that were attached to an assortment of cables. His chest and hips rested on leather cushions beneath him. "At least it's well padded," he thought .

"This is brilliant! BRILLIANT!" said the doctor, a phrase he uttered repeatedly that afternoon with the completion of each new battery of tests. "Yes, yes ..." was the other oft repeated phrase. Finally he stepped over to the laboratory door and shouted, "Mr. Wilde! Mr. Savage! Now! I'm going now!!"

Wearing oil-stained bib overalls and dirty work boots, the two bearded henchmen (last seen buggering Mr. Mately with considerable gusto on the floor of the gym) came bounding into the lab. "Plug him into the Master Mech, boys," said Dr. Raze. "It's time to finally extract payment from this wretched city!"

"What are you doing??" asked McGovern as he struggled to release himself from his bonds. He suddenly found himself curiously weak and helpless as Wilde and Savage moved him, machine and all, into a freight elevator at the rear of the lab. The threesome was joined by the doctor, and they started to descend.

"You probably thought I wanted you and your fellows to capture Lord Brightman just to keep him from interfering in my plans," the doctor said to Mr. McGovern. "Wrong! Even his power is no match for the Master Mech's energy assimilating armor. No, I wanted that flare-spitting nuisance captured to supply the super-power boost needed to give the Mech's ultra weapons system an extra charge of ascendant might! However, since my tests show that my energy siphon works perfectly well on you, and you have plenty of power to spare, it seems you will be able to stand in for the elusive champion of Clevington, leaving me quite free to begin my mad rampage of fire, destruction, and nihilistic naughtiness right away!" The elevator shuddered to a halt at the lowest level of the lair. Dr. Raze threw open the elevator doors. "Wilde, Savage, work quickly! I have a city to bleed!"

That night in the city of Clevington ...

The city's citizens were still growing accustomed to the concept of "nightlife." Or rather, the concept of a safe nightlife where bright gas lamps and a solid police presence made enjoying after-hours gatherings possible. No longer were evenings out the exclusive purview of scallywags and sneak thieves and far too many unsavory characters. But even the scum of the city were nothing compared to the explosive projectiles of a mad man with a mech.

Lord Brightman — who, in his unmasked daily life, was untitled and considered thoroughly unremarkable — was quite pleased with the sobriquet given to him by a journalist with a flair for the sensational. Being a "lord" in possession of such fantastic abilities filled him with no end of confidence. However, standing atop the Watson Bank Building, gazing toward the port he had so recently rescued from a devastating attack, his confidence was shaken by the sight of what he would later learn was the Razer II Master Mech.

The evening was a slight variation on a recurring nightmare: explosions and terror at the talons of an intimidating hell-spawn of anarchic science. But it was not a group of machines responsible for the panic this time, only a single, horrifying aggressor. The Master Mech had the appearance of a one-hundred-foot tall mannequin made of shiny silver. It was naked and scandalously accurate in its anatomy. In an unwise, but irresistible, fit of hubris, Dr. Raze had shaped the beast's head in his own image, down to its large metal goatee. The doctor himself was piloting the dangerous device from within its vanity-inspired noggin. Well below, a pair of shiny brass stabilization spheres hung beneath an enormous cannon that emerged from the metal man's crotch and was firing round after deadly round.

Lord Brightman (who no longer wore his flamboyant cape) flew into action and quickly discovered his energy attacks were useless against the new threat. Perhaps it was just the noise made by the automaton's metal joints, but it almost sounded as if the machine were taunting the luminous hero with a sort of hollow, mocking laughter.

Flying around the mechanical giant, Brightman noticed what might have been a way inside through a bolted iron sphincter in the monster's back end, obviously used to vent steam. He thought to himself, "Now here's an engineer with a sense of humor." Flying up the giant's metal ass, Lord Brightman blasted past steel joints and motion-making gears and into the cramped chest cavity. There he saw what looked like a fellow costumed (albeit barely costumed) hero being held hostage. "As much as I would like to seek favor in this situation," he said to the captive, "I'll simply use my powers to free you instead, citizen."

"No!" cried McGovern. "That will only reduce the mech's power. We've got to destroy this abomination! It's drawing energy from me. With your assistance, I can overload its systems! Take a tube of lubricant from my right belt pocket."

The big-muscled hero followed the instruction. "Is this what you're talking about? What do I do with it?"

"Smear some on your jonnie knob and pound my backside! Hurry!"

"Are you serious?"

"Very! Hurry up!!"

The champion of Clevington removed his uniform gloves and pulled off his tights. Employing his extraordinary strength, Lord Brightman ripped open McGovern's shorts baring his buttocks. After covering his staff with the professor's fine lubricant, Brightman entered the stranger and began rhythmically pumping and thrusting ... guiding his manhood in and out of Mr. McGovern's hole with abandon. Questions about the potential efficacy of the stratagem quickly evaporated. The hero knew from the first stroke that there was something very different about this man he was buggering, a certain overwhelming something that captivated his senses ... his surroundings became blurry, and soon he was sensing nothing but the feeling of ultimate arousal setting his loins ablaze. Brightman's hands moved over every inch of his partner's dark, muscular arms while he became even more deeply enthralled by the hot, smooth ass clutching his pecker and making his eyes roll back in their sockets. Surely, this was what heaven was like! Suddenly, the orgasm hit him like a sucker-punch from Shiva: Brightman shouted! He hollered! He bellowed! He roared! A geyser of cum exploded from his dick and endless waves of euphoric glee whacked and rapped his spinning brain box and sent a lightning shock of "FUCK YEAAHHH!" through his entire buff bod.

The hero of Clevington was barely aware of his partner's ecstatic shouts as boilers blew, cables snapped and the volatile systems of the Master Mech ruptured and fried. Every pressure valve holding the head of the massive monster to its neck exploded, sending the top of the beast, and its beastly pilot, sailing over the city.

A level of calm and order followed the dramatic defeat of the Razer II. The head of the Master Mech landed on the street between city hall and police headquarters. It required little imagination on the part of the constabulary to correctly deduce that "Linus Puckleby" was, in fact, the villainous Dr. Raze and immediately take him into custody. News of the evening's events reached the wicked mastermind's minions who, upon realizing they were suddenly unemployed, looted the lair and quickly left Clevington to seek greener pastures where they were not considered wanted criminals.

In the days the followed, Lord Brightman and Eustace McGovern (his Lordship's new masked crime fighting partner, nicknamed "The Energetic Cowl") quite irresponsibly allowed Clevington to go completely unprotected. The pair were far too busy fucking.

IMPOSTOR By Armand

I was spritzing the offensive brown stain on my green spandex costume with Shout when my boyfriend, Bobby, aka Helios, entered the room wearing only a towel and a sexy smile.

"Should I ask?" he jibed before heading to the kitchen for a bowl of melon.

"Chocolate," I quipped too bitchily. "After I helped the fire department with that overturned tractor trailer on the bypass, I thought I'd treat myself to a chocolate shake from the Pink Shack, and I spilled it on my costume."

"You know you shouldn't drink and drive." He dropped a piece of melon and bent over to pick it up. Concentrating with all my might, I wished hard for the towel to drop, but my power over gravity was not telepathic.

To distract myself from my tarnished costume, I clicked on the TV in hopes Deborah Norville would be reporting some delicious Hollywood scandal. Maybe a Ryan Gosling sex tape. Which I'd sell my mother to see! Instead of Gosling porn, there was something about a Kardashian. Kill me now! Before I could turn the channel, a banner came across the bottom of the screen with breaking local news: The mayor, Robert Parker — who happened to be Bobby's father — was being investigated for propositioning a fifteen-year-old girl in the park.

Unaware of his father's Weiner-esque behavior, Bobby strutted in front of the TV, dropped his towel, and said, "Whatta you say we have a work out before dinner?"

"Oh, Sweetie." I knew I should tell him about his father's unfortunate transgression, but then he turned and struck a pose like an Olympic god. Rather than bring him down, I decided to go down on him. It'd be easier to break the news post-coitus. "Let me throw this in the wash," I said as I held up my costume.

"Get your seamstress to make you a new one." He shot a burst of sun power and hit my crotch. "Now get over here and show me how much you love me."

\# \# \# \# \#

I was still pounding his ass hard and deep when his cell phone began playing the dirge. His mother was calling.

"Keep fucking me," he commanded. "I'm about to come."

The phone had momentarily broken my concentration, but, at my boyfriend's insistence, I returned to thrusting hard and steady into his muscle ass. He was a bossy bottom sometimes, but then he knew what he liked.

"Oh yeah," he exclaimed. "Oh yeah. Oh yeah. Fuck me, baby. That's it."

I knew I was hitting his spot. When he began to shoot, I started pile driving him because that drove him insane. He convulsed like he was having a grand mal seizure. Once he'd collapsed, I shot my load on his blond pubes and nearly hairless chest and belly.

Before we even had a chance to speak, the dirge started playing again.

"What the hell does she want?" he grumbled between breaths.

Bobby hadn't spoken to his parents in months, since his father canceled the gay pride parade because it "violated the city's morality code." Helios and Gravitar were supposed to be grand marshals of the parade — or grand poobahs, or exalted homos, or something. I didn't much care about the pomp and circumstance, but Bobby was really looking forward to it. I have to admit: even I had warmed to the idea of riding on that float in public with Helios by my side and adoring fans cheering for Plain City's queer supers. Sure the conservative nut bags would bash us, and I usually wanted to pretend no one knew Gravitar was gay, but seeing Helios' happiness would be worth it.

"What?" Bobby said into the phone. I knew she was sharing the news about his father's transgression in the park. After listening for a while, my boyfriend said, "He calls me a freak and then turns around and does this. A fifteen-year-old girl! Really, Mom!"

Oh how I love when the self-righteous fall. Maybe he could find Jesus while snuggling with a hirsute cell mate in Statesville Prison. Who's immoral now, Mr. Parker?

# # # # #

Though I should have been mildly pleased for Bobby's sake, I was a bit disheartened that Mayor Parker had a pretty rock solid alibi during the time someone looking like him propositioned that poor girl: He was holding a budget meeting with several staff members at a posh restaurant, and they had his signature on the receipt. At the meeting, he'd blown over a thousand dollars of the tax payers' money eating lobster and drinking champagne. There were no fewer than thirty witnesses who saw him there. Damn, I was hoping for a little Shawshank Redemption for Bobby's homophobic father.

Still, surveillance tape confirmed the fifteen-year-old girl's story. It certainly looked like the mayor leaving the park, but the image was grainy and distant. So how the hell could the mayor be in two places at one time? It must have been someone with similar features.

While I mulled over the doppelganger, I cleaned with the fury of Speedy Gonzales on meth. When Bobby came bounding in with the mail, I was levitating the couch with one hand and vacuuming underneath it with the other. My power over gravity often came in handy around the house — cleaning under heavy furniture, reaching a rarely used spice from the top cabinet, depositing the neighbor's horny Pomeranian on the roof, levitating my boyfriend in the air while I stimulated his prostate with my cock.

"It arrived today," he proclaimed as he proudly held aloft the newest issue of *Out Magazine* with Helios and Gravitar locking lips on the cover. "It's us, babe. On the cover! Look how hot we are."

He leapt over the back of the levitating couch and landed on it perfectly. If I'd have attempted the same move, my triple lindy would not have ended so well. I'd probably have bounced off the cushions, smashed into the coffee table, and landed indecorously with my legs akimbo, my tailbone broken, and my pride injured. Bobby, on the other hand, was reposed on his side, propped up on one elbow, legs crossed, wearing a Colgate smile. The magazine rested against his chest, and the cover really did look great. Sometimes I couldn't help but look at him and think he's so charming butter wouldn't melt in his mouth. Because of my own insecurities, he made me feel like a nelly queen and an oaf. But he loved me — insecurities and all.

"Why don't you put me down and then come over here and get me up," he stated in his best movie announcer voice.

"We going to shut the blinds first or give Mrs. Tillman a free BJ show?"

"I don't care about Mrs. Tillman. I just want you to make love to me." Make love? Only Bobby could say that un-ironically.

I grabbed his ankle with my right hand and kept him levitating in the air while I lowered the couch with my left.

"I love when you show off." He rubbed his semi-hard dick through his basketball shorts.

Sixty seconds later, I was feeding on Bobby's thick cock, tasting his pre-come while he vibrated the floor with his energy rays. With the power of a superhero, he grabbed me and pulled me into 69 position, and then we came simultaneously like good lovers do.

# # # # #

The next day, Bobby and I were sitting around a hideous orange laminated table at the Plain City Police Department.

"Uh, 1960 called and they want their table back," I said. Helios, wearing his yellow spandex costume and black eye mask, swatted my leg and shot me a parental glare.

"Thank you, boys, for coming." The officer's badge said J. Dahmer. How unfortunate to work in law enforcement and share a name with a serial killer. "We got a situation, and we thought you boys might be able to help."

The situation is that this table is hurting my gay eyes. Where's that cutie Nake Berkus when you need him?

Officer Dahmer's partner, who had introduced herself as Danita Frampton, sat across from Helios, opened a file, and slid two photos toward us as she spoke: "Yesterday around 1:00 pm the owner of the Lakeland Country Club cleaned out the registers and safe, said he was going to the bank, and then left the premises. Twenty minutes later the owner returns and finds out the money's gone and wants to know what happened. Swears he's not the one who took it. Claims he was getting a massage from one Ms. Ying Yang at Chang's Pleasure Emporium when the whole thing went down."

Went down. Sounded so cop-like and licentious at the same time.

"Mr. Steinman," Bobby uttered. "I worked at Lakeland Country Club in high school."

Before I could catch myself, I gave him a look of disdain. When Officer Frampton caught me, her brow furrowed suspiciously. Damn, she's a good cop and doesn't miss a thing. Despite her short afro, she reminded me of Queen Latifah — same skin tone, similar build, identical mannish gestures, tough attitude. I found myself imagining Officer Frampton in one of those 70s movies starring Pam Grier.

Conversely, the pudgy male officer with the serial killer name reminded me of George from Seinfeld. He said, "We got a dozen witnesses saying the guy who took the money was wearing different clothes and acting different, so we got ta thinking maybe it was a lookalike."

"Especially after what happened to the mayor," Frampton added.

"What are you saying, Coffy?" I was instantly mortified that the 70s blaxploitation name had escaped my lips. Fearing Officer Frampton's wrath, I fumbled to fix my gaff: "I mean, what do you think happened, ma'am, and can I get a cup of coffee?"

"Uh-uh," she responded while wagging her finger. "You do not want the sludge they got in the machines here. Tastes like dirty socks and soot. You best wait to get a cup around the corner."

Helios clearly didn't know what to make of what was happening, so he picked up a photo and said, "Mr. Steinman fired me one day because football practice ran over, and I got to work late."

"We think someone was pretending to be Mr. Steinman and the mayor," Foxy Brown said.

"Like Bruce Willis in that movie," her partner added. I presumed he meant *The Jackal*. Mmm, if memory served me, it featured a gay kiss.

"You think this is an actor?" Helios asked.

"Or the blue chick from X-Men," Dahmer retorted and chuckled at his joke.

"Actors," Foxy corrected. She slid another photo over. The picture was of a young woman with a tear-stained face and fuchsia hair that looked as if it had been cut by a third grader with safety scissors. "She says her beautician at the Hair Menagerie on Linden did that to her, but the beautician had car trouble and couldn't make it to work."

"That's Karen Graff, one of my girlfriends from high school," Bobby said.

"Hold the phone." The requisite queeny hand gesture accompanied my outburst. Sometimes one just cannot suppress the gay gene. "You dated her?"

"What the hell's going on here?" Bobby said to no one in particular.

# # # # #

The next evening Bobby slipped into the bedroom and caught me watching *My Little Pony* and eating walnut and chocolate chunk brownies in bed. "Brought you something," he said holding out a stuffed bear.

"Aww, that's sweet." I reached, but he didn't hand it over.

"I'll put it over here." Bobby placed the stuffed animal on the bookshelf where it sat with the blank stare of a Teddy Ruxpin. "Because now I want to fuck your sweet ass."

"You wanna what? Unless you roofied me and took advantage without my knowledge, you've only fucked me when I've lost a bet, and I ain't lost a bet."

"I don't fuck you?" My boyfriend's look of confusion was almost comical.

"No, because god gave you a big, beefy ass that needs to be plowed."

"Oh."

"Now get over here and I'll fuck some sense into you."

Bobby peeled off his "Hermione for President" T-shirt pulling it over his head by the collar. Normally he grabbed the hem and turned the shirt inside out as he peeled it off his body. Though it was such a small distinction, the change gave me momentary pause. Next, he dropped his pants, and I saw his naked penis.

"Oh, baby, no," I said. "No, no, no."

"What?"

"You know I don't like when a guy shaves off his pubes. It looks too prepubescent, which is not sexy. Is that the result of an unfortunate manscaping accident?"

"Uh, I guess."

I jumped up and kissed him; then I pushed him back on the bed, stripped off my clothes and reached for the lube. "You ready for some super lovemaking?" Rather than wait for a response, I grabbed his leg and levitated him off the bed.

"What the fuck is happening?" he exclaimed. "How are you doing …"

I let go his leg and watched him drop onto the bed. "You're not Bobby," I averred.

"You're Gravitar?" The man who looked like my boyfriend but clearly was not wore an expression akin to terror.

"What have you done with my boyfriend, and who are you?" My face was hardened with resolve. I wanted to kill the lookalike.

"So Bobby is Helios?" the lookalike asked.

I touched the impostor's leg and increased the pull of gravity so hard his body pressed into the mattress. A scream escaped the lips as the body shifted from Helios' into a woman's. "I didn't know," she gasped. "I didn't know."

I eased the gravitational pull. "Who are you?"

"Irene Polaski. I dated Bobby in college."

What's with the ex-girlfriends coming out of the woodwork? Hell, I'm already insecure enough without worrying Bobby might leave me for a woman.

Seeing her hairless vagina, I shuddered. Yep, I'm homo through and through. "Please cover that up." While she pulled the blanket over her privates, I reached for the Teddy Ruxpin lookalike. "A nanny cam?"

"I wanted Bobby to see you with another man, so he'd leave you. I was going to shift into another man's form while I fucked you in doggie position. I didn't realize he's the one … that he … that you …"

"You presumed I was the bottom? Why does everyone think Bobby's the Penetrator in bed, and I'm the Gaping Hole?" Clearly, I'd momentarily lost focus. For a second I felt as if I was in one of those cheesy TV *Batman* episodes. I expected to hear her say in the voice of Eartha Kitt, "You'll never see your boyfriend again, Boy Blunder." Then the word kerplunkt would float in the air as an announcer's voice said, "Can Gravitar save Helios before Jade Impostor uses her waxed vagina to turn him straight again?"

I said more forcefully, "Where's Bobby?"

"Somewhere safe."

"What have you done to him?"

"I'm a nurse and I have him hooked up to an IV — a little diazepam to keep him unconscious while I execute my plan. I've already punished his father and that pig Steinman and that slut Karen Graff. I just needed to get you out of the picture, and then Bobby would come back to me. If you don't let me go, he'll die."

"Hey, Luna Loonybin, Bobby's gay, and he's with me now. So where is he?"

"You're going to let me go, and I'll set him free."

I grabbed her leg and increased the earth's pull. "If I keep this up, the gravitational force will cause the bed to collapse; your lungs will cave in, and your bones will break. Now tell me now where he is."

She cried out as her body sank deeper into the mattress. "Okay, I'll tell you."

#

After I removed the IV, I woke Bobby and told him that he was safe and I loved him. Unfortunately, I hadn't shackled the impostor well enough, so Irene, the wily, loony shape shifter, escaped before the cops arrived to pick her up. Now it would be a waiting game to see if she exposed our true identities or kept our secret. My only hope sprang from the knowledge that in her own Swimfan way she loved Bobby.

The next day, I doted over my boyfriend, bringing him breakfast in bed and popping Burlesque in the DVD player.

"I'm fine," he insisted. "Come lay with me. But pull off my pajama bottoms first." That's one thing he'll never have to ask me to do twice. Seeing the trimmed thatch of blond hair above his penis, I breathed a sigh of relief. "Seriously, she was going to fuck you?" he asked.

"And record it." I pointed to the teddy bear. "That's when I was on to her. She clearly didn't know how much you like your booty plowed."

"If she'd have used a strap on, I might've stayed with her."

What!

He grinned at me. "Relax, babe. You're the one I want. I love you."

"I know." Trying not to let my diffidence show, I dug my toe into the carpet.

"Now how about you turn on that nanny cam and get over here and show me how much you love me." As if by command, his penis thickened and stood at attention. Then he lifted his legs and said, "Remind me why I gave up on girls."

That was a challenge I was willing to take.

About the Authors

A.J. DAMIAN likes writing steamy stories about hot men. She lives in England, and this is her second story for STARbooks Press. Contact her at: armanddesigns@gmail.com.

ARMAND has published a dozen stories in a variety of anthologies. His ultimate fantasy is to move to Europe, marry a nice Czech man, and write full-time.

DAVID CONNOR lives with his dog Max in rural New York. In the eighth grade, his creative writing teacher told him he should either write soap operas or porn; soap opera writing is really hard to break into. Schmooimax@aol.com.

DERRICK DELLA GIORGIA was born in Italy and currently lives between Manhattan and Rome. His work has been published in several anthologies and literary magazines. Visit him at www.derrickdellagiorgia.com.

EDWARD ARCOTT is a hitherto unpublished writer of fiction, a fan of steampunk and small press comics, and a shameless advertising industry whore. valthemus@gmail.com.

Residing on English Bay in Vancouver, Canada, JAY STARRE has pumped out steamy gay fiction for dozens of anthologies and has written two gay erotic novels. Contact: Jay Starre on Facebook.

JOSHUA SKYE is the author of the fantasy adventure "Xerxes Canyon." He lives in rural Pennsylvania with his partner Ray of fifteen years and their son Syrian. Visit him at http://joshuaskye.yolasite.com.

LOGAN ZACHARY (loganzachary2002@yahoo.com) is an author of mysteries, short stories, and over forty erotica stories, living in Minneapolis with his partner, Paul, and his dog, Ripley, who runs the house. www.loganzacharydicklit.com.

MARK APOAPSIS, in his secret identity, writes for a major daily publication in Metropolis and resides on his estate outside Gotham City with his youthful ward.

R. W. CLINGER has numerous books and stories published through STARBooks Press. He can be reached by e-mail: kenitorico@verizon.net.

ROB ROSEN, author of critically acclaimed novels, has had short stories featured in more than 150 anthologies. Please visit him at www.therobrosen.com.

THOBY MUSGRAVE is a novice writer living in Sydney, Australia. thobymusgrave@yahoo.com.

About the Editor

ERIC SUMMERS resides in West Palm Beach, Fla., and he has a special place in his heart for men in tights.

www.ingramcontent.com/pod-product-compliance
Lightning Source LLC
Chambersburg PA
CBHW031113030726
47496CB00002BA/525